THE FC

BOOKSHOP GIRLS

ELAINE ROBERTS had a dream to write for a living. She completed her first novel in her twenties and received her first very nice rejection. Life then got in the way until she picked up her dream again in 2010. She joined a creative writing class, The Write Place, in 2012 and shortly afterwards had her first short story published. Elaine and her patient husband, Dave, have five children who have flown the nest. Home is in Dartford, Kent and is always busy with their children, grandchildren, grand dogs and cats visiting.

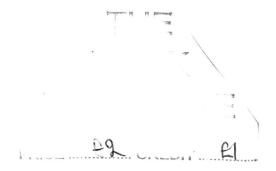

THE FOYLES BOOKSHOP GIRLS

Elaine Roberts

www.ariafiction.com

First published in the United Kingdom in 2018 by Aria, an imprint of Head of Zeus Ltd

9 7 5 3 1 2 4 6 8

A CIP catalogue record for this book is available from the British Library.

ISBN 9781788544856

Aria
c/o Head of Zeus
First Floor East
5–8 Hardwick Street
London EC1R 4RG

About *The Foyles Bookshop Girls*

London, 1914: one ordinary day, three girls arrive for work at London's renowned Foyles bookshop. But when war with Germany is declared their lives will never be the same again...

Alice has always been the 'sensible' one in her family – especially in comparison with her suffrage-supporting sister! But decidedly against her father's wishes, she accepts a job at Foyles Bookshop; and for bookworm Alice it's a dream come true.

But with the country at war, Alice's happy world is shattered in an instant. Determined to do what she can, Alice works in the bookshop by day, and risks her own life driving an ambulance around bomb-ravaged London by night. But however busy she keeps herself, she can't help but think of the constant danger those she loves are facing on the frontline...

Alice, Victoria and Molly couldn't be more different and yet they share a friendship that stems back to their childhood – a friendship that provides everyday solace from the tribulations and heartbreak of war. Perfect for fans of Elaine Everest, Daisy Styles and Rosie Hendry.

To my husband, Dave, and my son, James.
Without them, and their never-ending support and
belief, this story would never have been written.

Chapter 1

June 1914

Alice Taylor was a little breathless. A small bead of perspiration had formed on her forehead. She lifted her head slightly to enjoy the breeze that rippled along the river, breaking up the heat of the early morning June sunshine. Alice sighed. The summer of 1914 was going to be a hot one. The small heels on her ankle boots clipped the pavement purposefully as she hurried across Westminster Bridge towards Big Ben, leaving her visit to St Thomas' Hospital behind her.

The tall black ornate ironwork of the streetlights lined the bridge, high above the people walking along, each rushing to their destination. Horses pulled their carts, leaving piles of dung in their wake. The everyday pungent stench went unnoticed by everyone. Children leant against the sides of the bridge to enjoy the boats chugging along the river. Their arms were outstretched, waving, as they got nearer. Some mothers stopped to enjoy the scene, while others shouted to hurry their children along.

'Come on, we'll be late, you can watch them another

time.'

'Don't let me have to tell you again.' A woman snatched her child away from the side of the bridge and dragged him along the road, scuffing his worn shoes as he went.

On another day, she would have stopped to admire the boats and the sun glinting off the River Thames, but not today. If she didn't get a move on, she'd be late. An army of people had gathered outside the Houses of Parliament and Alice glanced over, intrigued by what they were all looking at. Shrill voices chanting 'votes for women' carried through the air. She took a step towards the crowd that was growing in size.

'Votes for women.' A single voice rang out.

Alice came to an abrupt standstill. That was Lily's voice, wasn't it? She stood on tiptoes, stretching her neck to see above everyone, but all she could see were the placards held high. She wrinkled her nose as the strong smell of coffee wafted around her. Crowds were building, spilling onto the pavement.

Men frowned and shook their heads as they were made to step into the road.

A deep voice shouted out, causing the spectators to look around. 'Get back to your kitchens.'

'It shouldn't be allowed. God help us all if women get the vote,' another yelled as he walked by.

Some women jeered in response, while others mumbled to each other. People stopped and stared. They all wanted to see what the commotion was about, but not wanting to get involved, they moved on quickly.

Alice wanted to push through the crowd to see if it was her sister's voice she'd heard. If so, she'd try to pull her away, but Lily's fiery nature would mean a commotion, drawing unwanted attention to them. Their father would be furious if Lily was involved in what he called 'that nonsense'. A stout, grey-haired woman walked through the crowd, wearing a tall, black, wide-brimmed hat. She was carrying a long white cotton bag with 'Votes For Women' emblazoned on the front of it. The bag rested against her long black skirt, while her white blouse rippled underneath the strap. She stood in front of Alice, thrusting a handful of leaflets at her. 'Take one, miss, this is all about you and your future, and your daughter's.'

Alice looked down at the white paper with 'Votes for Women' printed across the top in large, thick black letters.

The old lady moved her white-gloved hand nearer. 'Go on, you know it's important we all stand together.'

Alice reached out and did as she was bid. The woman smiled and moved on into the crowd. The loud musical chimes of Big Ben made her jump; she automatically glanced down at her wristwatch as they continued. Thank goodness they'd alerted her to how late she was going to be if she didn't hurry. Deciding against worrying about Lily's folly, Alice thrust the leaflet into her skirt pocket and turned right onto Whitehall. The tall buildings, with what her father liked to call 'architectural details' of pillars and scrolls, were invisible to her as she focussed on reaching W & G Foyles Bookstore, on Charing Cross Road, where she worked as a shop assistant. Alice's stomach churned and she felt nauseous thinking about the confrontation between Lily and their father, but she told herself she could say, hand on heart, and on a stack of bibles if her father insisted, that she hadn't seen Lily at the demonstration.

Two men in dark suits walked in front of her and lit cigarettes. She wrinkled her nose when the slight breeze caught the smoke and it wafted in her face. Their black trousers held sharp creases, which had been ironed in, front and back, matching their long sack coats. Bowler hats were perched precariously on their heads.

'What do you think then, about the Austrian being shot?' the smaller man asked his companion, tucking a newspaper under his arm.

'I can't see why the shooting in Sarajevo should affect this country.'

The man lifted his arm slightly, to adjust the position of his daily paper. 'No, let's hope not; we have enough problems...' he responded, pausing to listen to the women's voices as they carried through the air. 'Those women are causing havoc.'

The taller man laughed. 'I'm more concerned about the unions and the talk of a general strike.'

'Yes, the thought of strikes is worrying.' The other man sighed. 'The unions are getting stronger and if the miners, transport workers and dockers all stop work, it will bring the country to a standstill. The threat of it alone is already putting up prices. Mark my words, it won't be long before it affects my grocery business and I'll be the bad person when the prices go up.'

'We've noticed it at the factory too; it could be a rough ride ahead. My wife is already complaining she can't get what she needs from the milliners.'

Alice sighed. Anxiety threatened to engulf her. Having no desire to overhear their conversation, —the same one she had heard a hundred times over between her older brother, Robert, and her father— she stepped out into the wide road to pass the two men. All this talk of strikes, and now Lily getting involved in politics; at twenty years old, her younger sister wanted to take on the establishment. Alice shook her head. Talking to her feisty sibling, before she got arrested, was paramount. Their Grandpa Gettin was always saying Lily was like their mother, Sarah, when she was her age and she in turn reminded him of her mother, Alexandra, when she was alive.

Alice quickened her step. Her grip tightened on her empty shopping bag as it swung by her side, brushing against her black tulip-shaped, ankle length skirt. A red tram approached, she was convinced they were travelling faster than they used to. She stepped onto the pavement as it trundled past; the breeze blew a strand of her long brown hair across her face. Her slender fingers pulled it away and pushed it behind her ear, under her narrow-brimmed hat, before checking the small pearl earrings nestling on her earlobes.

The men's voices faded into the morning air as each step took her further away.

'Read all about it,' a newspaper boy yelled, pulling at his flat cap to keep the sun off his face. His brown jacket looked worn and threadbare. His black trousers sat an inch above his scuffed shoes. 'The heir to the Austrian throne and his wife shot dead in Sarajevo.' Men in suits swarmed towards the boy from all directions, frantically searching in their trouser pockets for the halfpenny needed to buy the newspapers that were under the lad's arm. 'Your change, sir.'

'Keep it.' The man stepped away, staring at the front page.

'Come on, lad, I'm going to be late for work.'

'Hold on, mate.' The boy handed over the paper and quickly pocketed the money.

Alice crossed Trafalgar Square, where the tall column was sited, with the famous admiral looking down on Londoners going about their business. The National Gallery stood tall and vast on her left as she made her way along Charing Cross Road. Drivers of the horse-drawn carriages were careful to avoid the motorcars as they drove past. The dull thud of the hooves clip-clopping on the tarmac provided the usual melodic background for the engines coughing and spluttering above them. Horse dung lay in a line along the road, the earthy smell mingling with the overpowering fumes from the cars. Shopkeepers said good morning to everyone they saw as they pulled down awnings to protect their produce from the early morning sunshine. As she walked by, Alice watched their practiced hands wipe down the windows with rags, reminding her of her father's wrath when he had caught her throwing away some worn bed linen. He'd lectured her about not wasting his hard-earned money, insisting the sheets were cut up, hemmed and used as rags, just like his mother used to do. Her mother hadn't said a word against him. She stored them away in a cupboard and his instructions were still waiting to be carried out. Alice had never met her father's family and neither had her mother. As a child, she had built fantasy pictures in her mind about them, and as an adult she had thought about visiting them in Norfolk, but she didn't want her father's anger to come down on her. He kept in touch by visiting them once a year, but he always went alone.

The chimes of Big Ben told her it was now quarter to nine. Alice shook her head, annoyed with herself for having gone to St Thomas' Hospital before work, instead of afterwards.

Chapter 2

Alice sighed with relief. Foyles Bookstore frontage was unmissable. The message was clear. They were the largest booksellers in London, with six floors. If a novel was purchased and returned after it was read, there would be a refund of two thirds of the price for each book. They had created quite a name since William and Gilbert Foyle started selling their own unwanted books in 1903. Everyone who started working there was told about their vision of having a bookshop for the people.

She paused for a moment to take a couple of deep breaths, hoping to lessen the heat on her face, catching sight of her reflection in a shop window. Her slender figure was slightly distorted by the glass as she patted down the wide, black-edged lapels of her white blouse. Her hand automatically ran down the small black buttons, twisting each one in turn. She took a deep breath, patted her pinned up hair and stepped towards the open doorway of the shop.

The shutters were being lifted and bookstands were being placed by the entrance and to the side of the store. Customers of all ages were already gathering.

'Morning, Miss Taylor.' A slim man towered above

her. 'You only just made it on time.' He frowned.

Her heart pummelled in her chest. She looked up at his stern expression. His grey hair was greased back. 'Sorry, sir, I foolishly went to St Thomas' before I came to work.' Colour flushed her cheeks; Mr Leadbetter was a stickler for timekeeping.

'Oh.' His face softened. 'Nothing wrong I trust?'

'No, sir, I've so many books indoors, I wanted to give some to the hospital...' Alice's voice faded to a mumble. 'For the patients.'

Mr Leadbetter raised his eyebrows. His hands linked behind his back, making his dark grey jacket gape revealing more of his blue tie and lily-white shirt. 'Very commendable.' He paused for a moment. 'You do know we sell second-hand books as well as new ones, don't you?'

The corners of Alice's lips lifted slightly. 'Of course, sir, I've worked here for a few years now. I just thought it would be a good thing to do, but I should have waited until my day off.'

Mr Leadbetter nodded and stepped aside for Alice to walk through the store to the staff room. Having removed her hat and left it with her shopping bag, she stood in front of a large white clock face with its wooden surround and pulled her clocking-in card from the individual slots next to it. She dropped it into a hole in front of the clock and pulled it out again. Alice looked down at the time stamp, realising she had only just made it on time. Quickly placing it back, she hurried into the shop.

Foyles had an air of a library about it as men, women and children lifted books from the shelves to look at the covers and read the first few pages. People whispered to each other, some louder than others, as their excitement grew. The bookshop had become a popular meeting place. There were shelves upon shelves of old and new books, priced from tuppence upwards. She took a deep breath, never tiring of the smell that came from them. She smiled, remembering how Mr Leadbetter had caught her with her nose in a book, her eyes shut, savouring the smell. He hadn't questioned her; he understood and they spent ten minutes trying to work out how to describe it. Was it woody? But then there was a trace of something else; maybe it was the ink or dust. If the previous reader had been a smoker, then that also clung to the pages. No one in the store thought it was odd; they were book lovers, after all.

Alice stepped behind the counter and placed her pad of bill payments in front of her.

'Morning, Alice, everything all right? I saw old Leadbetter talking to you.'

Alice looked up and smiled at Molly. 'Shh, don't call him that, he's quite nice really.'

'Huh, I am not so sure about that.' Molly pulled back her shoulders and lifted her chin, showing she was a head taller than her friend. She pushed back her blonde fringe and patted the bun that was neatly formed at the nape of her neck. 'I don't think he likes me.'

Alice laughed. 'He's probably heard what you call him.' She reached for a pen and placed it on top of her pad. 'Right, I'm ready.' Alice glanced over at the payment booth, expecting to see Victoria sitting there but it was empty. 'Is Victoria in yet?'

Molly shrugged her shoulders. 'Vic's nearly always late. I don't know how she gets away with it.'

Alice frowned. 'Don't call her that, she hates it.' She took a deep breath; the waft of carbolic soap hit her. In an attempt to clear her throat, she gave a slight cough.

Molly's bottom lip jutted out as she stared intently across at the payment booth. 'Well, you can't deny Miss Victoria Appleton seems to get away with things that no one else would.'

Alice sighed. 'Stop being mean, she has a lot on her plate, and anyway she probably gets docked fifteen minutes pay every time she's late.'

Molly's eyes looked heavenward. 'As always.' She frowned. 'If she's so poor, you wouldn't think she could afford to lose money like that.'

'Stop it. You or I wouldn't be able to cope with the things she does at twenty years old.' Alice glared at her friend for a moment before allowing her features to soften. 'Something's clearly bothering you but we can't talk about it now; maybe at lunch time.'

'What makes you think something's wrong?'

Alice laughed. 'You're obviously not in a good mood.' Glancing over at the payment booth again she saw Victoria stepping inside and locking herself in. She looked pale and weighed down. Alice smiled and waved at her friend but she wasn't looking her way.

'I'm in a perfectly good mood for a Monday morning, thank you very much.' Molly smiled through gritted teeth.

'What's happened?' Alice turned to give Molly her full attention. 'Didn't you have a very good weekend?'

Molly stared down at the counter, her fingers tracing the wood grain. 'It was fine.'

Alice shook her head. 'We've been friends since we were children; you do know you can tell me anything, don't you?'

Molly looked up and frowned. 'We have, but we come from very different backgrounds.'

'Not that different, and it's never been an issue before, so what's happened to make it one now?' Alice squinted at her, trying to read what was going on.

'Miss Cooper.'

Molly turned around to see Mr Leadbetter staring at her; she feigned a smile. 'Yes, Mr Leadbetter.'

'Is this your post for today?'

'No, sir, I'm just going there now.' Molly stepped past him without waiting for a response.

Alice watched him smile after Molly. The smile vanished as quickly as it arrived. He turned towards

Alice. 'We could be in for another busy day today, so please keep your eye on things. I don't want half the stock going missing.' He gave a curt nod and stepped aside, allowing a customer to be served.

Alice smiled at the lady standing in front of her. 'Good morning, isn't it a glorious day?' She took the book the customer was holding out towards her.

'It certainly is. Too nice to be shut inside.'

'You're right, but I do love being surrounded by all these wonderful books.' Alice smiled. She looked down and completed the bill payment form before giving it to the customer. 'If you would like to take this slip, together with tuppence, over to the payment booth.' Alice indicated to her left. 'Make your payment and then come back to me with your receipt.'

The lady gave a toothless smile. 'I will.' A gnarled hand reached out and took the slip of paper. 'Thank you.'

Alice watched her hobble over to the payment booth; she hadn't noticed her leaning heavily on a walking stick. She should have done and offered to take her payment over there for her. A low sigh escaped; it was too late now though, and she'd probably have been dismissed for trying to be helpful. Frowning, she recalled another assistant getting the sack for the same thing. They had all been reminded that it's clearly stated they were not to handle any money outside of the payment booth. With her smile permanently fixed, Alice moved onto the next customer.

Foyles was as busy as ever and the morning soon passed.

'Are you stopping for lunch?' Alice looked up. Tony Fletcher was smiling back at her.

She forced a smile. 'Hello, Tony, is it Molly you are looking for?' Apart from his tall muscular figure and obvious good looks, Alice couldn't see what Molly saw in him. She watched him move a little to the left, enabling him to see his reflection in the glass cabinet behind her. Alice shook her head. He could never love anybody more than he loved himself, but Molly was smitten. Alice had heard rumours about him flirting with every woman in town and had tried to tell Molly he wasn't good enough for her, but she wasn't interested in anything Alice had to say about him. Only last week, she had caught Molly writing her name as Molly Fletcher. They had joked about it but Alice knew she had to respect Molly's feelings for him.

'Why did you shake your head?' Tony's brows furrowed across his dark eyes.

'I didn't realise I had.'

His eyes sparkled and the corner of his lips lifted. 'Are you saying you don't want to have lunch with me?'

Alice's mouth straightened into a thin pencil line for a split second. 'Molly is my friend—'

'Yes, yes, I know that, but it doesn't mean we can't be friends.' Tony winked before giving her the benefit of his best smile.

'Don't you wink at me, Tony Fletcher. It's not appropriate.' Alice paused for a moment. 'You and I will only ever be friends because of Molly.'

Tony tipped his head to one side and gave her his best puppy-dog eyes. 'Ahh, don't you think you're being a little hard on me?'

'I've no desire to discuss this with you, not now or ever.' Alice scowled as she picked up her bill payment pad and pen.

'Hello, Tony.' Molly beamed as she came towards them.

Alice breathed a sigh of relief.

Tony turned around. 'Hello, Mol, I thought I'd surprise you and take you for a bite to eat.'

'That'd be lovely.' Molly's smile faded as her glance moved from Tony to Alice. 'Are you joining us?'

'No, thank you. I shall leave you two love birds alone.' Alice mustered up her best smile but nothing about this situation felt right. 'I'll have lunch with Victoria.' She was rewarded with a beaming smile from her friend. 'Has it been busy in the children's section?'

'Non-stop as always, but that's a good thing, it's lovely to see children so interested in reading books.' Molly rested her hand on Tony's arm. 'Give me five minutes to grab my bag.'

Tony nodded as he watched Molly speed through the store to the staff room, then turned his attention back to

Alice. He lent his arms on the counter separating them and swayed a little. 'I'm intrigued. Why do you always decline my invitations? Are you worried about being alone with me? Do you think you won't be able to control your feelings if you're in my company for any amount of time?'

Alice folded her arms over her stomach. Her eyes widened as she stared at him. 'You've an incredibly inflated opinion of yourself.'

Tony chuckled, pulling a cigarette packet out of his pocket. 'I can't help it if the ladies find me attractive.'

She unfolded her arms and raised her eyebrows. Her eyes twinkled mischievously. 'Although not as attractive as you find yourself.'

Tony stood up straight, towering a good six inches above her, and shrugged his shoulders. 'I don't mind you playing hard to get because it's all in the chase, and that's the best bit.'

Alice shook her head. 'You're despicable. If you hurt Molly I'll—'

'Ready,' Molly called out as she approached them.

Tony winked at Alice before turning to face Molly. 'You were quick.'

Molly gave him a beaming smile and tucked her arm in his. 'I don't like to keep my man waiting.' They took a couple of steps towards the door.

'Wait, did you remember to clock out?' Alice frowned as Molly looked back at her. 'You don't want Mr

Leadbetter after you again.'

'Yes, yes, stop fussing.' Molly laughed, leaning into Tony as they walked towards the open shop door.

Alice glanced over at Victoria, locked in her booth, busy processing payments. She wondered if her friend would ever recover from the dreadful events four-and-a-half years ago. Her complexion was ashen against her dark brown hair. The dark rings under her eyes told of many sleepless nights. Life had been draining out of her for four-and-a-half years. When her parents died that terrible day, something inside Victoria had died with them. The fun the pair of them had shared, preparing the surprise afternoon tea for Victoria's mother and father flashed into Alice's mind. They had made such a mess in the kitchen, but laughter had been the order of the day. That laughter hadn't been heard since. She momentarily closed her eyes, tears pricking at her lids as the feeling of grief for her friend washed over her. The need to help was overwhelming, but there was nothing she could do except be there when she was needed. Alice walked away from her counter, towards the payment booth, as Victoria stood up. A work colleague had come to replace her while she had lunch.

They sat together in the staff room, each nursing a cup of coffee. Alice placed her lunch on the small table before unwrapping the chicken sandwich Mrs Headley had made her that morning. The paper crinkling broke the silence between them. Her hand ran across it, smoothing out the creases, so it could be used again. She eyed her friend. 'Where's your lunch?'

Victoria gave Alice's sandwich a sideways glance before she folded her hands around her cup and gazed into the dark liquid. 'I forgot it. I was running late, so it's sitting on my kitchen side.' A slight flush temporarily coloured her cheeks.

Alice looked at Victoria under hooded eyes before sighing. 'Again? You'll fade away if you keep missing lunch.' She turned her attention back to her sandwich. 'Well I'm never going to be able to eat all of this, so we might as well share it. I fear Mrs Headley gets carried away; these slices of bread are so thick.' She peeled back the edge of the crust to look at the chicken. 'This is more like chunks than slices.' Alice shook her head. 'It's a shame to throw it away. Here, take half.' She pushed the paper it was sitting on in Victoria's direction.

Victoria looked longingly at it. After a moment she shook her head. 'No thank you, I'll be fine.'

Alice shrugged her shoulders. 'Well obviously I can't make you, but if you don't want it, I'll see if someone else does. It's a shame to throw good food away.' She picked up half of the sandwich but kept her eyes on her friend.

'You're right, it's a shame to waste it.'

Without a word, Alice pushed it nearer to Victoria.

'Thanks.' Victoria picked up the remaining half and eagerly bit into it.

Alice's eyes narrowed and a frown quickly formed as she wondered when her friend had last eaten. 'How's everything going?'

Victoria shrugged. 'We've been busy this morning so it's a never-ending queue to pay. Thankfully, most people are patient.'

Alice nodded. 'I know, but I didn't mean work.' She bit into her sandwich and a white chunk of chicken fell onto her paper.

Victoria's eyes were transfixed on her sandwich. 'Nothing changes. I don't suppose it ever will.'

Alice put down her sandwich and placed her hand over Victoria's. 'Is it Daisy and Stephen? Are they still giving you a hard time?'

Victoria laughed, but it wasn't a joyous sound. 'They're young. Stephen's only sixteen and hates his job at the boot factory. He wants adventure but I keep telling him we need the money he earns, otherwise we'll have to give up the house.'

'And Daisy?'

'Huh, she hates being in service. At eighteen, she could probably get a job here at Foyles but she doesn't want me spying on her, as she puts it.'

'What?' Alice's mouth dropped open.

'I know.' Victoria shook her head. 'I'm not sure how much longer I can keep going. I'm so tired. I don't know how people do it.' She blinked rapidly as her eyes welled up.

'What about if I talk to them?' Alice shook her head. Victoria's eyes widened, taking in her friend's elegant appearance, now so different from her own. 'I don't know if I can get through to them, but I'm happy to try.' Alice looked down at her half eaten sandwich, already knowing the answer to her offer.

Victoria stayed silent for a moment, staring down at the palms of her hands as though they had all the answers. She folded her arms in front of her stomach before looking across at Alice. 'Thank you, but they'll know I've been talking about them and that'll only make matters worse.'

Alice nodded. 'I'd suggest Lily, especially as they're a similar age, but I'm not sure she'd be a good influence right now.'

Victoria nodded. 'They're at a difficult age. They seem to want it all and I'm not sure where that comes from.'

Alice frowned as she glanced across at her friend. 'They do seem more confident than us.' She paused, forcing a smile. 'Do you remember when Molly's gran let us loose in the kitchen?' Alice chuckled. 'We made a right mess. If I remember rightly, we covered everything with flour.'

Victoria giggled. 'Yes, she was mad letting the three of us try our hand at baking cakes. I'm not sure I'd have been that brave.'

Alice laughed. It had been a long time since she had

heard her giggling. 'No, and it's not as though the cakes were up to much either.'

*

Mrs Headley opened the front door. Her old eyes squinted at the sunshine. Concern flitted across her lined features when she saw Lily looking dishevelled, with a uniformed policeman standing in front of her.

Lily painted on her best smile, roughly pushing her brown hair away from her face. 'Don't look so worried, Mrs Headley. I'm fine.' She feigned a laugh. 'But you might want to hold dinner and stay out of the way for a couple of hours. At least until his lord and master's finished with me or summonsed you.'

The policeman removed his hat and nodded at the housekeeper as he entered the four-storey Bloomsbury Street house. Without a word, he followed Lily. His heavy footsteps were silent on the floor tiles in the hallway, in contrast to the rhythm of the small heels she wore. They didn't stop at the front parlour, where guests would normally be taken. Instead, Lily carried on to the day room at the back of the house.

Mrs Headley's gaze followed them as she clicked the front door shut. Without a sound, she took the stairs to the scullery.

Lily took a deep breath, pulling up her five-foot-six petite frame. Her jaw clenched. She pushed open the door to the spacious, lavender-filled family sitting room.

The policeman stared straight ahead, trying not to gawp around the beautiful room. The oak fireplace was surrounded with blue ceramic tiles, standing directly in front of him, with a brass coal scuttle to the left of it. A large glass and silver bowl stood on a wooden corner cupboard, next to the French doors, allowing the early evening sunshine to cast shadows into the room. The green and brown chintz curtains that hung loose at the doors were at odds with the brown leaf design of the Queen Anne chairs and the brown square design of the rug. Family pictures hung on soft grey painted walls. His two-up, two-down house would fit into this room alone.

Sarah looked up. For a split second, horror flitted across her face. The book nestling in her lap was forgotten as she shifted her gaze from her daughter to the officer and back again. Lily's windswept head was slightly bent. Brown tendrils of hair had dropped down and obscured her face. She didn't look up to meet her mother's gaze; instead she concentrated on the rug under her feet.

Luke stood up, his body upright and rigid, showing the full six-feet plus of his height. His thin face was tight and unyielding, with hands clenched by his sides. They had never had a policeman in their home before.

'Mr and Mrs Taylor, I am very sorry to disturb you this evening...' The policeman moved his helmet to under his arm.

Lily looked up; defiance chased the anxiety away from her young features. She held her head high and jutted out her chin. Her dark eyes glinting a sharp steel-like quality, in anticipation of what was to come. She lifted her hand to smooth away the stray locks of hair that had escaped the roll she had pinned up that morning. A pulse was visible at the side of her temple.

'The sergeant asked me to bring your daughter home…'

Sarah jumped up out of her armchair, ignoring the thud of her book hitting the floor. 'Are you hurt, Lily?'

Luke stepped forward and held up his hand, signalling his wife to stop talking. 'Home from where?'

The policeman cleared his throat. 'Miss Taylor was brought into the Police Station when a fracas broke out outside The Houses of Parliament, sir.'

Luke glared at his daughter. 'Were you demonstrating again, even though I forbade it?'

Lily's face hardened under his scrutiny. 'Yes. How else are we going to get anyone to listen?'

'But I told you—'

'Sorry, sir, if I may. Your daughter hasn't been charged with any offence, but the sergeant asked me to forward his regards onto you both, and Mr Gettin. Apparently Mrs Taylor, his father held your father in high esteem.' He paused for a brief moment. 'I am correct in saying your father is Mr Edward Gettin?'

'Yes, officer, thank you.' Sarah nodded, taking a deep

breath in an attempt to stop the colour rising in her cheeks. 'I'll make sure my father gets the message.'

The policeman visibly relaxed a little, before a smile lit up his face. 'I hear a lot of stories about the Gettin family...'

Sarah's hands intertwined in front of her, her knuckles white with tension. A nervous laugh escaped. 'All good I hope.'

'Oh yes, all good.'

'Thank you for bringing our daughter home and I apologise for the problems she may have given you.' Sarah's words rushed over each other as colour crept into her cheeks.

The policeman gave Sarah a gentle smile. There was a fragility about her. He had the urge to protect her, but from what, he wasn't sure. 'She was lucky the sergeant was on—'

'Yes, thank you.' Luke took a step towards him, holding out his hand. 'We appreciate this has been handled with sensitivity.'

Disdain flitted across the policeman's face. He shook Mr Taylor's hand and nodded. He glanced across at Mrs Taylor. 'Well, I'm sorry to have disturbed you.' He turned towards Lily. 'Please take care, miss.' He nodded to the family before stepping towards the doorway. 'Goodnight.'

'Goodnight, officer.' Sarah and Luke said in unison.

The thud of the front door shutting jolted Luke into

action. 'Lily, we have never had any reason to have the police on our doorstep, and yet here we are tonight. You have brought shame on this family.'

'Father, don't you mean shame on you? I'm not ashamed, although I expect you are worrying about what your precious neighbours were saying as they sneaked a peek from behind their curtains.' Lily took a deep breath, her face crimson with rage.

Open-mouthed, Sarah lowered herself back into the armchair. 'Lily, you must stop. Your father has worked hard to provide for you, for us.'

'So I should be grateful, is that it?'

'Not grateful...' Sarah stopped as Luke's voice drowned her out.

'Yes,' Luke spat. His tone let them know he was reaching boiling point.

'I wish I'd been locked up like some of my friends.'

'So do I. Maybe it would have taught you a lesson.' Luke walked over to the sideboard that was nestling in the recess of the chimneybreast. The room had fallen silent. The chink from the crystal glass decanter as he lifted the stopper out of its neck echoed in the room. No one spoke as he poured himself a whisky.

Sarah glanced down at her book on the floor. She lowered herself to pick it up, but stopped halfway when she realised Luke had turned his steely gaze on her. She straightened herself and lowered her eyes.

'Evening.' Alice strolled into the sitting room and

flopped unlady-like, into an armchair. 'Ohh, my feet are killing me. It's been another busy day at the bookstore.' She was suddenly aware of the tension and scanned the room, trying to ascertain what was the problem. Her lips tightened. Lily, that's what the problem was.

Luke turned to face Alice, leaving the whisky on the sideboard. 'You left before me this morning; have you been at work all this time?' His sharp, steely-eyed expression belied his soft tone.

'Erm, yes, well pretty much.'

Luke's stare didn't waiver. 'Pretty much, what does that mean?'

Alice stared back at him. Her mind frantically searched its archives. Had she done something wrong? 'I didn't go straight to work. I went to St Thomas', to deliver some books for the patients.'

'That's right.' Sarah tried to sound jovial, but it didn't work. 'I remember you said you were going to do that.'

Luke didn't take his eyes off Alice. He ran his fingers through his thick mop of salt and pepper hair that just curled over his collar. 'So, you must have walked over Westminster Bridge.'

Lily feigned a cough and shook her head at the same time.

'Do you have something to say?' Luke arched his eyebrows at his youngest daughter.

Lily swallowed hard. She thrust her shoulders back as

she took a deep breath. 'I don't understand why you are asking Alice where she's been; after all, it's me that's in trouble, not her.'

'Yes, that is true.' Luke smiled at both of their troubled faces. They didn't smile back. 'The thing is, I think Alice was probably there and did nothing to put a stop to it.'

'What? Put a stop to what?'

Luke turned to pick up his glass.

'You don't think Alice could've stopped me, do you? What you feel now would be much worse if she'd tried.' Lily laughed. 'Bloomsbury Street would've been beside itself with gossip.'

He slammed his empty hand down hard on the sideboard. The thud made the three women jump simultaneously. 'I will not put up with your disrespect, do you understand me?'

Fear ran through Alice as she stood up, not noticing the leaflet fall from her skirt pocket as she took the couple of steps towards her sister. She placed a protective arm around her. 'I'm sure she didn't mean to be disrespectful, Father. Lily is just passionate in what she believes in. I'm sure one day she'll be running the country and you'll be so proud of her then.'

Luke sneered at his eldest daughter, before bending down to pick up the folded paper. 'That won't happen in my life time. Women are only good for one thing.'

Nausea swept over Alice. Anxiety tied her stomach in

knots. She had forgotten about the leaflet that had been thrust into her hand that morning.

Luke played with the paper before lifting his glass and emptying the contents, grimacing as the whisky's strong flavour warmed his throat. He placed the glass down on the sideboard.

Lily opened her mouth to speak, but Alice quickly jabbed her elbow into her sister's side.

'So, you didn't see Lily at the demonstration?' Luke didn't look at Alice. His eyes stayed focussed on his hands as he slowly unfolded the paper. It wasn't long before the large bold print became visible.

Alice closed her eyes and took a deep breath, waiting for the repercussions of not speaking to Lily at the demonstration.

Chapter 3

Alice turned and stared out of Lily's large bedroom window. Being on the top floor gave a good view of Bedford Avenue. It was bright and sunny outside, a stark contrast to inside. She unlocked the metal catch and pushed up the sash window; the beautiful gardens in Bedford Square were just visible when she leant forward slightly. She stood there for a moment and closed her eyes, enjoying the early morning air dancing on her skin.

Lily grappled with her white cotton sheets and red woven bedspread, smoothing them out before pulling them close under her chin. Her nightdress was hidden from view. Her arms wrapped around her knees, hugging them to her.

How Alice wished she were going to work. It wasn't the first time she'd yearned to work more than three days a week at Foyles. Her father couldn't understand why she wanted to work at all; after all, there was no financial need to, and if he had his way, she wouldn't. She had begged and pleaded with him. With her mother's help, and the suggestion that he could stop the equivalent of her wages out of her allowance, he had compromised, albeit reluctantly. Alice had grabbed it with both hands. He hadn't understood it wasn't about the money; she would've worked for free. It was about the freedom that working in Foyles gave her. Alice sighed and straightened the red curtains, before turning to face her sister again. She walked over, sat on the edge of the bed and glared at Lily. 'I don't know what you were thinking about.'

'What do you mean?' Lily sighed. 'Isn't it obvious?'

Without thinking, Alice straightened the three books lying haphazardly on the bedside table, before pushing herself up off the bed. 'Don't be obtuse, you know what I mean.' She paced, barefoot, around her sister's bedroom, the exposed wooden floorboards creaking under her feet. There was no opulence in this bedroom, or in hers. When the girls had asked to have pictures on the whitewashed walls, the answer had come back as a resounding no from their father. The only rooms furnished to a high standard were those visitors would sit or sleep in. The thick woollen pile carpet in her parents' bedroom was missing in their children's rooms. She stopped pacing to alter the position of the French antique freestanding mirror, which stood next to the heavy oak wardrobe. Both Alice and Lily had received one from their grandparents a few Christmases ago after it had come to light that neither of them had mirrors in their bedrooms. Their father had disapproved of the gift. Vanity was a profound sin. He had made it clear they were only allowed to remain in their rooms because they were antiques. Alice shook her head; clearly money or greed wasn't such a sin. She continued around the foot of the bed towards the chest of drawers.

Lily squeezed her hands tight over her knees. 'Alice, is everything all right?'

Alice stopped pacing and raised her hands, wrapping them around the china jug that stood centre stage, inside a large bowl on the chest of drawers. 'Apart from the obvious, you mean?' Her arms dropped by her sides and the tepid water stood unmoving, waiting for her sister to rise and wash herself.

Lily nodded. 'Yes, apart from the obvious.' She paused, watching Alice, noticing for the first time that her shoulders were hunched over. 'You shook your head after you straightened the mirror. I just wondered...' Lily paused. 'I'm sorry about yesterday. I just didn't think about you getting into trouble.'

Sighing, Alice continued to walk around the small room. 'No, and there lies the problem. If you'd thought about your actions, you would've known father would be angry, especially getting yourself arrested.' Alice stopped pacing and glared at her. 'What are you trying to prove?'

Lily held her gaze but stayed silent. She closed her eyes and lowered her head.

Alice immediately felt sorry she had berated her sister. 'There has to be another way. I'm not saying I have the answers, but life's going to be unbearable in this house if you don't work it out.'

Lily looked up and across at the window, the blue cloudless sky just visible. 'It's unbearable anyway.' She closed her eyes again for a moment before shaking her head. 'I don't know what is going on but mother looks like a scared cat most of the time.' Lily frowned before staring at Alice. 'What's happened to the spirit she always had? I remember her being great fun when we were children. Always laughing and playing, I don't understand what's happened.'

'I don't know. Father isn't his normal self either; maybe they're worried about the general strike I keep hearing about.'

'Hmm, I don't know, maybe.' Lily moved the bedcovers and lowered her legs. She wrapped her hand around her long brown hair and formed a ponytail before releasing it down her back. 'I don't understand why everything I do gets you into trouble.' She frowned. 'Nothing seems to make sense anymore.' Lily reached out and picked up the cup, leaving the matching saucer on her bedside table. Her hands clasped around the bowl of it, the warmth seeping through her fingers and steam spiralling into the air.

'Are you cold?'

Lily took a sip of the tea that Alice had gifted her. 'No, I just like the warmth.' She sucked in her breath as she replaced the cup onto the saucer. 'It needs to cool a little.'

Alice walked over and sat on the edge of the bed, taking Lily's hand in hers; the tingling warmth spread into her fingers. 'It's because I'm the eldest, so I should be protecting you, keeping you out of trouble.'

'I'm not ten. I'm twenty years old for goodness sake and you can't be with me twenty-four hours a day.'

Alice laughed. 'You and I know that, but I'm not sure father does.' She paused for a moment. 'I think he's old fashioned in his thoughts and probably believes we shouldn't be out without a chaperone, at any time, day or night.'

Lily scoffed. 'That is old fashioned. When do you think I'll be allowed to start taking responsibility for my own actions?' A tear trickled down Lily's cheek; she quickly wiped it away. 'When do you think he'll start seeing me as the adult I am?'

Alice sat silent for a moment stroking Lily's hand. 'Be careful what you wish for, because the moment he does he'll try and marry you off to someone influential, especially if he sees you as a problem to him.'

Lily stared hard at Alice. 'He hasn't you, but then I suppose you're not a problem child.' She paused, trying to glean information from her expression. 'He hasn't, has he?'

Alice laughed, but it wasn't a jovial sound. 'I've had some near misses and that's only because mother and grandpa stepped in for me.' She sighed.

Lily rubbed her hands over her eyes, trying to hide

the tears that were forming. 'Yes, and I suppose he didn't really want to part with any money either.' She frowned and mumbled almost to herself. 'He has old fashioned values, but only when it suits him.'

'Look, Lily, you have to find another way to make your mark on the world and try to keep father happy, for your own sake and mine.'

Lily tipped her head backwards to peer up at the ceiling. She looked back at Alice. Her chin trembled a little as she gave a half-hearted shrug. 'I'm not trying to prove anything. I'm just standing up for what I believe in, but that appears to be a crime.'

A smile crept across Alice's face. 'If I'm honest, I don't disagree with what you are doing, but if you tell anyone I shall deny it.'

Lily gave her a weak smile. 'Coward.'

Alice licked her dry lips and splayed a hand across her chest. Her heart was pounding with increasing volume. 'Through and through, but I prefer to think I'm more conservative, with a small 'c', in my actions.'

Lily smiled at her before taking a deep breath. 'I'm truly sorry you were dragged into it last night, Alice, but women should be able to vote on how our country is run. My only regret is him blaming you for what I'd done.'

'I know you are, don't worry about it.' Alice laughed, standing up and walking over to the dressing table. 'The leaflet that woman gave me didn't help matters. To be honest, I shoved it in my pocket and forgot about it.'

Lily scowled. 'Yes, and now he thinks you are a problem child too.' She chuckled. 'I can't imagine you as a problem child.'

Alice couldn't stop the smile from forming, but then she didn't want to. 'You do need to think about how it affects us all. Mother looked terrified when I came in.'

Lily frowned as she rubbed her arm. 'Do you think he hits her?'

Alice leant back slightly, wrapping her arms around her waist. 'I know father has a short temper, but I don't think he'd do that.'

'I'm not so sure.' Lily's lips closed into a thin pencil line.

Alice raised her eyebrows, surprised her sister was having similar thoughts to her own. She shook her head, deciding it might be best to change the subject, but nothing came to mind. 'I know you are in hiding but he's gone to work, so it's safe to get up.'

Lily laughed. 'I'm not hiding, just having a lie in.' Her eyes scanned the walls of her room. 'After all, it's so tastefully decorated, why would I want to leave?' The smile disappeared from her voice. 'And that's something else I don't understand.'

'What's that?' Alice turned away from her sister, sensing a rant was on its way.

'Why are our rooms a small whitewashed cell when we live in such a large house. Prisoners probably have better rooms than us. I bet they're allowed to put pictures up. Daisy's room is bigger than ours, and nicely decorated. I'm not saying she's lucky, because I clearly wouldn't want to be in her position, but she does have carpet. No splinters in her feet, I can tell you.'

Alice chuckled at her sister. 'The boys have the larger rooms upstairs.' She picked up the bottle of Narcisse Caron perfume that stood on the dressing table, amongst several other bottles. Her fingers gently rolled over the indentations of the white glass that were shaped into petals at the top of the bottle. She pulled off the flower-shaped lid and held it under her nose. The floral, fruity fragrance immediately assaulted her senses. She pushed the lid away and wrinkled her nose at it.

Lily laughed at her sister's face. 'Put some on your wrist and give it a few minutes to settle down.'

Alice pulled it back towards her for a second attempt. There was orange, with maybe a mix of jasmine and rose. 'No, I don't think I will, thanks.' She replaced the lid and stood it back on the dressing table.

'Aunt Emily bought that for me at Christmas. It's quite nice but when you put it on, it needs time to settle.'

Alice nodded.

'Didn't she buy you perfume as well?'

'Yes, I got Champs-Élysées.' Alice smiled. 'I think she buys them for the lovely bottles as much as the perfume.'

Lily took another sip of tea. She peered over the top of her cup at Alice, whose dark hair was hanging in loose waves down her back. She drained her cup before replacing it on the saucer. Lily sighed. 'I don't know if I should tell you this but Daisy was there yesterday.'

Alice's jaw dropped open for a moment before she gathered herself. 'What?'

Lily nodded.

'Oh my goodness, I should go round there. Victoria has so much to deal with already, looking after a younger brother and sister. Did she get arrested as well?'

'I know it's hard for you.' Lily frowned as she stared at her sister. 'But I don't think you should get involved. Leave them to work it out on their own.' She took a deep breath. 'They won't thank you for interfering.'

*

Victoria sat alone in the small sitting room of her home in Percy Street. The evening was warm and the air was still. The flame of the candle barely flickered. It cast shadows around the room, distorting the shapes and the colour of the furniture. The lack of money meant she had given up on gas lighting and returned to using candles. She stared at the flame, wanting to touch it, wanting to feel the warmth. It reminded her of the winter evenings spent with her mother and father in front of the open fire. They were bittersweet memories that hugged her, but also stabbed at her heart. Tears gently rolled down her cheeks. She wiped her damp face as laughter seeped into the shadows of the house, from outside. The pendulum clock chimed; she glanced at it sitting in the centre of the mantelpiece. Ten o'clock. Was that Daisy or Stephen?

Loneliness engulfed Victoria as the laughter drifted further down the street. Ted Marsden leapt to the front of her thoughts. She shook her head. It was too painful to think about him, even though he stood tall and strong in her mind. She could almost feel the soft curls of his black hair. What was he doing now? She wondered why she hadn't bumped into him around London. Perhaps he was avoiding her. Four years ago her future was with him and, although he was five years older than her, the love she felt for him at sixteen was as strong as ever.

Her brother and sister had taken her life, just as the rail crash had taken her parents.

*

It was five-thirty and the Foyles shop assistants were gathered around the machine in the staff room, waiting to clock out, each trying to reach the card with their name on it. The chatter and laughter amongst them filled the room. Alice took out her time card, pushed it into the correct position and when the mechanism dinged, she pulled it out and put it back in its slot. She moved aside and glanced across at Victoria, who was now following the same procedure. Molly had long gone, rushing to meet Tony. Alice knew she worried about keeping him waiting.

Victoria and Alice strode through the shop, eerily quiet with no customers. Mr Leadbetter stood at the now bolted door.

'Goodnight, Mr Leadbetter,' the girls said in unison, above the rattle of the bolt being pulled across.

Mr Leadbetter smiled as he opened the door wide. 'Goodnight, ladies, see you tomorrow. No doubt it will be another busy day, but that's what keeps us employed.'

They both nodded. 'See you tomorrow.'

The door closed behind them and the noise of the bolt being drawn momentarily followed them down Charing Cross Road.

The door to the George Tavern, on the corner of George Yard, was wide open. The maltiness of the ale, mingling with cigarette smoke, seeped out into the street, inviting passers-by to enter. Men's laughter and jeering coming from inside the small pub caught Alice's attention. 'Don't you just love the summer evenings when you've finished work and can just amble along without worrying about getting out of the cold, or being somewhere by a certain time?' Alice swung her brown handbag by her side, her free arm tucked inside Victoria's. 'Everyone is so much happier when the sun is shining, don't you think?' Her salmon pink and cream column dress hung neatly over her slim figure. The toes of her brown-buttoned ankle boots peeked out from under her skirt when they stopped to cross Sutton Street before continuing along Charing Cross Road. 'Shall we be little devils and walk along to Regent Street and have some coffee and cake in Monico?'

'Hmm, that does sound tempting but...'

Alice laughed and tightened her grip on the white silk blouse covering her friend's arm. 'If you are tempted, I am not taking no for an answer. My treat.'

Victoria glanced across at her friend's smiling face. 'I've known you nearly all my life and I don't think I've ever known you to be miserable.'

Alice laughed. 'You're joking with me, aren't you? Perhaps I should be on the stage, what do you think?'

Victoria laughed. 'Maybe.' Guilt swamped her and the laughter was quickly replaced by a frown. 'Or perhaps you've led a lucky life.'

Alice smiled. 'I think you're right. I've led a lucky life, especially when you compare it with what you've been through.' She paused, staring down at the pavement, wondering whether she should continue or not. 'Everyone has bad times you know; admittedly some are worse than others, but I've had my moments. Things aren't always easy.' She paused, casting Victoria a sideways glance. 'I worry about Lily and all this demonstrating she's doing.' She took a deep breath. 'My mother looked terrified when I got home last night and Lily was quite defiant.'

Victoria's arm squeezed her friend's hand. 'Lily's always been passionate in believing she's right, even when she isn't.'

Alice nodded. 'It's not that I disagree with the fundamentals of it all, but she'd been escorted home by a policeman.'

Victoria's jaw dropped and her eyes widened. 'I bet your father was furious. No wonder your mother was frightened.'

'Yes, he wasn't too pleased and, obviously, I got into trouble for not stopping her.'

Victoria shook her head. 'What? Is he sure? Doesn't he know Lily at all?'

Alice gave her a feeble smile. 'Apparently not. Lily, to her credit, spelt out the consequences of that action to him, but I think it made matters worse.'

Victoria gave a hollow laugh. 'Lily's always been strong willed, a bit like Daisy.'

Alice looked across at her. 'I'm glad you said that, and I don't want to tell tales but Lily told me Daisy was also at the demonstration.'

Victoria's pale features turned ashen; her eyes darted around as if searching for a memory.

'Lily didn't know if she'd been arrested, but I thought you should know.'

'She never mentioned it,' Victoria whispered, remembering she'd sat in the chair and cried until sleep rescued her. She hadn't seen her sister until that morning and had no idea what time Daisy and Stephen got home. She'd tried to talk to them but they'd flounced out of the house early, leaving her alone with her worries about what would become of them all.

'No.' Alice took a deep breath and slowly exhaled. 'I didn't know whether to say anything or not, but as you say, we've been friends a long time.' She paused, staring at Victoria's complexion and feeling a little bit scared she may have tipped her over the edge. Maybe Lily was more astute than she realised. 'I'll ask Freddie if he can find out, and maybe sort it out quietly.'

Victoria nodded. 'I don't want him to get into trouble, but I can't pretend that wouldn't be appreciated.' She gave a weak smile.

'How is Daisy?'

Victoria sighed. 'It's a constant battle. She hates working as a domestic so I offered to try to get her work in Foyles, but that didn't go down well.' Victoria looked down at the pavement for a moment. 'It's hard being a parent to an eighteen and sixteen-year-old, especially when you are only twenty yourself.' She sighed and looked across at Alice. 'You know, every time I make a suggestion or try to explain things, they just explode and tell me I'm not their mother.'

Alice nodded. No words came.

Victoria's eyes became watery. 'I miss my parents so much. It has been a hard four years without them.'

Alice's vision became blurred; she sniffed. 'I don't

know what to say. I'm afraid I don't have any words of wisdom. The only thing I'd say is you do a marvellous job and your parents would be proud of you, keeping the family together. I know I couldn't do it.'

Victoria's laugh was hollow. 'You don't know what you can do until you're thrown into a situation that's out of your control.'

Alice gave Victoria's arm a light squeeze. 'I expect that's true but you've proven yourself to be a strong woman and don't you forget that.'

They walked along Oxford Street in silence, neither stopping to look in the shop windows. Men stood in groups, puffing on their cigarettes, plumes of smoke swirling around them, before disappearing in the breeze. Their chatter followed the girls down the street, making it clear there was talk about the general strike action that was being planned.

Alice broke the silence. 'You know, if everyone isn't talking about the possibility of a general strike, then they are talking about whether we'll end up going to war.' She sighed. 'It seems to me it's all doom and gloom.'

'Yes, I must admit I'm thankful that if we do go to war, Stephen is too young to enlist.'

'I know what you mean because I have the same thoughts about Charles. To be honest, I try not to think about it.' Alice took a deep breath. 'Robert will make father proud, and mother distraught, by enlisting straight away.'

Victoria nodded. 'I expect you're right. Even as a child, I remember Robert as always being dutiful.'

Alice laughed. 'Dutiful? As the eldest of four, he's just plain bossy if you ask me.' She paused for a moment. 'He was always telling tales on us and he liked to pull the "I'm the eldest so I know best" phrase, but actually he doesn't always.'

'Maybe that's how Daisy and Stephen see me.' Victoria chuckled. 'Perhaps I should ask them.'

Alice tapped her friend's hand. 'Nonsense, you had no choice. The position was thrust upon you. Robert did though; he just liked being father's favourite and that's the difference.' She smiled. 'He drives Lily and Charles mad.'

They turned left onto Regent Street.

'Do you think Freddie will enlist?' Victoria frowned as she looked across at Alice.

Anxiety chased Alice's smile away. 'I don't think so; the police will be needed here.'

Victoria gave her a sideways glance. 'I'm surprised you and Freddie haven't got married by now.'

Alice laughed. 'He has to ask me first.'

'Well it's about time he did. Trust me, four years is an eternity.' Victoria frowned as she looked at Alice. 'It's definitely time he proposed.' She blinked rapidly as she stared hard at the pavement. He was a constant reminder that her friend's happiest moment was inextricably linked to the worst day of her own life.

Alice wanted to talk about Ted, to know whether Victoria had heard from him since he walked away from her within months of her parents dying, and whether she still had feelings for him, but she couldn't bring herself to rake through that pain again.

The two adjacent pyramid signs of the Café Monico were just ahead; people were milling around outside. Alice pushed the wooden door, which opened into a large room filled with round wooden tables and matching chairs. Arched mirrors on the wall gave the illusion of space, while the white roman pillars gave it grandeur. The panelled ceiling was edged with scrolled mouldings. Large potted palms were strategically placed around the room.

Victoria's jaw dropped. 'This is beautiful.' She looked around her. 'I haven't been in here before.'

Alice smiled as she watched her eyes moving around the room. 'I don't come much; only when I fancy a real treat.'

Their heels clattered on the tiled floor as they were shown to a table.

Alice smiled at the waitress, dressed in a floor length black dress with a pristine white apron tied around her waist. 'Thank you. I know what I want, do you, Victoria?'

Victoria pulled out her chair and sat down. 'I can never say no to a chocolate layer cake, if you have any.'

'Hmm, I'm tempted but I think I'll stick with a slice

of lemon cake please, and' Alice looked across at Victoria, 'we'll have two teas.' Victoria nodded her agreement.

Moments later, they were tucking into their slices of cake, before pouring tea from the white china pot.

'This is delicious; so light.' Victoria scooped another piece on her dessert fork. 'I love chocolate cake. My mother used to make it all the time so it's a bit of a weakness of mine.'

Alice laughed. 'Cake is a weakness full stop.' She picked up the lid of the teapot and gave the hot liquid a stir before replacing it. 'I'm always being told it's all in the brewing.' She lifted the pot and poured the golden hot liquid into the china cups.

Victoria added a splash of milk to her tea. 'It looks a fine cup.'

Alice followed suit before automatically picking it up to take a sip, but the steam warned her it was too hot. A shadow passed over Alice's eyes as she returned her teacup to the matching saucer. 'I can't remember the last time we were out shopping together. We used to spend most of our time in Liberty's and John Lewis, do you remember?'

Victoria patted her lips with the white linen napkin. 'The choice of embroidery threads from John Lewis is always wonderful, but I haven't bought any for a long time.' She smiled before continuing. 'We did use to have fun wandering up and down Oxford and Regent Street, especially in the milliners. What about all the hats the three of us used to try on, so many styles and colours, we used to spend hours in there.'

Laughter bubbled to the surface as the pair of them reminisced.

Victoria rested her hand on her chest as tears of laughter rolled down her cheeks. 'Do you remember Molly bought that awful wide brimmed lacy thing.' She giggled. 'I'm sure I've never seen it on her head.'

A clatter ricocheted around the coffee house, making Alice jump in her seat. She turned to see a red-faced waitress stooping to pick up some of the broken crockery.

Victoria shook her head. 'I expect the owners will make her pay for those breakages, so that'll be at least a day's wages lost.'

Alice watched the young girl; she momentarily looked up and caught her watching her. It was only then Alice realised it was the waitress who had served them. She picked up the large broken pieces and placed them on a tray, while another waitress appeared with a broom and started to sweep the residue away from the customers. 'If that's true, it's a shame.' Alice wondered if she could offer to pay for the breakages without insulting anyone. Perhaps she could speak to the owner, or leave a large tip for the waitress.

<u>Chapter 4</u>

Alice gave a weary sigh and pulled at the three-quarter length sleeves of her white blouse. She wriggled her toes inside her shoes. Her feet ached and tiredness swept over her. She glanced across at Victoria, who was still serving customers at the booth. It had been another busy day at Foyles and Alice hadn't had the chance to talk to her about Daisy. The sun being out hadn't stopped the customers from coming in and searching through the thousands of books. She caught sight of Mr Leadbetter leaning over, talking to a customer. Her mouth formed a ready smile when she remembered him reassuring and guiding a tearful customer out of the shop earlier that day. He had looked uncomfortable dealing with such emotions, but the lady had got lost on the third floor. It had happened to several customers since Alice had started working there. She began tidying up the counter and stacked the books that hadn't been collected, never understanding why customers went to the trouble of picking a book but then not coming back to collect it. When she had finished, she placed her pen neatly on top of her bill payment pad, ready to store it away when the shop closed for the evening.

'Here, let me.'

Alice stopped what she was doing and looked up. She watched the tall dark-haired man in a police uniform reach effortlessly for a book on one of the higher shelves. The three gold stripes on his arm appeared to sparkle against the dark blue of the uniform. A smile played on her lips as he passed it to the old lady stooped next to him.

'There you go. Is there anything else you need while I'm here?'

The old lady giggled. Her grey pallor took on a pink hue and her smile revealed crooked brown teeth. The tangle of her grey hair hid the soft curls from view. 'I'm sure there's a lot you could do for me, sergeant, but even the thought of it makes me come over all unnecessary.' Her cackle filled the shop. 'So I'm afraid I've to make do with D. H. Lawrence's Sons and Lovers.' She waved the book in the air.

'Cheeky.'

Alice giggled. There was something about Freddie Leybourne that attracted the ladies. She couldn't deny he was a handsome man. He was clean cut, which emphasised his kind brown eyes. She smiled as pride rushed through her veins. Of course, it might only be something to do with a man in a uniform. Whatever the reason, they all liked to flirt with him, particularly the older ones.

Freddie turned and beamed at Alice. 'Shall I escort

you to the beautiful lady behind the counter?' He held out his arm for the old lady.

The lady looked up at him; her blue eyes danced with mischief. 'This is definitely my lucky day.' She placed her arm through his. 'Do you think your wife would mind if I ran away with you?' Her raucous laughter was louder than ever.

'You,' Freddie Leybourne smiled at her, 'are a little bit naughty.' He tucked his own book under his other arm and held out his hand. 'Let me hold on to your book.'

She passed her book to him and then wiped a tear from her eyes with a handkerchief from the pocket of her threadbare coat. 'Actually, I can't run anywhere. It would have to be a very slow hobble.' The lady smiled and took a deep breath, inhaling a woody, citrus smell. 'Handsome and smells wonderful; someone's a lucky woman.' She stared ahead at Alice. 'So, is the beautiful lady your wife?'

Freddie opened his mouth to speak but the lady continued before he could form any words.

'No, that can't be so because once men are married, they generally stop seeing their wives as beautiful, so she must be your girlfriend.'

'I don't know if I agree with that, but the outcome is correct.' He laughed into her mischievous eyes and patted the fingers that were gripping his arm. 'I could do with you on the police force. Would you like a job?'

The old lady cackled. 'Do you know, I think I'm a little bit past my best years.'

Freddie was still smiling when he placed the two books on the counter in front of Alice.

The old lady stared at her. 'I hope you realise you're a very lucky young lady to be stepping out with this delightful police sergeant.'

The colour rose in Alice's face, but she couldn't help but smile at her cheekiness. 'Indeed I am.'

Freddie didn't take his eyes off Alice. 'I was thinking of taking her to Her Majesty's Theatre to watch Pygmalion next weekend.' A smile crept across his face as he looked down at the lady on his arm. 'What do you think?'

'You should snap him up lovey, before someone else does.' The lady winked at Alice. 'It might be worth my while getting arrested, just to have some time in his company again.'

Alice laughed as she picked up both books and her pen.

'The D. H. Lawrence book is mine.'

'You've made my day, so I think the book can be my treat.' Freddie grinned from ear to ear.

Alice nodded.

'No, I can't let you do that.' The lady frowned. 'I live on my own, so talking to you has been my treat.'

Alice hesitated, with her pen poised over her pad.

Freddie gave a slight nod in her direction.

She wrote the titles down on the pad, along with the price, and gave it to Freddie to take to the payment booth.

'There's a chair.' He patted the lady's fingers. 'Take a seat while I go and pay for the books.' He held onto her as she lowered herself onto the upright wooden chair. His eyes clouded when he glanced across at Alice. 'Did Lily get home all right the other night?'

Alice immediately flushed a bright pink. 'Yes, thank you.'

Freddie nodded. 'She's lucky I was on duty or she probably would've been charged, along with the rest of them.'

'I… I didn't realise.' Alice lowered her eyes, unable to look at him.

'Sorry, Alice, I thought you knew…'

'No, I didn't.' She took a deep breath. 'Was Daisy with them?'

'Daisy?'

Alice's eyes darted around the shop, quickly taking in the old lady sitting on the chair, thankful she was now rummaging through her bag and not paying them any attention. 'Victoria's sister,' she whispered. 'Lily said she was with them and I'm concerned she got arrested.' Alice frowned. Her eyes welled up as she remembered her friend's pale features. 'Victoria has had such a lot on her plate since her parents died, I'm not sure she could cope with any more.'

Freddie took a couple of steps towards Alice. 'Leave it with me and I'll see what I can do, but I can't keep favouring the two girls, because if word gets out, I could be in trouble.'

'Surely not, an upstanding citizen like yourself.'

They both looked around to see Tony.

His eyes were sharp as they looked from one to the other, and back again. 'Come on, you look as guilty as hell so please tell, what will you be in trouble for?'

Alice's gaze darted from Tony to Freddie. He was staring tight-lipped at Tony. She rested her hand on his arm. 'Freddie, you'd better go and pay for the books.' Fidgeting from one foot to the other, Alice turned her attention back to Tony. 'I didn't see you there, have you come to meet Molly?'

*

Luke Taylor pulled open the heavy door to the Gentlemen's Club in St James's Street. Although he had been a member there for nearly forty years, he still got a thrill every time he walked into the large entrance, with its magnificent marble pillars and high ceilings, above the wonderful oak and marble staircase. Every time he entered the prestigious club, it reminded him how far he had come, 'but only by association' a voice echoed in his head.

He was seventeen years old when he decided to travel

to London from Norfolk to look for work, not realising how it would change his life forever. His charm had quickly won over Arthur Gettin. Convincing him he had potential to be a great architect had been easy and it had secured him work as an apprentice in his son, Edward's, company. It hadn't taken him long to discover Edward would be missing for some time, as he was mourning the loss of his wife, Alexandra. Luke, unashamedly, used the time to his advantage.

The Gettins were well known in London and Luke quickly developed a life plan. He had been careful not to attract any scandal and there had been times when he had wanted to walk away, but his need to be part of their lifestyle kept him focussed. His charm had attracted Edward's daughter, Sarah. Her grandfather, Poppy, as she liked to call him, had over-indulged her and she had wanted for nothing. This had made courting her an expensive time, but he had been careful and found the money, through various means. No one appeared to question how his lifestyle was more extravagant than his earnings allowed for. He had fabricated a story about having money from his family and it was a notch in his belt that his plan had worked. With the maturity of an older person, meticulous perseverance and hard work, he eventually won her hand. The success brought perks into his life. Yes, he had four children with her, but more importantly, he loved the good life and the respect that came with being married to a Gettin.

'Good morning, Mr Taylor.' The concierge's voice echoed from behind the desk.

Luke stared blankly for a moment, before quickly gathering himself. He smiled before nodding his head. 'Morning.'

The concierge pulled his shoulders back and straightened the bottom of his navy-blue jacket, before tipping his head with a smile.

Luke's black leather shoes made no sound on the tiled flooring as he headed towards the staircase. Without any acknowledgement, he stepped past the large portrait of King George V, which hung in pride of place on the back wall, facing the front door. Gasoliers hung from the centre of the high ceiling. Their flames had left distinctive round soot marks, although they had faded with scrubbing. It had been rumoured they might change to electricity; although expensive, it was becoming more popular. Luke feared it wouldn't be long before Sarah and his feisty daughter, Lily, would be asking for it indoors, now all the streets were lit by it. Alice wouldn't dream of making demands of him though. He allowed himself a smile. She was a good girl and, although the leaflet gave him cause for concern, she was easy to control. She would make someone a good wife one day. The same couldn't be said for Lily; his smile vanished as quickly as it arrived.

As he mounted the stairs, he barely glanced at the

many portraits that filled the wall. Old and new members had achieved recognition from their peers and country for their endeavours. They hung proudly. He had been schooled by Sarah's family, particularly her cousin William, about the importance of trying to get your picture on the wall, but it didn't interest him. He didn't want anybody looking into his life.

A wide landing took him around to the left and into a large oak-panelled room. Leather armchairs were haphazardly placed, with small round tables nearby. He followed the staircase around to the coffee room. He stood in the doorway for a few moments, admiring the ornate curved ceiling with its hanging chandeliers. The round tables, covered with white tablecloths and the place settings of silver cutlery and crystal glassware added to the splendour of the room. It was a quiet morning with only a few occupants sitting down for breakfast. Despite the large open windows, framed with dark green curtains, cigar smoke hung in the air. He wrinkled his nose in distaste as he looked around, before walking over to a table in the corner.

'Edward, on your own? I didn't realise you were here.' Luke smiled at his father-in-law, dressed in casual black trousers and an open-necked white shirt.

Edward stood up and folded the newspaper he was reading. He held out his hand indicating his son-in-law should take the seat opposite him. 'Hello, Luke, I haven't been here long myself. I thought I'd have a change of scenery.' Edward sat down again. 'Aren't you hot in that jacket and tie?'

Luke followed suit, sitting down on the soft leather chair. 'One should always look smart. I'm surprised they let you in without a tie.'

Edward's lips lifted slightly at the corners. 'Indeed, one must. Maybe the Gettin name lets me off such formalities, or perhaps it's because I've been coming here since my teenage years.'

Luke's hackles began to rise, but he forced a smile. He nodded towards the newspaper. 'Any news in there?'

'The Daily Mirror? Not really, the last couple of days have been either about the shooting of the Austrian and his wife, a terrible state of affairs, or the pending strikes.'

'Hmm, so has The Times.' Luke frowned as he peered over at Edward. 'Robert is convinced we will be at war soon and is already talking about enlisting.'

'He shouldn't rush into it. I'm not sure it'll come to that, but it does make you wonder what the world is coming to.' Edward lifted his coffee cup and sipped the steaming dark liquid before placing it back onto the table. 'Are you eating or just drinking?'

Luke indicated to the waiter. 'Just a coffee please. Anything for you, Edward?'

Edward lifted his hand. 'No, I'm fine thanks.' He watched the waiter walk away before looking back at his son-in-law. 'How is everything in the Taylor household?'

'Fine, well as fine as it can be with a daughter like Lily.'

Edward laughed. 'You sound just like my cousin, William, when he used to talk about his sister. He was always moaning about Emily and how she needed to be married, mainly because she didn't fit into the way they thought. But then William was always a bit strange.'

Luke waited until the waiter had left his coffee, before glancing across the table at Edward. 'Well I can't pretend I haven't had similar thoughts myself.'

'What?' Edward raised his eyebrows. 'You can't just marry Lily off because she has spirit.' He stared at Luke; disdain crept across his face. 'You mean it, don't you?'

'Yes, I do.' Luke sighed. 'You know she was escorted home by a policeman the other evening because she had been demonstrating outside Parliament?'

Edward leant forward and slapped his knee as his laughter took hold.

'I don't know why you are laughing so much. If Freddie hadn't been on duty, I would have been bailing her out of jail.'

Edward wiped his eyes as he gulped for breath. 'Oh, bless her.'

Luke ran his hand through his hair. 'Oh, bless her?'

'My father would have enjoyed this moment, as indeed would his sisters; well maybe not the eldest.' Edward paused as he looked at Luke. 'My Aunt

Elizabeth was always telling the girls in the family that they came from a long line of spirited women and they had to continue with it and not become downtrodden.'

Luke shook his head. 'Wonderful! I am so glad she is not here to encourage Lily.'

Edward started laughing. 'They had some stories to tell.'

'Well, I'm looking out for a potential husband for Lily. She can be somebody else's problem.'

The smile vanished from Edward's face. 'Does she know?'

'No.'

Edward stared at Luke. 'Does Sarah know?'

'No, and I would appreciate it if you didn't say anything.' Luke picked up his coffee cup and took a gulp of the hot black liquid.

'That's not how I work, Luke. I don't believe in arranged marriages and Sarah's mother would never forgive me if I stood by and let that happen.'

Luke's eyes narrowed. 'I don't recall Jane commenting either way.'

Edward took a sharp of breath as anger flitted across his face for a split second. 'I'm not talking about Jane, I'm talking about Alexandra. She wanted me to protect Emily, so I'm quite certain she'd want me to protect our own grandchildren.'

*

The late evening sunshine cast shadows across the sitting room in Bloomsbury Street. Freddie scraped his hand through his short hair as he sat on the edge of the Queen Anne armchair. He peered through his lashes at Alice's father; his stomach churned as his nerves took over. He took a deep breath and wrinkled his nose as the lilies, sitting in a vase in front of the window, overpowered the aroma of beef coming from the kitchen.

Lily giggled as she stood in the hall and pressed her ear up against the closed sitting room door.

'Shh, we'll get caught.' Alice grinned at her sister as she crouched down and pressed her own ear to the door.

'Do you think he's going to ask father?' Lily whispered, nervously looking around for her mother.

'I don't know. He hasn't said anything to me, but why else would he want to talk to him.' Alice peered up at Lily and also gave a quick look over her shoulder. 'Unless it's about you and your antics, of course.'

'Freddie would never talk to father about me.' Lily gave her sister a huge grin. 'He loves me far too much.'

Alice groaned. 'You keep your eyes off him.' She laughed. 'He's mine.'

'Eww, no, you can have him.' Lily's eyes sparkled with mischief.

Alice shook her head. 'We'll miss it if we don't listen.'

They both turned their heads sideways and leant into the door.

'Let's hope we don't get splinters.' Lily giggled. 'That

would take some explaining.'

Alice attempted to stifle the laughter that was threatening to spill over. She took a couple of deep breaths and tried to concentrate on what was being said in the sitting room.

'Mr Leybourne.' Luke coughed to clear his throat. 'I want to thank you for your discretion the other night when the constable brought my wayward daughter home.'

Freddie rubbed his palms down the legs of his trousers. 'That's all right, Mr Taylor.'

'I can assure you it is far from all right.' Luke removed the stopper from the crystal glass decanter and poured himself a whisky before turning to Freddie. 'Can I get you one?'

'No, no thanks.' Freddie laughed but the noise was alien to him. He raised his eyebrows and looked around his feet, wondering if he'd trodden on a cat's tail. He shook his head; the Taylors didn't have any pets. 'I don't drink much these days. I suppose I'm basically never off duty.' He forced a smile to his thin lips.

Luke swallowed the golden liquid, emptying the glass. His lips tightened into a thin straight line as the heat from the alcohol warmed his chest. He placed the glass back onto the silver tray before moving to the large window, which looked out onto the street.

'What are you two girls up to?'

Lily and Alice jumped at the sound of their mother's

voice. They both stepped away from the door and looked round, guilt written all over their faces.

Sarah scowled at them, standing inches away from them, with her hands on her hips. 'Whatever you're up to, you look guilty. Eavesdropping, I'd guess.'

Alice lowered her eyes and bit on her lower lip. 'Sorry, I know it's rude to listen in on people's conversations.'

Lily laughed at her sister's pitiful expression. 'Stop it, will you.' Her guilt had been quickly replaced by excitement as she looked at her mother. 'We think Freddie is going to ask if he can marry your perfect child.' She grinned as her gaze bounced between her mother and sister, knowing they would immediately want to defend her statement.

Alice held her head high. 'I don't think...'

Sarah shook her head before she took a step nearer to the door. 'Don't, Alice, you should know your sister by now...'

Lily's laughter echoed around the hall.

'You can't stay now, your father would have heard you,' Sarah whispered, pulling them both away. 'Come on, you two, before your father comes to see what the noise is about. Anyway, they say eavesdroppers never hear anything good about themselves.'

The laughter from the hall filtered into the sitting room. Luke looked round from the window and settled his gaze on the closed door before turning back to the window. 'I find I am drinking more, that is unless someone else in the house is helping themselves.' He pushed the sash window up further, allowing the cool evening air into the room. 'Sarah does like to keep these windows almost shut.'

The chatter and laughter of people walking by seemed to fill the room, momentarily easing the tension that had wrapped itself around Freddie. He looked at the man standing in front of him and fidgeted in his seat, before taking a deep breath. 'Mr Taylor, I wanted to talk to you about Alice's future.'

Luke lifted one eyebrow as he crossed the room and sat on a matching armchair. 'Go on.'

Freddie stood up and began pacing, his hands clenched together in front of him. He glanced under his eyelashes at Luke, wishing he'd never started this conversation. He took another deep breath. 'Well, I was —'

'You were what, Mr Leybourne? Please sit down. I don't expect to have to follow you around my sitting room.' Luke stood up and poured himself another whisky. 'You know the talk at the club swings between the general strike and how it's going to bring the country to its knees, and going to war, which could well end up being the better option of the two.' He sighed as he sat down on the chair he had just vacated. 'Did Alice tell you her brother has already signed up?'

'No, sir, she didn't.'

'Yes, it was a proud moment when Robert came in and said he had enlisted.' Luke smiled for the first time that evening. 'His mother wasn't impressed, mind. Robert is convinced it is only a matter of time before we go to war, but I don't know.' He eyed Freddie for a moment. 'Are you going to enlist?' He lifted his glass to his lips.

'To be honest, sir, I hadn't thought about it...'

Luke lowered his glass and raised his eyebrows. 'Well maybe you should, because if it does come to fighting for your country, you will be judged if you stay behind.'

'Yes, sir.' Freddie looked down at the carpet. 'Surely there's no reason to think it'll come to that, is there?'

Luke stared long and hard at Freddie. 'Who knows? The papers are full of what the Germans are up to. It's probably about time we stood up and be counted; this country hasn't done that for a long time.'

'Yes, I've been reading about it all but, to be honest, I didn't think it would affect us. It's not our fight and I assumed, as a police officer, I'd still be needed at home.'

Luke took a sip of his drink. 'Hmm, I expect so, we can't have anarchy, can we?' A smile formed on his lips. 'I'm not sure what the future holds for any of us right now, never mind Alice.' He gulped down the whisky until his glass was empty again.

Freddie swallowed hard, trying to remove the lump that was forming. 'Mr Taylor, I'd like your permission to marry Alice.' His words tumbled over each other, in their rush to escape.

Luke gave a hearty laugh. 'It has taken you long enough to ask. You are lucky she is still available, because I had considered finding her a husband.' He stared into his empty glass for a moment, before looking up at Freddie. 'She will make someone a good wife, unlike Lily.'

Freddie's feet systematically tapped up and down. His knuckles were white as one hand clutched the other. 'Yes, sir. I've taken my time, but wanted to make sure I could give Alice a good life. My job is secure, with prospects, and my love for her is not in doubt.'

'Love, huh, well, I don't see why not. She could do much worse than a police sergeant, and it means there will be one less woman in this house to drive me mad.' Luke paused for a moment. 'Actually, she is the least of my worries; can't you marry Lily instead?'

'No disrespect to Lily, but I'd rather marry Alice.'

'Wise man.'

There was a light knock on the sitting room door just before it opened and Alice stood in the doorway. 'Mother asked me to let you know dinner is ready.'

Freddie's face lit up and he jumped to his feet. He sniffed the air. 'Let me guess.' He paused while he sniffed a couple of more times. 'I reckon it's roast beef.'

Alice grinned at Freddie. 'I believe so.'

He beamed as he reached for Alice's hand, forgetting Luke was still in the room. 'Lovely, Mrs Headley is a great cook.'

Alice laughed at his enthusiasm. 'You and your food.' She smiled at him. 'We are definitely lucky to have her. From what I've heard from the family, good help is hard to find. One of my great aunt's infamous quotes was that "it was easier to find a husband than a good butler"'. Alice laughed.

Freddie laughed with her. 'She sounds like a character.'

'By all accounts, they all were. I should get Aunt Emily to tell you a few stories about them. They were strong, spirited women.'

Luke cleared his throat behind them.

Freddie jerked round. 'Thank you, sir.'

Luke had his back to the room as he lifted the whisky decanter, concentrating on pouring another drink. 'Yes, well we don't need to make the aunts into something they probably weren't. After all, they were probably bitter spinsters, and Lily certainly doesn't need any encouragement in that direction.'

Alice immediately dropped her head. 'No, Father.'

Freddie squeezed her hand and gave it a reassuring shake.

Luke moved sideways to walk past them. 'Anyway, with all this talk of war, your mother might need to learn to cook, in case we lose Mrs Headley.'

Alice looked up at her father. 'Why would we lose her?'

'Who knows? But you just don't know what's coming.'

Alice stared after her father as he left the sitting room. She wondered if he knew something, or whether he was just scaremongering.

Freddie shook her hand again. 'Are you all right?'

Alice turned her head to look up at him.

'You look sad now; don't let your father get to you.'

'I'm fine.' Alice forced a smile to her lips. 'You know, when Grandma Jane married Grandpa, and a few years later the cook retired, she decided to have a go at doing her own cooking. Apparently she liked it and now believes every man and woman should be self-sufficient. Consequently, I think mother is going to ask her to teach her all she knows.'

'But the most important question of all is will your mother pass on all that important information?' Freddie laughed as his stomach made a gurgling noise.

Alice's laughter filled the room. 'Don't worry, you won't starve.'

*

'Don't you love the summer evenings, Freddie?' Alice smiled as they walked towards Trafalgar Square. 'Doesn't the sunshine lift your heart?'

Freddie laughed as he turned to face her, soaking up her smooth pale complexion and her long dark hair, which covered her ears and was piled high on top of her head, with soft curls cascading down. The pearls of the teardrop earrings she wore were just visible, bobbing with each step she took. Alice had discarded her hat today, in favour of a white bandeau, decorated with pale blue and white roses, which complimented her column style dress, partially hidden beneath her silk shawl with its tantalising fringe that swayed in the slight breeze. 'You are always saying that, yet you are always a ray of sunshine.' He stopped walking and stared at her. 'What I love is your view on life. I am going to call it the sunshine outlook from now on.' A humourless laugh escaped as he started walking again. 'Everyone I speak to is talking about the possibility of war, the general strike and women wanting the vote, but not you.'

Alice's smile vanished. 'I could talk about all those things if you want me to. I also talk to people and read the newspapers, but I choose not to worry about things like that. After all, it may not happen.'

Freddie frowned. 'I wish I could be like that.'

'My mother told me Poppy—'

'Poppy?'

Alice laughed. 'Apparently, she started calling her grandfather Poppy when she was a small child and it stuck. She still calls him that, even though he's no longer with us. I don't remember him, but my mother has some wonderful memories.'

Freddie's smile crept across him as he watched her

face light up.

'When we were children, she and Grandfather were always relaying stories about him.'

They took a couple of steps in silence. Nelson's Column towered above them, a familiar shape in the skyline, with the four bronze lions sitting at its base. Freddie placed his hand on her elbow as they weaved between other people going about their business. 'It's always so busy around Trafalgar Square.' He guided her past the National Gallery and down Pall Mall East. 'Sorry, you were saying?'

Alice gave him a blank look.

Freddie laughed before shaking his head. 'Poppy?' He watched her eyes crinkle and her lips lift at the corners. She laughed, reminding him of birdsong, and he couldn't resist joining in.

She took a deep breath and exhaled slowly. 'Sorry, it wasn't anything important. I was only going to say Poppy was quite philosophical about life. He used to say family are the most important thing of all, but don't let them or anyone else swallow you up. Be yourself and don't worry about things that you can't change.'

'Good advice, but I expect that's why Lily got taken to the police station.'

Alice stared hard at his straight-laced expression, before a smile broke out. 'Probably, but she's right to stand up for what she believes in, no matter how upset father gets.'

'And yet you're not doing the same thing. Does that mean you don't believe in the cause?'

Alice's smile vanished. 'No, it doesn't.' She sighed and looked down at her white-gloved hands gripping the silver mesh purse. 'No, it means I'm not as brave as Lily.'

Freddie nodded. 'It doesn't do for us all to be the same.'

The hair on the back of her neck bristled. 'Do you think chaining myself to railings, getting thrown into Holloway Prison and refusing to eat so I'd be force-fed would achieve much more? Then, of course, there's always throwing myself in front of the King's horse at the Derby like Emily Davison did last year.' Alice shook her head.

Freddie's jaw dropped as he stared at Alice. 'My goodness, I had no idea you were so passionate about it, but it sounds like they have your support.'

Her eyes held a steel-like quality when she looked at Freddie. 'I'm fighting my own battles of not having an arranged marriage and being able to go out to work. I want Lily to have a freedom of choice to do what she wants with her life and not be stuck in the Dark Ages.' Alice took a deep breath. 'The vote is obviously important, but good women are dying, or at best making themselves ill and losing their children in the process. It's all such a waste. There are other ways. We'd be better off to become doctors and judges.' She glanced down at the pavement. 'So, no, it doesn't do for us all to be the same, but I should stand up and be counted.'

'You will, when the time's right for you.' He gave Alice a sideways glance. 'Your father used those same words when he talked about the possibility of war. He asked me whether I'd considered enlisting.'

Alice stopped in her tracks and stared at him. 'I hope you told him you won't be.'

'He said judgements would be made on the men that don't fight for their country.' Freddie paused as he took a deep breath. 'I told him there's every possibility I'd be needed here as a police officer.'

Alice nodded.

'Freddie.' Tony's voice rang out behind them.

Alice groaned, wondering if they could pretend they hadn't heard him. She looked across at Freddie; his jaw was clenched. Without a word, their pace quickened.

Freddie frowned. 'We should've come out earlier and maybe had a meal before the theatre. We could have eaten at The Café Royal.'

'Freddie, Alice,' Tony shrilled down the road at them.

People turned and stared. Alice's colour began to rise up her neck. There was no choice but to stop. The alternative was acute embarrassment.

'Sorry,' Freddie whispered as they slowed down their pace.

Alice thinned her lips and shook her head slightly as they came to a standstill. She painted on her best smile before turning around.

Tony raced up to them, a little breathless, but grinning from ear to ear. He turned and beckoned to Molly. 'Come on, slow coach.' She was a few feet behind Tony and had a sullen look about her.

'Hello, Tony, Molly.' Alice smiled at her friend but Molly's grim expression didn't change. Alice wondered what was going on with her lately. She seemed so unhappy. Perhaps she should organise a night out for the three of them, maybe the theatre or the music hall might be fun. It was about time Victoria threw herself back into socialising.

'Where are you two off to?' Tony pulled a packet of cigarettes, along with some matches, from his jacket pocket. Molly joined them and, without a word, placed her arm in Tony's.

Freddie stepped aside, so someone could pass him. 'We are going to see Pygmalion at His Majesty's Theatre. I've heard some good reports about it. Apparently, Mrs Patrick Campbell is excellent as Eliza Dolittle and George Bernard Shaw is receiving equally wonderful reviews—'

'What a coincidence,' Tony interrupted, before beaming at Alice. 'We're going to see that as well. Wouldn't it be great if our seats were next to each other?'

Molly openly glared at Tony, before turning to scowl at Alice. 'That is unlikely, especially as the tickets weren't bought at the same time.'

'Well, we can walk to the theatre together.' Tony grinned at the three of them, but no one returned his enthusiasm.

It was clear Molly wasn't happy. Alice knew she should talk to her, but now wasn't the time and she wasn't sure Molly would tell her what the problem was. Their friendship had hit a rocky road without a cross word being said. Alice hoped her father and mother, Jack and Charlotte, were not in bad health. Although, with Jack being held in high esteem by the family, she felt sure she would've heard on the grapevine if something were wrong. Alice suspected it had something to do with Tony.

Chapter 5

August 1914

The early morning sunshine was already showing its strength as Alice stepped over the threshold into Foyles bookstore. Once inside the shop, her eyes took a moment to adjust to the dullness. She wondered why she insisted on working at all, instead of soaking up the glorious weather, but then remembered her conversation with Freddie. Beads of perspiration were gathering on her forehead. She felt hot and sticky as she walked purposefully to the staff room to clock on, hoping she'd have time to splash her face before heading towards her counter.

Once in position, she took a deep breath. She brushed her hands down the soft black tulip-styled skirt, before straightening the black lace edged collar of her silver-grey blouse. The black buttons down the front added the finishing touch.

'Morning, Miss Taylor, it is showing all the signs of being a warm day, don't you think?'

Alice turned to see Molly, her face deadpan but her eyes struggling to hide the twinkle in them. 'Good morning, Miss Cooper.' Alice's formal tone played along. 'The weather certainly looks promising; let's hope it stays that way for the weekend.'

Molly beamed from ear to ear. 'Let's hope so, especially as we've an extra day off for the bank holiday. I expect you've plans already; what are you doing?'

'I don't know.' Alice paused for a moment. 'There'll probably be the usual discussions, it's the same every year.'

Molly laughed. 'So, what will win?'

'Ah, let's see now.' Alice lifted her finger and placed it on her lips, tapping it lightly. 'The choices will be either the cricket match that's held every year at The Oval, or doing something much more exciting like going to Southend.' The girls both giggled.

'Sounds like it's Southend.'

'Are we going to the seaside then?' Tony chirped up behind them. 'Hmm, someone smells lovely, let me guess.' He paused to sniff the air, leaning into Molly before moving towards Alice and back again. 'Is it jasmine or rose I can smell?'

'It's probably rose.' Molly tucked her arm through his. 'This is an unexpected pleasure.' She beamed up at him.

Alice lifted her chin and her eyebrows drew together. 'You shouldn't be in here, Tony. Molly will get into trouble.'

'I only wanted to see my favourite girl for a few

minutes.' His eyes flitted from Molly to Alice, giving her a suggestive wink.

The hair on the back of Alice's neck bristled while Molly's smile got broader, as she gazed adoringly up at him.

Alice glared at him. 'Don't you have a job to go to?'

Molly frowned. 'I don't want you to go, but Alice is right.' She quickly looked around her. 'And anyway, you'll be late for work.'

Alice couldn't stop her smile from forming. It was a good job Freddie wasn't here; it looked like a crime was about to be committed.

Molly moved from side to side as she tried to see down the aisles. 'We are not open yet and if old Leadbetter catches you, we'll all be in trouble.'

Tony smiled at Alice before moving his gaze to Molly. 'We can't have that now, can we, sweet pea?'

Alice shook her head. She didn't consider herself a violent person but she had a strong urge to slap his face. Whatever his game was, she wanted no part of it. 'Molly, best you get Tony out of here before we get caught.' Alice walked around the counter in front of her and started preparing for the shop to open. After a few minutes, she looked up to see Molly guiding Tony to the back of the shop. She shook her head again; perhaps she should have a word with Molly, but it wasn't something she relished doing. Tony wasn't good enough for her friend, but Molly was clearly smitten.

'Is everything all right?'

Alice hadn't heard Victoria approach and gave a weak smile. 'I don't know.' She sighed, glancing at Victoria, before watching Molly disappear between the bookshelves. 'I worry about Molly's infatuation for Tony. I'm sure she could do much better than him; he's such a womaniser.'

Victoria followed her gaze. 'You can't get involved in their relationship, even if it's for the right reasons.'

'I know, but it's hard to do nothing and he'll hurt her in the end, it's just a case of when and with whom.'

'You have to remember, not everyone's as confident as you. Molly feels her parents owe everything to your family.'

'That's nonsense, and by all accounts, her father helped save my great uncles, cousins and great grandfather from acute embarrassment. I don't know the details, because it was a family secret that everyone actually kept. To be honest I think the older generation took it to the grave with them.' Alice paused; her friend's vacant expression told her she was rambling. 'So, by all accounts, if anything, we owe Jack Cooper everything.' Alice turned and smiled at Victoria. Her heart reached out for her friend as she took in her grey complexion and dull eyes. Her vibrancy had died along with her parents. Alice had been with Victoria when Freddie delivered the tragic news. Although neither of them had met him before that fateful day, he returned daily to check on them both. Alice had stayed with her until after the funeral, but four years on she was still lost in her grief. 'Anyway, how are you today? I did enjoy our amble to Monico. We should do it again sometime.'

'Yes, it was lovely to just have a wander. I don't know if I said so at the time, but thank you for the tea and cake. It wasn't a place I'd normally go into.' Victoria's fingers rubbed the material at the side of her black skirt.

'You did thank me, but it was entirely my pleasure.'

Victoria furtively looked around in case Mr Leadbetter was hovering nearby. 'I don't know whether you know or not but yesterday, one of the customers told me there was going to be a peace march in Trafalgar Square on Sunday.'

Alice wrinkled her nose slightly and frowned. 'A peace march?'

'Yes, apparently they're trying to persuade the government against getting involved over Germany and Austria declaring war on Russia. I think there's more to it than that. Belgium is in the mix somewhere. I don't really understand it all.'

Alice frowned. 'I didn't know.' She clasped her hands together on the counter.

Victoria's fingers wrung the side of her black skirt. 'I'm only mentioning it because of Lily. I know she likes to get involved with these things.' Her fingers twisted and turned, until they found a small hole by the seam.

Alice tried to laugh, but it fell short. 'Yes, she's become quite a little activist, much to my father's annoyance. Perhaps I'll try and get her to come to Southend with us.'

Victoria nodded and relinquished her hold on her skirt.

Alice arched her eyebrows. 'Thanks for telling me about it.' She took a deep breath, wondering if she would get a chance to talk to Lily before the march.

'Is that what you've decided to do then?' Victoria forced a smile. 'I mean go to Southend.'

'Probably. Will you come with us? It's been a long time since we spent the whole day together, outside of work that is.'

Victoria's eyes darted around Alice, before she looked straight at her. 'I don't think so. My money won't stretch that far, and then there's Stephen and Daisy to think about.'

Alice nodded. 'I know you have the responsibility of looking after them, but Daisy must be eighteen now. What age do they have to be before you can start going out and having fun again, Victoria? You used to be the life and soul whenever we went out.'

Something flitted across Victoria's face but Alice wasn't sure what it was. 'If it weren't for my brother and sister, I wouldn't have anything to live for. I don't earn enough to feed us all properly and pay the rent. The day my parents died, I also lost the man I loved, because it was all too much for him. So forgive me if I don't have the urge to be full of fun and laughter.' Tears tripped over Victoria's long black eyelashes and trickled down her cheeks.

Alice fought the urge to scoop her into her arms. 'I'm sorry, Victoria, it was quite insensitive of me. I just want to help you, but I don't know how.'

Victoria sniffed and ran her hands over her face. 'Appreciate what you have, Alice; it can all be taken away in the blink of an eye.'

*

The train trundled towards Southend, the tall grey city buildings gradually diminishing, to be replaced by nature's greenery. Freddie sat close to Alice. The train swayed them back and forth as it chugged along the tracks. She watched her impeccably turned out man brush his hand down his trouser leg, adjust his position to tug at the ironed-in pleat and straighten his jacket. His leg brushed against hers, hidden under her long pale blue skirt. Freddie reached for her hand; she gazed up at him and their eyes locked. She longed for him to hold her, to rest her head on his chest. Her stomach immediately somersaulted. Alice wondered if he felt the same way. As if he could read her thoughts, he lifted her hand and lightly brushed his lips on the top of it. She shivered at the butterfly touch. Blood raced through her veins. His dark hair was begging to have her hands run through it.

'I'm so excited,' Molly burst out loudly.

Alice's attention was immediately pulled from him; the moment had been ripped away from them. She frowned. Would he ask for her hand in marriage today? Had he asked her father's permission to do so? Why had no one mentioned it to her? Maybe that wasn't what they'd been talking about. He was a policeman after all, so they could have been talking about anything.

Freddie looked up; the love and want was clear. He sat up straight and gave a slight nod. A smile crept across her face.

'What are you excited about?' Alice laughed.

Molly's eyes sparkled with happiness. 'Look out of the window.'

Alice did as she was bid. The clear sky bounced off the blue of the sea; it looked inviting. 'It does look beautiful,' she murmured to herself.

'We have to go paddling.' Molly tapped Tony's arm next to her. 'Tony, can we go paddling, can we?'

Tony opened his eyes and stared blankly at Molly, before following her gaze out of the window. He adjusted his sitting position and leant forward. 'It certainly does look inviting.'

Molly turned her adoring eyes to him. 'Can we please?'

Tony leant back in his seat and smiled at her. 'You

can do whatever you want, love.' He looked over at Alice. 'Are you going to take a dip?'

Alice felt her colour rise. 'It does look like you could throw yourself into it, so I may paddle with Molly.'

Freddie laughed. 'I may join the pair of you.'

It wasn't long before the train began to slow down, gradually coming to a standstill at Southend Victoria station. They gathered their things together and proceeded to alight from the train. The heat of the day took Alice's breath away and seared her skin, but the sea breeze immediately gave a cooling effect.

Tony grabbed Molly's hand. 'Come on, let's go to the pier; someone told me you can get a train that runs the full length of it.'

Molly raised her eyebrows as excitement took hold. 'I wonder if there is a Punch and Judy show on there. I love watching them.' Her laughter bubbled over. 'How does it go? "That's the way to do it."'

The four of them giggled at Molly's impression of the puppets.

Alice caught her breath. 'You can't come to the seaside and not have an ice cream, so that's what I'd like to do before we go home.'

They walked along, each with a spring in their step, until the pier came into view. Alice and Freddie joined others leaning against the wrought iron railings, soaking in the view.

Molly pushed herself back off the railings. 'We are

going to move on. Shall we catch up with you later?'

'If we miss each other, I think there is a train around four o'clock.' Alice sighed; she could look at this view all day.

Molly nodded and pulled Tony away.

Alice returned her attention to the intimidating brick-built archway that led onto the pier and to the pavilion. She watched the small sailing boats bobbing up and down on the waves. Children screamed with delight as the sea lapped around their feet. Dads were helping to build sandcastles, while the mums unpacked the picnics. Alice smiled. 'Isn't it beautiful? I could stay here forever.'

Freddie straightened his back. 'It is certainly idyllic. You could forget there were any problems in the world, standing here.'

'Not today, Freddie. Let's just enjoy what we have.'

He put his arm around her waist and kissed the top of her head. He forced a smile. 'Let's go find an ice cream, shall we?'

*

Alice laughed as she placed her dessertspoon in the dish in front of her. 'So Grandpa, which cricket match won today, was it Canterbury or the Oval?'

'I followed tradition and watched Surrey take on Nottinghamshire at the Oval.' Edward gave Jane a sideways glance before continuing. 'I thought, as it's Canterbury Cricket Week, I might be able to sneak down there in a few days, but don't tell Jane.' He smiled before winking at Alice.

Jane laughed. 'I can hear you, you know.'

Edward laughed. 'I always used to go to the cricket with your great grandfather; I could tell you some stories. He thought he was a regular ladies' man.'

'Grandpa, you're always telling us funny stories about your father. I'm sure they can't all be true.' Alice picked up her glass of dessert wine and sipped it, shuddering as the sweetness wrapped itself around her mouth. She glanced around the rectangular mahogany table, hoping no one had noticed.

The dark wood of the table was barely visible underneath the crockery and glassware. It was a contrast to the dove-grey on the walls, which had white mouldings at the top, hiding where they met the ceiling. Artwork and photographs were hung around the room to break up the colour. The fireplace was surrounded by blue brickwork-style enamel tiles, which were protected by a wooden mantel. A black marble hearth twinkled in the candlelight, casting shadows around the room. The heavy winter curtains at the large sash windows had recently been replaced with lighter, red floral ones.

'Poppy was a fine man, wasn't he, Sarah?' Edward smiled at his daughter sitting next to him at the end of the dining room table. 'Although he wouldn't understand why you've never employed more people to help with the cooking and cleaning.'

'No, and I don't think you do either, although I do have help come in every day and Mrs Headley is a wonder.' Sarah laughed. 'When I think about it, he put up with quite a lot from me.' Her smile faded and her eyes looked sad for a moment. 'When mama died and you went away, he worried about me so much. Poppy was concerned about cousin Emily too; that dreadful, although extremely handsome, man she was about to marry, but thankfully didn't.'

Alice leant forward and clasped her hand over her mother's. 'It must've been awful for you.'

'It was a terrible time, but Emily was very good to me; she and my mother were very good friends.' Sarah's face lit up as she looked across at Jane. 'As much as I hated losing my wonderful mother when I was so young, I've been fortunate to have Jane step into the breach.'

Luke raised his eyebrows and sighed at the other end of the table.

Jane laughed. 'I think at the time, we all needed each other. I'd say we've all been very lucky.'

Luke picked up his wine glass and gulped down the contents. 'So, Edward, all this sentimentality is fine, but forgive me, I have heard these stories a hundred times before.' He peered into his empty glass. 'I feel a more important discussion right now is whether you think we will be at war tomorrow? Now that's a burning question we all want to know the answer to.'

The room fell silent. Alice's stomach churned. Her eyes darted to Lily, who was biting her bottom lip and fiddling with the pendant around her neck. Charles opened his mouth to speak but flinched when Alice kicked him under the table.

Edward's eyes widened as he lifted his chin. 'It might be a burning question, Luke, but I don't think it is appropriate to ask it now, especially not in front of the children.'

Alice frantically searched her mind for a safe subject to discuss, as she noticed her father swilling back the wine.

'They are not children anymore. They are fully grown; even young Charles is sixteen...'

'Seventeen,' Charles whispered.

Luke glared across at Charles. 'That's what I said, seventeen. If there is going to be a war, then they are very much a part of it.'

'Charles is too young,' Sarah cut in, blinking rapidly, trying to stop her eyes from welling up. 'Isn't it enough we have one son that couldn't wait?'

Edward clasped her hand in his.

Luke picked up the carafe. 'I've heard it said there were crowds outside Parliament, trying to find out what was going on, and the Foreign Secretary, Edward Grey, sent the Germans an ultimatum. Nearly everyone seems to be in favour of going to war, well everyone except this household that is.' Luke poured himself another glass of red wine.

'That's not true, Father.' Lily took a deep breath. Her eyes held his. 'There's been a peace rally in Trafalgar Square. Those people don't want war. They don't want senseless killing, because some politician or other has decided their sons, brothers, and fathers should fight.'

There was a sharp intake of breath from around the table, but Lily didn't flinch.

Luke drained his wine glass before placing it back on the table. 'I suppose you were participating, ready to bring more problems to our door?'

Lily lifted her chin. 'Actually, I didn't.'

Luke stared at her for a few moments before he took in the rest of the occupants around the table. 'Robert did the right thing. You should be proud that we have a patriotic son who wants to fight for his king and country.'

Edward's nostrils flared as he tightened his grip on his daughter.

Sarah pulled her clammy hand away from her father's and rested it on her lap. 'He's my baby, so I struggle to be proud.' She looked down; under the table, her fingers were busy twisting a napkin.

Luke shook his head. 'Well, he's not your baby, he is twenty-eight years old. I had moved away from home, across country, and was working for your father before I was his age.'

'Yes, I know, but that is not the same as going off to war.'

The room fell silent.

'Maybe it's time we left.' Jane picked up her napkin and started to fold it neatly into a square, before placing it on to the table.

'Nonsense, Jane, you haven't had coffee yet.' Sarah forced a smile to her lips, but she glared at her husband. 'I'm sure everything will be all right. I'll just go and make the coffee, then we can move away from such talk.' Sarah stood up. Alice and Lily followed her lead and started to clear the dessert dishes from the table.

'It was a delicious meal.' Jane smiled at Sarah.

'Indeed it was; the beef was most succulent and that suet pudding and custard means I can't possibly move for at least six months.' Edward laughed, keeping his focus on his daughter.

Sarah forced a smile. 'Thank you both. I'm glad you enjoyed it. Now for coffee.'

Alice frowned and her lips thinned as her father poured another glass of wine. She frantically searched her mind for a safe subject to talk about. 'Oh, I forgot to tell you, Freddie took me to see Pygmalion at His Majesty's Theatre.' Alice smiled as she remembered Freddie holding her hand under the darkness of the show. 'It's about Professor Higgins trying to educate a flower girl, to pass her off as a duchess. It was wonderful, Grandpa; you should take Grandma to see it.'

'I've read the reviews on it and they're all very good, but I think it's ending its run soon.' Jane frowned. 'Perhaps we should try and get tickets for it.'

Edward smiled at his wife. He never had the intense love for Jane in the way he had for his first wife, Alexandra, but she knew that when they married. They were happy together and had produced two more wonderful children, Aimee and James, who in turn had given them grandchildren. 'I'll try to buy some tomorrow.'

'Grandpa, I haven't told you about our day in Southend.' Alice beckoned Lily to join in. 'You should've seen the children queuing up to jump off the pier.'

'It was a warm day, so I expect they all wanted to cool off.' Jane smiled.

Lily raised her eyebrows in disbelief. 'And believe it or not, Alice told me they were charging the boys a tanner each for the privilege.'

'Sixpence, shocking, there's always someone ready to take advantage of the situation.' Jane shook her head. 'It's all about making money.'

Lily nodded. 'I've heard said it's a sign of the times.'

'Did you go as well, Lily?' Jane looked down the table. She admired Lily, but hoped her modern outspoken views wouldn't mean she would end up a lonely spinster.

Lily's laughter filled the room. 'What, and act as a chaperone for the love birds? No thanks.'

'You could have come, we weren't on our own, Molly and Tony were with us.' Alice forced a smile, aware her father was sitting at the table and, thanks to Lily, it was no longer a safe subject.

'Is she still with that womaniser?' Lily frowned, unable to hide her disgust.

Alice glared at her sister, before shrugging her shoulders. 'They seem happy enough.'

Lily nodded. 'Well, that's all that matters.'

'It's a lovely pier though; we had great fun.' Alice smiled at her grandparents. 'We got on the train that took us the full length of it; it's very long. I read somewhere, it's over a mile.'

Edward's silver spoon clanged against the blue and gold-rimmed porcelain dish as he placed it inside. He leant back in his chair and took a deep breath, before placing both hands on his stomach. 'I don't think I should've had seconds.' He pulled himself upright. 'Southend is popular and I understand the pier gets a lot of use.'

'It was certainly busy. I wish I could've persuaded Victoria to come along with us.'

'How is she? I do feel for her, carrying such a heavy load on her own.' Jane frowned. 'It's a shame we can't help in some way.'

'She struggles to make ends meet, not earning enough

to pay the rent and buy food. I don't think she wants to move to a smaller place because it's full of childhood memories, although she may have to.' Alice sighed as sadness engulfed her. 'She won't accept any help from me; she's too proud.'

Jane nodded. Glancing at Edward, she remembered how difficult it had been to tell him her family had money problems. 'Is that why she didn't go to Southend with you?'

Alice lowered her eyes for a moment. 'That, and going on a train would've probably reminded her of the crash that killed her parents.' She sighed. 'The problem is, I didn't think of that when I asked her to come with us and she did get upset. I felt dreadful.'

Jane reached across the table and rested her hand on Alice's. 'It's not your fault. That derailment at Stoats Nest was a tragic accident.'

Alice shook her head. 'I couldn't disagree more. I'm meant to be her friend, so I should think of these things. The trouble is, I don't know what to do to help.'

Chapter 6

'I'm pleased you and Grandma decided to stay last night. I think Mother was too.' Alice pulled the curtain across, to shut out the sun that was blinding her when she sat at the dining table. 'Is the sun in your eyes, Grandpa? I can pull the other one.'

'No, I'm fine.'

Alice made sure the curtain was hanging correctly before walking over to him and resting her hand on his arm. 'It's a shame to shut it out, but at this time of day it gets too much.'

Edward nodded. 'I'd have taken you all out for lunch, but I don't think your mother is up to it today.' He frowned, biting down on his lip.

Alice nodded. 'She has taken all this talk of war hard. She hasn't said as much, but I believe she is worried sick about Robert, never mind what Charles might try to do.'

'All we can do is hope sense will prevail.'

Sarah walked in, carrying a tray of cold meats, followed by Lily, with a basket of bread and a large gravy boat.

Edward jumped up. 'Allow me.' He grasped both sides of the silver platter and placed it at the centre of the dining table. 'It looks and smells delicious.'

Sarah smiled at her father. 'It's only cold meats. Jane is bringing in the vegetables and Charles is hopefully following her with the potatoes.'

Edward's eyes twinkled. 'It doesn't matter. It's a feast fit for a king.'

When the table was finally covered with plates of food, they all sat down. Sarah looked across at the empty seat that would have been Robert's and sniffed, before taking a deep breath. Edward pulled her chair out and beckoned her to sit down. Sarah hesitated, but caught Luke's glare. She sat herself down and Edward patted his daughter on the shoulder, before taking up his own seat next to her. One by one, they passed the dishes around and loaded their plates. For a few moments, the only sound in the room was cutlery hitting the crockery as they all ate their fill.

Alice's head jerked up. 'Can you hear that? It sounds like a whistle, and someone shouting.'

Chairs scuffed back from the dining table, over the red and blue floral carpet, the lunch things forgotten. Charles rushed to the window and pulled the curtain away from the edge, to get a better look. 'I don't know what's going on, but everyone is out on the street and a police officer is just getting off his bicycle. He's the one blowing the whistle, obviously trying to get everyone's attention.' The curtain dropped back into position as he ran to the front door. Edward and Luke reached him as he pulled it open.

Edward looked up and down Bloomsbury Street. The uniform black front doors were wide open and it was awash with people murmuring to each other. The policeman had propped his bicycle up against the house railings and removed his helmet, hanging it over the handlebars. He stood poised, in his navy blue uniform, with his whistle between his lips.

Luke turned to the well-dressed elderly man, who had his hand clasped around a whisky glass. 'What's all the commotion?'

'Be blowed if I know.' He lifted his glass and gulped at his drink, pursing his lips as he swallowed the strong amber liquid. 'Probably something to do with that daft peace demonstration on Sunday. Mind you, it was so wet, I'd be surprised if anybody turned up for it.'

Luke looked around, waving to his neighbours as he did so, before turning to Lily. 'Were you at Trafalgar Square on Sunday?' His eyes were razor sharp as they stared at her. 'If you have brought the police to my front door again, I will not be responsible for my actions.'

Lily paled. 'I... I haven't, Pa, honest.'

Luke didn't take his eyes off her. 'If they arrest you, I won't be bailing you out. You'll be finished as far as this family is concerned, do you understand?'

Lily nodded.

'Do you understand?' He spoke through gritted teeth. His voice was low and menacing.

'Yes,' Lily whispered.

'It must be important, to keep blowing that damn whistle and shouting.' The older man emptied the contents of his glass.

'What's going on?'

Luke turned around at the sound of Sarah's anxious voice. The whole family had followed him outside. 'I don't know.'

The policeman blew hard on his whistle, causing those nearest him to cover their ears. 'Ladies and gentlemen, can I have your attention please.' He waited for the talking to stop. 'The Germans invaded Belgium and Great Britain has declared war on Germany.'

Everyone remained silent for a moment.

'It's about time the Empire started flexing its muscles; we can't let the Huns walk all over everyone,' the old man shouted. 'I'd shoot the lot of them.'

The silence was broken and everyone in the street appeared to start talking at once.

'It's wrong to go to war; killing is a terrible thing.'

'I wonder if there'll be a food shortage?'

'Do you think the Germans will make it to London?'

'Of course not; we are perfectly safe.'

The police officer blew hard and long on his whistle. He held up his hands. 'Well, I can't answer your questions, but they do say it'll be over by Christmas.'

Luke turned to Sarah, his face lit up like a Christmas tree. 'Robert was right. As a regular soldier, he will be one of the first to go.'

'I want to enlist too, Father.' Charles peered up at Luke. He grinned as his excitement began to take hold. 'I want to fight for my king and country. I might even get to see France and meet a French girl.'

Luke beamed. 'I bet not everyone's sons are as patriotic as ours, Sarah.'

Jane put her arm around Sarah.

Alice glared at her father; anger rose inside at his insensitivity.

Charles looked around for Lily and Alice. 'Come on, you two. I bet everyone's going to Buckingham Palace; let's go, the king might come out onto the balcony.'

'You two go. I'll stay, just in case...'

Lily looked at her parents. Her mother's tense face held a fixed smile as she tried to hide the fear in her eyes. In stark contrast, her father looked like the cat that had got the cream. She turned her attention back to Alice. 'Are you sure? It doesn't seem very fair...'

'Don't worry. Just go, before father puts a stop to it.'

Lily and Charles looked at each other and laughed, before disappearing into the throng of people. Their next-door neighbour came out with pots of tea and plates of Victoria sponge. She started wandering around, offering it to the people in the street, then another neighbour followed suit.

Alice looked at her mother's ashen face. Jane was at her elbow, with her father standing on the other side of her. Alice stepped in close to her and whispered. 'Shall we go in, Mother? You look like you should sit down, before you fall down.'

Sarah looked up at Alice and nodded.

*

Alice looked behind her; the dining room was quiet and the house was still. Her grandparents had gone home to Russell Square the evening before, although she had a feeling they hadn't wanted to leave her mother, telling her to let them know if she had any concerns. She sat very still, holding her breath, listening for her father's footsteps, before picking up the Daily Mirror. He liked the paper in pristine condition and everyone was under strict instructions not to read it before he did. She laid it flat on the dining table, carefully smoothing out the coarse folds with her hands. She turned her hands over, checking for ink. The headlines on the front page were in capital letters, declaring Great Britain was at war. There was a large picture of torpedo boats sailing close together, so they could send messages to each other with megaphones. Pictures of Admirals and Field Marshalls were underneath that, followed by one of a submarine rising to the surface. The paper rustled as she turned the page, making her look behind her. She quickly noticed a picture of the King and the Prince of Wales on the balcony of Buckingham Palace.

'It was wonderful, Alice; you should've come with us.' Charles grinned at her startled expression as she looked over her shoulder at him.

Alice shook her head. 'I wish you wouldn't creep about. I thought you were father. You know what he's like about his precious newspaper.'

Charles laughed. 'As he is with everything.' His eyes were sparkling as he read the paper over her shoulder. 'It's so exciting; I can't wait to join up.'

Alice looked up from the newspaper and stared at her young brother for a moment. 'It's not glamorous, you know.' She looked back down at the newspaper. 'People are going to get killed. People are getting killed.'

'Only the Germans; we're going to get those Huns.' He laughed as he sat down next to her at the table and started buttering some toast on Alice's side plate.

She gave him a bemused look and shook her head. 'They're all someone's sons, brothers or husbands.'

Charles looked thoughtful. 'I suppose when you put it like that.' His face lit up again. 'But it has to be done.'

Alice shook her head. 'Don't you think it's bad enough Robert is going off to fight?'

'I shall miss him, although he does get more like father every day. It's hard to breathe when he's around, let alone have fun, but what an honour. Father is so proud of him for enlisting.' Charles paused, staring down at his toast and holding his knife to attention. 'I want him to be proud of me too.' He carefully placed the knife across the plate and bit down on the cold toast, covered with an inch-thick layer of butter. Crumbs immediately fell on to the white tablecloth. He placed the toast down and brushed them into his hands, before letting them fall onto the plate.

Alice watched him brush up each speck, feeling sure other boys his age wouldn't take the trouble to be so meticulous. 'He is proud of you, and not everyone can go and fight.'

'Huh, we both know that's not true, and anyway, if it's going to be over by Christmas, there won't be time to hang around.'

Alice looked at her younger brother and a smile crept across her face. 'You'll have to "hang around" as you put it, because you aren't eighteen yet, so you can't enlist.'

Charles frowned for a moment and then his face lit up. 'I bet I could if father signed something or other, giving his permission, and he'd definitely do that.'

Alice could feel her eyes welling up. 'You are too young to go to war. I can't lose both of my brothers. This is all too dreadful.' She slammed the paper shut and the spine folded up at the bottom. Alice sensed her brother's eyes boring into her as she stared hard at it, wishing she had the courage to leave it in that condition. She took a deep breath; it wasn't worth the commotion that would follow, so for the same reason Charles cleared his crumbs, she opened and straightened the newspaper, before carefully closing it again. Her eyes inspected it, checking for any imperfections.

Charles placed his buttery fingers on top of hers. 'Everything will be all right, you'll see.'

Alice gave him a weak smile, understanding why he wanted to escape, but unable to let him go without a fight. 'You'll be needed here and there'll be plenty to do; the country still has to run.'

'Like what?'

'I don't know, but men will be needed.'

'Do you think Freddie will join up?' Charles' boyish charm quickly turned to excitement. 'He could. I would if I was him.'

'I don't know. He mentioned it the other day but until then, I hadn't given it any thought.' Alice frowned, wondering how Charles could be so excited by the turn of events. 'I don't think so. After all, the police will still be needed here.'

'Yes, you could be right. Gosh, I'd be upset if I was Freddie.'

'That's because you see it as an adventure and an opportunity to get away from home.'

Charles' eyes clouded over and he lowered them for a moment. When he looked across at Alice again, there was a sparkle to be seen. 'It was packed at the Palace last night. I've never seen so many people in one place before. Everyone was singing, "we want the King", and they were all so happy and excited.' Charles sighed. 'Lily and I couldn't get close enough to see him. He was like an ant to us, on his balcony, but we all sang the national anthem. We sang at the top of our voices.'

Alice shook her head. 'I have to go to work.' She sighed. 'I expect that's all everyone will be talking about today.'

'Don't worry, Sis, there's talk that Lord Kitchener will be appointed War Minister in the next day or two, so that'll get things moving along.'

'How do you know such things? Father hasn't mentioned that.'

'I saw cousin Harry yesterday and Uncle William was telling him. He might be getting on a bit, but he still knows what's going on.'

Alice frowned as a feeling of foreboding swept over her. 'And I expect he'll be filling Harry's head with nonsense about doing the right thing.'

Charles sighed as he looked across at Alice. 'Well that's right, isn't it?'

'Obviously it is important to do the right thing, but Grandpa has no time for him and he's quite easy going, so there has to be a reason for it.'

'Yes, I know.'

Alice rested her hands on the arms and pushed back the chair. 'I have to go, otherwise I'm going to be late for work.'

Charlie reached out and grabbed her arm, before quickly dropping his hand. 'Sorry, I just wanted to say, don't worry about things. Everything's going to be fine.'

Alice stared at him for a moment, before nodding. 'You're not going to try and do something stupid, are you?'

Charles laughed. 'Does that sound like me? All right, maybe it does, but I just don't want you to worry, that's all.'

Mrs Headley appeared, carrying Alice's hat. 'Thank you, Mrs Headley.' Alice placed the hat on her head and gave herself a cursory glance in the mirror above the fireplace. 'I have to go, Charles, but we'll continue this conversation when I get back.'

Charles nodded. 'Take care.'

Alice stared at him for a moment, wondering what was going on inside his head. 'And you,' she whispered, placing her hand on his shoulder, before walking towards the hall and the front door.

The sun had already burnt away any early morning clouds, giving signs it was going to be another hot day. The familiar sweet malty smell from the Horseshoe Brewery in Tottenham Court Road told her she was approaching Charing Cross Road. As she crossed the street, the pungent smell hung in the air, letting her know the spent grain had been left to ferment in the storage bins.

'Hello, Alice, you're out early.'

Tony Fletcher's deep voice stopped her in her tracks. Alice inwardly groaned; she couldn't pretend she hadn't heard him.

She turned to see Molly and Tony walking arm-in-arm towards her.

'Everything all right, Alice.' Molly frowned. 'You look a little flushed.'

'Yes.' Alice tried to muster up a smile. 'I'm running behind and probably going to be late for work.' She looked from one to the other. 'What are you two doing up and about so early?'

Molly smiled and gazed up at Tony's face with puppy dog eyes. 'We're going to Greenwich for the day.' She laughed. 'Sit in the park and eat ice cream.'

Alice smiled at her friend's contagious laughter. Molly was truly smitten. 'It sounds fun.'

'Why don't you come with us?' Tony slipped his free hand into his pocket and pulled out a packet of Players Navy Cut cigarettes. He let go of Molly's hand and opened the box to pull one out.

Alice looked at Molly's face. Her eyes were downcast. The smile had become tight lipped.

'It'll be fun.' Tony winked at Alice before he placed a cigarette between his lips and struck a match to light it.

Alice pulled her lips together. Her free hand clenched by her side. 'No thank you. As I said, I have to go to work.' She forced a smile as she made a note to be there when Tony finally broke her friend's heart. 'But enjoy your day. I believe the weather is going to stay fine.'

Molly's eyes lit up and she tucked her hand through

Tony's arm. 'Shall we go?'

Smoke swirled down Tony's nostrils. The tip of his tongue peeped out between his lips, so his finger and thumb could lift off the tobacco sitting on it. 'Of course.'

'Have a good day, Alice. Make sure you enjoy the sunshine while you can.' Molly beamed.

*

Alice leafed through a stack of books behind her counter in the Foyles bookstore, running a soft yellow duster over the covers as she went. Looking over her shoulder, she watched Molly sorting the books in publisher order, ready to be put on the shelves. 'Did you enjoy your day in Greenwich Park?'

'Ahh.' Molly stopped dead and looked up to the ceiling, as though she was seeing stars. 'It was lovely; in fact, it couldn't have been better. We sat under a tree and watched the world go by. Tony rested his head on my lap and I stroked his hair.' She shivered, before looking across at Alice. 'Greenwich is a beautiful place; you and Freddie should go one day.'

Alice smiled at Molly's far away expression. 'Perhaps we should.'

Molly's look of love was quickly chased away by a frown. She stared across at the stack of books Alice was dusting and putting to one side. 'Where do all these books come from? I have to find somewhere on the shelves to put them all and they're already bursting at the seams. I never knew there were so many, and we're just one shop.'

'I know, and yet we sell hundreds every day, but I suppose we are a popular store.' Alice looked over her shoulder, watching her friend move to sort through the books that had no bill tickets in them. 'It's a good idea, selling second hand ones alongside new publications. I wish I'd thought of it. I could live in a bookshop. It's my idea of heaven.'

Molly wrinkled her nose. 'There's a musty smell to some of them, but it's certainly a place to meet people, I'll give you that. We certainly don't have many quiet days, but I suppose that'll change now.' Molly lowered her voice. 'There won't be any men around soon. They're enlisting in their droves, especially since Lord Kitchener's poster appeared on the front cover of the London Opinion magazine.'

Alice sighed. 'I don't know why you are getting upset about it; your Tony is still here. Robert enlisted before war was even declared and goodness knows, I don't trust Charlie not to do something stupid.'

Molly turned and stared at Alice, anguish written all over her face. 'I know I sound selfish, but,' she bit down on her lip, 'that's just the point. With everyone going, there'll be even more women after Tony and I struggle to hold his attention as it is.'

'Molly, stop worrying. If he loves you, he won't be

interested in anybody else.'

A humourless sound escaped Molly's lips. 'We all know he doesn't. He's a womaniser, Alice, but the problem is, I do love him.'

Alice placed her arm around her friend; her rose scent lingered in the air around them. 'I know you do. It's obvious to anyone watching you when Tony's around.'

'Do you think they'll get called up?' Molly's eyes welled up. 'It scares me. I'm frightened I'll lose Tony.'

'Who knows? All you can do is make the most of the time you have together. This war is a dreadful business; let's hope they're right and it is over by Christmas.' She paused and dropped her arm from Molly's shoulders. 'You know, I think Robert is already in France. Goodness knows what he is going through.'

'Alice, Alice...'

Alice spun around at the hysterical voice, quickly taking in her mother's tear-stained face. 'What is it?'

Sarah gulped for air. 'It's awful, it's truly awful.'

Molly frowned at Mrs Taylor and gently pushed Alice towards her. 'Take her into the staff room and I'll look after the counter for you.'

Alice nodded and put her arm around her mother. 'What is it? Robert's all right, isn't he? Nothing's happened to Grandpa has it?' Her mind was jumping all over the place, trying to second-guess what had caused her to act so out of character.

Sarah nodded and shook her head, almost at the

same time. She took a handkerchief out of her bag and wiped her eyes, before running it over her cheeks. 'I don't know if I can bring myself to say the words out loud.'

Alice could feel the colour drain from her face. 'Tell me.'

Sarah took a deep breath. 'Charles has enlisted. He left for training today.' A shudder racked through her body.

Alice stopped dead. Her mind was racing; she felt unable to move. She should have said something after her conversation with Charles the morning after war was declared, but she didn't think they'd allow him to enlist. Sarah put her arm through hers and pulled her along the corridor to the staff room.

'He... he's too young.' Alice stopped and grabbed her mother's arm, not noticing the softness of the grey jacket she was wearing. 'There must be a mistake.'

Sarah sighed as she frowned at her daughter. 'No, there isn't. Apparently, he signed up with Harry, and I think Stephen was with them as well.'

'Oh my God. Harry and Stephen are only sixteen. Aunt Emily and Uncle George must be beside themselves, let alone his parents. Does Victoria know?'

Sarah sniffed as she tried to keep her composure. 'I don't know about Victoria, but everyone is distraught. I wanted to tell you and Lily myself. I didn't want someone else mentioning it to you first.'

Alice shook her head. 'I don't understand how they could accept him when he's under age; Harry and Stephen even more so.'

Sarah turned and held Alice's hand tight in hers. 'Emily thinks they must have lied about their ages.'

Alice gave a wry smile. 'I should've thought of that. Charles was so keen to enlist and he wanted Father to be proud of him, like he is of Robert.'

A tear tripped over Sarah's lashes. She sniffed and quickly brushed it away. 'Charles is so young and trusting, innocent to the ways of the world. It can be a cruel place.' She looked away from Alice. 'I can't understand why the men around us all think it's a good idea to put their children's lives on the line. I must be missing something.' She sighed. 'I hope he'll be all right.'

Alice shook her head. 'Perhaps we could stop them from going.'

Sarah's eyes lit up for a second and she grabbed Alice's hand in hers.

Alice's enthusiasm for her plan was taking hold. 'You know, go to the recruitment office and make a fuss.'

Sarah's sparkle disappeared as quickly as it had come. 'Charles would never forgive us, and neither would your father.'

'To be honest, I don't care what Father thinks.' Alice's hope quickly vanished. 'It's his fault that Charles signed up in the first place; all that talk of patriotism and doing the right thing.'

*

Wearily, Victoria pushed her front door key into the lock at Percy Street and turned it. The door sprung open. The scent of the lavender plant situated at the bottom of the stairs had overpowered the enclosed space and rushed to meet her. She wrinkled her nose and stepped into the hall. Her heels tapped on the black and white tiles. She placed her keys on the console table, immediately noticing an envelope propped up against a silver candleholder. She picked up the envelope and examined her name, written in blue ink across the middle. It looked like Stephen's spidery writing. Victoria frowned. She bit hard on her bottom lip until blood seeped into her mouth. Tension twisted her insides. Her heart pounded in her chest. Why would he be writing to her? Her head began to throb. She walked into the sun-filled sitting room and slowly sank into a high back chair. Her fingers gripped the letter. A tear tripped over her lashes. She didn't need to open it; she knew what Stephen had done.

Chapter 7

Alice had tossed and turned all night and finally gave in as dawn broke through her bedroom curtains. She dragged herself out of bed and pulled back the heavy blue floral curtains, before looking out on the pavement below. It was a grey, wet beginning to the day; puddles rippled as the wind caught them. The rain had lashed down all night, thudding against the window. She blamed it for keeping her awake, but deep down she knew it had nothing to do with it.

Not being able to face breakfast, Alice left home early. The house was quiet with the boys gone. She had kept waiting for Charles to walk through the door with his usual vigour and sparkle. She walked briskly along Bedford Avenue, pulling up the collar of her black coat.

The early morning sun held no heat as it tried to break through the clouds. The leaves on the ground were a testament that autumn had arrived. The familiar sweet, malty smell from the Horseshoe Brewery in Tottenham Court Road hung in the air, igniting memories of Aunt Emily's stories of her own mother's fixation about moving from Percy Street. It was partly because of the brewery, especially when the spent grain had been left to ferment in the storage bins, but mainly because Lilian had always wanted the status of living somewhere with a garden view, like Russell Square, which is where Alice's grandparents' family home had always been.

Alice turned into Percy Street and the large four-storey houses came into view. She glanced up at the house that had been Emily's childhood home. It was still in impeccable condition. Emily had known Victoria's mother since they were children and was devastated when she died. Victoria stepped out and shut her front door. Alice waved frantically and increased her speed. Her footsteps were deadened on the wet leaves covering the pavement. As her pace increased, her feet gave way on the slippery surface of the leaves and she just managed to prevent herself from falling. 'Victoria.' She tried to shout but her upbringing prevented her from doing so.

Victoria turned away from her front door before stopping to look round. 'Morning. What a miserable day. How come you are walking this way to Foyles?'

Alice rested her hand on her chest as she gasped for air. 'Sorry.' She paused to catch her breath. 'I wanted to see you before we got to work.'

Victoria frowned as she placed her arm through Alice's. 'What is it?' She moved to walk forward, but Alice stayed rooted to the spot.

'Did Stephen come home last night?'

Victoria's eyes began to water. 'He left me a note.'

She took a deep breath. 'It said he couldn't face me, but knew he was doing the right thing.'

Alice's eyes widened. 'Oh God, it's true then. I was hoping—'

'I know.' Victoria blinked quickly. 'The note said he went with Charles and Harry; is that true?'

'My mother is in a terrible way.'

'Molly told me she came to the shop to see you yesterday, and how distraught she was, but didn't know what had happened.' Victoria gave Alice a feeble smile. 'Being the coward that I am, I couldn't bring myself to ask you.'

Alice pulled gently at Victoria's arm and they started walking towards Charing Cross Road. 'My mother said yesterday she'd heard Stephen might be with Harry and Charles, but wasn't sure. I'm sorry. I should have said something then, but I kept thinking it couldn't be true, because they were all under age.'

Victoria took a handkerchief out of her coat pocket and dabbed her eyes. 'I was shocked and upset when I read Stephen's note, but once I had time to digest it, I realised I had no right to be surprised. He made it no secret he'd join up at the first opportunity.'

Alice nodded. 'I should have been with you; I'm sorry I let you down.'

Victoria pulled her collar up slightly. 'No, you didn't. From what I hear, you had your hands full with your mother.'

Alice laughed but it was a bitter sound. 'Like you, once I had thought about it, Charles had left enough clues as to what he intended to do. I just didn't hear them, and what's more, I am shocked they were able to get away with it.'

Victoria gave her friend a sideways glance. 'I know exactly what you mean, but we can now only pray for their safe return.'

Alice nodded again. 'You're right, of course, but I've had enough of the damn war already. It's only just begun and it's pulling families apart.'

Victoria squeezed Alice's arm against her body. 'Let's hope they're right and it is over by Christmas.'

'Let's hope.' Anger began to flow through Alice's veins; she took a deep breath. 'I blame my father for Charles signing up. Him and his "I'm proud my son is patriotic and prepared to fight for king and country" rhetoric.'

'I know what you mean, but it wasn't just him, Alice, so don't be too hard on him. Look around at all the posters pasted on every advertising space and wall you see. I've even seen them in shop windows and they're all encouraging men to enlist, implying they're cowards if they don't.'

Alice nodded her agreement and for a moment they walked on in silence. 'How did Daisy take the news?' Her mind was firmly fixed on Lily's reaction, which caught her by surprise and didn't help her sleepless night.

'She was upset.' Victoria gave a little laugh. 'We cried together and probably talked more than we've done in years.'

Alice looked across at Victoria. 'I'm glad you weren't on your own.'

Victoria's eyes welled up. 'I'm terrified, but we have to stay strong for them. How about Lily? Did she explode when she found out?'

Alice looked down at the pavement, momentarily studying the varying shades of brown leaves that were littering it. 'It was worse than that, much worse.'

Victoria's head jerked up, her eyes wide. 'What do you mean, worse than that? I didn't think it could get any worse than Lily on one of her rants. Oh my God, she hasn't killed your father, has she?'

Alice laughed. 'No, but in a way, it felt worse than that.'

Victoria stared at her expectantly before sighing. 'And?'

'Sorry. Lily didn't say a word to him. She just kept staring at him with unbridled hatred. I was on tenterhooks all evening, waiting for her to explode, but she didn't. At one point her eyes looked watery and I thought tears were about to come, but no, she sat in silence. I don't know what's worse.'

They walked on, each lost in their own thoughts. Victoria relived the situation and understood Lily's rage.

'I expect your father was thrilled, wasn't he?'

A sound escaped from Alice, an involuntary noise of something trapped and unable to break free. 'Actually, he didn't say much. With a house full of angry women, I think he was scared, and rightfully so.'

Victoria nodded. 'It's all about survival now, Alice. We have to stay positive for them and look after ourselves for when they return.'

Alice sighed. She had no words of wisdom.

'Do you think Tony will enlist?' Victoria held out her hand in front of her. 'Can you feel rain?'

Alice followed suit, thankful for the change of subject. 'No, and I don't think Tony will enlist either.' She couldn't resist a smile. 'Molly's very concerned about him staying behind though, because there'll be all these single women chasing after him, due to the man shortage.'

'What?' Victoria gave a belly laugh. 'Doesn't she know he already chases everything in a skirt?'

Alice's smile faded. 'Yes, she does. It's quite sad really, because she's well and truly smitten with him, but he'll break her heart. It's just a question of when.'

'You're right, it's sad. I had no idea she was that smitten.'

'She told me she loves him, even though she knows he doesn't love her.' Alice swallowed hard as a lump began to form in her throat. 'When the time comes we just need to be there to help pick up the pieces.'

*

Freddie and Alice took a leisurely stroll in the unexpected evening sunshine, along Shaftesbury Avenue to Leicester Square and the Odeon Cinema. He looked across at her and frowned. The sparkle he loved seemed to have been doused with the cold water of reality. Her sunny outlook appeared to have been buried under a heap of worry. He rubbed his chin, the stubble growth from that morning scratching the palm of his hand. He wasn't sure what was showing, but he was hoping it would be something to bring a smile to Alice's face. She hadn't spoken since they had left Bloomsbury Street. Someone at work had told him David Garrick was showing, but he'd rather have a good laugh at a Charlie Chaplin film.

Freddie rested his hand on top of Alice's, which lay limply on his arm. 'Your father was telling me how your Uncle William's son, James is it, tried to enlist but got turned down because of his height. Your father seemed to find it quite funny although, apparently, William wasn't amused. In fact, from what I can gather, he's beside himself with shame.' Freddie gave Alice a sideways glance. Her pale face was unreadable. The dark lines under her eyes were new. 'At least Lily and Daisy should be safe for a little while, now the suffragette movement have called off all protest marches and demonstrations.' He coughed. 'The general strike's been called off too. The message is about the country pulling together in support of our men at the front.'

Alice stared blankly ahead.

'Look, that man and woman have no clothes on.'

Nothing.

Freddie tried again. 'Of course, when we marry and have six children, you won't have time to work in Foyles.'

Still nothing. Freddie stopped walking.

Alice jerked back in surprise. 'What's wrong?'

Freddie raised his eyebrows. 'That should be my question. You haven't heard a word I've said in the last half an hour.'

'I have. I just didn't have any comment to make, that's all.' Alice adjusted her light blue woollen cardigan.

Freddie threw back his head and laughed, almost hysterically.

Alice stopped fiddling with her cardigan and stared at him. 'What is so funny? I only said—'

'Oh I know what you said.' Freddie wiped the tears from his eyes. 'I haven't laughed that much in ages.'

'I don't understand—'

'No, and that is because you clearly weren't listening.'

Colour flooded Alice's face; she lowered her eyes as shame washed over her. 'I'm sorry.'

Freddie smiled as she stood forlornly in front of him. 'And then you lied about it, and I might add, not very well.'

Alice looked up. 'I'm sorry, I was miles away. What did you say?'

'Nothing important, but enough to know you'd have commented if you'd been listening.' Freddie sighed. 'I was initially talking about your cousin James not being accepted in the army, because of his height.'

Alice nodded. 'I expect Uncle William was furious about it, and he's probably trying to pull strings as we speak, instead of being thankful he's safe at home.'

Freddie nodded. 'Well, your father seemed pleased about it.'

'That's because both his boys are patriotic and fighting for King and country. He'll probably dine out on that for a long time.' Alice sucked in her breath. 'I'm frightened what'll become of Robert and Charles. Even if they survive, they'll not come back the same men. If they don't survive, mother will be devastated and I'm not sure how I'll cope with her, let alone my own grief.'

Freddie grabbed both her hands in his. 'They'll be all right, but remember you're not alone; whatever happens, you won't have to cope on your own.' He paused and squeezed her hands. 'I read in the London Daily Newspaper at work that David Lloyd George gave a speech in the Queen's Hall. I think they called it the Road Hogs of Europe. Apparently, he said that the Germans had left Belgium bleeding and broken. They had killed women and children. They say that has spurred men on to join and fight. They got something in the region of thirty-three thousand recruits in one day. At that rate it'll soon be over.'

Alice's eyes opened wide and her jaw dropped slightly. 'That's awful. Is that what we're going to see on Pathé News at the cinema?' She closed her eyes for a second. 'If it is, I don't want to watch it. I can't sleep at night as it is, for worrying about my brothers, and everyone else.'

'I don't know.' Freddie hesitated. 'But you're right, it is awful. You must see why we can't stand by and let it all just happen; wouldn't we be thankful if other countries came to help us in our moment of need?'

She took a deep breath and slowly let it out again. 'Yes, I suppose so.'

'Alice, I've something to ask you...'

'What?'

Freddie fidgeted from one foot to the other. 'I'm afraid this isn't how I thought I'd do it but—'

Alice narrowed her eyes as she stared at him. 'What?'

'Will you marry me?'

'What?'

Freddie gave a nervous laugh. 'As I said, this wasn't how I wanted to ask you but things have changed and I —'

A smile crept across her face; her eyes sparkled with happiness. 'Yes.'

'Oh, that's brilliant.' He beamed. 'I've already asked

your father's permission.'

'So, we can fix a date then?' Alice gave a little jump off the ground and clapped her hands together.'

Freddie hesitated, staring at her smile, capturing it in his mind's eye.

'This is wonderful. Lily and I wondered if that's why you were in the sitting room with him but...' Her sparkle was quickly replaced with anxiety. 'Freddie, what is it?'

His smile disappeared and his tone changed to a whisper. 'Alice, I've something else to tell you...'

She looked up at him, her eyes wide and full of fear. 'What?'

His shoulders hunched over as his head dropped. He breathed in and stared down at the pavement. 'I was going to wait to tell you but I suppose now's as good a time as any...'

'What?' Alice closed her eyes and breathed deeply, trying to control the hysteria that was rising in her chest.

Freddie took another deep breath and held both her arms in his hands. 'I've enlisted.' He blurted out the words before he changed his mind about telling her.

Alice's legs buckled and he tightened his grip, pulling her towards him. 'I'm sorry, Alice but my conscience wouldn't let me not.'

She pushed away from him. Her eyes were watery when she looked up at him again. 'But you're a policeman. I thought...'

Silence stood between them like an insurmountable wall. Freddie searched her face, waiting for acknowledgment that he'd done the right thing, but it wasn't there. 'That's not all. I leave tomorrow for training.'

Alice stood silently in front of him. Tears cascaded over her lashes and the saltiness rested on her lips. She made no attempt to wipe them away.

'So when…?'

Freddie couldn't take his eyes off her and wished he hadn't mentioned it, but to just disappear would have been worse. 'I shall have leave, so we can do it then.' He grabbed both her hands and gently shook them. 'I don't want us to wait any longer than we have to. I love you, Alice Taylor.' He pulled her towards him and wrapped his arms tightly around her. Fear suddenly gripped his heart; would this be the last time he'd hold her in his arms?

Chapter 8

October 1914

People were gathering in Whitehall, patiently waiting and listening. The familiar skyline of the Houses of Parliament, Big Ben and Westminster Abbey were visible in the distance. They were all there, waiting to watch and cheer the hundreds of men march along the wide road, in their full army uniforms, passing the statue of Prince George, Duke of Cambridge.

When Lily, Alice and Sarah arrived, the crowd was already six deep along both sides of the long road. Many were gaunt and serious as they waited, stretching their necks to peer down the road, looking for a sign that the soldiers were coming. The chill of the air disappeared as people moved forward, each pressing closer to the person next to them, so others could join the throng. If one person moved, so did everyone. They were as one, body odour fusing with soap and cologne.

Lily had nagged Alice and her mother about going.

'Is that the men coming?'

'I can't see any coming this way.'

In the distance, a faint sound of people cheering

carried up the road towards the waiting crowd, preceding the soldiers.

A child's voice rang out. 'I can see them, they are coming.'

As one, everyone stretched their necks to see. Some stood on tiptoes and children were pushed to the front. Women, children and older men clapped and cheered, drowning out the thud of army boots hitting the road as the soldiers passed them. There was almost a party atmosphere in the crowd as women threw children's shoes at the soldiers, for good luck.

'You'll be back before you know it.'

'See you at Christmas, boys.'

'We're proud of you.'

'Give the Huns what for.'

'For King and country boys, for King and country.'

Alice strained her neck, moving right then left, trying to see through the crowd. Was Charles one of them? If he was, then Stephen and Harry must be too. Her heart was pounding as she prayed for a last glimpse of her brother, before he went off to war. She stood on tiptoes, trying to see the soldiers' faces. The men in uniform stared straight ahead as they kept in formation. Alice frowned; they all looked the same from her position. A tear rolled down her cheek as it hit home they may not see Charles again. She had never told him how funny he was, or how proud she was of him, let alone how much he meant to her.

Sarah's voice cut into Alice's thoughts. 'Do you think Charles is one of them?'

Alice ran her hand over her face, before turning to look at her mother. 'I don't know, it's hard to tell.' She paused, looking through the crowd again. 'They all look the same in their uniforms.' Alice wondered if her mother was having similar thoughts to her own. She gave her mother's arm a squeeze. 'He'll be all right; he's too bright a star to be dulled by all this.'

Sarah gave a weak smile. 'I hope you are right; he is so young.'

An old lady with a mop of grey hair, wearing an expensive tweed coat, stood next to Alice and cheered enthusiastically. She turned to Alice and shouted above the noise around them. 'Come on, lovey, you've got to let them know they've got our support, otherwise they're fighting for nothing.'

Alice stared hard at the smiling face of the old lady, as she cheered and clapped the soldiers. Her words echoed Lily's, earlier that morning. 'Do you think it's right, the war I mean?'

The old lady's toothless smile immediately disappeared as she went silent, before looking Alice straight on. 'It doesn't matter what I think. As my late husband used to say, it's a done deal, and you can't let these lads go off without the country's support behind them. They're all someone's sons, brothers and husbands.'

Alice nodded and gave her a faint smile. She looked across at Lily joining in with the crowd's enthusiasm, to give the boys a good send off. Alice smiled at her. She may have been younger, but she was probably wiser. She lifted her hands up and started cheering and clapping. Sarah followed suit.

The old lady gave a toothless smile at Alice. 'That's it, lovey, let them know we care. Hopefully, it'll be over soon. You know, even the young Princess Mary has made an appeal for money, so the troops can have a Christmas gift each. Now that's sweet, don't you think?'

Alice stopped clapping and slowly lowered her hands. 'But I thought they were hoping it would all be over by Christmas.' Her heart plummeted – would she ever see the boys again?

*

Molly fastened her coat as another busy day at Foyles came to an end. 'I'm dreading going outside; the temperature has really dropped.' She looked across at Alice, who was pulling a scarf around her neck. 'I haven't seen Freddie in here for a while. Has something happened? Are you two not together anymore?' Molly asked, as Victoria joined them.

Alice pulled on her soft woollen gloves and took a deep breath. 'He has enlisted.' Her shoulders hunched over. 'He went a couple of months ago.'

Molly grabbed her hand. 'Why didn't you say something?'

Alice pulled her hand away and folded her arms across her stomach. 'What was there to tell?' She shrugged her shoulders. 'He felt, like thousands of others, he wouldn't be doing his duty if he didn't enlist.'

Victoria remained silent as she studied Alice.

Molly raised her eyebrows. 'I can't pretend I'm not shocked. I thought, as a policeman, he'd stay here and do the things policemen do.'

Alice gave a wry smile. The usual sparkle in her eyes was gone. 'Yes, me too, but his sense of duty to his country took hold.'

The two younger girls glanced sideways at each other, each nodding encouragement to the other.

Molly lifted her chin and pulled her shoulders back. 'But I suppose he must have already had that sense of duty, to do the job he did.'

Victoria stepped forward and rested her arm around Alice's slumped shoulders. 'Silly question I know, but are you all right?'

Alice nodded. 'You know, this is happening to every family, all around the country. I've just got to get a grip and keep myself busy.'

Molly shook her head. 'I'm sorry, Alice. I truly thought you and Freddie would set a date to be married in the next year, but I suppose...'

Alice closed her eyes for a moment, before opening

them wide to stare at her friends' expectant faces. 'We've set a date, but the trouble is, I don't know when it is.'

'What?' they asked in unison.

Alice's eyes clouded as she remembered the happiness his proposal had given her, then the cold water he had quickly drowned her excitement with. 'He proposed the evening before he went away.' Alice couldn't bring herself to tell them that he had followed it with news of his going away for army training. 'He said he wanted to get married at the earliest opportunity, so it'll happen as soon as he returns. The problem is, he doesn't know when that will be.'

Victoria grabbed Alice's arm. 'Let's go for tea and cake. This is a crisis and a celebration all in one.'

Alice could feel her eyes becoming blurry. 'I need to go...'

Molly grabbed her other arm. 'That sounds like a good idea, Victoria; let's go to that delightful tea room in Oxford Street. I forget what it's called, but it's my treat.'

Victoria tugged a little on Alice's arm. 'Come on, allow us to be your friends.'

Alice gave her a watery smile and nodded.

The three of them walked arm-in-arm, along Charing Cross Road towards Oxford Street. The shoppers and the many people trying to get home made it a busy thoroughfare. Molly turned the handle on the street door of the tearoom and a bell chimed; a waitress immediately walked over to them.

'A table for three please.' Molly began unbuttoning her coat. 'We'll have three teas and the best chocolate cake you have.'

The girls all laughed as Molly took control of the situation. 'In times of crisis, it's always good to eat chocolate in any form and my mother, of course, swears by drinking tea at such a time.'

The waitress showed them to a white-clothed table, near the window. They all removed their coats before sitting down. By the time they were all comfortably seated, the waitress had returned with pots of tea and plates loaded with large pieces of chocolate cake.

Alice stared down at her plate. 'Oh my.'

Molly laughed. 'Doesn't it look delicious?'

'It certainly does.' Victoria scanned her plate. 'Although I have a feeling I won't need to eat for a week when I've eaten this.'

The girls laughed and picked up their dessert forks.

Molly stabbed at her cake, separating a small piece. 'So come on, let's discuss your wedding.'

Alice didn't touch the feast in front of her. She placed the fork onto her plate. 'There is nothing to discuss. I can't plan something that may not happen; after all—'

'No.' Victoria raised her voice and looked sternly at Alice. 'We'll not have that sort of talk, thank you very much. None of us know what is going to happen, but I for one cannot think about Stephen not coming home again, so we should carry on as if they're visiting family or something.'

Alice's jaw dropped a little. 'I wondered how you were managing to deal with it so well.'

Victoria nodded. 'It's the only way I can.' She paused and looked down at the chocolate cake. 'I've even wondered if Ted enlisted. Of course, he could be married with children by now.'

Molly and Alice gave each other a quick look, before turning to stare at her.

Molly coughed and returned her attention to the cake that was calling out to her. 'So Alice, we need to find out how you get married without knowing when it will take place.'

Alice tilted her head at Molly before returning her attention to Victoria. 'You can talk to us about Ted. I know we haven't mentioned him, but that was because we didn't want to upset you. At the time, you had enough to deal with. In fact, it certainly puts my self-pity into perspective.'

Victoria's lips lifted at the corners. 'There is not a day when I don't think about Ted, but don't feel that what you're going through is less important. You've been a good friend and now it's my turn to return the favour.'

Molly nodded, but Alice didn't take her eyes off Victoria. 'You've been through so much; I wish I had your strength.' Alice shook her head.

Victoria laughed. 'Oh Alice, I didn't choose this. We

all have strength, but we just don't know it until we are tested. Now this is meant to be a crisis and celebration tea and cake for you, remember.'

They all laughed, before picking up their forks again and tucking into the light, sweet sponge.

Victoria closed her eyes. 'Hmm, this is quite decadent.'

Alice and Molly laughed and they both mimicked her.

'Well you must admit, it is.'

'So Alice, about your wedding.' Molly returned to the question in hand. 'Do you know what you want to wear?'

Alice shrugged. 'I can't allow myself to think about it, because it may not be for years, if at all.'

Victoria poured the tea into each of their cups. 'Look, it will happen. As my mother used to say, I can feel it in my water.' She placed the china teapot back onto the metal stand. 'If you don't want to buy a wedding dress, what about your mother's?'

'I don't know if it would fit, or actually, if she still has it.'

Molly laughed. 'I expect she does; my mother still has hers. I think she hopes I'll wear it one day.'

Alice tilted her head again. 'Ahh, I'll have to pop round to see your mother and father; they are so lovely.'

Molly laughed. 'All families are lovely, when they're not your own.' She looked sideways at Victoria. 'Sorry.'

'It's all right.' Victoria paused. 'Stop worrying. It's about time I moved on and Alice's wedding could be just the antidote I need.' She gave her best smile, chasing away the jealous thoughts that immediately invaded her mind. She felt sure there would be no wedding for her. With no Ted, and no father to walk her down the aisle to the man she loved, fate had dealt her a mean blow. She took a deep breath and concentrated on the cake in front of her. 'Anyway, back to the dress; you should ask your mother, and I don't mind doing any alterations that might be needed.'

Alice shook her head. 'Thanks, Victoria, but I don't even know whether my mother still has one.'

Molly picked up her cup and took a sip of the hot liquid. 'Well then, that is your first step.'

Confusion swept across Alice's face. 'What is?'

Molly tutted. She put her cup back on its saucer. 'To ask your mother if she still has her wedding dress, and then try it on, if she's happy for you to wear it.'

Alice gave a strange laugh. 'I haven't told her that Freddie has proposed.'

'What?' they answered in unison.

Alice's lips thinned. 'I don't expect you to understand, but Freddie went away the following day and I just thought…'

Molly shook her head. Her eyes sparked with impatience. 'Did he say he wanted to wait until the end of the war?'

'No, actually he said he didn't want to wait and when he gets leave, he wants us to marry.'

'There you go then, we've work to do.' Victoria rested her hand on Alice's arm. 'This is so exciting. I can't wait; you'll be the first of the three of us to get married.'

Alice laughed at her friend's excitement. 'Well, we don't know that yet. It could be years away.'

'Or weeks,' Victoria corrected.

'Or days.' Molly laughed.

Alice shook her head as she joined in their laughter. 'You two are incorrigible.'

Molly held her fork, laden with cake, in mid-air over her plate. 'Well, I certainly won't be getting married before either of you.'

'You don't know that,' Alice whispered.

'I think I do.' Molly laughed again, but it was a hollow sound. 'Tony and I are finished.'

Alice's mouth dropped. 'Finished?'

Molly let out a big sigh. 'Yes, to cut a long story short, I called him a coward because he hadn't enlisted.'

Victoria rested her hand on Molly's. 'Why did you do that? Surely you'd be grateful that the man you loved was safe.'

A grating sound filled the space between them. 'Yes, I know that now. I've since heard he's enlisted, but he didn't tell me. I haven't seen him to say goodbye.'

Alice placed her hand on Molly's and the three sat in

silence, holding on to each other, deep in their own thoughts.

<u>Chapter 9</u>

December 1914

Luke walked into the library of the Gentlemen's Club and scanned the room. It was busier than usual; cigar smoke hung in the air and the room was buzzing with whispered conversation. The walls were stacked with shelves from floor to ceiling, each packed with leather-bound books. On each wall, a ladder stood to one side, attached to a runner. The grandeur of the room was lost on him; only the newspaper headlines filled his thoughts. He noticed Edward and another man, sitting with their backs to him, at a small round table by one of the large sash windows. Heavy dark green curtains hung in tight folds to the floor. The window was open a fraction at the bottom; the cold wintry breeze caused the curtains to flap and papers to rustle.

Luke weaved his way through the many tables and chairs, nodding at the occupants as he passed. 'Morning, Edward.'

Edward looked up from his newspaper and placed his empty cup back on its matching saucer. 'Morning, Luke, pull up a chair.'

Luke nodded and glanced at the other man. 'Sorry, George, I didn't realise it was you.' Luke paused as he sat down. 'How's Emily?'

George gave a wry smile. 'Probably the same as most grandmothers, mothers and sisters at this time. Christmas is just two weeks away and they're worried sick about their menfolk. Emily is fixated on the fact they said it should be over by then.'

Luke shook his head. 'I have to say, that's not how it's looking.' He raised his hand and beckoned to the steward. 'Anyone for coffee or something stronger?'

Edward looked at his watch. 'No thanks, it's a bit early for something stronger and we've just ordered a pot of tea.' He closed and folded the newspaper, laying it on the table.

'Very civilised,' Luke mumbled, glancing at the steward. 'Just a coffee.' He turned back to Edward. 'This place is busy today.'

Edward gave a hollow laugh. 'Yes, I think the war is good for business.'

Luke smiled at his father-in-law. 'Well I suppose it's somewhere to talk about it, without having women crying all over you.'

George's eyes widened and his mouth dropped slightly.

Edward shook his head. 'The headlines make for worrying reading, that's for sure.'

Luke's shoulders went back and his chest puffed out.

'It has to be done though.'

The steward returned with a porcelain pot of coffee. A couple of Lincoln biscuits had been placed on the saucer carrying his cup.

'So they say.' George sighed. 'You know our grandson wrote to Lord Kitchener.'

Luke nodded as the steward placed the drink and crockery on the table in front of him. 'Thank you.'

Edward frowned at George and leant forward in his chair. 'Why?'

'Was he objecting to the war?' Luke laughed. 'These youngsters don't understand the importance of it.'

George stared hard at Luke, momentarily watching him pour his coffee into the cup. The steam spiralled upwards while the strong aroma escaped into the air around them. 'I'm not sure I agree with that, Luke. However, he wasn't objecting about the war.' He paused as he held Luke's gaze. 'He wanted to enlist.'

Luke's laughter brought a chorus of shush from the occupants of the room. 'Well good for him. You should be proud.' He placed the pot back onto the table.

George's eyebrows furrowed together. 'He's eleven.'

'I think it's brilliant.' Luke carried on chuckling as he picked up one of the biscuits, his fingers running over the dots patterned all over it. 'What did he think he could do?' Luke bit into the hard, crunchy biscuit and crumbs immediately fell onto the table.

'He wanted to be a runner, you know, carry

messages.' George glanced down at the newspaper headlines and sighed. 'Apparently, David told Kitchener he was the fastest runner around here and he could ride a bike as well. Thankfully, Kitchener sent him a lovely letter, saying that he couldn't enlist, but they'd bear him in mind as and when other duties come up.'

Luke wrapped his hand around his cup, ignoring the handle. He sipped at the hot, strong black liquid. 'Don't you think it's wonderful, Edward? You should be very proud of him, George.' He held the cup for a few seconds, until his fingers became too hot and then, without a word, he placed it back on the saucer.

George stiffened in his seat as he sucked in his breath. 'Proud? I don't know how you can say that, Luke. This is an eleven-year-old boy that war has been glamourised for.'

Luke shook his head. He lifted his hands chest high, with his palms facing George. 'Oh please, tell me you are not one of those conscientious objectors, are you?'

George frowned and his lip curled as he stared at Luke. 'No, I'm not.'

Edward's gaze flitted between the two men. 'Luke, we all know you're passionate about the war, but not everybody feels the same as you and you need to learn to respect that.'

A smile crept across Luke's face. 'Quite the contrary, Edward, I believe everyone needs to get behind our boys and support them. I make no apology for that.' His chin

145

lifted as he nodded towards the newspapers sitting on the table between them. 'From what the headlines are saying this morning, several people, including women and children, have died on the east coast from yesterday's bombings.'

Edward shook his head. 'Yes, I just read about it here in the Daily Mirror. Apparently, Scarborough was badly hit; they say fifty shells fell on it.'

George sighed. 'It must have been terrifying for them. I assumed only London would be hit, which I know sounds stupid, but I thought it's the seat of power and royalty, so in my head it made the most sense.'

Luke nodded. 'I'm inclined to agree with you, but it wasn't just Scarborough that was hit, so was Hartlepool.'

Edward picked up the newspaper. 'Hartlepool isn't that surprising really, because it's a shipbuilding area.' He opened the paper on page four. 'It says three east coast towns were bombed.'

George and Luke leant forward to peer over the edge of the newspaper, both trying to read it upside down.

Edward shook his head. 'It says here that even a church was hit, during a service of communion.'

George leant back in his chair and shook his head. 'It will be hospitals next, you mark my words.'

*

Victoria patted the bun at the nape of her neck, before pulling a woollen scarf around her. 'I am dreading leaving the shop; the weather has turned bitterly cold.' She paused as she tied the scarf in a loose knot under her chin. 'I worry more and more each day about Stephen and Charles. I do hope they're all right.'

Alice frowned while straightening the books on the shelf, preparing for when Foyles opened in the morning. 'I know what you mean. We don't talk about the war at home because it starts Father off on one of his patriotic speeches about the empire, and Mother always looks like tears aren't very far away.' She pulled an old rag from her skirt pocket and ran it along the layer of dust that had sat unnoticed on the shelf. 'I had hoped getting some Christmas cards might lift her spirits. You know, give her something else to think about, but I've come to the conclusion it's making things worse.' Some of the dust particles ran free, rising in the air, not unlike a fog, as they escaped the cloth. Alice folded it in half and moved on to the next shelf. She took a deep breath and the mustiness filled her lungs. Her fingers rose to her mouth, running along it, trying to remove the stale unpalatable taste. She licked her lips. 'I just try to keep myself busy. To be honest, I don't know what else to do.'

Victoria watched her for a moment, before shaking her head. 'It's the nights that are the worst. If it isn't that police constable riding his bicycle up and down the street, ringing that bell of his, shouting for us all to take cover, it's my own thoughts keeping me awake. I lay in bed and my head is in a spin, wondering where Stephen is and what he's doing. I hope and pray every night that God is keeping him safe and that my parents are watching over him.' Victoria clasped her hands together; the knuckles were white as her fingers clung to each other. 'I couldn't cope if anything happened to him, and Daisy won't talk about the war. I think she's secretly as worried as I am.'

Alice looked across at Victoria and tilted her head slightly. 'Bless her. I can totally understand why; as a family, you've already been through so much. I must admit, when we were waving the soldiers off, I did wonder if Stephen, Charles or Harry were among them, but I wasn't close enough to see.' She pursed her lips for a moment. 'I suspect Robert is already fighting in France, but we haven't heard from him. We have to assume no news is good news. It's all about trying to stay positive; after all, what else can we do?'

Victoria nodded. 'It's difficult, but I'm sure it must be worse for them.' She gave a little smile. 'I've moved our beds to the basement. At least if we have to stay there all night, we might as well get used to it and be comfortable.'

Alice laughed at her friend's sheepish expression. 'What, are you sleeping permanently in the basement?'

Victoria laughed. 'Yes, Daisy and I did it at the

weekend. At least now, we don't have to worry about hearing the policeman.'

Alice giggled. 'Perhaps I should suggest that to my family.'

'It might be more difficult for you. Don't forget there are only two of us.'

'That's true.' Alice smiled. 'Can you imagine my father's face if I suggested sleeping in the basement? He'd be horrified.'

The two girls giggled like a couple of schoolgirls who were up to no good. Victoria put her hand over her mouth and took a deep breath. Alice looked around her, before following suit.

Victoria watched her scanning the shop. 'Don't worry, Mr Leadbetter has already left for the evening.'

'That's unlike him. He's always the last to leave, not the first.'

Victoria loosened her scarf from around her neck. 'I hope he hasn't had bad news about his son. I heard him talking to a customer about him joining up.'

Alice frowned. 'Don't say that; it's too dreadful to think about.'

'I know.' Victoria's chin began to tremble. 'I've been thinking, with our brothers probably off fighting in France, I feel I should be doing something to help, but I don't know what.'

Alice gave her a thoughtful look. 'Hmm, on my way here the other day, I saw a Women and War Guide on how to knit and crochet for our soldiers; perhaps we should knit for them. It only costs a penny, so perhaps I'll pop in the shop tomorrow and buy one or two for us to share.'

Victoria's face lit up. 'At least I'd feel as if I was doing something to help the men.'

'What are you two talking about?'

Alice jumped as Molly's voice startled her. 'We were just wondering what we could do to help our menfolk.'

A smile crept across Molly's lips. 'With Christmas around the corner, we could send food parcels to them.'

'That's a great idea.' Alice beamed. 'We could put in some of their favourite things, maybe chocolate and some cigarettes.' She looked around the shop before laughing. 'And books.'

Victoria smiled. 'We certainly have enough books to choose from.' She looked across at Molly. 'Alice has also come up with a wonderful idea. Knitting.'

Molly laughed. 'Knitting?'

Victoria frowned at Molly's reaction. 'Yes, we could knit socks, gloves, scarves and balaclavas.'

Molly shrugged her shoulders. 'I don't know how to knit,' she mumbled.

It was Victoria's turn to laugh. 'That's all right, I don't mind teaching you. At least it will while away the long nights and I'll feel like I'm doing something to help.'

Molly frowned, unsure about this knitting malarkey.

Alice laughed. 'Don't worry, Molly, it isn't that difficult. We can get together one evening and follow the patterns together.'

Molly nodded. 'Count me in. I've nothing else to do, with Tony gone.' She looked down at the wooden floor and fidgeted from one foot to the other. 'I regret encouraging him to sign up now. I wish I hadn't told him about the embarrassment I was feeling, because he hadn't gone when the others did.' Her foot scuffed along the floorboards.

Alice dropped her rag on the shelf and grabbed both of Molly's hands, shaking them gently. 'I'm sure he understood. You were just being like everyone else – patriotic.

'Yes, well I don't feel very good about it.' Molly's watery eyes looked up at Alice. 'I keep getting this awful feeling in the pit of my stomach.'

Victoria stared hard at Molly. 'You're not pregnant, are you?'

Molly's eyebrows rose under her fringe. 'I don't know what type of girl you think I am, Victoria, but I am not that sort.'

'I'm sorry.' Victoria stepped nearer to Molly and rubbed her arm. 'I didn't mean it.'

Molly wrapped her arms around herself. 'I just get this feeling of foreboding.'

Alice stepped forward and hugged her friend. The coarse wool of her coat was rough on her hands; it began to itch her arms through her blouse. She stepped back and left her hands on Molly's shoulders. 'You do know we all feel the same. Victoria was just saying how she couldn't sleep at night, for worrying about Stephen, and I'm trying to keep myself busy, so I don't have to think about Freddie, let alone Charles and Robert. If my mother loses two sons, then she'll probably follow them.'

Molly closed her eyes and took a deep breath. 'All right, count me in for knitting. I can't promise I'll be any good at it, but at least I'll be doing something instead of watching that wretched Pathé News all the time.'

Alice dropped her hands to her side as she and Victoria laughed.

'That's the spirit.' Victoria smiled.

'From what I've read in the papers Father buys, I think Pathé News is meant to make us feel better about what's going on.'

Molly lifted her eyes heavenward. 'Well it isn't working for me. Watching so many men going off to war is heartrending. Let alone this awful weather, and the trenches they have to dig and live in. It all sounds horrendous to me.' Her eyes became watery. 'I don't think I'm going to see Tony again.'

*

Victoria sat in the payment booth in Foyles Bookstore.

Her lips trembled as she turned the envelope over in her clammy hands. It had been folded in her pocket all day. The small brown envelope had been lying on her hall mat when she got home from work yesterday. It hadn't left her thoughts since she found it. Staring at the unopened letter for about the hundredth time, she was convinced it wasn't Stephen's handwriting; it was too neat. Had something happened to him? Was someone from the government writing to her?

A man cleared his throat.

Victoria looked up at the elderly gentleman waiting to be served. 'My apologies, sir, I didn't mean to keep you waiting.' She rammed the envelope into her skirt pocket.

'You were somewhere else. I hope it's not bad news.' The man tilted his head and gave her a sympathetic smile.

Victoria's eyes welled up. 'I don't know. I can't bring myself to open it.'

The elderly man closed his eyes for a moment, before speaking. 'Let me tell you, young lady, it doesn't matter how long you take to open it, the contents will be the same. Trust me when I say don't torture yourself by wondering. Treat it like you would removing a plaster; it's less painful in the long run if you rip it off quickly.'

Victoria nodded. 'I'm just scared.'

The man put a couple of pennies and a bill payment slip under the pane of glass. 'I know. It's written all over your face, but you never know, it might be good news.'

She forced a smile to her lips. 'Maybe.'

The gentleman picked up the slip confirming he had paid for his book. 'I'll pop in again, in a day or two, to see if you've opened it and to make sure you're all right.'

'You're too kind, sir, but there is no need. I'm sure I'll be fine.'

The man chuckled. 'Trust me, it isn't kindness. It lifts an old man's heart to look at someone who is as pretty as a picture.'

Victoria found herself chuckling with him, as colour rose in her cheeks.

He'd turned to walk away, but glanced back. 'That's better; music to my ears. Now open the letter and I'll come and see you tomorrow.'

Victoria nodded. She watched him walk away. His shoulders were hunched over. Was he carrying a great weight as well? She sighed. Wasn't everyone?

The rattling of the steel shutters told her that the store was closing. She cashed up her till and let herself out of the booth.

'Everything all right, Victoria?'

Victoria's head jerked backwards. She turned on her small heels to see Alice standing in front of her. Her hand flew to her chest. 'Alice, you startled me.'

Alice lifted her hand and lightly stroked Victoria's arm. 'That doesn't surprise me; you seemed miles away.'

Victoria gave a small nod and her chin began to

tremble.

Without a thought, Alice dropped her hand, which clenched into a tight ball behind the folds of her skirt. She flicked her tongue over her lips. Her legs started to shake. Did she know something? Had something happened to Stephen? Did it mean Charles had the same fate? 'Do... do you have news?'

Without a word, Victoria pulled the brown envelope from her skirt pocket. She unfolded it, to show her the sealed letter.

A gasp escaped as Alice lifted her trembling hand to cover her mouth. She reached out to touch Victoria's hand. 'You need to open it.' She looked down at it. 'I don't think it's what you're thinking.'

Victoria also stared down at the envelope. Her gaze fixed on it until her vision became blurry. 'It's not Stephen's handwriting,' she whispered.

'No, but that doesn't mean it's...' Alice couldn't bring herself to say the words out loud.

'Why else would I have a letter?' Victoria raised her troubled eyes, to look at Alice.

'I don't know, but... but I think it's normally a telegram,' Alice whispered. 'Let's get out of here so you can open it in private.'

Victoria nodded.

They both clocked out and grabbed their coats, hats and scarves.

Alice was still wrapping her scarf around her neck as

they left Foyles. She hated the dark winter evenings, but was thankful it wasn't snowing. A shiver ran through her. She tightened the woollen scarf around her neck and pulled up the collar of her coat. Her heart was pounding in her chest. If only she was as calm and confident as she pretended to be. 'You need some privacy. Let's go into St Mary's Church; it's just up here.'

Victoria followed Alice. Her heart was pounding and her legs were trembling as they strode past the school gates. Her lungs fought for oxygen. She bowed her head in a bid to stop it from swimming. Her back pressed hard against the stone of the church wall, the cold creeping through her coat, while Alice pulled open the large oak door. There was no one about as they quietly slid into the pew at the back, dropping their heads to give a silent prayer for their family and friends. They looked up as one, both staring straight ahead at the altar and the stained-glass window of the Virgin Mary. Each of them alone with their own thoughts, each too scared to say the words out loud.

Alice could feel beads of sweat forming on her forehead. She wondered if a letter had arrived for her parents. She had to fight the urge to run home to find out, as she unwrapped her woollen scarf from around her neck and undid the buttons of her brown tweed winter coat.

Victoria parted the bottom of her coat and thrust her hand inside her skirt pocket. The corner of the envelope stabbed at her finger as she pulled it out. Her jaw clenched as her grip tightened. As she unfolded it, the rustle echoed in the church. Her eyes never left the paper. She ran her hand over the creases she had created. After a moment, she looked up at Alice, who nodded her encouragement. Victoria turned the letter over. What had the man said, 'treat it like removing a plaster; rip it off quickly, it's less painful'. She took a deep breath. Without waiting another second, she forced her index finger underneath the seal. She pulled out what looked like brown wrapping paper. It was neatly folded in three, with the top of the page in full view.

My dear Victoria,
I know my behaviour four years ago was unforgivable and I cannot offer any excuse for it, except my immaturity.

Her heart was pounding. Pain gripped her chest. She quickly unfolded it and scanned to the bottom of the letter. 'It's from Ted,' Victoria gasped. 'Why is he writing to me after all this time?' Her eyes jumped back to the top of the page.

There hasn't been a day go by that I haven't regretted my decision to walk away from our friendship, and I believe, our love for each other.

157

Alice gasped for air. She hadn't realised she had been holding her breath. 'Don't worry about why at this stage; at least it isn't about Stephen.'

Victoria's tears began to flow, leaving saltiness on her lips. She gulped to catch her breath. Alice wrapped her arm around her friend, holding her tight as she sobbed into her coat, patiently waiting for the four years of pent up grief and tension to slowly evaporate.

Chapter 10

Christmas had finally arrived at Bloomsbury Street. The tree stood tall and proud in the corner of the sitting room, the woody freshness of pine scented the air. With Charles absent, Lily had placed the star on the top of it last night. The red and silver glass baubles reflected the candlelight into the room. Alice had tied some of her mother's childhood embroidered ornaments to the tree and tinsel had been draped over the branches, to add sparkle. Greeting cards hung from the picture rail, while red ribbon and festive scenes decorated the walls. The deep, shiny green of the holly, together with its small red berries, stood side by side with the white berries and the paler green leaves of the mistletoe, on the mantelpiece and every other available space. The fire, blazing in the hearth, gave the room warmth that wrapped itself around everyone who entered.

Alice picked up the next present to be wrapped. She examined the plain cream cover of the book, The Dubliners by James Joyce. Her grandfather shared her love of reading, so she hoped he'd enjoy the short stories.

Sarah walked in, her gaze immediately drawn to the

base of the tree.

Alice gave a little chuckle. 'Is it time for your tree inspection this evening, Mother?'

Sarah jumped and forced a smile. 'I know everyone thinks it's funny, but I worry the pine needles might fall off before Christmas is over.'

Alice smiled. 'I know, and it's a good job someone checks it, but you do know Mrs Headley cleans before you do your inspection, don't you?'

'Of course I do.' Sarah frowned. 'I don't know why I worry about it; it's not as if it has ever happened.'

Alice shrugged her shoulders. 'We all know why you worry about it, Mother.' She paused, taking in her mother's anxious expression. 'I'd say it's because you are not happy unless you are worrying about something, but under the current circumstances I don't think that can be true.' She smiled. 'Have you checked the one in the dining room yet?'

'Yes, you and Lily did a good job decorating them. They look lovely.' Sarah smiled. 'In fact, this whole room looks quite wonderful.'

Alice smiled across at her mother. 'Thank you, I'm sure Lily will be as happy as I am to know you like it.' She continued to wrap her presents with colourful paper, tying the soft, silky red ribbon around them and finishing each one with an elaborate bow. 'It's not the same though, is it?'

Sarah's eyes clouded as she hung her head. Her

shoulders hunched over. 'No, I really wanted to believe they'd be back for Christmas, but that clearly isn't going to happen.'

'I know. I did too, but you know the boys wouldn't want us to be unhappy, especially not at Christmas,' Alice whispered.

Sarah nodded and sat down in the armchair nearest the fire. 'No, I know. I suppose we just have to get on with it.' She gave a little smile. 'Hopefully, they received the parcels we sent them.'

Alice glanced up and smiled at her mother. 'The parcels were certainly laden, what with cigarettes, the tinder box, chocolate and let's not forget my effort of knitting a balaclava.' She gave a hearty laugh. 'I'm sure Charles will have something to say about it when he returns.'

Sarah couldn't resist joining in; her laughter was filled with memories. 'Yes, I'm sure he will.' Her smile faded. 'The government couldn't have got it more wrong when they said it would be over by Christmas.'

Lily flounced into the room and flopped in an armchair. 'What are you two talking about?'

Alice glanced at her mother before looking back at Lily. 'Just Christmas.'

Lily sat tight-lipped as she gazed up at the tree, before letting her eyes travel between her mother and Alice. 'I've been meaning to ask whether either of you donated any money to Princess Mary's appeal?'

'Yes,' they answered in unison.

'So did I.' Lily looked back at the tree. 'I hope they all manage to celebrate Christmas in some way and stay safe.'

A thud reached the sitting room. Lily straightened her seating position.

Luke strode in, his newspaper folded under his arm. Without a word, he walked over to the tree before letting his gaze drop to the carpet. He turned and gave Sarah a curt nod before pouring himself a whisky. 'Have you heard?' His voice rose as exhilaration took hold. 'Rumour has it, the Germans have dropped bombs in a garden in Dover this afternoon. It's thought they were heading for the castle but dropped the bombs too early.'

Sarah leant forward in her chair. 'Oh goodness, has anybody been hurt?'

Luke took a swig of his whisky. 'I don't know for sure, but it is thought to be unlikely.'

'Evening, Father.' Lily stared hard at him. Her father's love of the war was only matched by the hatred for him that ran through her veins. He never asked if there was any news about the boys, or how any of them were holding up under the immense strain and worry they felt each day. He didn't care that they were dreading Christmas. She would even welcome Robert bossing her about again. She missed Charles' infectious smile and laughter, his take on life. As far as she was concerned, it was entirely her father's fault. It sat squarely on his shoulders. He'd driven them away. She lifted her head and jutted out her chin. 'Would you like a cup of tea, Father?'

Alice took a deep breath. Biting hard on her tongue, she looked down at the parcel sitting on her lap and concentrated hard on tagging it.

Sarah's eyes widened as she shook her head at Lily.

Colour flooded Luke's face as he squared his shoulders. 'I am fine, thank you.'

Lily looked across at her mother. Her hands were clenched and a vein pulsating at the side of her forehead was the only sign of the anxiety she was feeling. Her mother appeared to have aged since the war began. She looked quite frail. Lily forced a smile to her lips. 'I assume you've invited Victoria and Daisy again this year.'

Alice took a sharp intake of breath. 'Actually, none of us talked about Christmas.'

Sarah shook her head. 'That's understandable. There's so much worry around, people aren't focussing on Christmas this year, but she's come every year since her parents died, so wouldn't she know to just turn up tomorrow?'

Lily laughed. 'You mean, like you would?'

Sarah gave her younger daughter a look of frustration, before smiling. 'You're quite right, Lily, I'd never dream of just turning up without a proper invitation, not even to family, but young people are different these days.' She moved her gaze to Alice. 'Best you get round to Percy Street and let Victoria and Daisy know they're welcome here, as always.'

*

Luke carried the golden-brown goose into the dining room on a silver platter, to a chorus of ooh and aah from everyone sitting around the table. He placed the tray in front of him, at the head of the table. He pulled back his chair and picked up the carving knife and fork.

Edward sniffed the air. 'That smells wonderful.'

Sarah frowned. 'With us taking longer to leave church this morning, I thought it might be a little overcooked, but thankfully it doesn't look like it is.'

Jane licked her lips. 'It looks to me like it's been cooked to perfection.'

Sarah laughed at them both. 'Anyone would think you two haven't eaten for a week.'

Any space on the table was gradually filled with bowls of roast potatoes, sprouts and other vegetables. A couple of gravy boats were squeezed on at either end of the table. The carving knife cut through the dark meat with ease and Luke placed several slices on each plate; in turn, they were handed around the table. Everyone loaded their plates as if food had evaded them for a long time.

Edward looked down at his packed plate. 'I wonder if

I could squeeze on another couple of roast potatoes.' He smiled at his daughter. 'You know I love them roasted in goose fat.'

Sarah shook her head and laughed at him. 'You are incorrigible.' She smiled, watching everyone tucking into Christmas dinner. The food bowls looked as though they had been invaded by a swarm of locusts; not even a sprout was left. 'Make sure you leave room for the Christmas pudding and custard,' she shouted above the buzz of conversation. 'We've mince pies as well.'

Alice watched her mother; pleased she was throwing herself into enjoying the day. She gave herself a minute to look around the dining table trying not to think about the people that were missing. Victoria and Daisy appeared to be enjoying themselves and Lily was keeping them entertained. She shuddered to think what she was saying to them, but there was a lot of laughter from that part of the table. Alice wondered what was in the letter from Ted. Victoria looked happier than she had seen her in over four years, but she couldn't help worrying he was raising her hopes, only to grind them to dust again. She eyed her father and wondered why he was so subdued. It intrigued her, but not enough to ask. She was thankful for his silence and gave a silent prayer for everyone's safe return to the family fold. Nobody mentioned them at all; the brave faces were firmly set in place.

After everyone had eaten their fill, Sarah, Alice and

Lily cleared the table to make way for dessert and coffee.

Alice returned to the dining room and clapped her hands. 'May I have your attention, as Mother gives you the pièce de résistance.'

Sarah followed her daughter into the room, to thunderous applause. She carried a silver tray with the Christmas pudding sitting proudly in the middle of it, ablaze from the ignited brandy that had been poured over it. The pungent fumes hung in the air, gradually fading with the blue flame. Sarah started to spoon the dark, rich, fruity pudding into dishes. 'Help yourself to custard and watch out for those little sixpences. I don't want anyone choking, thank you. Hopefully you'll all get at least one; I think I went a little mad with them this year.'

The Christmas pudding disappeared in seconds.

Edward leant back in his chair and rubbed his stomach. 'I've eaten far too much. I think it was those extra potatoes that did it.'

Sarah laughed at her father. 'Not the two helpings of pudding then?' She stood and picked up her coffee cup. 'Let's take our drinks into the sitting room, where we can sit in some comfortable chairs and exchange presents.'

They all stood up and made their way to the sitting room, leaving the dirty dishes where they sat.

As they entered, they each stared at the pile of presents, all shapes and sizes, under the tree in an array of coloured Christmas paper. They each claimed a chair, but they sat in silence.

Alice stood up. 'Shall I play a few chords on the piano before we open the presents?'

'Yes,' they chorused, relief spreading around the room.

Sarah gave Alice a watery smile. 'Perhaps we could sing some carols.'

Jane clapped her hands together. 'That sounds like a wonderful idea. I do love a carol.'

Alice walked over and lifted the lid of the piano, running her fingers over the keys. 'How about Away in a Manger?'

Victoria smiled. 'That's one of my favourites.'

Edward laughed. 'Then that's where we shall start, to be quickly followed by Good King Wenceslas, Ding Dong Merrily on High, then God Rest Ye Merry Gentlemen and finally The First Noel.'

The room suddenly filled with laughter.

Lily wiped away the tears as her laughter died down. 'Are you sure you haven't forgotten one?'

'Have I?' Edward laughed. 'Of course, I don't want to be demanding. Feel free to throw in your special requests. I am sure Alice won't mind.'

Alice laid her fingers on the black and ivory keys. 'No, I don't mind, although I have to say I wasn't expecting such enthusiasm to my suggestion. Right, let's start with Away in a Manger then.' She started playing and the room was suddenly full of song.

It was three hours later, with the daylight long diminished, that Sarah looked across at Lily with a forced smile, but her eyes clouded over with sadness. 'Lily, as you are the yo... will you do us the honour of handing out the presents this year?'

Lily gave a tight-lipped smile as she cast her eyes towards Alice, who nodded her encouragement. The excitement was missing this year, as Lily took up the reins of doing the youngest's job of searching for and handing out the presents. When she had finished, she sat down to begin unwrapping the gifts she had received.

Alice looked down to the pile at her feet, before looking back at the tree. 'Lily, there are still some presents sitting under the tree.'

Lily frowned. 'They're for the boys.' She took a deep breath. 'Victoria, there are some for Stephen as well, so you might want to take them home for when he returns.'

The room fell silent. Victoria nodded as all eyes stared at the unopened presents.

Luke lifted his wine glass. 'It's time for a toast.'

Everyone picked up a glass or cup; no one cared, because none of it mattered.

'To absent friends and family.'

Everyone followed Luke's lead. 'To absent friends and family.'

The rustling of silk and satin sounded around the room, as the ladies rummaged in their pockets for their handkerchiefs. As one, they dabbed their eyes, to stop the onslaught of tears.

Chapter 11

January 1915

Sarah sat in her favourite chair in the dining room, nearest the fireplace. The crackle of the coal and the smoke swirling up the chimney did not distract her from the envelope in her hand. She looked at the spidery handwriting and a smile spread across her face. It was from Charles. With nervous fingers, she ripped open the seal and quickly unfolded the letter.

Dear Ma,

I hope this letter finds you all right and father is being nice to you all. It's very wet here in the trenches and we have seen our fair share of rats, but we are keeping well. I'm not spending much of the twelve shillings and sixpence the army pay me; there aren't many shops around here, ha ha. I received the parcel, thank you. It was great to eat chocolate again, as we seem to be living on bully beef at the moment. When one of us receives a parcel, we share the contents; it lifts our spirits to have a treat. Can you send me some socks because my feet are permanently cold and wet? Some of the chaps here are wearing two or three coats. It would be good to be warm again. Tell Alice the balaclava fits a treat, although the shape of it did make me laugh before I put it on.

It was strange being here on Christmas Day. I missed you all. The Germans lit some lamps on Christmas Eve and started singing carols, so we followed suit. No shots were fired. It was strange sleeping in such silence when we have been used to the constant barrage of bombs and gunfire. On Christmas Day, we were all terribly brave, left our trenches and talked about our families. You know Ma, they are just ordinary men, like me; some have small children. It makes you see things a little different. Some of the chaps played football with the Germans. The next day, it all returned to normal, although I am not sure how hard we all tried to kill each other. Somehow, things are different now.

Before I go, I want to tell you about a gift box I received from Princess Mary, no less. The brass box had some ciggies in it, as well as a pipe and tobacco, along with a tinderbox and a Christmas card. I'll try and send it home, so it can be kept safe.

I haven't seen Robert, but Freddie and Stephen are around here somewhere. I am hoping to get leave soon. It'll be lovely to sleep in a proper bed and eat some home cooking. Say hello to everyone for me and hopefully I'll get home to see you soon.

Your loving son

Charles xx

Sarah's vision became blurry as she tried to read the letter again.

Dear Ma,

She chuckled. The cheeky boy, calling her ma; when did he assume that was all right? She ran her fingers across the words he had written. Her baby was safe, and that was all that mattered. She stopped trying to read and hugged the letter close to her chest, hoping he was right and she'd see him soon, to judge for herself. She would show the girls. They'd be thrilled to hear from Charles, and Alice would be happy to know that Freddie was with him, and more importantly, safe.

'What's that you have there?' Luke's voice carried in the silence.

Sarah jumped in her seat.

'And why are you hugging it?'

She clung on to the letter as she lowered her hands onto her lap, the folds of her black skirt wrapped around them. All excitement and happiness was immediately washed away by his cold tone. 'It's... it's a letter from Charles.' Sarah wondered if she should offer it to him, but she couldn't bring herself to let go of it.

Luke sat down at the dining table. Once comfortable, he wrapped his hands around the china teapot, before pouring himself a cup. 'The post arrived early this morning. Was there anything else?'

'No, at least I don't think so.'

Luke sighed. 'What do you mean, you don't think so? Either there was or there wasn't.'

'There wasn't,' Sarah mumbled.

'What? Stop mumbling. Speak up.'

Sarah took a deep breath and pushed her shoulders back. 'No, there wasn't any post, other than this letter from one of our sons.'

Luke arched his eyebrows as he stared across the room at her. 'That's better.' He picked up his cup and sipped the hot tea, before placing it back on its saucer.

Sarah turned the letter over in her hand. 'Would you like to read it?'

Luke shook his head. 'Not particularly. There won't be anything about the war in there because all the post is monitored, in case it falls into the wrong hands.'

Sarah's eyes widened as she fought to know what to say. 'He says he might be home soon. He talked about a Christmas ceasefire and the men playing football with the German soldiers.'

'Football? They are the enemy.' Luke shook his head again. His voice rose with frustration. 'I bet Robert wasn't involved in such shenanigans. They are meant to be fighting them, you know, keeping everyone safe.'

Sarah kept her focus on the letter, determined he wasn't going to spoil her happiness today. 'They all received a lovely gift from Princess Mary, which was very kind, don't you think?'

'If you ask me, it's all nonsense. They aren't children.'

Sarah stood up and colour raged into her cheeks. 'That's just it, Luke, some of them are only children.'

'When I was Charles' age, I was—'

'Yes, yes, we know, you had travelled across country on your own. We've all heard it before.' Sarah took a deep breath. 'Many, many times, Luke.'

Luke pressed his fingertips down on the table and slowly stood up, never taking his eyes off her. 'How dare you talk to me like that?'

The soft tone sent ripples of fear down Sarah's spine. 'I dare because you may not care whether your sons come home safe or not, but I do. To know that Charles is safe is everything, it's your fault he joined up in the first place.'

Luke eyed her, daring her to keep talking. 'I might have known it would be my fault.'

'If he hadn't been so desperate to impress you, he'd still be here, so yes, it is your fault.'

Luke scuffed back his chair. 'I can see there is no talking to you today; best you sort yourself out before I get back. I will not tolerate such behaviour from you, or anyone else in this household.' He glared at her, hands clenched by his sides. 'Do you understand? Have I made myself absolutely clear?'

Sarah nodded.

'I can't hear you.'

Sarah slumped back into the chair she had only recently vacated. 'Yes, very clear.'

*

Alice sat in the family sitting room with a closed book on her lap. Her mother sat opposite her. They both stared into the flickering light that came from the golden flames of the open fire. The logs crackled and every so often a spark would fly onto the hearth.

'The letter was wonderful, wasn't it?' Sarah kept staring ahead into the flames.

Alice smiled. 'It was, Ma.'

Sarah laughed. 'That is a title I will not be keeping.'

Alice chuckled. 'To just know they're all safe is wonderful news. I wonder if Robert will write to us, although he hasn't so far, so I suppose it's unlikely. We've to assume no news is good news.'

Sarah glanced at Alice and nodded. 'I wonder where they are and what they're doing.'

Alice shrugged her shoulders. 'In some respects, I'd rather not know.' Her mind instantly went to the Pathé newsreel she had seen at the cinema with Freddie. The men at the front, standing in trenches flooded with water, smoking their cigarettes, some waving and smiling for the camera. She couldn't tell her mother that Robert and Charles were certainly in that situation.

175

The front door slammed shut. Neither looked around, both assuming it was Lily.

'Is this how you greet your prodigal son?' Charles kept his voice low.

Sarah and Alice both jerked round and jumped up out of their chairs, ignoring the books thumping to the floor.

'Please tell me I'm not dreaming. I do believe I've just willed this to happen.' Sarah stared wide-eyed at her son.

Alice's eyes filled with tears. Her emotions became too much for her to handle.

'There's someone else I've picked up along the way.' Charles stepped back, turning his head to the doorway and shouted. 'Come in.'

Alice's legs began to wobble. She sank down into the chair she had just vacated. There he stood, next to her brother, both of them in full army uniform. 'I can't believe it. Is it really you?' she whispered. She closed her eyes, squeezing them tight before slowly looking through her lashes to see if he was still standing in front of her. 'Oh Lord, it's true.' She was rooted to the spot, staring at his grey pallor. He had lost weight since she had last seen him, he looked older and his eyes were dull. She didn't want to think about what had happened to him. Tears rolled down her face. 'I've dreamt of this moment so many times.'

Freddie didn't take his eyes off her as he took a step

forward.

'Come on, Sis, give the man a cuddle.'

Alice looked across at Charles, as though seeing him for the first time. He and Freddie had the same worn-down and lifeless look about them.

Sarah stepped forward, tears flowing freely down her cheeks. She wrapped her arms around her youngest son. 'I can't believe you are here.'

Charles gave out a breathless noise. 'Not so tight, I can't breathe.'

Sarah laughed and stepped back. She glanced across at Alice, who was openly sobbing in Freddie's arms.

'I was so frightened I wouldn't see you again,' Alice whispered in between her sobs. She gulped for air. The dampness, along with the metallic smell of blood and the body odour of someone that hadn't washed in a long time, clung to his uniform. It was rough under her soft hands, which gripped him tightly. 'I've been so frightened.'

His eyes squeezed shut as he held her tight in his arms. He never wanted to let her go. Slowly, he opened them and rested his finger under her chin to lift it up. His other arm held her tight to him. He tilted his head as he lowered it. Their noses brushed as his lips rested gently on hers.

Alice moved her hands higher so her fingers could lose themselves in his hair, which had lost its softness. All thoughts of her mother and brother were forgotten as she pushed his head down, letting him know she wanted more. Her heart wanted to leap out of her chest as her body moulded to his. The bristles around his soft mouth scratched her skin, but she didn't care. She could taste smoke on his lips and mint on his breath.

Charles gave an awkward cough. 'All right, Freddie, put my sister down.'

Freddie and Alice both jumped back. Colour flooded Alice's face.

'Sorry, Mrs Taylor, I didn't mean to—'

Sarah laughed. 'Don't worry, Freddie, I do understand. Just don't let Mr Taylor catch you.'

Freddie smiled and reached out for Alice's hand. 'I won't, Ma'am.'

Sarah beamed from ear to ear. 'It's good to see you both, although it looks like you could do with a good bath and something decent to eat.'

Charles laughed. 'That's true. We've been living on tins of bully beef.'

'I can't believe you're home,' Sarah and Alice said in unison.

'It's not for long, Ma; we only have two days, then we are on our way out again.'

Sarah and Alice's faces dropped.

Freddie pulled Alice's hand up to his lips before turning it and kissing her palm. 'Alice, I want us to get married before I go away again.'

'But... but... nothing has been organised. I didn't

know when you were coming home.'

'Neither did we, but the opportunity came up, so we jumped at it.'

Alice frowned and looked straight at Charles. Was she allowed to be as happy as she felt right now. 'Are Stephen and Harry home?'

Charles nodded. 'I suspect they are by now.' He laughed. 'They were dreading the stick they were going to get from their families.'

Sarah smiled. 'I expect they'll just be pleased to see them; we've been so worried about you all.'

Freddie gave Alice's arm a little shake. 'So, are you going to marry me tomorrow? Are you going to become Mrs Alfred Leybourne?'

The corner of Alice's mouth lifted. 'I want to, but I haven't spoken to the vicar or organised what to wear, and Molly and Victoria wanted to be my bridesmaids as well.' Alice's words tumbled over each other, in a bid to be heard.

Freddie lifted his hand. 'I spoke to the vicar before I went away, so he'll be fine about it. He knew it would be short notice.'

'Really, I wasn't even sure you'd remember wanting to marry me when you came back. Molly and Victoria wanted to organise things, but I wouldn't let them.'

Sarah gazed lovingly at her eldest daughter. 'Alice, stop worrying about things.' She tapped her index finger against her mouth. 'I know, while the boys have a bath and freshen up, you can always try on my wedding dress.' She paused. 'That's if you want to. I know it's not the same as having your own, but it was my mother's too, so I suppose you could call it a vintage look, but it's up to you.'

Alice beamed at her mother. 'The thought of it makes me nervous because it's important to you, but I'd love to wear it, if it fits.'

Sarah shook her head. 'You know it means a lot to me because it was my mother's, but in the last few months, I've come to realise there are other things that are far more important. It's just a dress.' She lifted her finger and tapped her temple. 'My memories are all in here and I know my mother would be over the moon at the thought of you wearing her dress. Family was everything to her.'

Charles gave his mother a squeeze as he grinned at her. 'Well, Ma.'

Sarah laughed and playfully hit Charles' arm. 'You can stop that, young man. I'll have none of it.'

Charles laughed as he rubbed his arm. 'Mother, it looks like there's going to be a wedding tomorrow.'

Lily stood in the doorway, blinking rapidly. She couldn't believe what her eyes were telling her. 'Any excuse for a party.'

Charles spun around as Lily ran towards him, their arms colliding as they wrapped them around each other. 'Hello, Sis.'

*

Lily had spread the news last night and, consequently, the house in Bloomsbury Street was a hive of activity at seven o'clock that morning. An eleven o'clock wedding didn't leave much time for preparations. As the women's excited chatter grew, Luke folded his newspaper and decided to take himself off to the Gentlemen's Club for breakfast.

Sarah followed him into the hall. 'Make sure you're back by ten o'clock, won't you?'

Luke pulled his coat on over his suit jacket. 'I will be back when I am ready, and not when you tell me.'

Sarah closed her eyes and took a deep breath. 'I don't want Alice's big day ruined.'

'And it won't be.' Luke pulled up his collar before opening the front door. The biting wind rushed in and whooshed around the hall. He nodded before slamming the door behind him.

Sarah rubbed her hands as she walked back into the warmth of the fire in the dining room.

Lily gave her mother an anxious look. 'Don't worry, he's better off out of the way.'

Alice laughed. 'Charles is certainly enjoying his lie in. Did father ask whether he would've liked to have gone with him?'

Sarah shook her head. 'Charles is better off resting as much as he can, before he has to leave again.'

Lily frowned. 'It would have been good for him to spend some time with Charles, to find out what the war is actually about, instead of glorifying it all the time.'

Alice nodded her agreement. 'It would be nice for Charles to get some respect and for Father to let him know how proud he is of him.'

Sarah sighed. 'Your father won't change now, and today isn't the day for worrying about it. There's a lot to do.'

Molly arrived first, sitting Alice in front of her bedroom mirror before proceeding to roll, curl and plait her hair, within an inch of its life. It draped down her back in soft waves and curls. The hair at the front and sides had been pulled away from Alice's face and held in place by a large silver and diamond flower hair slide.

'I wonder where Victoria and Lily are?' The white vapour of Alice's breath hung in the air. She looked in the mirror, not recognising the lady staring back. 'Molly, have you spoken to Victoria?' She frowned. So did the person in the mirror. 'Is Stephen home?'

Molly laughed. The warmth of her breath was also a stark contrast to the air in the room. 'Stop worrying. It's your wedding day. Everyone will be here soon enough.'

'I haven't seen my mother either, at least, not since about seven-thirty this morning.'

'She's busying herself. After all, the mother of the bride has a lot to organise and you must admit, it has been very short notice.' Molly tweaked a curl around her finger. 'She didn't want to leave you, but I told her to do whatever she had to do and I'd look after you.'

Alice lowered her eyes and nodded, but she couldn't help wishing her mother was there with her. 'And Lily?'

'I suspect she's helping your mother.' Molly sat on the bed and looked around the room, letting her eyes rest on the wedding dress hanging on the back of the door. 'Your grandmother's dress is beautiful.'

Alice smiled as she looked across at it. She fleetingly wondered whether Molly was shocked at the sparse decor of her bedroom. If so, she was too good a friend to say so. 'It is beautiful and an honour to be able to wear it. It means so much to my mother. I was really surprised how well it fitted last night.' The thought of being Freddie's bride sent tingles hopping and skipping over her body. 'You know, I really want to marry Freddie today, but I feel that all this is wasting precious time. It's time I could be spending with him.'

Molly tilted her head and gave Alice a faint smile. 'I know, sweetie, but it's an early wedding so there will be lots of time afterwards, and it's obviously important to Freddie.'

Alice hunched her shoulders and her chin dropped to her chest. Colour burnt her cheeks. 'Molly, I'm so sorry. I've been so wrapped up in myself, I haven't asked...' The bedroom door creaked as it swung open, causing them both to look around.

Victoria stood in the doorway with dresses resting

over her arm. There was still a fragility about her, but her eyes were alive, sparkling like stars on a clear night. 'Here we are.' Her face was crimson, while her chest heaved, as she gasped for air.

Alice jumped up and wrapped her arms around Victoria. The winter's cold, fresh breath was still on her skin. As their cheeks touched, Alice shivered and pulled away. 'You're freezing. Come in, not that it's much warmer in here.' She smiled, stepping back so her friend could walk into the bedroom. 'What have you got there?'

Victoria laughed. 'Your mother insisted we went to the shops this morning. We actually went to Liberty's and she bought Lily, Molly and me a dress each, so we'd match.'

'Oh, how lovely.' Molly jumped off the bed, removed the dresses from Victoria's arms and laid the three of them on the bed.

'Your mother and Lily will be up shortly to help you into your dress,' Victoria rasped as she stepped over the threshold, pushing the door to, behind her. 'Oh, is that it?' Victoria stared at the beautiful white taffeta dress, with its layers of trumpet sleeves and lacework on the bodice, ending at the base of the neck. 'It's beautiful.' She turned to Alice. 'You're going to look stunning. Freddie's a lucky man.'

'I'm the lucky one.' Alice could feel her eyes welling up and blinked rapidly, still in disbelief that in a couple of hours, she'd be Alice Leybourne, Mrs Alfred Leybourne.

Victoria stood at the end of the bed and stared down at the dresses. 'Mrs Taylor wanted to buy flowers as well, but I told her not to worry about them, because we could carry our bibles.'

Molly nodded. 'That's a good idea.'

'I wondered where you were. I was beginning to worry, in case something was wrong with Stephen.'

Victoria laughed. 'No, he's fine. You'll see him later, and Daisy.' Her upturned face beamed and her eyes danced. 'He's enjoying having a lie in and sleeping in a proper bed. It was wonderful to have him come home so unexpectedly.'

'I know what you mean. I thought I was imagining things when Freddie walked into our sitting room.' Alice paused. 'Did you tell him off for joining up?'

'No, I probably should have done, but I was so pleased to see him…'

Alice laughed. 'Yes, it was the same here when Charles walked in; all the anger and worry evaporated.'

Molly looked up from examining her dress. 'These are beautiful.' Molly ran her fingers over the soft, dark blue lace that overlaid the pale blue dress. The long sleeves were cuffed with the same detail. She let her fingers rest on the hard surface of the navy sequins, which had been sown onto the lace appliqué. 'I hope it fits me; I'm going to be devastated if it doesn't.'

'I'm pretty sure it will. It is rather fabulous isn't it? And we've matching navy blue hats.' Victoria laughed at Molly's wide-eyed expression.

Sarah quietly opened the bedroom door and watched the girls. Their excitement and happiness was evident. Luke had better not be late back, she thought with a sigh. Surely he cared enough to be on time. She shook her head, concentrating on the girls' excitement as they examined the dresses. She moved slightly to watch Alice; she would miss her when she moved into her own home. The room became blurry; perhaps she'd be able to get her to stay, at least until the war was over. 'Is everything all right in here?'

Alice turned around and gave her mother a huge smile. 'Thank you. These dresses are beautiful. What are you going to wear?'

Sarah walked over and gave her daughter a hug. 'It's my pleasure. There may be a war on, but I still want you to enjoy your day, and don't worry about what I'm wearing. Now let's get you dressed.'

Chapter 12

Freddie stood tall in his army uniform as he looked around the church and its stained-glass windows. The sanctuary had seating for around two hundred people. The altar was small and the aisle narrow; perhaps he should have chosen a bigger church, but he enjoyed the intimacy of this one.

Twisting a gold button on the front of his khaki jacket, Charles looked across at Freddie. 'It won't be long now.'

Freddie turned and grinned at him. 'Thanks for being my best man.'

Charles became flushed with colour. 'It's an honour to be asked.'

'I'm not sure about that, but it's great to have you standing here, next to me.' Freddie's smile faded. 'We've been through a lot since we left here a few short months ago.'

Charles nodded before frowning. 'I suppose, in Robert's absence, it must be my job to warn you to look after my sister and treat her right.'

Laughter echoed around the church and Freddie immediately put his hand over his mouth.

His eyes crinkling at the corners and his shoulders moving up and down told Charles the laughter was barely contained. 'It's not that funny.'

'No, sorry.' Freddie took a deep breath. 'I don't think you realise how much I love your sister.'

'Hmm.' Charles arched his eyebrows. 'It took you a long time to ask her to be your wife.'

Freddie nodded. 'I was waiting for the right time and I wanted to be able to offer her everything, but this war has taught me there are other things much more important than money.'

Charles nodded, before patting Freddie's arm. 'I hope you're both very happy.' He looked up and grinned at him. 'And I'm pleased you've got your hair cut for the occasion. Very smart.'

Freddie chuckled as he ran his hand down the back of his head. 'Yes, it does feel so much better.'

Sarah walked through the church doorway, shivering, as she stood in the vestibule, glad to be out of the bitter wind that had been gathering momentum. The dark oak door was pushed back against the grey stone of the church wall. She lifted her gloved hand to check her hair, patting the French roll she had expertly styled that morning, before straightening her silver-grey tulip-style dress under the matching coat. A piece of paper blew around her feet; she stooped and picked it up, leaving it on a small table to her left. The girls giggled as they followed Sarah. Luke escorted Alice through the doorway. Molly tweaked at Alice's hair and veil, while Lily and Victoria straightened the bottom of her skirt.

Alice gave a nervous laugh. 'Stop fretting; I'm fine.'

'Alice, you look wonderful.' Lily beamed, her eyes welling up. 'Be happy. Freddie is a good man.' She raised her eyebrows. 'Even if he is a policeman.'

Alice laughed, shaking her head at her sister's quip.

Colour flushed Lily's cheeks. 'He's not like some, he's a good, honest man.'

Alice's tears pricked at her eyelids. She reached out and grasped Lily's hand. 'Thank you.'

Sarah removed her glove to straighten the lace on the trumpet sleeves of Alice's gown, before beaming at her daughter. She lifted her hand to touch the soft skin of her cheek. 'You look beautiful. Freddie's a very lucky man.' Tears filled her eyes. 'My mother would be happy to see you wearing her dress; it looks like it was made for you.'

They all stood motionless for a moment. Luke cleared his throat.

Alice momentarily closed her eyes to stop her own tears from falling. 'Thank you,' she whispered, opening them again. She glanced towards her father, who offered no words of wisdom as he stood to one side, reading the notice board. Alice returned her gaze to her mother, before taking her hand and holding it in hers. 'You've worked so hard to make this day possible.'

Colour began to fill Sarah's cheeks. 'We're all staying

at Russell Square with your Grandfather and Jane this evening.' She lowered her voice to a whisper and patted Alice's hand. 'So the house is yours and Freddie's tonight; you'll not be disturbed.' She released her hand from Alice's and fanned her face as she looked away, wondering if she should step outside into the cold air.

Alice blushed. 'But...'

Heat seared through Sarah's cheeks. 'The guest room is more suitable...'

Alice looked away, pulling at a strand of hair that had broken free of the clip. 'I don't know what to say.'

'No words are needed. You don't have long with Freddie before he and Charles have to return to their regiment, so make the most of it.' Sadness engulfed Sarah as she gazed at the aisle in front of her, Charles and Freddie standing proud in their uniforms. She forced a smile. Honeysuckle immediately conjured memories of her own wedding, over thirty years ago. She had been so happy then; how things had changed. Sarah shook her head as she glanced across at her husband. 'I suppose we shouldn't keep Freddie waiting any longer.' She turned on her heels and pushed back her shoulders, before stepping forward. Her shoes clattered on the stone floor as she walked towards the front pew. She nodded at her family and Molly's parents, Jack and Charlotte, before taking her seat.

The priest stepped forward and the chords of the pipe organ filled the air. The congregation stood up as one, and with Lily leading the way, the three bridesmaids slowly walked down the aisle, in single file, towards the waiting priest, in step with each other and Mendelssohn's Wedding March. The navy lace and pale blue satin underlay of the column dresses swished around their black kitten-heel shoes with every step they took. They each held their own bibles in front of them, the covers worn and the edges of the pages crinkled with use.

Jack and Charlotte stood, watching their daughter with pride, as she followed Victoria towards the altar.

Freddie stood pensively, with Charles by his side. His brow furrowed as the girls approached them. His gaze darted beyond the girls, but he couldn't see his bride. He clutched his hand in front of him; the knuckles were white as the bone tried to break free of his skin.

Lily nodded and beamed at him as she stepped across the front pew, past her mother.

Alice stood in the vestibule with her father, gazing up at him. 'Are you so disappointed that you've nothing to say to me?'

'No, not at all.' Luke cleared his throat. 'I am sure you and Freddie will be very happy together. You know how to do as you are told, so I think all will be well.'

Alice stared at her father as disbelief ran across her face. 'Freddie doesn't want me to do as I'm told. He treats me like an equal.'

Luke jutted out his arm for Alice to tuck her hand

into. 'I'm sure that will change once you are married.'

Before Alice could say anything, they were walking down the aisle together.

Charles and Freddie gasped as one, when Alice came into view. Freddie's eyes began to fill as Alice stepped nearer to him. He smiled, trying to remove the anxious set of her lips. The look on her face reminded him of when Charles had enlisted. They finally drew level with him. 'You look beautiful. I love you so much, Alice.'

Her eyes lit up and she smiled back at him. 'I love you too, with all my heart.'

The priest cleared his throat and nodded at the pair of them.

They nodded back in unison.

'Dearly beloved, we are gathered here today...'

*

Alice's eyelashes fluttered as daylight started to seep through them. A weight across her midriff pinned her to the bed and her eyes flashed open, immediately taking in the plush deep red curtains, where the grey day was trying to break through. The walls, painted a soft green, had framed canvasses hanging from the picture rails. A wedding dress lay in a crumpled heap on the brown rug, in front of an oak chest of drawers, with an army uniform just visible amongst its folds. One black sock hung over the arm of the chair, sitting in the corner of the room. Alice fleetingly wondered what had happened to the other. The rhythmic breathing next to her, and the arm draped across her, was a reminder of why she was sleeping in the guest bedroom. She was a married woman now. Mrs Leybourne, Mrs Freddie Leybourne. Alice smiled to herself. It had all come about so quickly. She wondered if there'd be talk about her condition; maybe that's why there had been no words of wisdom from her father.

Alice lay still, enjoying the feel of his warm, naked body next to hers. His musky scent had settled on her skin, fusing with her own rose-scented perfume. Maybe she'd wear them both every day, to remind her of the wonderful night they had spent together.

Freddie had been gentle; he had worried about hurting her. Any fears she may have had soon disappeared. Alice closed her eyes and rested her hand on top of his, as her thoughts strayed to the previous day. Thanks to her mother and grandfather, there had been no arranged marriage for her. She had willingly walked down the aisle, towards the man she loved.

At the front of the church, Freddie had stood tall and proud. His eyes glistened as he watched her every move.

'I now pronounce you man and wife.' The priest's voice had rung through the church.

Alice had lifted her chin; her lips parted as a slow smile had crept across her mouth. Without waiting to be asked, Freddie had taken Alice into his arms and kissed her. The light, butterfly kiss ignited the promise of what was to come.

Alice gave a contented sigh as she snuggled further under the white cotton sheets and the red eiderdown.

Charles had slapped Freddie on the back, bursting their bubble, reminding them they were still in the church. 'Congratulations.'

Freddie had raised his hand and caressed her cheek, before turning to face Charles and hold out his hand.

The young man had laughed. 'We don't shake hands; we are brothers now.' Charles wrapped his arms around Freddie, giving him a bear hug.

Alice squeezed Freddie's hand under the bedclothes. Her fingers ran over the soft dark hairs on his fingers.

She smiled as she remembered the girls giggling around her, each hugging their congratulations.

Sarah had wrapped her arms around her. 'Be happy,' she whispered before stepping back.

'Congratulations. I can't believe my granddaughter is married, and to a police officer.' Edward had laughed as he enveloped her in his arms. 'We're all going to Russell Square. Jane has excelled herself on the food front and there's enough to feed an army.'

Sadness engulfed Alice as she realised Freddie would soon have to return to the front line. She wondered if she could lock him away in the attic; no one need ever know he was there.

'Morning, Mrs Leybourne.' Freddie's sleepy breath

brushed her shoulders.

Tingling swept up the back of her neck. 'Morning, Mr Leybourne,' Alice whispered. All thoughts of him leaving were swept away.

Freddie pulled her tighter to him. 'Hmm, this is where I want to be.' He paused for a moment. 'Here with my wife.' His fingers walked across her stomach.

Alice's breath quickened as heat ravaged her. She shivered as her whole body became alight with desire. She rolled over to face him, her eyes soaking in his features, every line etched into her memory. 'They could be back soon,' she murmured.

He propped himself up on his elbow and nodded. 'But they are not here now.'

She moved her head to one side as he slowly lowered his mouth on to hers. The bristles of his morning beard scratched her skin as the passion grew. Alice wrapped her arms around him, clinging to him, for fear she'd drown in the desire that was rising inside her.

*

While Luke had silently eaten his breakfast, the sky had turned a menacing dark grey. The wind had chased away any brightness that had been trying to break through and the lone bird singing outside had disappeared. Within minutes, the first silent drops of rain that had slowly dribbled down the window had begun to gather force and batter the glass. The heavens had opened, allowing the rain to fall in biblical proportions. Puddles of water flooded the pavements. The wind huffed around the windows, from time to time, giving an odd whistling noise.

Alice sighed. 'This weather is dreadful.'

Lily put down the knife she had been using to butter a slice of toast. 'At least it wasn't this bad for your wedding day, Mr and Mrs Leybourne.' She gave a throaty chuckle as she picked up her toast, stopping to lick the small globular knob of creamy butter from her finger.

Alice giggled. 'That's true; we were lucky.'

Freddie leant towards Alice as he rested his hand on top of hers, to give it a gentle squeeze.

Charles arched an eyebrow as he looked across the table. 'Yes, Freddie certainly has a spring in his step this morning.'

Freddie's usual musky scent transported Alice back to the previous night. Heat rose slowly in her face, turning it a delicate shade of pink. She was thankful no one could read her mind.

'Charles!' the ladies in the room chorused as one.

The young man laughed. 'What? Just saying, he looks very happy.' He paused, giving his sister a mischievous grin from the opposite side of the table. 'And Alice doesn't look too sad either.'

Lily nudged her brother. 'You didn't look too sad

either, last night.' She smiled. 'I spied you deep in conversation with Molly.'

Luke sighed and shook his head, before putting down his empty teacup. He glanced across at the clock sitting on the mantelpiece.

Freddie looked amused. 'Don't worry, Mrs Taylor, I'm very happy. I wish I hadn't wasted so much time worrying about being financially secure, before marrying Alice.'

'So what were you and Molly talking about?' Lily persisted.

A flush crept across Charles' cheeks. 'I've asked her to write to me. It lifts you to receive a letter, doesn't it, Freddie?'

Freddie turned to his wife, his eyes full of love. 'It certainly does and it's going to be hard to leave today.'

Luke pulled at the chain to his fob watch, releasing it from his waistcoat pocket. 'Everyone has to make sacrifices; that's life.' The top of his watch sprung open and he stared at the face for a moment, before snapping it shut and returning it to its home.

Freddie stared at Luke, wondering what sacrifices he was making for the war effort. He pondered as to how well his father-in-law would have coped in the trenches, but decided not to ask. 'Yes, sir.'

Luke pushed his chair away from the dining table. 'I had better get going if I am to make the train from Liverpool Street. I don't want to arrive at Sandringham too late, especially now, as thanks to the war, nowhere is lit.'

Sarah frowned. 'Would you rather not wait and see if the rain slows down? It sounds dreadful out there.'

Luke stood up in one movement. 'A little bit of rain won't kill me.'

Sarah lowered her head and raised her eyebrows, looking down at her boiled egg. 'No, but sitting on a train in wet clothes will,' she mumbled.

'Sorry, did you say something?' Luke stared hard at his wife.

The colour drained away from Alice's face. She looked down at her arm, expecting to see the tiny hairs standing on end as she moved her hand away from Freddie's, hoping he wouldn't notice how clammy it had become. Alice glanced through her eyelashes at Lily. Her skin was ashen and all her bravado and laughter had momentarily disappeared. Alice knew their father had the same effect on them both. They just handled it differently.

Charles lifted his hand to his mouth and gave a small cough.

Alice stiffened in her seat as she wondered if he was clearing his throat to say something.

Sarah lifted her head and pulled back her shoulders. 'I said it won't do you any good sitting in wet clothes.'

Alice watched Charles wipe his mouth with his napkin before opening his mouth to say something. Her foot sprung into action and kicked him under the table.

'Ouch,' Charles shouted, dropping his napkin.

'I'm sure I will survive.' Luke stepped away, not giving his son a second glance. He placed his seat back into position.

Sarah immediately stood up, the tension already forgotten. 'What's wrong? Are you all right?'

Nerves took hold and Alice let a giggle escape. 'Sorry, Charles.' She grinned at him. 'I was just stretching my legs under the table; I didn't mean to catch you.'

Charles pushed his chair out, to examine his shin. 'Catch me? I'll be lucky if I can walk again.' He rubbed his leg vigorously, before eyeing her suspiciously.

Luke sneered at his son. 'Perhaps we should be sending Alice off to fight the Huns and you should stay here to clean the house.'

Colour filled Alice's cheeks as she jerked her head around, to face her father. Her finger nails dug into the palms of her hands.

Freddie jumped up. He grabbed his chair as it started to topple backwards on to the floor. 'Thank you for allowing me to stay, sir.'

Luke turned his attention to Freddie and nodded. 'I suppose, now you are family, you had best call me Luke or Father, whichever you choose.'

'Thank you...' Freddie hesitated, '... Luke, for everything.'

There was a light knock on the dining room door.

'Yes!' Luke bellowed.

The door hinges squeaked as Mrs Headley pushed it open and came in. A long woollen grey scarf swung from her arm as she walked. Her arms were weighed down with Luke's black winter coat and her fingers gripped his hat.

'Ah, now that's what I like – punctuality.' Luke gave a rare smile. 'Excellent, Mrs Headley, right on time.'

Luke wrapped the scarf around his neck, before shrugging his arms into the coat that Mrs Headley held open for him.

She waited until he was buttoned in before passing him the hat and watched him place it firmly on his head, at a jaunty angle. 'I'm not sure the wind won't whip that right off, sir.'

'Thank you, Mrs Headley, I am sure I will be fine.'

She gave a little bow. 'As you wish, sir.' Mrs Headley turned on her heels and left the room.

Alice, Lily and Sarah stood up as one. Each stood in line, waiting for the perfunctory kiss on the cheek, which was duly given.

Luke grasped the handle of his worn, brown suitcase and juggled it on his fingers for a few seconds as he looked at his son. 'I will see you all in a few days.'

Charles remained seated and didn't look up at his father.

The thud of the front door signalled Luke had left the house. The noise resonated into the dining room, hanging in the air like shards of glass waiting to fall on them as they took their seats again at the table. No one spoke of Luke's comments, or of the rucksacks packed and standing in the hall, waiting to be transported to the front line. Freddie and Charles hadn't been seen out of uniform, a constant reminder that their time at home was temporary. Each knew that, in a few minutes, they'd be saying goodbye to their loved ones.

Chapter 13

Alice sat in the sitting room at Bloomsbury Street, with her mother and Lily. Sarah had taken advantage of Luke's absence and the fire had been lit in the middle of the day. The smoke's grey tendrils curled around the coals and the black ash. She stared into the flames that licked up the chimney; the flickering colours held her mesmerised. She didn't flinch when a spark escaped onto the hearth, leaving an ember's glow slowly dying. The coals crackled and warmth spread into the room, with each of them lost in their own thoughts.

Alice's embroidery lay untouched on her lap. The shine of her new wedding band caught her eye. She absently turned it on her finger as worry filled her head.

Lily stared out of the sash window. The sombre grey sky pressed down, emulating the sadness in the room. The trees had long since lost their leaves so the bare branches reached up, disappearing into the low cloud. People rushed past the window with their collars up, not stopping to talk to one another, giving curt nods as they sped by. Men in uniform walking along the road were now commonplace, some stopping to chat to children who played war-games in the street. Lily fidgeted in her seat. Her book snapped shut on her lap, but it didn't register with her. 'The house is so quiet, it's hard to believe they were ever here.'

Sarah looked across at Lily. 'Yes, Charles does light up a room with his laughter and his mischievous comments.' She frowned as she turned and stared into the flames that were licking up the chimneybreast. 'We certainly crammed a lot into the couple of days.'

Alice picked up her embroidery and sighed. The smokiness in the air filled her nostrils as she breathed in. 'If I wasn't wearing the ring on my finger, it would be easy to think it was all a dream; a lovely dream, but a dream all the same.'

Lily looked over at her sister. 'It's obvious we all miss them, but I think we need to do something to give ourselves a lift.'

A smile played on Alice's lips as she looked up. 'Well, it must be the cure-all then.' Lily frowned as confusion flitted across her face. 'Tea and chocolate cake it is.' Sarah and Lily laughed. 'I've discovered it doesn't matter whether it's crisis or celebration, it does the trick.' Their laughter filled the room, chasing away the dark clouds hanging over them.

The house shuddered at the violent banging on the front door. The three of them were pulled out of their reveries. The brass knocker hit the door again, quickly followed by knuckles rapping hard. They jumped to their feet, ignoring the thud of a book hitting the floor and the embroidery frame falling softly onto the carpet.

Stunned into action, Sarah pulled open the sitting room door and called out from the end of the hallway. 'Who on earth...?' The clatter of heels on the stone tiles announced that the ladies were on their way, before anyone came into view.

Mrs Headley, red faced, reached the front door first and swung it open.

Molly fell in through the open doorway. The housekeeper reached out and just managed to catch her. Molly stretched out her hands in a bid to save herself. Her normal bright sparkling eyes were red raw and her pale face soaking wet.

Mrs Headley held on tightly to Molly's arms, momentarily forgetting her position in the household. 'Come in, Miss Cooper. What on earth is the matter?' She wrapped her arms around Molly, pulling her further into the hall, while stretching out her foot to nudge the door closed, shutting out the cold air that had ripped into the hallway.

'I'll fetch Miss Alice for you.'

The clattering ended as the three ladies stopped dead by the stairs. Lily frowned towards her mother, reaching out to clutch her warm hand, but she was gaping at Molly.

Alice rushed forward, keeping her eyes firmly on her friend. 'Molly, what is it?'

Mrs Headley was suddenly aware she was holding

the girl's weight. 'Miss Alice, I think she may have fainted.'

Sarah turned to Lily, grasping her hand tightly. 'Go and pour a little of your father's whisky into a glass.'

Lily arched her eyebrows as she stared at her mother.

Sarah let go of her daughter's hand. 'Go, quickly.' She looked over as Alice and Mrs Headley tried to put their arms around Molly's waist, so they could get her into a chair. 'Don't move her. I'll fetch a dining chair. It's not ideal, but we can't carry her.' Not waiting for a response, Sarah sped off down the hall.

'I wonder what's happened, Miss Alice?'

Alice shook her head. 'I don't know, but it certainly isn't good news.' She tried to adjust her grip around Molly's waist.

'Here.' Lily ran down the hall holding a glass containing some amber liquid.

Sarah appeared, carrying a wooden carver chair and dropped it next to Alice. 'Sit her down.' She arched her back and gasped for air. 'Hopefully, the arms will stop her from falling off.' She watched Mrs Headley and Alice try to manoeuvre around the chair, with Lily shouting instructions at them.

Lily scowled. 'Mother, you should've fetched the whisky while I got the chair; it is too heavy for you to carry.'

Sarah nodded, giving her a weak smile, as she tried to take in the air her lungs were aching for.

Lily placed her arms around her mother. 'Perhaps we should be getting you a chair.' She passed the glass to her sister.

Alice looked down at the glass, then back to her sister.

Lily pushed out her bottom lip and shrugged her shoulders.

Sarah laughed at the two of them. 'Place a little bit of the whisky on Molly's lips and, as she starts to come round, give it to her to sip.'

Alice followed her mother's instructions and wafted the glass under her nose, hoping it would work like smelling salts. Slowly, Molly's eyes began to flutter. The ladies let out a collective sigh.

'Mrs Headley, could you please make some tea; I think we're going to need it.'

The housekeeper looked across at Mrs Taylor. 'Yes, Ma'am. Would you like cake to go with it?'

'One can never say no to your cake, Mrs Headley.' Sarah visibly relaxed as Molly showed signs of coming round.

Lily laughed. 'I say never mind tea, we should be drinking father's whisky.'

Molly's eyes suddenly opened, showing the full impact of her tears.

*

Alice lifted the shiny brass doorknocker and let it drop from her fingers. It gave a thud on the black front door. Drops of water spattered, before it bounced up and fell again. She wiped a splash from her face, before stepping backwards onto the wet red and black tiles of the path to Victoria's terraced home. She stared at the once pristine house in front of her. What had been dust were now black rivulets, swirling down to the path. The white paint on the windows had blistered, allowing the rain to form pools of water underneath. Alice had heard women make judgments on how clean a family was by their doorsteps. It would have amused her at one time, but today her mind was full of Molly's distress. She shook her head. Here she was making judgments, based on the cleanliness of a step. The creak of the door broke into her meanderings.

'Hello, Alice.' Victoria's gaunt, ashen face stared at her through the crack of the door.

Alice forced a smile. 'Hello, Victoria.' She paused for a moment, taking in her grey pallor. Thoughts immediately raced around her head. Had she also received bad news? 'I hope you don't mind me popping round unannounced, but we haven't had much chance to talk since before the wedding.'

'No.' Victoria hesitated for a moment before opening the door wider. 'Please come in.' She stepped aside. There was no welcoming smile in her eyes. 'Excuse the mess, but I've been a little slow in getting started today.'

'I don't mean to intrude.' Alice frowned. She'd thought her friend had turned the corner recently. Receiving Ted's letter appeared to have lifted Victoria's spirits, but maybe it had turned back time and opened old wounds.

Victoria gave a faint smile. 'No, it's fine. Please go through to the sitting room.'

Alice stepped through the doorway on her left. It was a smaller version of her parent's home. She tried to stifle a gasp, as the stench of stale perfume and damp hit her. The heavy brown curtains hadn't been opened to let in the sunshine that was trying to break through the morning's grey clouds. There was less furniture than she remembered from previous visits. The room was cold and unloved. Had it been that long since the house had heard laughter?

'Please sit down. I'll make us some tea.'

Alice turned, her eyes wide with horror as she stared at her friend. 'I'm sorry, Victoria, but I have to ask.' She paused and looked around the room again. 'Where is your furniture, and your mother and father's belongings you treasured?'

Panic rushed across Victoria's face. 'I've just been having a clear out; it's nothing to worry about.' Her eyes became watery and she blinked rapidly, to stop the tears from falling. 'Now, tea, no sugar, isn't it?'

Alice lowered her eyes. She once again felt she had let her friend down. 'Yes please.'

Victoria hesitated, holding her hand tight in front of her waist. She opened her mouth to speak, but changed her mind and turned to leave the room, wanting to put off her friend's questions for as long as possible. Victoria sighed as she filled the kettle and lit the gas flame under it. She loved Alice dearly, but didn't understand why she couldn't see, or wouldn't accept that their lives were different. She'd lost everything when her parents died. They'd protected their children from life's realities, but that meant her life had been turned upside down when those harsh realities had hit home. They were never going to be living the same life again. Victoria took a deep breath. She didn't know how she was going to tell her friend that she had to stop reminding her of all the things she'd lost. A tear tripped onto her cheek. The only way that could happen was if they stopped being friends.

Standing in the sitting room, Alice squeezed her eyes shut for a moment, wondering what she could do to help her friend. She turned and opened the curtains wide. Daylight streamed in. Alice fought the urge to turn around and look at the room. She remembered how Victoria's parents had been full of life. She swallowed hard, trying to dislodge the lump that was beginning to form in her throat. She shook her head; this wasn't about her. It was about Victoria and her younger brother and sister. Without another thought, she unlocked the sash window and pushed it up. The cold air flooded the room, quickly chasing away the musty dampness that had taken hold. The muted chatter of people walking by brought life into the room.

'Thank you,' Victoria whispered. 'I hadn't got around to opening them yet.'

Alice jumped. 'I hope you don't mind.' She turned around to face her friend, but her eyes darted around and colour flushed her cheeks. 'You need to talk to me, Victoria. What's happened?'

'Please take a seat.' Victoria placed the tray with the floral china tea service on the small table at the side of the room. 'It should be brewed in a moment.' She sat down on one of the three high-back chairs in the room. She leant her head back and momentarily closed her eyes as a sigh escaped.

Alice leant forward and rested her hand on Victoria's arm. 'What is it? You can talk to me; we're friends.' She gripped the arms of the chair next to her, before slowly lowering herself into it.

Victoria opened her eyes and gave a tight-lipped smile. 'Life is just hard, that's all.'

'I can't pretend I know what you're going through, but what I do know is that I couldn't manage in the way you do.' Alice's eyes stung, as tears began to form. 'You're doing a wonderful job and I hope your brother and sister appreciate what you've done for them.'

Victoria gave a hollow laugh. 'If only.' She clenched her hands together in her lap. 'You know, it was hard keeping a roof over our heads even before Stephen joined the army, but now…' Victoria shook her head.

'Is that why you've been selling your furniture and the precious memories of your parents?'

Victoria didn't look up. Tears splashed onto her hands. 'Some are sold, but I pawned what I could.' Her pale face became flushed with colour.

Alice's eyes widened, the only sign of her despair at her friend's predicament. 'Have you kept the tickets?'

Victoria's head jerked upwards and her nostrils flared. 'Of course.' She snatched open a small drawer in the side table next to her chair and pulled out a wad of tickets. 'I know you're shocked.' She sniffed. 'You don't have to pretend otherwise, but I couldn't bring myself to sell the things outright.' She took the handkerchief that Alice offered and blew her nose.

Alice reached out her hand and let it rest on Victoria's arm. 'Let me get the things back for you,' she whispered.

Anger flew across Victoria's face. 'I'm not a charity case.' She flung the tickets back in the drawer.

Alice stared at her friend, before shaking her head. 'No one is suggesting you are, but everyone has times when they need friends and this is that time for you.'

Victoria nodded, twisting the handkerchief around her fingers, her eyes concentrating on her lap. 'Since my parents died, you've been a very good friend to me. In fact, I probably couldn't have got through the aftermath of the train crash if it wasn't for you, but I cannot allow you to waste your money on my problems. Besides which, my agony is emphasised every time I see you. It's having a constant reminder of what my life used to be like, and what I no longer have.'

Guilt washed over Alice. If she'd stopped to think, it was obvious, but she hadn't. 'Victoria, look at me.'

Ignoring her friend, Victoria stared down at her clenched hands, the fingers tightly intertwined with the handkerchief. 'You know, Stephen wanted to do something exciting, but he was well paid at the factory and we couldn't afford for him to just give it up.' She blinked rapidly. 'The ten shillings and six pence he gets paid in the army is less than he was earning before.' Victoria paused. 'Maybe if I hadn't been so insistent, he wouldn't have been so eager to join up.'

'Don't punish yourself like this. You couldn't have stopped him. They all thought it was an adventure.'

'Maybe, but I knew he hated it at the boot factory.' She looked up and took a deep breath. 'I just thought he was young and didn't realise how lucky he was to get that job.'

'Try not to fret. His job will still be there when he comes back, and I'm sure things will settle down once he gets used to working there.'

Victoria returned her gaze to her hands, clasped together on her lap. 'The trouble is, he may not come back.'

Alice leant forward, unable to stop her voice rising an

octave. 'Don't say things like that. He'll return...' Her voice trailed off as she lowered her eyes. 'They all will.'

Alice watched a tear trip over Victoria's lashes and, for a brief moment, she wondered if her friend had received the same news as Molly. 'Have you heard...?' She couldn't bring herself to finish the sentence.

'Heard news, like Tony's parents?' Victoria took a deep breath. 'No, thank God, but it could've been any of them.'

'You've heard then.' Alice paused, studying her friend's delicate features. 'Molly literally dropped in on us yesterday.' She shook her head, swallowing hard, trying to remove the lump restricting her throat. 'She was in a terrible state.'

Victoria shrugged her shoulders. 'I'm not surprised. He wouldn't have enlisted if she hadn't shamed him into it.'

'That's a bit harsh,' Alice whispered.

'Harsh but true,' Victoria snapped. 'Any one of us could have received that news. As they say, "there but for the grace of God go I."'

Alice nodded. 'I know, but you should have seen her. We couldn't get anything out of her for ages. She just kept repeating the words "it's Tony".' She shook her head as the tears pricked at her eyes. 'We had to guess the rest. Apparently, he died on his first day on the front line. He didn't stand a chance,' she murmured.

They sat in silence for a moment, each lost in their

own thoughts.

'I'm sorry I remind you of what you had. I can't do anything about that, but if you think I'm just going to walk away from our friendship, you're sadly mistaken. You can walk away, but I'll fight for it, because it's important to me. We have to stick together more than ever now.' Alice thrust her chin out. 'Friendship is important, especially in times like this. It's all a mess. You feel guilty, I feel guilty and Molly feels more than guilty enough, without anyone telling her it was her fault he enlisted. Judging from the mess she was in, she knows that already.'

Keeping her head bent, Victoria gave her friend a sideways glance.

Alice sighed. Her energy was draining away. 'Look, there is no doubt in my mind we're all friends, and one day you'll be my crutch to lean on, but today, you need to lean on me.' They sat in silence for a moment. 'I'm sorry, I can't sit here and do nothing. Actually, I'm not sorry. You're my friend and I'm going to help you, whether you like it or not. I can't let your pride get in the way of keeping your family's things.'

'I've never known you to be so... forthright before.' Victoria looked back down at her hands, clenching the handkerchief tight on her lap. 'It's been a hard four years and needs must.' She sniffed and looked up at Alice. 'Life has become a constant battle.'

Alice stared at her friend's pale face, the dark circles

under her eyes letting her know she wasn't sleeping well. She had to think about how she could help her proud friend. 'Why didn't you let me know? I assumed, albeit wrongly, that once everything had calmed down, and with Ted writing... well, you seemed much happier.'

Victoria wiped the handkerchief over her face. 'It was lovely to hear from Ted, but...'

Alice stood up, poured the tea and passed a cup to Victoria.

*

Three golden spheres were suspended at varying heights from an ornate wrought iron bar. Alice looked up and down Victoria Street. She stood outside the pawnshop, fidgeting from one foot to the other. The Railway Express Parcels Services horse-drawn wagon trundled past. The cars chugging along in front and behind it drowned out the clip clop of the hooves. Dark smoke coughed from exhaust pipes. Alice moved aside as a man approached on a bicycle. The pavement was getting busy with stallholders setting up to sell their wares.

A scruffy lad, with an unruly mop of brown hair, shouted the newspaper headlines out from over the road. 'Bombs drop on Sandringham and Yarmouth.' People rushed to buy papers, before going about their daily business, while others stopped to chat.

Alice stood frozen to the spot. Fear held her captive.

Her body automatically sucked in the cold air. Pedestrians turned to stare at her, but carried on walking. How would she find out whether her father was safe? The need to find out carried her across the road. She handed the boy a halfpenny, which he grasped with his fingers, hidden inside his threadbare woollen gloves.

He handed her a folded Daily Mirror newspaper. 'Zeppelin raid on Norfolk.' The boy's voice rang out, making her jump as she took it. 'Sorry, love.' The boy flashed a set of uneven brown-tinged teeth, giving her a cheeky smile.

Alice nodded, but no smile came. Her face was fixed on the newspaper she was holding. She scanned it, before frantically opening it up and finding the details on page three. Two people reported dead in Yarmouth. Two houses had been demolished at Kings Lynn and a teenager had died in one of them. Alice searched for news of Sandringham, where her father was staying. There it was; several bombs dropped, but no damage reported.

'Those poor people,' Alice mumbled as she stood by the boy, reading the news.

'They were brave, miss.' The boy frowned. 'It says the police and special constables were scrambled from every direction, to help those that had been bombed.'

Alice looked up at him. 'It's terrible.' She had to get home before her mother heard the news.

'Yeah, it's terrible all right. The houses that survived had all their windows smashed in, but the Zeppelin was shot down. Thankfully.' The boy paused and took a deep breath, before raising his voice again. 'Read all about it, Norfolk bombed by the Germans.'

Alice jumped and stepped away from the boy, as others rushed over to buy from him. She looked back at the shop and took a deep breath. Victoria had probably stood at this same spot. Alice wondered if she had been filled with the same apprehension. She pulled at the collar of her coat as the winter wind lifted the flap, chilling her to the bone. She had come early, hoping no one she knew would see her, but she had underestimated how many people were around at nine-thirty in the morning. Her father would've been livid if he'd seen or heard about her entering such premises, but this wasn't about her. She needed to do this for her friend. She placed the newspaper in her shopping bag and tightened her grip on it, as the wind built its momentum.

Victoria didn't know Alice had taken the tickets when she took the tea tray back to the kitchen, but she couldn't let her friend's pride get in the way. They'd argue it out when everything was back where it belonged. She glanced up and down the road, before purposefully stepping towards the shop doorway. She pushed hard on the door and a chime rang out. Heat started to rise up her face, with the realisation of how desperate Victoria must have been to come into one of these shops. The long counter stretched out in front of her. Shelving behind it was cluttered with a variety of objects. All kinds of items, from clocks, glassware, and china to walking sticks and spades, spilled from shelves around the shop. Clothes of varying sizes and colours hung from a rail. There were boxes of gloves and scarves, waiting for someone to rummage through them. Mustiness sat in the corners, daring anyone to disturb it. The jewellery was kept on display, in a glass cabinet.

The elderly man behind the counter looked up from his newspaper. 'Can I help you, madam?'

Alice's colour deepened. 'I've some tickets.' Alice paused, aware that the portly man was staring at her.

He straightened his position and closed the newspaper. He arched his brows as he watched her open her bag and thrust her hand in, fumbling around before trying to peer inside. Eventually, she pulled out a bundle of papers.

'Ah, here they are.' She put them down on the counter. 'I'd like to buy all the items back please.'

'All of them?' The man picked up the papers and began reading them. 'This'll come to a tidy sum of money.'

Colour rose in her cheeks. 'I am aware of that, thank you.' Alice watched as he started to search around the premises.

Gradually, the items were brought together, from porcelain ornaments to brooches, along with wedding and engagement rings. The man's grubby fingers picked up a pen and placed the nib into a pot of ink. He wrote the value of each ticket on the paper in front of him, before slowly adding them up. He stopped and held up a ticket. 'This belongs to a table and six chairs, so you'll have to arrange to get them picked up. Once you've paid for it, there'll be a charge for storage, until it is collected.' He returned to his column of figures.

Alice stood transfixed, staring at his dirty fingernails as his hand moved up and down the figures.

'That'll be seven pounds, ten shillings and six pence.

Alice took a deep breath. 'I shall give you five pounds, sir.'

'No,' the old man blustered. 'It adds up to over seven pounds and that is what I want.'

'Sir, I am taking more off your hands today than you'd probably get rid of in a year, so five pounds it is.' She took a deep breath, trying to keep her embarrassment at bay. 'For every minute it takes you to decide, I shall take away another ten shillings, so be quick before my offer is four pounds ten shillings.' Alice took out her purse and counted out five one-pound notes onto the counter. She stared hard at her money, unable to bring herself to look at him.

Moments later, he picked up the notes. 'You drive a hard bargain, miss. There's a job here for you, if ever you are in need.'

Alice placed the items into her shopping bag. 'Thank

you, sir, but hopefully I will never have that need. I'll arrange for the table and chairs to be collected tomorrow.'

'I'd say it's been a pleasure doing business with you, miss, but I think you've fleeced me.' The man smiled at her.

Alice nodded and, without another word, she left the shop. The chiming of the door followed her down the street. With her eyes downcast, she paced along, her bag weighing heavily on her, but she didn't slow down. The impressive gothic architecture of Westminster Abbey didn't capture her attention in the normal way. Her heart was pounding and her head was starting to throb when the Houses of Parliament came into view. Relieved, she slowed down. Her arms ached and her lungs burnt, as she gasped for air. All she had to do now was face Victoria's wrath.

*

Victoria stared vacantly out of her sitting room window wondering, not for the first time, how everybody's lives could carry on as normal. It didn't seem right. The clouds were low and getting darker, so the threat of rain was growing and the grey day reflected her mood. She didn't want to go out but, contrarily, she didn't want to stay in either. The house was bare of her parents' personal possessions; it no longer felt like home. A child screaming broke into her thoughts. Leaning forward, she peered through the dust that clung to the glass, her nose almost touching it. Victoria looked up and down the street, trying to discover what had happened. A grey-haired woman was helping a young girl up off the pavement. The child clung to her, as tears ran down her face. She stared at the scene and a tear trickled down her own cheek. Her parents were never going to meet their grandchildren. Angrily, she swiped the tear away. It wasn't fair. It suddenly dawned on Victoria that Sarah Taylor must have been equally heartbroken when her own children were born. Her eyes widened as she spied Alice approaching the house. Victoria watched her walk past the little girl, heading purposefully towards her home. Alice's shoulders were hunched over and her eyes stared at the pavement. The straps of the bag she was carrying looked strained, stretched to breaking point. Victoria sighed. She's probably bought more books. Alice looked up and Victoria quickly jerked back, behind the heavy curtain. Twice in a couple of days, she couldn't face her again. She was immediately overcome with guilt; after all, Alice was only trying to help.

Alice raised her hand to lift the doorknocker in Percy Street, but dropped it again. Victoria was fiercely independent and Alice feared she was going to be furious with her. She wanted to run. 'You did it for the right reasons' the voice yelled in her head. Surely her friend would know that, wouldn't she? She straightened her shoulders and lifted her chin, bracing herself for what was to come. She shook her head, wishing she had thought it through, instead of acting impulsively. Seeing her friend smile again was what this was about, and surely there was no better way to do it. Her jaw clenched shut. She lifted her hand and before she had time to change her mind again, the doorknocker thudded down.

Victoria groaned. She wanted to ignore the front door and her unwanted visitor. She could hear her mother telling her off.

'Don't be rude Victoria, Alice is a good friend to you.'

She stood rooted to the spot. The door thudded again.

'Don't turn your back on people that care, she's doing her best.'

Victoria shook her head. 'I know you're not here, Mother, so does that mean I'm going mad?' She ran her hand over her face, before taking a deep breath.

The door thudded again. Victoria sighed. 'I'm coming,' she yelled as she walked towards the hallway. She gave a wry grin; if she was hearing voices, then maybe she did need her friends. She swung open the door. 'Hello, Alice, I wasn't expecting to see you again today.' She stood aside, so Alice could step in.

Alice frowned. Victoria's hair was a tangled mess and dust was smeared across the side of her face. She stepped inside the house, wrinkling her nose as she inhaled the stale air. 'No.' She paused. 'I've been a little impulsive, so I hope you won't be angry with me.' Her fingers trembled as she tried to undo the buttons of her black winter coat.

Victoria took it, hanging it on the peg in the hall. She indicated for her to walk into the sitting room. 'What have you done?'

Alice did as she was bid. Their skirts rustled, matching the tap of their heels on the tiles. The carpet deadened their footsteps as they entered the sitting room. Alice walked over to an armchair and lifted the bag on to it.

'That looks heavy. How many books have you bought today?' Victoria forced a smile to her lips.

Alice stared hard at her friend, before lowering her eyes. Without a word, she opened the bag. Tension flowed through her veins. Her heart pounded in her ears. She couldn't bring herself to look at Victoria, so began taking out the figurines she'd recovered from the pawnshop, slowly standing them side by side on the chair, and the small table next to it.

'That looks like...' Victoria stopped as jewellery was placed on the table. 'How...?'

'I took the tickets from your drawer and I—'

'You had no right,' Victoria gasped. 'Who do you think you are? You come into my home and help yourself to my things, without a word...'

'I... I thought you'd be happy to get your parents' things back.'

Tears streamed down Victoria's face. 'Get out!' She screamed.

Alice stood rooted to the spot.

'I said get out.' Victoria turned her back on Alice. 'You've no idea about what I'm going through.' She paused for a moment before whispering, 'I've already said goodbye to these things once.'

Alice blinked rapidly as she looked across at Victoria's hunched back. Her fingertips were just visible as they gripped her tiny waist. 'I know. That's why I thought you'd be happy to see them.' She sniffed, taking a step towards the hallway. 'Your table and chairs will be delivered to you tomorrow.'

Victoria spun round, her face contorted with rage. 'You know I hate you, and you don't even realise it. You just can't see that you have it all; parents, husband, money. You even met Freddie, the love of your life, because of that damn train crash, and I lost mine.' She sobbed. 'I lost everything. It's not fair.' She sniffed. 'Get out and don't come back. I'm not some lost dog or charity that you can keep throwing your money at. Get out.'

Alice could feel her body trembling. The urge was strong to run away from the raw pain that has being hurled at her. She took a step towards Victoria. 'You've got to stop blaming me. It's not my fault. I didn't make the train derail. I didn't expect to fall in love with Freddie. None of this is my fault, and what's more, I refuse to take the blame, especially when I'm only trying to help.'

Victoria turned her back on Alice.

Alice stepped into the hallway, her heels echoing in her ears. Tears tripped over her lashes as the front door slammed shut behind her. Surely this couldn't be how their friendship would end.

Chapter 14

February/March 1915

Lily sat in the armchair nearest the unlit fireplace. Ash mixed with blackened wood and the grey coal from the previous evening's fire. The woody smell and charcoal mingled with the citrus of the orange blossom her mother had put on that morning. The silence in the sitting room, at Bloomsbury Street, was only broken by the pitter-patter of the rain hitting the windows. She peered down at her embroidery, examining her handiwork. She poked and pulled at the silk thread; the small red roses were proving to be tricky. She sighed and glanced across at Alice, sitting opposite her. Lily frowned. Her sister had been very quiet, even by her standards. Her eyes were red, ringed by dark circles. Lily wondered if she'd missed some news about her brothers. She squeezed her lips together, hoping she hadn't.

Alice stared down at the white pages of the book sitting on her lap. She kept reliving Victoria's rage, and without realising it, she shook her head. It hadn't occurred to her that Victoria would find it difficult being around her and Freddie. The hard, red cover of the book nestling in the folds of her blue skirt moved and the corner jabbed into her thigh. Alice altered its position and rubbed her leg. She peered down and read the same line again.

'What's going on?' Lily's voice rang out, startling Alice.

'Sorry?'

Lily's eyebrows knitted together. 'Don't pretend nothing's wrong. You haven't read a word of that book all afternoon.'

'That's not true.' Alice straightened her shoulders and lifted her chin.

'All right, let me say it another way.' Lily paused. 'You haven't turned a page of that book, all the time I've been sitting here, which is a good hour.' Lily stabbed her sewing needle into the canvas she'd been embroidering and placed the stiff material at her feet.

Alice sighed.

'Is the book rubbish?' Lily smiled at her sister.

'No, definitely not, it's Phantom of the Opera.' Alice closed her eyes and leant back into the chair, resting her head against it. Unfortunately, and much to her father's disgust, her French was never good enough to read and understand the original version. 'I just can't concentrate, that's all.'

Lily could feel her lips begin to tremble as she took a deep breath. 'Has there been news?'

Alice's eyes flew open. Her sister's tears weren't far

away. She immediately leant forward and rested her hand on Lily's knee. 'Oh no, at least, not that I'm aware of.'

Relief flooded Lily's face, as her body sunk into the chair. 'So, what is it then?'

Alice frowned. She adjusted her sitting position and closed her book. 'It's Victoria.'

'What about her?'

Alice stared down at her fingers, intertwined on her lap. 'She got angry with me and asked me to leave her home, telling me never to return.' Her eyes welled up. 'I wouldn't mind, but I was trying to be helpful.'

Lily sighed. She had been on the end of some of Alice's help before. It usually involved her telling Lily to behave and not rock the boat otherwise they would all suffer. 'What did you do?'

'Nothing.' Alice instinctively knew Lily would agree with Victoria.

Laughter filled the room. 'Well, I knew you didn't like confrontation, but lying as well...'

'All right, all right.' Alice's eyes glinted when she looked up. 'I don't need you making me feel worse than I already do.'

'So, tell me.' Lily frowned. 'It couldn't have been that bad.'

Alice steeled herself and relayed the story to her sister. '... and then she screamed at me telling me how much she hates me. She told me to leave and never return.' Alice broke off, sniffing, as tears fell onto her cheeks.

Lily's mouth was set in a thin line as she shook her head. 'I know you meant well, and I have to say that will be on your headstone, but I'm not surprised she told you to leave. I'd have thrown something at you, so she showed more restraint than I would've done.'

'I was just trying to help, you know, be a friend.' Alice sobbed. 'The trouble is, she's so damn proud.'

Lily gave a hollow laugh. 'You must see that she does her best, and you helping yourself to something that wasn't yours to take, and also trying to rescue her from a situation, doesn't resolve it. All it does is make her feel she's not coping very well.' Lily gave a little laugh. 'If you ask me, you're lucky you were able to walk out of there.'

Anger began to rise in Alice. She could feel colour flooding her cheeks. 'I just wanted to see her happy again and don't know what else I could've done, but thanks for your support.'

'Look Alice, you'll always have my support, you know that, but Victoria needs time and space to heal. She needs a friend, someone whose shoulder she can cry on.'

Alice sighed. 'I tried to be that friend, but she said I was a constant reminder of what she didn't have.'

Lily nodded. 'I can understand that. All you can do is be there when she needs you.' She paused, staring at

Alice. 'She carries a heavy burden, especially with Stephen going off to war.'

'I know.' Alice shrugged her shoulders. 'I feel so inadequate. I just want to help.'

'That's two of you feeling inadequate, then.'

The front door thudded shut. Both girls lowered their heads and returned to their reading and embroidery.

*

Alice took a deep breath as she walked through the entrance of Foyles. Her normal excitement at being around so many books was missing, as sickness washed over her. 'Morning, Mr Leadbetter.' She forced herself to smile in his direction as she removed her black gloves and began unbuttoning her winter coat.

The floor manager of the bookstore frowned as he watched her walking towards him. She had lost the spring in her step and her eyes were shadowed with dark circles, against her pale skin. 'Morning, Mrs Leybourne. Is everything all right?' It occurred to him that he hadn't seen her talking to Victoria Appleton in the last couple of weeks and wondered if it was connected.

A smile played on her lips. Yes, she was Mrs Leybourne. She had often wondered if those wonderful two days with Freddie, a couple of months ago, had been a dream. She pulled herself upright. 'Yes, sir.'

Mr Leadbetter nodded, deciding she didn't look well,

but knowing it was best to keep his own counsel as he watched her walk towards the staff room. He'd keep a fatherly eye on her.

Alice walked into the staff room and was immediately hit with the strong smell of coffee. Nausea rose in her throat. She held her breath, quickly hung up her coat and clocked on, before moving towards the shop and breathing deeply. Her hand reached out and clung to the doorframe as a wave of dizziness washed over her. She closed her eyes and tried to steady her breathing. She hadn't been right since the argument with Victoria a couple of weeks ago. Even though she missed her friend and their early morning chats, Alice had made no attempt to contact her. After all, she'd made her feelings quite clear. Alice took the couple of steps to her counter and began preparing her pad and pen for customers. She glanced up and saw Mr Leadbetter walking towards her.

'Has your father got back from Sandringham?'

Alice gave a weak smile. 'Yes, thank you, sir. He stayed longer than normal, which worried us. Thanks to the newspapers, I was able to reassure my mother he was probably safe, but yes, he's back now.'

Mr Leadbetter took a step towards Alice. 'It's a shame he didn't write to her. I've been going to the picture house to watch The Pathé News, but they don't give much away. Did he say whether there was much damage up there?'

Alice looked up at his tall, black suited frame; his

lined features looked grey in colour. 'He didn't say much, but I get the impression other areas were much worse off.'

Mr Leadbetter nodded, approving of her father's silence. 'It must have given you all quite a scare, but still, he's back now.' He turned and headed up some steps, towards another section.

Alice turned to the table behind her, and the books that hadn't been collected from the previous day. She moved them to one side, ensuring they didn't get mixed up with today's.

'Morning.'

Alice peered over her shoulder to see Molly at the counter, with Victoria standing just behind her. Nausea and dizziness swept over her for the second time that day. 'Morning.' She tried to take some deep breaths as she leant forward, gripping the side of the table.

'Right, I'm putting my foot down with you two.' Molly grabbed Victoria's arm and pulled her forward. 'I don't know what has occurred between you, and I don't need to know.'

Alice closed her eyes, steadying herself, before releasing her hold on the counter. She forced a smile to her lips, before turning around to face her friends. Her legs started shaking and she leant back for support.

Molly looked from one to the other. 'All I know is, since Tony died, you two haven't been speaking. You're both my friends.' She paused before shaking her head.

'You know, I felt so guilty when Tony died and if nothing else, it taught me to treasure my friendships and family more.' Molly arched her eyebrows and gave them both a piercing look. 'There's a war on, for God's sake. We could all die tomorrow. Whatever's gone on can't be that bad that you wouldn't want to clear the air before we all die.'

Alice smiled. 'It's clear someone's feeling better. It's good to have you back.'

'Actually, I still feel pretty awful but I have to say you look as bad as I feel, so please sort it out before it makes you really ill.' Molly turned on her heels and walked away.

Alice's eyebrows knitted together as she watched her disappear between the rows of bookshelves. She glanced at Victoria, before turning back to her things on the counter. 'Well, that told us didn't it? She's always had a flair for the dramatic.'

'Yes, yes it did.' Victoria paused, looking at Alice's unyielding back. 'Look, Alice, I'm sorry. I know I said some terrible things. It's important you know I was so happy for you on your wedding day.' She hesitated, searching for words. 'You must understand, it was a shock when you turned up on my doorstep with nearly everything I'd pawned. I over-reacted and shouldn't have done. We haven't spoken for weeks now and I don't like it. In fact, I really miss you. Please forgive me.'

Alice slowly turned around. Her shoulders slumped.

Her eyes were moist.

'Has something happened?' Victoria ran her hand down the silk sleeve of Alice's dress. 'Are you all right?'

Alice blinked quickly. She reached into her black skirt pocket, pulled out a white handkerchief and dabbed her eyes. 'Everything is fine. I don't know what's the matter with me today. I don't feel too good.'

Victoria kept her hand on Alice's arm. 'You do look pale; shall I get you a seat?'

Alice gave a watery smile. 'I'm fine, honest. I'm sure it'll pass in a minute.'

'I don't suppose all this has helped, this morning.' Victoria's eyes darted over Alice's face. 'I just want you to forgive me, so we can get back to normal.'

Alice closed her eyes and took a deep breath, as another wave of nausea gripped her. 'There's nothing to forgive.' She opened them and looked at Victoria. 'I was in the wrong, but I was just trying to help, in my own clumsy way. It's hard watching someone you care about struggling, when you can do something about it, but I accept I shouldn't have stolen the pawn tickets. In my defence though, I know you wouldn't have willingly given them to me.'

Victoria gave a humourless laugh and sighed. 'It was my pride that got in the way of our friendship.' She lowered her hand and rested it on her friend's. 'It must have been hard for you going to the pawn shop. It was hard for me, and I was desperate.'

'Yes, it was hard, but there's nothing I wouldn't do for you.'

'It was a good thing that you did for me and my family,' Victoria whispered. 'Thank you.'

Alice's lips straightened into a thin line. 'Don't thank me. You don't know what else I've been planning to do, under the guise of helpfulness, but I suppose while we are talking, you may as well know everything.'

Anxiety flicked across Victoria's face. 'That sounds ominous.'

'Well I don't think it's a bad thing, but after this conversation, you might see it as pretty bad.'

Victoria frowned, before giving a faint smile. 'I know you mean well and will always have my interests at heart.'

A sound escaped from Alice. 'Let's hope you still think so when you've heard the rest of it.' She lowered her eyes, before lifting them again quickly and staring at Victoria. 'I have been thinking about asking my grandfather if we could buy your house...' She held up her hand when Victoria opened her mouth to speak. 'So you can live rent free, at least until Stephen's back and this dreadful war is over.'

Victoria stood open-mouthed, but said nothing.

'We are open, Miss Appleton. You should be in the payment booth by now. There's a queue forming and we don't want that, do we, Miss Appleton?' Mr Leadbetter scolded from the rows of bookshelves in the middle of the shop.

'Sorry, sir.' Victoria looked over her shoulder, before looking back at Alice. 'You know, Alice, many people live a lot worse than I do.' She spun around and, without a backward glance, headed towards her workstation.

An old gentleman coughed, jerking Alice back to her work. 'I'm sorry to keep you waiting, sir.'

'Don't worry, lass.' He winked at her. 'This war is preoccupying everyone these days. I noticed today, posters are appearing everywhere, calling for women to do some of the men's work.' He shook his head. 'I don't know if I've been slow in noticing them, but isn't it enough we are losing our children hand over fist, without putting our daughters, wives and mothers at risk too?' He paused for a moment. 'Whatever next?'

Alice gave him a feeble smile. 'I suppose, with all the young men fighting at the front, there's a shortage of people to do the work, and we keep hearing how we all have to pull together for the good of the country.'

'Yes, I know, but my father would turn in his grave if he could.' The old man laughed. 'Take care of yourself, young lady. You don't look too good. Have you been overdoing it?'

'I don't think so.' Alice gave him a smile. 'My mother and I have been at Victoria Station every evening, serving tea and biscuits to the wounded soldiers returning from the front. It breaks your heart to see them.'

The old man nodded. 'Yes, I've heard that.' He sighed. 'My son won't be coming back.'

Alice's eyes widened. 'I'm so sorry.'

The man straightened his lips and blinked quickly. 'I won't be the only parent losing a child in all this mess.'

Alice reached out and rested her hand over his. 'I know, sir, but that doesn't make it all right.'

The man nodded. 'Perhaps I should try and do something for those less fortunate. After all, with my wife and now my son gone, I've all the time in the world to sit and think. I should be putting it to good use.'

Alice nodded and squeezed his hand. 'Well, you can always join us at the station every night. Although I understand they welcome people to sit with patients at the hospital, to chat or read to them. Some of them have no one.'

'Thank you, young lady.' He paused for a second, before giving her a toothless grin. 'Thank you for taking the time out of your busy day to talk to an old man and making him feel better, because he has something to offer in this dreadful war.'

'No, sir.' Alice smiled. 'It should be me thanking you, and I look forward to seeing you again.'

The old man nodded and gave a wave as he made his way over to the payment booth.

The day passed quickly, with a steady stream of customers. The war hadn't affected the sale of second hand books; it seemed everyone wanted to lose themselves in a story. The conflict was on everyone's lips and Alice was glad when the shop door was finally closed, for the last time that day. She walked purposefully over to Victoria, in the payment booth. 'We need to talk,' she said. 'I keep messing up, but I'm trying to help you in the only way I know. If that's not right, then you should be explaining it to me, instead of marching off in indignation…'

Victoria looked up from the handful of pound notes she was holding. 'Breathe, Alice, before you have a heart attack or something.' Victoria frowned as she looked back at the notes in her hand. 'You're right. I keep letting my pride get in the way of everything, but that's because it's like I'm letting everyone down by not managing.' Her eyes glistened when she looked across at Alice. 'I feel a failure and most of it's caused by money, or the lack of it.'

'Victoria, you're far from being a failure. You've raised your brother and sister for five years or so. I couldn't have done that, certainly not at your age, and probably not even now.'

'You don't know what you can do until life throws something at you.' Victoria sniffed. 'It feels so unfair.'

Alice nodded. 'I've nothing to offer except money; that is the only way I can help.'

Victoria shook her head. 'No, it isn't, Alice. No, it isn't.'

Alice shook her head, as Lily's voice echoed Victoria's words in her head.

*

Sarah and Alice laughed as Lily stood in the middle of their sitting room, in line with the fireplace. The heavy curtains shut out the dark evening, along with cold and damp.

Lily frowned as she looked from one to the other. 'What's so funny?'

Sarah gasped, trying to catch her breath, leaning her hands on the soft wool that was resting on her lap, while the end of the knitting needles jabbed into the arms of the chair. 'Oh, you obviously can't see it.' Laughter spluttered from her again, as she wiped the tears from her eyes with the side of her hand. 'Oh dear.'

Lily's voice rose an octave. 'What?' She lifted her foot slightly, but quickly put it down again, hoping no one noticed. 'I don't understand.'

'Sorry, Lily, it's just a little ironic.' Alice smiled at her sister's bewildered face. 'You still haven't got it, have you?'

Sarah nodded. 'I'm sorry, we shouldn't be laughing at your news.'

Lily looked bewildered as she shook her head, glancing from one to the other. 'Am I being a little bit dense?'

Sarah and Alice spluttered with laughter again.

'No, you're not.' Sarah caught her breath. 'The irony is that you nearly got arrested demonstrating with the suffragettes, and yet here you are, telling us you've joined the police.'

Lily gave a wry smile. 'Yes, I can see why you think it's funny, but at least it tells you I've done the right thing. It's all about right and wrong.'

Sarah pushed aside the socks she was knitting, before pulling herself out of the high-back armchair and walking over to her troublesome young daughter, wrapping her arms around her. She pulled back slightly to look at Lily's face. 'You do know the police isn't about what's your idea of right and wrong, don't you, darling? It would be terribly embarrassing if we had to bail out a policewoman, don't you think?'

Lily laughed. 'Yes, Mother, but I thought you'd be pleased. From what I hear, some girls have given up being in service and gone to work in the munitions factories in Silvertown and Woolwich, because they pay well.'

Sarah stepped back, looking from Lily to Alice and back again. 'Well it's very commendable, but I'd rather you were a policewoman.'

Lily smiled and gave her mother another hug. 'That's what I thought.' She stepped back and frowned across at Alice. 'I hope Victoria feels the same, because Daisy came with me.'

Alice's jaw dropped slightly. 'What, Daisy joined the police as well?'

'Yes, do you think Victoria will be angry? It's my fault, I encouraged her.' Lily looked down at her feet. 'She was saying how they're struggling without Stephen's wages, so I thought it would be a way of her earning more money than she does cleaning houses.'

'I'm sure she'll be glad of the extra money in the household pot.' Alice raised her eyebrows. 'As long as Daisy puts it in, that is.'

Lily nodded. 'She talked as though she would. We had quite a talk and I think she has begun to realise what Victoria has managed to do for them all since their parents died.'

Alice nodded. 'I hope you're right. I do worry about Victoria, because she doesn't seem to be eating. She hasn't said anything, but I'm convinced she can't afford to pay the rent and buy food.'

Sarah stared down at the brown carpet. 'I wish there was something we could do.'

Alice stared into the crackling fire before a sigh escaped from her. 'She's very proud, Mother, trust me. I've already had her snap at my offers of help.'

Lily clapped her hands together. 'Well, enough of Victoria. Alice, are you thinking of signing up for anything?'

'I already have.'

'Oh no.' Sarah shook her head. 'What? Please tell me

you won't be putting your life in danger.'

'Mother, there's a war on.' Lily sighed. 'All our lives are in danger, even here in this sitting room.'

Sarah patted Lily's arm. 'I know, dear. I just can't stand the thought of all my children putting themselves at risk. It's bad enough the boys are...'

'Don't worry, Mother, I'll be quite safe.' Alice gave her a reassuring smile. 'I'm the coward of the family, remember.'

Sarah tried to return the smile, but her eyes were full of fear. 'We should have discussed the options before you both signed up, but I suppose you're modern girls, with minds of your own.'

'That's true, Mother, but that's because you and Grandpa brought us up to think for ourselves.' Lily plumped the cushion and adjusted its position, before sitting down in the nearest armchair.

Sarah followed suit and looked across at Alice. 'So, what are you going to be doing?'

'I'm learning to drive an ambulance.' Alice beamed with excitement.

'Wow, that's excellent.' Lily grinned. 'Wish I'd thought of that.'

'Well, we already go to Victoria Station most days or evenings, so I may as well drive the injured to a hospital at the same time.' Alice paused as sadness crept across her face. 'I know it's exciting for us to have these opportunities, but the soldiers we've seen look so broken and lost. I just want to help them in some way.'

Sarah nodded, as images of her sons invaded her thoughts. She squeezed her eyes shut and silently prayed they were safe; she couldn't allow herself to think otherwise.

Alice looked across at her sister. 'When do you start?'

Lily smiled. 'Tomorrow. I'm quite excited at doing something worthwhile and earning a little money of my own.' She paused and looked across at her mother; the colour had drained from her face. 'Don't worry, Mother, we're all going to be all right'.

Sarah nodded, before picking up her knitting again.

'Do you think Father will be angry about me joining the police? I know he wasn't happy with Alice working.'

Sarah sighed. 'I shouldn't think so, because it helps the war effort and of course, he'll be able to tell everyone that all of his children are doing their bit for king and country.'

'What helps the war effort?' Luke stood in the doorway, scanning the room. 'Certainly not using excess coal to light the fire all the time.' He strode over to the fireplace. 'We seemed to have got through more of it while I was at Sandringham.'

Sarah winced. 'Sorry, that was my fault. I got carried away, because it has been so cold.'

Luke scowled at her. 'Well, you need to remember the price of coal is going up, so we need to be more frugal with it.' He picked up the poker and waved it around in front of him. 'That goes for all of you. Put some extra clothes on.'

The three women nodded, each wondering how much of their conversation he had overheard, as they watched him thrust the poker into the fire. There was a crackle and hissing as the ashes dropped inside the grate and grey smoke swirled up the chimney.

Luke leant the poker against the hearth. 'Now what's this about the war effort?' He stretched his back and turned to face the three of them. 'What won't I mind?'

'We were...' The three of them spoke at the same time.

Luke held up his hands. 'One at a time.'

'I've joined the police force,' Lily blurted out, before anyone could say anything. Colour filled her cheeks. 'With the men going off to war, they need women to do their jobs. That's only until they return.' She was rambling, but previous experience told her she only had one shot at getting everything out.

Luke's chest rose. He coughed as he took in the smoky air by the fireplace.

'I've joined up to drive an ambulance,' Alice exclaimed, hoping to deflect him from Lily.

Luke looked from one to the other, before scowling at Sarah. 'Did you know about this?'

'No,' she whispered.

'Lily and I didn't discuss it with anyone, not even each other, until tonight.'

Luke nodded, but remained silent for a moment. The girls looked anxiously at each other and then at their mother, who glanced up at him before shrugging her shoulders.

'Well, it's to be commended that you are doing something for the war effort. Well done.'

The three of them let out a sigh of relief.

Chapter 15

April/May 1915

The only noise to be heard inside the house was the muffled sound of Mrs Headley moving around downstairs. Alice stared blankly out of her bedroom window. The golden rays of the sun filtered through the glass, warming her skin and caressing the floorboards. The green leaves on the tops of the trees in Bedford Square were just visible. The square would be worth a visit later, to see the bright yellow daffodils. In previous years, she had enjoyed the new beginning that spring brought with it. The flowers and the trees brought a splash of colour that was always missing during the greyness of winter, but this year, all she could think of was the men fighting for their lives somewhere in France or Belgium. The squeals and raised voices of children caught her attention. They no longer appeared to play with a ball or chase each other, but now carried sticks as guns. Each wanted to be the hero, as they played their war games, arguing who were going to be the Germans, and therefore get shot or blown up. Alice shook her head, wondering if this was how it was for Victoria all the time, always alone with her thoughts. Running her hand over her stomach, she sighed. 'Why does everything have to be so complicated?' she yelled into the empty room. 'This should have been a wonderful time for us.' A tear spilled over her lashes and she swiped it away, angry for feeling sorry for herself. The picture of Molly falling into their home, when she had received news that Tony had died, invaded her thoughts. 'I am luckier than most,' Alice mumbled to herself. 'I know that,' she argued, stepping back and sitting on the edge of the bed. 'I know I am'. She sighed. 'What about those broken men every night, at Victoria Station? The walking wounded.' Alice blinked rapidly as her vision became blurred. 'They'll never be the same again, no matter how much they pretend.' *No*, a voice screamed in her head, *but they were pleased to see a friendly face, and at least they're home with their families.* She shook her head again. Maybe working at Foyles during the day, as well as driving the ambulance in the evening, was too much for her. 'No, you've just got to pull yourself together. There are others in a much worse position, so stop feeling sorry for yourself.'

Unable to settle, Alice stood up and paced around the room, oblivious to the many books propped against the wall, threatening to topple over. She eventually stopped to pick up bottles of perfume that had been given as gifts. The reflection of a gaunt woman, staring at her through the mirror, made her stop and stare back. This woman looked ill. Thick dark circles under her eyes emphasised the translucent complexion. Alice didn't recognise the thin face that stared back at her. Shaking her head, she moved away and returned to the window, looking out at the people going about their business. This was probably what millions of people were doing, wondering if their brothers, fathers and husbands were safe.

'Mrs Leybourne, are you in there?' Mrs Headley's voice came from the other side of the door, quickly followed by a couple of raps in quick succession.

The noise catapulted Alice out of her meanderings. 'Come in, Mrs Headley.'

The brass door handle squeaked as it slowly turned. 'Sorry to disturb you, miss...'

Alice smiled. 'Don't worry. I was only staring out of the window, lost in my own thoughts.' She walked over to the bed and sat down.

Mrs Headley frowned. 'I was beginning to worry, because I'd knocked a couple of times and thought something must be wrong.'

'Sorry...'

Mrs Headley shook her head. 'Oh no, miss, you don't need to say sorry to me. I should be apologising to you, for talking too much.'

Alice laughed. 'Don't worry. As far as I'm concerned, you're part of the family, so you talk away.'

Mrs Headley lowered her head. 'That's very kind of

you, miss, but I shouldn't overstep the mark.' She suddenly remembered her reason for knocking on the door. 'Oh, I almost forgot, the post has arrived. I came up straight away because there's one for you.' She held out her hand containing the envelope.

Alice kept her eyes on the letter as she licked her dry lips. 'Mrs Headley, do you have any family fighting in this dreadful war?'

Mrs Headley shook her head. 'No, miss. I suppose, at this time, with the war on and all, I am quite fortunate to be on my own, although I wouldn't have said that last year.'

'I never realised you had no family around you,' Alice whispered.

'There is no reason that you should, miss.' Mrs Headley paused, looking down at the envelope in her hand. 'I wasn't blessed with children and my husband died some years back. Something to do with his lungs I think; they did say, but I didn't understand it.'

Alice looked up for the first time. 'You must miss him?'

'You get used to it, miss.' Mrs Headley looked up and saw the pain etched on Alice Leybourne's face. 'Let's face it, you don't have any choice.'

'No, I suppose that's true. At least, that's what Victoria, Miss Appleton says.' Alice's eyes filled with water. She blinked rapidly, in a bid to stop the floodgates from opening.

Mrs Headley offered the envelope again. 'You've got to look after yourself, miss, especially if...'

Alice stared wide-eyed at the housekeeper. 'If what?'

Mrs Headley tightened her lips. 'No, I've said too much already.'

'You can't leave it like that.' Alice's voice could have broken a dozen glasses. 'What do you know? What aren't you saying?' Pain gripped her chest. She wrapped her arms around her body and found herself swaying back and forth. Did the housekeeper know what was in that envelope?

Mrs Headley frowned for a moment, before giving Alice a smile. 'I could be wrong, but I think you could be blessed with a great gift, miss.'

Alice frowned. 'What?' She jumped up, but instantly sat down again as the room began to spin.

'Are you all right, miss?' Mrs Headley walked over to the jug of water and poured a small amount into a glass. 'Here, sip this and sit still until it passes.'

Alice did as she was told; pleased she wasn't on her own. 'This keeps happening to me. What with that and the nausea, I feel ill all the time. I think it may have started when I began driving the ambulance. Perhaps I'm overdoing it and just need to rest more.'

Mrs Headley smiled at her. 'I think you'll find it started earlier than that and you might need to rest more, but I don't think you are ill, miss'. She hesitated for a moment, before continuing. 'I think you could be carrying the next Leybourne generation, miss.'

Was Mrs Headley right? Alice added up the weeks since her wedding night. Was it possible? Surely she'd have known, wouldn't she? She tried to remember when the sickness had first started. Alice ran her hand across her stomach. Had it changed shape? She thought not.

Mrs Headley fought the urge to wrap her arms around Alice. 'The sickness must be nearly over.'

'I don't know...' Alice stopped, to try and focus her thoughts. 'It hadn't occurred to me...'

'You should probably get the doctor to check you over.' Mrs Headley clucked, wanting to make a fuss of Alice. 'Do you want to lie on the bed, perhaps have a rest?'

Alice gave a little chuckle. 'Thank you, Mrs Headley. I'm fine, just shocked. I don't understand why it never occurred to me.'

Mrs Headley frowned. 'Too busy worrying about everyone else, that's why. You need to start taking care of yourself and eat properly, because when that husband of yours comes home, he isn't going to want to find his wife is ill, or even worse, that he's a widower alone with a child.'

Alice looked across at the housekeeper and laughed.

'You may laugh, but these men can't raise children. It's not what they're meant to do, which is why they can't do it as well as a woman. What's more, you've got to think about that baby now. It isn't just about you;

251

there's life growing.' She sighed as her eyes welled up. 'Trust me when I say cherish it. It may be the only chance you get.'

'You seem to know a lot about these things, Mrs Headley,' Alice whispered, fighting the urge to give the housekeeper a cuddle.

Mrs Headley wiped her eyes with the front of her apron. 'I may not be wealthy, miss, but I've seen a lot in my time.'

Alice nodded, longing to ask more, but not wanting to pry.

Mrs Headley thrust the letter in front of Alice. She sat transfixed. Was it giving her bad news? Could she be receiving two lots of shocking news in one day? She wanted to take the envelope, but fear kept her rooted to the spot. Instinctively, she ran her hand across her stomach.

'I've noticed you do that a lot.'

'Sorry,' Alice whispered. 'Do what a lot?'

Mrs Headley smiled. 'Protect the baby you didn't know you were carrying. I think it must be instinct.'

Alice smiled. She looked down at her hand resting on her stomach. 'Freddie would be over the moon if he knew.' Her eyes dropped to the letter, wondering how an envelope could instil so much fear.

'Don't worry, miss,' Mrs Headley said. 'It's not a telegram.'

Alice's eyes didn't leave the envelope as she reached

out to take it. 'Thank you, Mrs Headley,' she whispered. 'For everything.'

Mrs Headley nodded. 'I shall be downstairs, should you need me.' Turning and walking towards the doorway, she twisted around to give Alice a last look, but she was transfixed on the letter, rotating it over and over in her hands. Mrs Headley shook her head, before quietly closing the door behind her.

Alice took a deep breath as she slipped her index finger under the seal and tore the envelope open. She pulled out the piece of paper. Her lips straightened before she unfolded it.

To my darling Alice,

A drop of water landed on the top of the paper.

I have been receiving your letters and they are a great comfort to me. Charles has received a few from Molly, so we share our news. I think she could be writing to him every day, which pleases him. Unfortunately, I can't tell you where we are, but Charles and I are sharing the same trench so we are both well, although we are tired of having wet feet and share it with a few rats as well. I want you to know you are never out of my thoughts, even though I am not writing to you as much as I would like. Charles and I spend our spare time talking about family and the things we miss, like hot water, clean clothes and food other than the tins of bully beef we seem to be living on.

We have heard rumours that the Germans are going to use a poisonous gas on us and, apparently, the gas masks are on order. In the meantime, we have been told to pee on one of our socks and hold it over our noses with the other sock. It's not something I shall look forward to, but if it keeps me alive, I shall do it. Huh, it's all great fun.

I keep reliving our wedding day, and of course the night we spent together. I can't wait to wake up in your arms again. Until I can write again, please don't forget I love you with all my heart. One day, I will be home and our life together can start.

Always yours,

Freddie.

Alice clutched the letter to her chest. A sob escaped as tears ran down her cheeks. He was alive and with Charles. She laughed and cried at the same time. They were safe. No one had heard from Robert and no one mentioned it, for fear of upsetting their mother, or starting their father on a rant about how he would be too busy to write. They had to keep hoping he was safe, at least until a telegram arrived to tell them otherwise. Alice shook her head. She had watched the boy who delivered the bad news rest his bike against railings, knock, leave the telegram, quickly run back to his bicycle and pedal away. Before the war, he would have waited to see if a response was needed, but not anymore. She pulled the letter away from her, silently giving thanks it was not a telegram. She stared at Freddie's scrawled handwriting. She chuckled, likening it to a spider crawling across the page, but she didn't care. It was her letter, to be cherished forever. She pulled it towards her body and hugged it. A smile slowly formed on her lips as she wondered whether she should read the letter to their baby, and whether she should tell Freddie he was going to be a father. Doctors first, decisions later.

*

Alice drove the ambulance up to the arch of Victorian Station. Her heart was pounding. Her fingers adjusted the stiff belt around her calf-length, khaki coat. She had accompanied her mother there many times, to give the wounded soldiers cups of tea and soup. She'd never spoken to any of them. Her job was to pour the hot liquid into the cups. Alice trembled as she remembered the shock at seeing so many broken young men, some more lucid than others, their faces weather-beaten and lined from their experiences. Their boots and coats were caked in dried mud from the trenches. She had soon grown used to the stench of unwashed bodies; it no longer made her retch. Her mother had shown care and compassion, giving a few kind words to reassure them they were home now and would be well looked after. Some didn't want to talk. Some couldn't talk.

Perhaps signing up for this had been a mistake; this was more Lily's type of thing than hers. The initial excitement she'd felt about being a policewoman and talking to people on the streets was being fulfilled.

Freddie and her brothers leapt into her mind. She closed her eyes. Wouldn't she have wanted someone to help them, someone to be brave? Her mother had been brave, listening to their stories of the horrors they'd seen and the shock of seeing the men next to them blown up. Sarah never once mentioned that she had two sons and a son-in-law fighting. Alice shook her head; she wasn't as strong as her mother. The stories had kept her awake at night. Her mother told her to try and detach herself in some way. She had no choice, if she was going to survive looking after the soldiers.

Alice parked and took a couple of deep breaths, trying to stop her chest from pounding. She was on her own now; her mother wasn't there to make up for what she lacked. 'Come on, you can do it.' She took another deep breath and got out of the vehicle. A dog barking startled Alice, as a car sputtered into life behind her. *But this isn't just handing out drinks*, the tortured voice in her head screamed back at her. *You'd want someone to be nice to the people you loved. Stop thinking so much and get on with it.* She nodded, but didn't notice the lady nodding back as she walked past. Alice painted on her best smile and stepped onto the station concourse. Thick grey smoke billowed from the trains, swirling around in the air. It would linger on her clothes long after she had left the station.

'Hey fellas, now that's what we've been missing, beautiful ladies with a beautiful smile.' A soldier grinned.

Alice flushed with colour as she turned to look at him. His leg was covered in a bandage, spattered with mud, and blood was starting to seep through.

'Damn these bandages. I can't see,' another one shouted out. 'Describe her to me.'

Alice lifted her chin and took another couple of steps.

'She's a cracker.'

A tiny voice came from behind her. 'Please tell us you're here to help us, miss.'

Alice turned to see another man lying on a stretcher. 'Yes, I am,' she whispered.

'Don't let these men frighten you. They're just glad to be back in dear old blighty and to see a friendly face.'

Alice nodded, before taking another deep breath. 'All right.' She raised her voice a little.

'You need to speak up, sweetheart; we can't hear you up this end,' a mysterious voice called out. 'Especially Private Tanner; he's deaf.' Everyone laughed.

Alice blushed.

'Don't be embarrassed, love. It's just our humour. It's either laugh or shoot ourselves.'

Alice cleared her throat. 'I'm going to be taking you all to Charing Cross Hospital, which is just off The Strand. I can't take you all at once, so I'll have to assess the urgency. Do you understand?'

'You can assess my urgency any time you like, love.'

Colour crept up Alice's neck as the soldiers all laughed.

*

The girls sat in the plush surroundings of Café Monico, in Regent Street. The constant buzz of conversation filled the room. The waitresses, wearing black dresses covered with white aprons, edged with wide frills and a white cap, moved around the room like a well-rehearsed dance troupe.

'I love this place.' Victoria looked around her. 'Although I'm not sure I like seeing myself in the arched mirrors on the wall.' She patted the bun nestling at the nape of her neck.

Molly followed her lead and looked around her. 'It does feel very grand, probably too grand for me.'

Alice laughed. 'Nothing's too grand for us, Molly Cooper.'

Molly raised her voice a little. 'It's obviously a popular place.'

Alice looked through the spirals of smoke that reached up to join the cloud above their heads. 'That's because of their chocolate cake.'

'Hmm, it is lovely.' Molly fidgeted in her seat and straightened her light blue, three-quarter-length jacket, before loosening the wide belt that pinched in her waist. 'Don't you just love the shorter skirts?' Molly giggled.' My father went berserk when he first saw me wearing the calf length. He thought I was turning into a woman of the night.'

The girls laughed as one.

'That sounds about right. Your father sounds as bad as mine.' Alice smiled. 'And yet I always thought of him as being more relaxed about things.'

Molly tilted her head in thought. 'I suppose he is, except when it comes to his daughter.'

The waitress brought over the tray of tea things, carefully placing the blue floral china crockery in front of them. She bobbed before she turned and walked out of view.

'I'm pleased to say you look a little better today, Alice. A couple of months ago, I thought you were on your way out.' Molly laughed. 'You'll hate me for saying this, but I think you've even put on weight.' She held up her hand to stop Alice from talking. 'I wanted to say you look so much better for it.'

Alice laughed, raising her eyebrows. 'Look at you, holding your hands up to stop me from talking. Only my father gets away with that.'

Victoria smiled as she opened the lid of the teapot

and placed the teaspoon inside, watching the hot liquid swirl around as she stirred it. Listening to them made her realise how much she had missed their company. Shame consumed her when she thought about the dreadful things she'd yelled at Alice, that day.

Molly laughed. 'Sorry, but I knew you weren't going to let me finish.'

'I can't imagine Alice, or anybody else for that matter, being able to stop you in mid-sentence.' Victoria giggled.

Molly watched the tea turn a lovely shade of brown as the leaves brewed. 'Very funny, Vicky.'

'Don't call me Vicky It's Victoria. I was named after the great queen.'

Alice sighed. 'Will you two stop squabbling and just pour the tea. Our cake will be here soon.'

Victoria removed the spoon and replaced the lid of the teapot. 'Shall I pour?'

Molly looked at Victoria and laughed. 'Go on then, you be mum.'

Alice looked at her two dear friends and smiled mischievously. 'I think you'll find, that'll be me.'

Both girls looked across at Alice, confusion running across their faces.

Molly folded her arms in front of her. 'What?'

Victoria moved her hand away from the china teapot. 'You can pour if you want. I only offered because I'd been stirring it.'

Alice laughed. 'No silly, I'm going to be a mum.'

The girls' jaws slackened as they tried to take in the information.

Molly's hand grabbed Alice's arm. 'You're going to be a mum, as in Freddie's going to be a dad?' Her frown deepened with every word she said.

Alice's laughter got louder. She placed her hand over her mouth. 'Yes, I'm going to have a baby. Freddie and I are having a baby.'

Laughter erupted around the table. Other customers looked across, whispering to each other.

'Sshh,' Alice whispered. 'We're getting some disapproving looks.'

Molly looked around the room. 'I know there's a war on, but when good news is announced, we need to make the most of it.' She spoke loudly, not caring everyone could hear her. 'God knows, we've all had enough bad news.'

The waitress appeared, carrying three tea plates, each holding a large slice of chocolate cake.

'Oh, this looks delicious.' Molly gazed adoringly at the plate that had been placed in front of her, accompanied by a silver cake fork.

'It certainly does, and I think you'll find it tastes delicious too.' Victoria picked up the fork, but didn't touch her cake. She looked across at Alice. 'This is really exciting news. How long have you known?'

Alice stared pensively at her cake, before looking up.

'About a month, but you're the only ones I've told, so you must keep it to yourselves.'

'Haven't you even told your mother or Lily?' Victoria's eyes widened as the words sunk in.

'No, I will, but I wanted to hug it to myself for a while.' Alice laughed. 'It sounds stupid, but I didn't realise I was pregnant. It was Mrs Headley who told me, and the doctor confirmed it a couple of days later.'

'Mrs Headley?' Molly arched her eyebrows.

'Eat your cake.' Alice laughed. 'It's a long story, but she delivered a letter from Freddie and guessed I was pregnant, mainly due to my sickness and lack of appetite.'

Molly stabbed at her cake. 'I can't believe it. Have you told Freddie?'

Alice shook her head. 'No, I haven't told anyone.'

'Oh yes, you said.' Molly put the fork laden with cake into her mouth. She momentarily closed her eyes, before putting her hand in front of her mouth. 'Mmm, this is delicious, so light and chocolatey.' She opened her eyes and lowered her hand, before continuing to eat the sponge.

Victoria smiled at Molly before turning to Alice. 'I assume you're going to let Freddie know.'

Alice shrugged her shoulders. 'To be honest, I can't decide.'

'What?' the girls responded in unison.

Alice shook her head. 'I don't want him to have the

distraction of worrying about me and a baby. It's more important his thoughts are about surviving and coming home safe.'

Molly shrugged her shoulders, before tilting her head to one side. 'I can see what you are saying, but don't you think he has a right to know?'

Alice sighed. 'Obviously, and in normal circumstances I'd be shouting it from the roof tops, but I want him to come home; that's more important.'

'I can see both sides of the argument and it's a difficult decision to make.' Victoria picked up the teapot and poured the hot amber liquid into a silver tea strainer, which she rested on each cup in turn. 'You can add your own milk and sugar.' She put the heavy pot down on the iron stand and sat the strainer on a small silver dish.

Alice added a splash of milk to her tea. 'I beg you not to say anything to anyone until I've decided, one way or another.' She passed the jug to Molly.

'Your secret is safe with us, isn't it, Vicky'

Victoria raised her eyebrows. Molly laughed as she shook her head. 'It is. Not a word of it will pass my lips, that is until you say I can, and then I'll tell everyone.'

Molly looked from one to the other of her friends. 'Look at us all growing up. Does it scare you, Alice?'

'It did at first. I was plagued with thoughts of being on my own with a child.' Alice frowned. 'But there are lots of women in that situation, with several children, and they had theirs before war was even mentioned.'

Molly nodded. 'That's true; this war has torn families apart, and none of us chose it.'

Victoria looked at them both, her eyes glistening and her fork poised in mid-air. 'You have to live your life. In my experience, you never know when everything is going to be ripped away from you.'

'That's very true.' The girls spoke as one.

Victoria gave them both a watery smile. 'It's exciting news, Alice, and it'll certainly give us something else to focus on. I wonder if it'll be a girl or a boy?'

'I hope it's a girl.' Molly laughed. 'I don't want boys.'

Alice laughed. 'I don't think you have any say in it. You get what you get.'

Victoria giggled. 'Yes, you can't send it back you know.'

'I know. I'm just saying I'd prefer a girl. What about you, Alice?'

'I really don't mind, as long as everything's all right.' Alice sighed. 'It'll be a part of Freddie that I'll always have, no matter what.'

The girls nodded and each placed a piece of cake on their forks.

'Anyway.' A sheepish look crept across Molly's face. 'While we are confessing all, I've a secret to tell.'

There was a clatter of forks hitting the tea plates, the cake momentarily forgotten.

'What?' the girls chorused.

'Please don't tell us you're expecting a baby too,' Victoria said with a laugh.

Molly's bottom lip jutted out for a moment. 'I don't know what sort of girl you think I am, Victoria Appleton, but as I said to you once before, I'm not that sort.'

The girls laughed at her indignation.

'Victoria's only playing. Come on then, share your news; it's all very exciting.'

Molly frowned at Alice. 'I hope you think so when you find out.'

'You make it sound very intriguing.' Victoria picked up her cup and sipped the strong dark brown liquid, before carefully replacing it on the matching saucer.

'Alice, I'm telling you in a public place, so you can't be too mad with me.'

'Come on, spill it. It can't be that bad.' Alice wondered what it could be that had Molly so concerned.

Molly took a deep breath. 'Since your wedding, I've been writing to Charles.' Her words tumbled over each other, in their bid to escape.

Victoria smiled. 'Is that it? That's a lovely thing to do. I thought it was going to be something terrible.'

'I must admit that so did I,' Alice laughed. 'You did give it quite a build-up.'

Molly picked up her cup. 'I thought you'd be cross. I know how protective you are of Charles,' she mumbled into her tea, before taking a sip.

Alice pushed the plate aside, the cake hardly touched. 'Molly, you and Victoria are like my family. I'm not going to be cross because you're writing to him.'

Molly smiled. 'We chatted quite a lot at the wedding...'

Victoria laughed. 'I noticed you two were getting cosy at Russell Square.'

Molly gave Victoria a scathing look, before continuing. 'Anyway, he asked me to write to him and I said I would.'

Alice nodded. 'That's good, it'll help remind him of home.' She hesitated, but decided not to mention that she already knew because Freddie had told her in his letter. 'Make sure you don't tell him he's going to be an uncle, because he'll tell Freddie.'

'I won't. That's your news to tell, when you see fit.' Molly looked at Alice's plate. 'Are you going to eat that cake?'

Alice laughed. 'No, you can have it.'

'It's a shame to waste it.' Molly picked up the plate and placed it in front of her, on top of her empty one. 'So, Victoria,' Molly spoke slowly, giving great emphasis to the name. 'While secrets are being told, do you have any you want to share?'

'No.' The answer came quickly.

Molly looked at Alice, then back at Victoria. 'That was a very quick answer. Too quick, I'd say.'

'No, I don't have any secrets. None.' Victoria looked

down at the remains of her cake.

Alice smiled. 'Who was it that said "thou doth protest too much", or something like that?'

Molly shrugged her shoulders and yawned, letting Alice know this wasn't the subject under discussion. 'Who cares? I want to know Victoria's secret.'

Victoria sighed. 'Neither of you will like it.'

'Ah, so there is a secret. I knew it.' Molly nodded with satisfaction.

'All right, Sherlock, but just for the record, you didn't know, you guessed.' Victoria gave Molly a scathing look.

'I don't care about that. I was right, and that's all that matters.' Molly beamed at Victoria.

'Anyway,' Alice interrupted. 'What are you doing that's so bad, you think we aren't going to like it?'

Victoria coughed to clear her throat. Her whole mouth was parched. She picked up her cup and emptied the contents, hoping it would give her the courage to face their disapproval. The chink as she placed the cup back on its saucer was lost in the lively café. She took a deep breath, but didn't look up. 'I'm writing to Ted Marsden.'

'Isn't that the little scumbag that ran out on you when you needed him most?' Molly's words burst out, her cheeks turning crimson.

It was Alice's turn to raise her hand, to stop Molly from talking. 'How long have you been writing to him?'

Victoria looked sheepishly from one to the other, before looking back down at her plate. 'Since that first letter I opened in church,' she whispered. 'Molly, he regrets running away. He begged for my forgiveness. He joined the army, so he has been at the front since day one.'

Molly sat open-mouthed, staring at Victoria. 'Well, you've managed to do what many have tried and failed to do, make me speechless.'

'Well now, that is a good thing.' Alice laughed, letting her smile gradually fade away.

'To be honest, I think the first letter was because he thought he might not make it back home and wanted forgiveness for letting me down. I never mentioned it, because it was obvious both of you wouldn't approve and, if I'm being honest, I wanted to write to him.'

Alice reached over and rested her hand on Victoria's. 'You shouldn't worry about what others think. You've to do what's right for you, and you alone.'

Victoria closed her eyes for a moment. 'Apparently, he ran because he was scared and didn't know how to deal with the death of my parents, let alone handle the thought of taking on two young people as well.'

Molly nodded. 'I suppose that's understandable.'

Victoria glanced at Molly through watery eyes. 'If my letters can help him to survive, isn't that a good thing?'

'Of course it is.' Molly sighed. 'What concerns me is that you still love him and I don't want him hurting you all over again.'

Alice nodded. 'I must admit, I do agree with Molly, but you clearly want to give it another chance so, as your friends, we should support you. We will, won't we, Molly?'

'That goes without saying.' Molly closed her eyes for a moment, before looking at Victoria. 'I know neither of you had any time for Tony, but I was smitten and you both allowed me to be. Deep down, I knew I was never going to be his wife.' She looked across at Alice. 'I know he fancied you.'

Alice opened her mouth to speak, but Molly held up her hand again.

'It wasn't your fault, Alice. I know you never encouraged him. Blimey, you were too busy being smitten with Freddie, but my point is that you allowed it and accepted you'd be there when it all fell apart, which it was always doomed to do.' Molly continued, 'What I'm trying to say is, in my own clumsy fashion, if it's what you want Victoria, we'll all be there for you. Make no mistake.'

Alice shook her head. 'I couldn't have said it better myself.' She lowered her eyes, hoping Victoria wasn't reopening old wounds.

Chapter 16

June 1915

The clicking of knitting needles stopped. Sarah frowned as she looked down at the pattern she was trying to follow; she should have stuck to socks. Humming quietly to the Irving Berlin record playing on the gramophone, she looked across the sitting room at Alice, her pale features concentrating as her needles moved back and forth. 'You've got quicker at knitting. I think I'm the opposite.' Sarah folded the wool around the needles and laid it on her lap. 'Lily works at quite a speed too.'

Alice laughed, not taking her eyes off the wool wrapped around her fingers and the needles moving in and out of each stitch. 'I don't think you've got slower, Mother. It's because you've decided to try and knit something more complicated than a pair of socks.'

Sarah smiled at her daughter's concentration. 'Hmm, maybe I got too ambitious with it.' She glanced down at her pattern again.

Alice pushed her stitches further down and poked the needles into the ball of wool, before laying them on the small table next to her. 'Perhaps you should try knitting booties.'

'Hmm.' Sarah carried on studying the pattern abbreviations. 'Why would I do that?'

Alice patiently watched her mother, waiting for the penny to drop. She couldn't resist a smile when her mother's head suddenly jerked up.

'Ohhh, ohhh, ohhh, my goodness.' Sarah's jaw dropped, her eyes wide as they focussed on Alice. 'Are you saying what I think you are saying?'

Alice laughed. 'That depends on what you think I am saying.' She couldn't resist a little tease. 'If you think I'm saying I'm expecting your grandchild at the end of the summer, then yes, I'm saying what you think I'm saying.' Her lasts words were drowned out by Sarah's laughter.

'What's going on in here?' Lily walked into the sitting room, carrying her police hat under her arm. The navy jacket to her uniform was unbuttoned, revealing her white shirt, navy blue tie and the top of her blue calf length skirt. She was grinning from ear to ear. 'There's an unusual amount of laughter coming from you, Mother.'

'It's wonderful, wonderful news. Your sister's expecting a baby.' Sarah jumped up and wrapped her arms around Alice. 'Isn't it wonderful, Lily? There's going to be a baby in the house.'

Lily laughed as her eyes followed her mother, who

was bouncing around the room.

Sarah's eyes sparkled as she clapped her hands together. 'I can't believe it. It'll be lovely to hear a baby again, but hopefully not too much crying.' She beamed.

Alice watched her mother's excitement growing, fearing she'd burst at any moment.

Sarah bounced from one foot to the other, before hugging herself tight. Her fingers disappeared into the soft folds of her silk blouse. 'Oh Alice, there's nothing better than a child gurgling and laughing, let alone the smell of talcum powder.'

Lily laughed as she walked over to Alice and gave her sister a squeeze. 'Congratulations to you and Freddie.' She paused for a second as the news sunk in. 'Oh goodness, I've just realised I'm going to be an aunt.' She smiled at Alice. 'Does that mean I now have to become more responsible?'

Alice chuckled at her sister. 'Lily, you do know you are standing in the sitting room, dressed in a policewoman's uniform?' She grinned as her sister looked down towards her feet. 'I don't think you can become any more responsible than that.'

'I guess you're right. Somehow, when I wasn't looking, I became respectable.'

'Lily, you are funny.' Alice laughed. 'You were always respectable, it's just that now you've something to focus on.'

'Who's got something to focus on?' Luke's deep voice

resonated around the room.

Sarah turned to face him. Her smile faded. 'Sorry, I didn't hear the front door.'

Luke frowned. 'That is hardly surprising with the racket you three are making in here.'

Alice stood up. 'It's not a racket, Father, it's called laughter. That's something we used to do a lot when we were children, do you remember?'

Luke stared hard at his eldest daughter, wondering what had happened to bring out a side of her he had never seen before. He always expected backchat from Lily, but Alice…

'Sorry, Luke.' Sarah took a deep breath and shook her head at Lily, before grabbing Alice's hand. 'But Alice has some wonderful news for us.'

'Yes, Father.' Lily stared hard at him, daring him to give them a difficult time for laughing. 'We're just happy and excited.' He glared at the three of them in turn, but they each held their position. 'We don't have much to be happy about these days, so we have to make the most of any good news we may get.'

Alice smiled at Lily's words, so reminiscent of Molly's.

Luke walked over to the sideboard with the silver tray sitting on it. Turning over a small crystal tumbler, he pulled the stopper from the glass decanter. In his haste, the lid chinked against the top. He poured himself a whisky, gulping it down without a backward glance.

'Sit down, Alice,' Lily whispered, pulling a chair close, to sit down next to her. She placed her hand on her arm. 'Have you told Freddie yet? Is he pleased?'

Alice looked across at her father, with his back to the room. He stood rigid, in the same brown suit he wore every day. She wondered if he had a wardrobe full of identical suits. His dark hair was longer than usual, curling over the edge of his collar. Heat began to rise in her face. She searched the caverns of her mind, trying to understand why he hadn't asked what the news was, why there was no interest at all, but there was nothing. She jutted out her chin and clenched her fists.

'Alice.' Lily nudged her. 'Is Freddie pleased with the news?' Clenching her jaw, she followed her eye line. 'Alice?'

Alice took a deep breath, turning her head to face her sister. 'I haven't told him yet.'

'Why not?' Sarah whispered.

Alice's lips lifted at one of the corners. 'I just want him to concentrate on staying safe. I don't want him to have any distractions.' She closed her eyes for a moment. Freddie was there, enveloping her in a bear hug. The tears were like pins pricking the back of her eyelids. There was no doubt he'd worry about her. No, she was certain, the news had to wait. She opened her eyes, stunned to see nothing had changed. Her father hadn't even turned to face the room.

Sarah nodded.

Lily shrugged her shoulders. 'I can see what you're saying, but it might keep him going, give him something to look forward to.'

A humourless laugh escaped from Alice, the fun of her announcement long gone. 'I hope having me waiting for him will be incentive enough.'

'Of course, I didn't mean—'

'I know, Lily, I'm sorry.' Alice gave Lily a watery smile. 'I've decided not to tell him until he comes home.'

Lily nodded.

'For that reason, you can't tell Charles or Robert either. I'm sorry.'

Sarah and Lily nodded as one.

'Well, we've a lot to do before the baby arrives, so that'll keep us busy.' Sarah smiled at Alice. 'Everything will be all right, you'll see.'

*

The Gentlemen's Club was as lively as ever; the war hadn't taken away the men's need to relax and unwind. It was predominantly filled with older men, with most youngsters having enlisted as officers, fighting for their king and country. The talk was of money being made, as women took over jobs for less pay. Some had talked of their shock at how hard the women worked, and how capable they were. The savvy businessmen among them had been happy for their factories to be converted into controlled establishments, making guns, wagons and shells for the war. Luke shook his head. He had been slow on the uptake. With the right premises and investment, he could have made a pretty penny out of the war. He shouldn't have stayed so long in Sandringham, allowing family issues to fill his thoughts.

Raucous cheers could be heard as Luke walked towards the Card Room, where money was being won and lost. He had never been a gambler himself, but had witnessed hundreds of pounds being forfeited on the turn of a card. He looked through the doorway as he walked past. The afternoon sun shone through the large windows, fighting its way through the haze of cigarette smoke. The green table tops had playing cards scattered haphazardly around them. Men were on their feet, patting each other on the back. Laughter rang out as someone was handed a cigar. He shook his head and continued walking along the landing, ordering a coffee from the passing steward, as he entered the library. He looked around before claiming a seat. Edward waved from his favourite position in the corner, by a window. A newspaper was folded on the table in front of him.

Luke sighed; he had the family do-gooder with him. He painted on his smile and walked over to them. 'Afternoon, Edward, George.'

'Afternoon to you too, Luke.' George looked up at him. 'Pull up a chair. I haven't seen you since the wedding. How's everyone?'

Luke shrugged his shoulders. 'I will be glad to have Robert back home. Dealing with women all the time is quite exhausting.' He nodded to the steward, as he placed his coffee in front of him.

George frowned and looked from Luke to Edward. 'I expect they're worried about their loved ones.' He paused. 'Emily gets herself into a terrible state almost every time Harry's name is mentioned. She can't bear the thought of anything happening to him, let alone the things he might be witnessing.'

Edward nodded. 'I know what you mean. He and Charles are so young.'

George nodded. 'I must admit I feel exactly the same, but I hold it together better than Emily, bless her.'

Luke shook his head. 'You should be proud. I am. I think Alice takes after me, because she's not as emotional as the rest of them.' He picked up the silver spoon, the metal cold against his fingers, and began stirring his coffee. The steam spiralled up, only to disappear into the air around him.

George and Edward looked across at Luke. Edward shook his head as he watched him replace the spoon onto the saucer and pick up the cup. 'I'm not sure that's true. She just doesn't voice it, and that probably isn't very good for her.'

Luke shrugged his shoulders. 'Whatever the reason, it suits me.' He held the cup for a few moments, smelling the rich aroma, before taking a sip of the hot liquid.

'Hmm, that's strong.' He placed the cup back on its saucer. 'I must say, they do a lovely coffee here.'

Edward stared hard at his son-in-law, wondering what Sarah had ever seen in him. He cleared his throat, remembering he'd vowed years ago to never get involved in their relationship, unless invited to. 'George and I were just catching up with the news.'

Luke frowned. He hoped it wasn't more family news; it was all so tiresome. 'News?'

George arched his eyebrows as he looked down at Luke's coffee cup. 'Yes, we were just talking about the Lusitania being sunk and all the people dying. It must've been quite frightful for them.'

Luke nodded. 'Yes, I must admit that was a shock. The Zeppelins bombing London overnight as well. Apparently, they looked quite spectacular in the sky. I'm not sure how many were injured or died though.'

Edward thinned his lips. 'It brings it home, doesn't it? We now have a couple of beds in our basement, so when the police come through on their bicycles, ringing their bells, we move down there until we get the all clear.'

George nodded. 'We were thinking of doing the same thing.'

Edward gave a little laugh. 'Jane thinks we should just sleep down there every night and that would save moving. I think Victoria told her at the wedding that she and Daisy now permanently sleep in the basement.'

George lifted his hand to summon a steward.

'Victoria's got a good head on her shoulders, but then I suppose she's had to grow up quickly, providing for her brother and sister.' The man appeared by the chair in seconds. 'Edward, would you like a coffee?'

'Yes, I think I will, thanks.'

'Luke?'

'I'll have a top up, thank you.'

George looked up at the steward. 'That'll be three coffees then, please.'

The steward gave a small bow and turned to walk away.

Edward's fingers formed a steeple and rested on his chin. 'Well, Jane certainly thought sleeping in the basement was a good idea; perhaps we should listen to the youngsters more often.'

Luke's lip curled. 'If you start doing that, it will be the beginning of the end.' The steward appeared at their table and placed three coffees in front of them, before silently turning and walking away. 'I suppose we are lucky to still have stewards here. It's a wonder they haven't brought in women to do their jobs as well.' Luke let out a humourless laugh. 'That would be something wouldn't it, having the gentlemen's club, somewhere to escape the women in your life, only to be served by more cackling women, probably blathering on about babies and children.'

Edward took a deep breath and slowly counted to ten. 'I think you'll find most men come here to do business, not to escape the women in their lives.'

Luke sneered. 'What's your excuse then? You have long retired from the business world.'

Anger bubbled away and Edward could feel his heart pounding in his chest. 'I come here to discuss things that either wouldn't be of interest to Jane, or would frighten her, like the war.' He paused for a moment. 'Not that I need to justify myself to you.'

George shook his head. 'Luke, there are times when you sound quite bitter and yet you've had a good life, thanks to the Gettin family.'

Colour rushed into Luke's face. 'Thanks to the Gettins? I'll have you know, I have worked hard for what I have.'

'Nobody is disputing you've worked hard since joining the family firm, but you were given that opportunity and when you married Sarah, that set you up for life.' George took a breath. 'The house came with the bride, along with a dowry, so yes, I do think you owe your good life to the Gettins.'

The do-gooder of the family had struck. The duel gauntlet had been thrown down and Luke willingly picked it up. 'Unlike your good self, I suppose.'

George laughed. 'That's right, unlike my good self. I had already made my money and I didn't want or ask for anything from Henry Gettin, apart from his permission to marry Emily, and maybe his acceptance of my bright shirts at the time.'

Edward chuckled. 'I remember them. Cousin William couldn't get his head around your taste in clothes.' He paused and looked Luke straight in the eye. 'I think you'll find you're the only one out of the three of us that didn't marry for love.'

Luke fidgeted in his seat. He needed to buy himself some time. He could feel Edward's eyes boring into his soul. He sighed. 'It would seem I am going to be a grandfather.'

Laughter burst out of Edward and George. There was a chorus of shush from around the room.

Edward stretched out his hand to shake Luke's. 'What excellent news. You wait, when Jane finds out we're going to be great-grandparents.'

George reached out and patted Luke on the back. 'Congratulations, it's an exciting time.'

Luke frowned as he let his gaze wander from one to the other. 'Yes, let's hope Freddie gets back in one piece.'

*

Alice and Victoria strolled along Bloomsbury Street, the June sunshine beating down on them. The fringed parasol did little to alleviate the brightness that sparkled off every surface. The tassels' only movement was the bobbing that came with their footsteps. The air was still. Dogs could be heard barking in the distance, mingling with the usual clatter of horses pulling carts, interrupted by car engines firing into life. The sun had brought the children outside. Some raised their voices as they played their war games, arguing who would be the enemy. It seemed no one wanted to be a German. Men dressed in army uniforms often stopped to talk to them. Squeals of delight carried from the gardens and could be heard above the birds singing. People smiled and nodded as they walked past. Muted conversations could be heard from open windows. The sunshine had definitely lifted people's spirits.

Victoria glanced across at Alice. 'Molly appears to have come through the worst of her grief.'

'I hope so. The guilt was ripping her apart.'

'Yes, I know.' Victoria sighed. 'I think writing to Charles must be helping.' She paused. 'I get the impression she writes to him every day.'

Alice smiled. 'I never realised she was writing that often, but I'm pleased for them both. Charles is a happy and uplifting character, so they're probably helping each other.' She pulled her handkerchief from the pocket of her pale blue, ankle-length dress. 'Is it because I'm carrying an extra person around with me, or is it as hot as I think it is? My body is sprouting leaks everywhere.' She ran the thin piece of lace across her forehead.

'No, my friend, it's hot.' Victoria laughed. 'And it's only the beginning of the month.'

Alice groaned. 'I know we shouldn't moan, especially

after the greyness of winter, but I feel like I'm going to die in this heat.'

Victoria frowned as she looked across at Alice's red face. 'Are you drinking plenty of water?'

'Yes. Who'd be pregnant in this heat?'

Victoria squinted as she looked ahead. 'Hopefully, it won't be this hot all month.'

Alice groaned again. 'What a thought, and I haven't made it to August yet.'

'Never mind.' Victoria beamed. 'When you're cuddling your little bundle of joy, you'll think it was all worth it.'

'Let's hope you're right.' Alice smiled. 'I know one thing though.'

'What's that?'

Alice laughed. 'I've got to stop moaning.' She took a couple of short breaths. 'I hope you don't mind me asking, but how are you managing now, with Daisy in the police?'

Victoria looked down at the ground, purposely slowing her pace as a line of ants distracted her. They carried a crumb on their backs, which looked ten times bigger than them, as they marched across her path. 'Of course I don't mind you asking.' She looked up and smiled. 'Daisy loves being a policewoman and seems to get on well with everyone.' She paused. 'I never did thank Lily for taking her along with her that day.'

Alice smiled. 'I'm sure there's no need, but you know,

Lily seems to love it too.'

'Well, it certainly changed things for us.' Victoria paused, but only for a moment. 'Daisy has no trouble getting up and going to work. She seems to love what she does and most of her earnings go into the family pot.'

'It sounds like she's a different person.'

Victoria laughed. 'A reformed character, without doing the prison time.'

Alice chuckled. 'I'm really pleased. You certainly seem to have been happier.' Alice held up her hand. 'I know you won't be happy until Stephen comes home, but you definitely look healthy and like a weight has been lifted from your shoulders, so that makes me happy.'

They walked on in silence for a moment.

'I've been thinking about putting some paint or paper on the walls, before Stephen returns, a sort of welcome home present for him.' Victoria lowered her eyes and cleared her throat. 'You know, I've been meaning to thank you.'

Alice frowned. 'Thank me for what?'

The corner of Victoria's lip lifted a little, wrinkling the side of her nose. 'Over the years, you've been a wonderful friend to me. I definitely couldn't have got through half of it without you or your family.'

Alice squeezed her friend's arm. 'Trust me, we're good friends to each other. I've made mistakes, for which I'm truly sorry, but it always came from a place of love and was meant well at the time.'

'I know, but none of that matters now. We have a little one that we can focus our attention on.' Victoria laughed. 'In between knitting for the soldiers, I'm also knitting bonnets, booties and little cardigans.' She giggled. 'You should see them; they are so tiny.' She held up her hand and positioned her thumb and forefinger about two inches apart.

'It's scary isn't it?' Alice's eyes widened. 'Can you imagine me in charge of a baby?'

'You'll be fine, and your mother is on hand to help, bless her.'

They walked on, each lost in their thoughts about the baby that was on its way. Alice watched a boy cycling on the footpath. She could hear the squeak of the brakes before his feet hit the ground, stumbling because the bike had come to a complete standstill. He leant it up against the railings of her home. Her hand dropped away from the parasol handle. She stopped, rooted to the spot and gripped Victoria's arm.

'What? What is it?' Victoria's voice rose. 'Are you in pain, has something happened?'

Alice silently lifted her arm and pointed to the bike leaning against the railings, and the boy standing at her front door.

'Oh dear,' Victoria whispered. She quickly bent down and picked up the parasol, which was lying upended on the pavement. 'Come, we must get you home.' She took Alice's arm and virtually pulled her along, fighting the urge to run in the opposite direction. Fear gripped her chest and her mind bounced around, in its bid to escape the turmoil that was taking over. She realised leaving her friend at the house wasn't an option for her. Everyone knew it wasn't good news when a boy on a bike came calling. It was just a question of who the telegram was for. Which one of them was going to be lost from them, Robert, Charles or Freddie?

*

'Missing.' The words repeated themselves over and over in Alice's mind. She rocked back and forth in her armchair. What does that mean? Is he dead, but they haven't found his body? Is he a prisoner of war? The front door thudded shut. She prayed it was her mother, and not her father.

Victoria walked in carrying a glass of water. 'Here, sip this.' She frowned at her. 'Your father has just walked in. He didn't say anything, but he raised his eyebrows when he saw me.'

Alice groaned. She was going to be in trouble for opening the telegram but, for once, there had been no self-control. She stared down at the crumpled paper in her grip, wishing she had left it alone.

'It may not be as bad as you think.' Victoria thrust

the glass in her direction. 'Doesn't it say he may have got separated from his regiment?' She knelt down beside her. 'Come on, sip this.' She paused, glancing over at the sideboard. 'Perhaps you should have something stronger, for shock. You've lost your colour. Maybe a drop of your father's whisky would be more appropriate.'

A feeble smile played at the corners of Alice's lips. 'The water's fine, thank you.' Aware that Victoria was examining her, she took the glass and sipped the lukewarm liquid.

'What's occurring here?' Luke's steely tone from the sitting room doorway caused Alice to jerk in her seat, spilling water onto her skirt. He stared from one girl to the other. 'What's happening, Alice?'

Alice took a deep breath. She pushed her hands on the arms of the chair and tried to stand up. Victoria pressed her fingers on Alice's shoulder, preventing her from moving.

'Mr Taylor.' Victoria stood upright and straightened her shoulders. 'Alice has had a funny turn, probably to do with the baby. I expect she'll be all right, but she needs some peace and quiet.'

Luke nodded and turned, walking into the hallway. Victoria could hear Sarah and Luke's mumbled voices, followed by the clicking of heels on the tiled floor. Seconds later, Sarah dashed into the sitting room, her black skirt trailing behind her in the breeze she caused.

'Alice, are you all right?' Sarah frowned as she rushed

to her daughter's side. 'Your father said you had a funny turn or something.'

'I'm fine,' Alice whispered. Her eyes concentrated on the telegram she was clutching. 'Mother, you might want to sit down.'

'Why?' Sarah didn't move. 'What's happened?' Fear ran across her face; she closed her eyes for a second. 'What's happened?'

'Charles is missing,' Alice whispered. She held up the telegram for her mother to read.

Victoria guided Sarah to an armchair. Returning, she unfolded Alice's fingers from the paper. Releasing it, she passed it to Sarah. 'It does say he may have got separated from his regiment or be a prisoner of war, so he could be on his way home.' She tried to sound optimistic, but wasn't succeeding.

Sarah stared down at the creased paper that was sitting on her lap. 'When did it arrive?'

Alice gave her mother a watery glance and closed her eyes, squeezing them tight.

Victoria cleared her throat. 'We saw the boy at the front door. He didn't wait for a reply; I believe the envelope is marked in some way, so they know whether to wait or not.' She gave a nervous laugh. 'Sorry, I'm rambling.'

'Mother, I panicked and opened it.' Alice paused. She sucked in the air around her. 'I'm sorry, it wasn't addressed to me, but I saw a telegram and I suppose I couldn't wait. Fear took hold.'

The telegram held Sarah transfixed for a moment. 'Does your father know?'

Alice shook her head.

'That one will be my fault.' Victoria fidgeted from one foot to the other. 'I'm afraid it was me who told him about the funny turn. Alice obviously knew she had done wrong, opening something that wasn't addressed to her, and I was just trying to protect her.'

Sarah nodded but didn't look up. 'You're a good friend, Victoria.'

Colour rose in Victoria's cheeks. 'Charles will be all right. We have to stay positive, for all of them.'

Sarah stood up and walked over to the window. She watched everyone going about their business as normal. 'I don't know whether we should tell your father or Lily.' Her chest was suddenly in a vice-like grip. A groan escaped as she tried to take some deep breaths, but the pain was too great.

Alice jumped up, all self-pity forgotten, as she strode to her mother's side. 'Are you all right? Come and sit down.' She put her arms around her waist and took her back to the chair, gently lowering her into the seat. Victoria, can you ask Mrs Headley to find my father?'

Victoria nodded and swept out of the room, to return only minutes later.

Luke followed Victoria through the doorway. 'What's happening?' He frowned and knelt down by his wife's feet. 'What's wrong?' He took her thin hand in his.

'I can't... I can't catch my breath.' Sarah gasped, all colour now drained from her face.

'Try Sarah, you must try.' Luke's eyes darted over her. 'It might be wind. Try giving a little cough; that might clear it.' He moved to the side of her and rubbed her back.

'It's passing.' Sarah gulped for air and lent back in the chair.

Luke stroked his wife's hand and watched as colour began to return to her cheeks. 'What has happened to bring this on?' He turned to look at Alice. 'Your mother isn't a strong woman and needs protecting at all costs.'

Alice frowned as she and Victoria exchanged glances. 'Father, there's been some news about Charles,' Alice ventured.

Luke stood up, giving Sarah a sideways glance, before taking a deep breath. 'Oh, what is it?'

Sarah held up the telegram. 'Charles is missing.'

He stared down at the words on the paper. His lips straightened into a thin line, almost disappearing from view. Luke looked down at his wife. 'You made him soft, Sarah.' He turned away and picked up a photo of his youngest son from the mantelpiece. Luke studied it for a moment; the boy was always smiling. 'Charles gets lost walking around the house.' He looked round and smiled at her. 'He'll turn up. He's like the proverbial bad penny; he won't be missing for long.'

Sarah eyes glistened as she nodded.

Luke knelt at her feet again. He took her hand and rested it between his palms. 'You have to keep your strength up, because the boys will need you when they return.'

Sarah took a deep breath. 'God will keep them safe; he has to,' she whispered. 'The thought of them not coming home again...'

'Try and stay positive, Mrs Taylor.' Victoria's energy had drained away. 'We must all pray for their safe return.'

Alice nodded. She didn't speak of Charles and Freddie sharing the same trench. She wasn't sure what it meant. Had Freddie told the army he was now married? Would she receive a telegram if Freddie was also missing or killed? Her head started to swim with unanswered questions.

Chapter 17

August 1915

Alice's feet ached as she walked along Charing Cross Road. She struggled to catch her breath in the early morning sunshine, longing for a wisp of a breeze. Her hand reached up and fluffed the bottom of her wavy hair; glad it was off her neck. In her mind, she had been brave to have her long hair cut off and hoped Freddie would like it when he got home. The new style meant it now sat just below her ears. The pearl droplet earrings swayed gently as she waddled along. The baby moved and her pink dress kicked outwards, giving her an unusual shape. She slowly moved her hand across her swollen stomach. There was no hiding that she was around seven months pregnant. She sighed, wishing Freddie was with her to share the excitement and the movement of their forthcoming child.

'Alice, wait,' Victoria boomed out behind her.

Alice stopped and slowly turned around, her features breaking into a smile. 'That was a little unladylike.'

Victoria laughed. 'Never mind, I don't think anyone noticed.'

'Oh trust me, someone would have done.' Alice smiled.

Victoria shrugged her shoulders. 'Why are you going to work?' She half ran the couple of steps towards Alice and placed her arm through hers. 'You look like you can hardly walk.'

'Mr Leadbetter said he'd find me a chair to sit on, if I could make it into work.' Alice frowned as she looked down at her feet. 'The problem is, my feet and ankles are swollen, so it makes walking a little uncomfortable.'

'All the more reason why you shouldn't be on your feet, if you ask me.' Victoria glared at her friend. 'This heat won't be helping, but I'm surprised your mother allowed you to leave the house, Mrs Leybourne.'

'Mrs Leybourne.' Alice laughed. 'You know, if I weren't pregnant, I could easily believe my wedding had been a dream.' She tightened her arms across the baby growing inside her. 'You know, I'm still sleeping in the same single bed, in the same drab room. It doesn't feel like anything has changed.'

Victoria bit down on her lip as she looked at her friend's watery gaze. 'It will. Freddie will be home soon and you'll set up home together, with your little son or daughter.'

Alice smiled. 'I'm saving every penny I can, so when he does get home, we can look for our own place. It'll be good for little Freddie or Freda.'

Victoria frowned. 'Is that what you're going to call

the baby?'

Alice laughed. 'I take it from that look, you don't like those names.'

Colour started to rise up Victoria's neck. 'No, no I wouldn't say that.'

'Well you're quite right.' Alice squinted in the sunlight. 'I haven't thought about names at all. I keep hoping Freddie will come home and we can choose together.'

Victoria nodded. 'He might. You never know, but I think you need to start thinking about some, just in case you have to decide.'

Alice nodded. 'I haven't heard from Freddie.' Her voice rose. 'I'm frightened something has happened to him and I haven't been told, because they don't know he got married.'

Victoria squeezed her friend's arm. 'Think about what you're saying, Alice; Freddie used to be a policeman, so I'm sure he's a stickler for paperwork.'

Alice gave a little laugh. 'I expect you're right.' She frowned and her chin trembled a little. 'But with Charles going missing, it has frightened me, because Freddie told me they were together.'

'Have you told Molly that Charles is missing?'

Alice shook her head. 'I didn't want to worry her. I think the letter-writing has meant they've grown quite close.' She sniffed. 'I find myself checking for him at the train stations, and asking at Charing Cross Hospital when I go there every night. I keep hoping he'll make his way home.'

Victoria nodded. 'I think you're right not to let Molly know, although she'll probably be pretty angry when she finds out.' Victoria smiled. 'We'll probably need to be wearing a soldier's helmet when she does.'

Alice laughed. 'I'll be all right, I'm pregnant. You're the one who should be worried.'

Victoria grinned. 'Oh thanks; I thought we were friends?'

Alice smiled. 'You know, this time last year, we were carefree, wondering what to do with ourselves over the Bank Holiday.' Her smile faded. 'Tony and Molly came with us to Southend.' She paused as they started to slowly step forward. 'I feel bad now, because at the time he annoyed me so much, but now he's gone.'

Victoria patted Alice's arm. 'It's no good thinking like that. You wanted to protect Molly, as indeed we all did.' She hesitated for a moment. 'At the time, none of us knew our loved ones were going to be whisked away to war.'

'I know. How things have changed in the last year.'

'Indeed they have.'

They both walked on in silence for a few minutes.

'This'll make you smile,' Victoria said. 'I saw my neighbour and she had a huge key, dangling on a chain around her neck. My eyes kept getting drawn to it.' She paused and gave a little laugh. 'My imagination started to run away with me and I wondered if she had a man locked inside the house.'

Alice chuckled. 'Did you ask her? I bet you couldn't resist.'

Colour rose up Victoria's cheeks. 'I got caught looking.' She gave a nervous laugh. 'I was so embarrassed.'

'What did she say?'

'She told me outright, saying she felt like a jailer, but with food shortages kicking in, she had no choice but to keep the larder key with her at all times.' Victoria laughed. 'Apparently, her children kept helping themselves to anything they could get their hands on.'

'Aw, bless. I didn't realise things had got that bad.'

Victoria nodded. 'I expect people are stockpiling food, and that's what's causing the shortage.' She looked up at Alice. 'Have you bought anything for the baby yet?'

'No,' Alice admitted. 'Mother is very excited and wandering around the shops, looking at different bits and pieces. She's knitting little booties in white or yellow, because we don't know whether it's a girl or a boy, and heaven forbid you should put blue booties on a little girl.'

*

The evenings were lighter and cooler than the heat of the

August days. Alice was grateful for this as she drove the ambulance close to the platforms, at Victoria Station, as she did every night. The Government was urging people to pin black material up at all windows, to prevent the Germans negotiating their way across the country, but this made it harder and more tiring for her when she drove at night. As the weeks passed, it took her longer to get in and out of the vehicle, her baby bump just squeezing in behind the wheel. She was used to the disapproving looks from some women, but she didn't care. Others smiled their approval of her efforts. This was her only avenue for trying to find Charles and she had to keep the hope alive inside her. If she could find him, then not only would she know he was safe, but he might also have some answers about Freddie.

Alice stepped onto the concourse. The baby changed position, causing her to stop and catch her breath.

An elderly lady approached her. 'Are you all right, lovey?' The lady frowned. 'Is that baby giving you jip?'

Alice rested her hand on the baby's foot or elbow that was protruding. She smiled. It reminded her of something out of a scary film. 'He's just kicking, letting me know he's around.'

'They clear take your breath away at times. Do you need to sit for a moment?'

Alice shook her head. 'I'm fine, thank you. I've just got to try and take it easy.'

'Take your time. You can rush all you want, lovey,

but it won't change anything.' The lady nodded and started to walk away.

'Thank you.' Alice watched her.

The old lady turned and waved. 'Take care.'

'And you.' Alice stepped forward, careful not to make any sudden movements. The soldiers were sitting propped up against a wall. All had various bandages on them, each spattered with blood and dirt, as others had been before. A lady handed out packets of cigarettes and matches to the men, helping some of them to light them. Spirals of grey smoke joined the steam from the trains waiting patiently at the platforms, before slowly disappearing into the roof. There were murmurs of thanks. Then there was silence amongst them. Some hung their heads with exhaustion, while others leant back onto the fencing and closed their eyes.

One man had his head and eyes covered with bandages. His head jerked up as she approached. 'Who's there?' he shouted out. 'Make yourself known.'

The men around him sprung to life, some leaning forward to see what was going on, while others described what they could see to the man sitting next to them.

Alice stared down at him. The anxiety she tried to bury every time she made the journey rose to the surface. She looked down the line of men. Their faces were etched and hardened by their experiences. Her little bit of kindness made a difference to them. Looking back down at the man, Alice wondered if his vulnerability, his lack of control was worse than anything else he had experienced. 'My name's Alice,' she whispered. Stooping next to him, it dawned on her she might not be able to get back up again. Alice smiled at her predicament as she rested her hand on his gnarled knuckles, briefly wondering who'd help her. 'I'm here to get you to a hospital. You're in safe hands.'

A smile slowly spread across the man's face. 'A beautiful name to match what I'm sure is a beautiful woman. I don't think I've ever had such soft hands touch mine before.'

The soldiers either side of him jeered at his cheesy comment. 'Take no notice of them, miss. None of us have seen a woman in a long time...'

'Nah mate, and you're not seeing one now.' All the men joined in the laughter that followed.

Alice smiled. 'You're a mean lot.'

The soldier chuckled, but ignored the banter that was going on all around him. 'And we certainly haven't had someone speak to us with such a gentle voice.'

'Mind you, you're right, she's a cracker, but you're out of luck. By the looks of things, she's carrying a baby and I don't think it's going to be long before it pops out.'

The soldier's mouth straightened as he squeezed Alice's hand. 'Ah well, never mind, you can't be lucky all your life, and I consider myself to be very fortunate right now.'

Alice laughed. 'I've a couple of months to go yet, so there's no need to worry. I'm not about to give birth on Victoria Station.'

The man lifted his hand and touched the bandage wrapped around his eyes. 'But someone is a blessed man.'

Alice smiled, but it didn't quite reach her eyes. 'Let's hope we're all blessed and God takes care of us all.'

'Amen to that,' the men chorused. Like time ticking away, their cigarettes gradually burnt down to their fingers.

*

Alice sighed as she took the cups out of the boxes and lined them up on the buffet table. She felt breathless; maybe it was all getting too much, in her condition. Perhaps she needed more than a day between driving the ambulance and serving tea and cake, and then there was her work at Foyles. Her feet ached and her ankles were swollen. Perhaps she should sit for a while.

''Ere, excuse me, lovey.'

Alice looked up from the table and glanced over at the people milling around the entrance of Victoria Station. An old lady was shuffling forwards, leaning heavily on her walking stick. Her grey hair hadn't seen a brush for a long time and her face was smeared with black marks. A young boy brushed past her and she waved her stick menacingly in the air. Alice held her breath. She couldn't watch. The screech of metal against metal alerted everyone a train was slowing down. Grey smoke swirled upwards from the funnel, trying to escape into the air. A deafening whistle travelled through the station as the train came to a standstill. Alice looked around her. It wasn't the train carrying the soldiers home. People stood around, some chatting to the person next to them, while others stood in silence, but they all looked pale and pensive.

'Lovey.' The old lady's voice carried above the din of the trains.

Alice looked across again but the woman didn't look familiar. The lady was hobbling in her direction. The fringed shawl, slung carelessly across her hunched shoulders, looked as though it had seen better days. Her long black skirt was crumpled and stained, while the cuff of her once white blouse was torn. Alice wondered whether to go and help her, but she was slightly dubious of the stick she had been waving around.

'Yer could 'ave met me 'alfway.' The old lady stopped just short of the table. Her breathing was laboured.

'Let me get you a seat.' Alice picked up a wooden chair and ran to the other side of the table. She placed her hand under the lady's elbow and eased her down. Alice's nose wrinkled at the stench of stale smoke.

The lady gasped for air. 'I've seen yer 'ere before.'

Alice's lips formed a smile, but wondered what the old lady wanted with her. 'I'm here most days, in one capacity or another.'

'I know.' The lady lowered her head and took a couple of deep breaths, before finally looking up. 'Yer drive an ambulance when you ain't dishing up tea and cake.'

Alice nodded, hoping the old lady wouldn't notice her taking a step backwards. The smoke, mingled with body odour, was too overpowering for her. She didn't know what to say; this lady had clearly been watching her, but why?

'I come 'ere most days too, 'oping my grandson will get off one of them there trains that steam in 'ere every day.' She sucked in some air, before pursing her lips and shaking her head. 'It ain't 'appened though, I'm still waiting. I just 'ope he's safe, that's all.'

Alice's chest tightened. Isn't that why she does this every day, so she can find the men she loves and bring them home safely? Will they come home on one of the many trains that arrive here every day? She shook her head, before forcing a smile. 'I hope he is too. It's what we all want, isn't it?'

The old lady lowered her wrinkled, almost translucent eyelids. 'Yes, well time will tell.' She concentrated on her hands resting in her lap, one gripping the top of her walking stick, as though it was her lifeline for getting home. She looked up and eyed Alice. 'Was yer driving yer ambulance last night?'

Alice frowned at the unexpected question. Her jaw tightened, while her hands clenched by her sides. 'Can I ask why you need to know?'

The old lady cackled. 'Yer know, my mother used to rap my knuckles for answering a question wiv a question, but you youngsters seem to get away wiv it these days.'

Alice lowered her head. 'I'm sorry, it's just that I have to be careful driving an ambulance, because of the equipment and things.'

'Don't worry lovey, yer equipment's safe wiv me.' The lady's eyes squeezed shut for a second. 'I just wondered if you would 'ave been called to Leyton Midland Road Station last night.'

Alice had a bad feeling. Her stomach knotted as her pulse raced. 'No, I wasn't. Why?'

'Them Germans bombed it last night; the booking office is flattened, along wiv the billiard 'all.' A tear dropped onto her cheek. 'I fink me bruvver was in there playing.'

Alice wanted to say something but her throat was too constricted.

The lady frowned. 'Fing is, I fink 'e's still buried under all the rubble.'

Alice shook her head and grabbed the lady's hands, squeezing them between her own. 'He may not have been in there.' Her thumb gently rubbed the susceptibly soft skin on the top of her hand.

The old lady gave a laugh. 'Yeah, 'e would've been. 'E's been going there every night since 'e was a kid. Me ma always said no good would come of it, and she was right.' She paused for a moment. 'I've been there today and did try to move the rubble, but I'm just an old woman who can't do what she used to.' The tears fell again. 'I was more of an 'indrance, so I left and came 'ere instead. You should see it; so much rubble. People's 'omes 'ave been destroyed.' She shook her head. 'I 'ate to fink 'ow many people were injured, or worse still died. Some bloke said the Germans 'ad been successful, because there'd been no moon, so it was right dark.' The tears stopped and her eyes sparked. 'Them blooming 'uns. If I was twenty years younger, I'd be shooting them out the sky, I would. Robbing us of our families.'

Alice found herself blinking quickly. 'I could try and find out about your brother,' she whispered.

The old lady shook her head. 'Nah, don't worry, lovey. That bloke I were chatting to said 'e'd let me know, but I know 'e's gone. I can feel it.' She chuckled. ''E's 'ad a good innings. I'm sure 'e's 'appy playing billiards in the sky, wiv me ma telling 'im off for wasting 'is life.' She grabbed Alice's arm and pulled herself up off the chair. She slowly straightened herself, but wasn't able to get fully upright. 'You do a grand job, miss. Look after yourself, and that baby of yours. Life's precious, yer know.'

Alice watched the lady hobble away. She should have broken the rules and offered her a cup of tea and a piece of cake. That's what Lily would have done, but she wasn't Lily. She shook her head and lowered her eyes, while resting her hand across her bump, slowly rubbing it to and fro. She couldn't help wondering what kind of world she was bringing her child into.

Chapter 18

September 1915

Alice sat on the edge of her unmade bed. She took a deep breath as she looked around her dreary bedroom; she had to tackle it before her mother and Mrs Headley did. She had to try and make space for the baby's things. That meant removing the many books that were stacked in every corner and gradually creeping further into the room. The piles appeared to have grown, since Freddie had been away. Perhaps working in a bookshop wasn't a good idea, but she was saving her money, in the hope they could buy a house when he returned. She stared at the books. She had seen the union jack poster several times on her way to work, telling the public to do their bit by giving old or new books and magazines for the sick, the serving soldiers and the sailors at sea. All she had to do was sort them out and take them to the Post Office; they didn't even want them wrapped. She frowned at her books. 'Easy'.

Standing up, she placed her hands on her hips, stretching her back, trying to alleviate the ache that she had woken up with. Alice caught her reflection in the mirror and smiled. She never did gain the rosy glow that women were meant to have when they were pregnant. 'Right,' she spoke to her reflection. 'Books.' Alice turned away and frowned at one of the piles. She waddled over to the nearest stack and stooped to pick up the top book. 'Ah, Pride and Prejudice. Jane Austen wouldn't be happy for me to give away Miss Bennet and Mr Darcy.' Smiling, she placed the book on her bed before bending to pick up the next. 'Jane Eyre and Mr Rochester, another great story'. The Charlotte Bronte novel was placed on the bed, next to Jane Austen's. Next was Jules Verne's Around the World in Eighty Days. Alice sighed. This was going to be difficult. She hated parting with her books, no matter how good the cause.

A minute later, the bedroom door creaked as it flew open and Lily rushed in. 'Alice.'

Colour drained from Alice's face. 'What's the matter? Is everything all right?'

Lily smiled. 'Of course. Why wouldn't it be?'

'Well,' Alice raised her eyebrows, 'for one thing, you rushed in as if the house was on fire.'

'Sorry.' Lily gave a sheepish grin. 'I didn't mean to frighten you, but you don't have the monopoly on worrying about people, you know.' She flopped on the bed and picked up the three books, neatly stacking them on the bedside table. 'Anyway, I thought I'd come and see what you are up to. We don't see much of each other these days.'

Alice gingerly lowered herself onto the bed, next to her sister. 'That's true. I've missed our little chats.' She sighed. 'I thought I'd be good and try to make room in here for the baby.'

Lily glanced around the room. It was bigger than hers, but not by much.

'I know it's going to be tight, so I thought I'd start by sorting out the hundreds of books I have...'

Lily nodded. 'But you're finding it difficult.'

Alice laughed. 'Well, I thought I'd put my 'keep' pile on the bed.'

'That's good, there are only three.'

'I don't know how to tell you this.' A frown creased Alice's forehead. 'They're the first and only ones I've looked at.'

Lily doubled up with laughter, gulping for air as she hugged her sister. 'That tells me it's not a job you can do by yourself.'

'Maybe, but I thought I'd do what those posters are saying. You know, pass them on to our soldiers and sailors.' Alice's chin trembled a little.

'Don't get upset.' Lily reached out and patted her sister's arm. 'I'll help you, but you mustn't argue with me, all right?'

'All right.'

Lily stood up and purposefully strode over to a pile of books, picking up as many as her arms would allow. 'Right, out of this pile of, what...' She paused looking down the stack she was holding, '… ten or twelve books, you can keep one.'

'One?' Alice shouted.

Lily smiled. 'No arguing, remember?'

'What about negotiating? You didn't say anything about that.' Alice stared at Lily. She pushed out her bottom lip in a bid to win her sister over. 'Can't I keep three?'

Lily dropped the books on the bed. 'No, look around you.' She waved her arms around the room.

Alice did as she was bid. 'All right, you win, but it's hard to choose.'

'If you want my help, don't keep giving me those sad little girl looks, because they won't work.' Lily laughed at her sister. 'Right, you can keep two out of these books.'

A smile spread across Alice's face as she clapped her hands together. 'Thank you.' She glanced at the three books that were already on the bedside table. 'But that doesn't include the three I've already chosen.'

Lily laughed again. 'You're a nightmare.' She shook her head. 'Yes, you can keep those three as well.' She smiled as she looked at the books stacked around the room. 'I can see this is going to be a long job.'

'I promise to be good. I just hate parting with them.' Alice smiled up at her sister. 'When Freddie and I have our own house, I'm going to have a library, where I can sit and read for hours on end.'

'Hark at you, lady of the manor.'

They both laughed, before stopping and staring at each other. 'It seems a long time since laughter was heard in this house,' Alice remarked.

'Yes, I'm not sure how mother will cope when you do move out. She is so excited about the baby.' Lily frowned. 'Why do you think we haven't heard from Robert?'

Alice shook her head. 'I don't know. I miss him in a funny sort of way, but it's strange he hasn't written to us.' She sighed. 'It's like we can't even mention his name, but we haven't had any bad news, so hopefully he's safe.'

Lily nodded. 'I suppose they'd soon tell us if he wasn't.' She gave her sister a sideways glance. 'I take it Charles hasn't been found yet?'

Tears stung the back of Alice's eyelids. 'I didn't know you knew he was missing.'

'I overheard the end of the conversation. What did Father say, "Charles gets lost in the house"?' Lily paused as colour rose up her neck. 'I couldn't go into the sitting room because I was so angry with him, so I went out again.'

Alice reached out and stroked Lily's arm. 'I'm so sorry. I should've told you, but I was trying to protect you.'

The corners of Lily's lips lifted slightly. 'I know, but I'm a grown up now. I'll have you know, I uphold the law in this town.'

Alice laughed. 'You are funny.' She ran her hand across the small of her back. 'But I do understand the point you're making.'

Lily frowned. 'It can get quite scary out there sometimes. I haven't said anything to Mother, because I don't want to worry her.' She paused, looking down at the stack of books on her lap. 'Daisy and I had to break up some trouble a couple of days ago. The pair of us make a good team.'

Alice raised her eyebrows. 'What sort of trouble?'

'People were refusing to buy their groceries from a corner shop that was owned by an old couple. It seems everyone thought they were German and accused them of being spies.' Lily shook her head. 'It got totally out of hand and the language and abuse that was being hurled at them was something else.' She gave a little laugh. 'I learnt some new words, I can tell you.'

Sadness crept across Alice's face. 'Those poor people. Were they German?'

'No.' Lily smiled. 'People are stupid; they hear an accent so assume the worst.'

Alice frowned as she reached out and rested her hand on her sister's arm. 'Don't worry, I won't say anything, but please be careful out there. This war is causing so much misery. I think fear is making people act out of character and Mother certainly can't take much more worry. Thank goodness for the distraction of a grandchild.'

Lily nodded. 'Do you think Charles is still alive?'

Alice rubbed her lower back again. 'As blunt as ever.' She sucked in her breath. 'I have to believe he's still alive. It's too dreadful to think otherwise. I check every soldier that comes into Victoria Station, hoping one day he'll be amongst them, but...'

'He'll turn up. Freddie would have looked after him.' Lily looked across at Alice's troubled expression. 'Are you in pain?'

'Not really, I just have a severe backache.'

'Right, enough of this maudlin conversation, let's get on with our negotiations about these books.'

*

Alice winced as she gingerly lowered herself into the armchair, her face etched with pain. She closed her eyes and took a couple of deep breaths, hoping the support of the upright chair would ease the increasing ache across her back.

Lily watched Alice closely. 'Is it still playing up?'

'Yes, I've probably overdone it with those books.' Alice gave a feeble laugh. 'That, or else the baby must have changed position and is lying awkwardly.' She sighed. 'If that's the case, I wish it would move back again.'

'I'll ask Mrs Headley for some tea or something.' Lily

turned to leave the room, but looked back again. The honeycomb glow of the mid-afternoon sun radiated into the room, its shafts of light bouncing off the glassware. Alice had her eyes closed, but the beads of perspiration were visible as her head rested back on the chair. Her hands were gripping the wooden arms. She looked washed out. Lily frowned. Surely, it was too early for her to give birth. Lily tried to do a quick calculation from the wedding day; eight months at best. Fear took hold. She turned away and took a couple of deep breaths. 'Stop panicking, everything will be all right.' She whispered the mantra a couple of times, on her way to the kitchen. *What do you know about these things?* a voice in her head countered.

Mrs Headley nodded as she approached her in the hall. 'I was just coming to see if you wanted afternoon tea, miss?'

'Afternoon tea?' Lily's eyes widened. 'Oh, er, yes, I suppose.' Lily paused. 'Thank you.'

Mrs Headley nodded and turned to walk away.

'Mrs Headley?'

The housekeeper turned back. 'Yes, miss.'

'What do you know about pregnancy and childbirth?' Lily's words fell over themselves in a rush to be heard.

'Is everything all right?'

Lily gave a tight-lipped smile. 'Possibly.' She paused, wringing her hands together. 'Alice woke up with backache this morning and it appears to be getting a whole lot worse. I'm probably just panicking. In fact I know I'm panicking, but the baby isn't due yet, and of course it might be nothing...'

Mrs Headley held up her hand, a gesture she knew would ordinarily get her the sack, but she had to stem the rising panic in Lily's voice. 'I'm sure Mrs Leybourne will be fine. It's quite a natural process, you know.'

Lily stopped wringing her hands and took a deep breath. She gave the housekeeper a faint smile. 'Yes, yes, it is, isn't it?' She took another deep breath. 'I must try and stay calm.'

Mrs Headley smiled. 'Would you like me to get hold of the midwife or doctor?'

Lily's eyes darted from side to side. Her hands each sought comfort from the other as they clenched together in front of her. 'I don't know. I wish Mother was back from her hospital visits. She'd know what to do.' She gave Mrs Headley a pleading look. 'Would you come and see what you think?'

The housekeeper nodded. 'I'm not sure what use I'll be. I've never had children, although I've helped deliver a couple.'

Without thinking, Lily threw her arms around Mrs Headley. 'Thank goodness, that's good to know.'

Mrs Headley laughed and enjoyed the warmth of the hug. It had been a long time since anyone had held her in that way. She didn't rush to pull back, as her grey curls rested against Lily's soft skin. Her arms crept round the young woman.

Lily pulled back a little, but left her hands on the housekeeper's shoulders. 'Sorry, Mrs Headley, I didn't mean to embarrass you by overstepping the invisible line.' She gave a chuckle. 'My father would've had a fit if he'd walked in then.'

Mrs Headley arched her eyebrows. 'Yes, miss, I'm quite sure I'd have been sent packing, but there's no need for you to be sorry.'

Lily laughed. 'Oh I'm not sorry for hugging you, and if he'd walked in, I'd have taken full responsibility for it.' She paused. 'I was apologising for embarrassing you.'

The housekeeper shook her head. 'I can assure you it was nothing of the sort. It was very nice. Now, let's go and check on Mrs Leybourne, then I'll get your tea.'

Lily nodded.

Mrs Headley followed Lily into the sitting room.

'Ah, Lily, I wondered where you'd gone.' Alice groaned. 'I might go upstairs and lie on the bed for a little while. It's definitely getting worse.'

'I've brought Mrs Headley to look at you.' Lily's voice rose with each word. 'I don't know whether to fetch the doctor.'

Alice tried to smile at her sister. 'I'm sure I'll be all right, but the pain in my back is becoming unbearable.'

Mrs Headley walked over to Alice. 'Do you mind if I touch your forehead?' She paused as Alice squeezed her eyes shut. 'I just want to see if you have a temperature.'

Alice shook her head.

Mrs Headley laid her flat palm over the area. 'I think you're right to suggest lying down. Your skin is quite damp; you definitely have a temperature.' The housekeeper turned to Lily. 'Can you help Mrs Leybourne upstairs and I'll get hold of the doctor.'

'You aren't going out.' Lily's eyes glistened. 'I can't do this by myself.'

'Stop fretting. I'm not going anywhere.' She touched the young girl's arm. 'I'll come upstairs as soon as I've found someone to fetch the doctor.'

Lily nodded. 'Right.' She took a deep breath, before reaching out to grip Alice's arm. 'Right, come on Alice, I'll help you up the stairs.'

Alice groaned. 'I don't know now. I'm not sure I can walk, never mind climb the stairs.'

Mrs Headley moved to the other side of the chair. 'Now I'm sorry, but you definitely need to be upstairs.' She looked across at Lily. 'Miss Taylor...'

'Oh God, please just call me Lily.'

Mrs Headley nodded. She had to keep them both calm until help arrived. 'Lily, hook your arm under your sister's and I'll do the same this side, then we can support her while we lift her up together.'

Lily did as instructed. 'Say when.'

Mrs Headley looked into the frightened eyes of the young girl. 'On the count of three. One, two, three.' They both lifted as one.

Lily smiled, her fear momentarily forgotten. 'There, we can do this, Mrs Headley.'

The housekeeper nodded. 'Now we need to get her upstairs, and we can't do it three wide. If I help as far as the stairs, can you manage, while I sort out the doctor?'

Lily nodded, but the fear was back for all to see. 'I'll try.'

Alice looked from one to the other. 'I'm sure I can manage. I just feel a little weak, but I'll have the banister to hold on to.'

Lily's face relaxed a little as she stared at her sister. 'If you hold the rail, I'll be right behind you, in case you slip.'

Mrs Headley nodded before giving Lily a smile. 'Let's go then, before her waters break.'

'What? You think she's about to give birth?' Lily burst out.

Mrs Headley shrugged her shoulders. 'Who knows? Babies come when they are ready, and I think this little one is at least making preparations to pay us a visit.'

Lily beamed. 'Do you hear that, Alice? You might be a mother by the end of the day.' Her grin faded with the excitement. 'I'll get her upstairs, if you can sort out the doctor.'

The housekeeper nodded and sped out of the room. 'I'll boil some water and find some towels as well.'

Alice bit down on her lip and blood oozed into her mouth, leaving a metallic taste in its wake. She leant heavily on Lily, stopping every minute or so. 'Come on Alice, you can do it. It won't be long before you can hold on to the banister.'

A cry burst from Alice.

Fear wrapped itself around Lily's chest. 'What is it? Alice, what is it?'

Alice looked down at the floor. 'I don't think there's going to be time for the doctor.'

Lily looked down at Alice's feet; she was standing in a puddle. 'Mrs Headley,' she screamed. 'The baby's coming. Where are you?'

Mrs Headley ran into the hall. 'Upstairs quickly,' she said breathlessly. 'Otherwise you'll be giving birth in the hall.'

*

The curtains kept the threads of early morning sunlight out of Alice's bedroom. One of her drawers had been emptied and placed on the floor, next to her bed. Alice looked down at the makeshift crib and smiled. Only Mrs Headley would have thought to line an old wooden drawer with newspapers, before covering them with a sheet folded many times. She vaguely remembered Lily bouncing between groaning with worry, and squealing with delight. The doctor hadn't arrived until after Mrs Headley had cut the cord and she was holding her adorable little bundle. The black curls had been matted with blood but Alice hadn't cared. She was exhausted, but elated; she had given birth to a son. Lily and Mrs Headley had done a good job looking after her.

'Well, little one, what are we going to call you?' Alice smiled. She stared down at her son's button nose. His long dark eyelashes rested on his cheeks, while the perfectly formed lips pursed as he slept in her arms. His tiny fingers opened when her hand touched his. He stretched them, before wrapping them around her index finger. Lowering her head, she kissed his soft, pink forehead. A tear ran down her cheek. She sniffed, before giving a watery smile. 'Wait till your father sees you, Master Leybourne.' Alice cuddled the soft bundle close to her and closed her eyes, allowing his sweet, milky scent to fill her. She jolted at the knock on her bedroom door. Before she had time to respond, the door flew open.

'Good morning mummy, and my wonderful little nephew.' Lily beamed.

Alice couldn't resist smiling at her sister. 'My son and I would like to thank you for last night.'

Lily laughed. 'I don't think it's me you need to thank, but Mrs Headley; she's a bit of a dark horse, that one. Thankfully, she took total control and I just did as I was told.'

'That's a little ironic when you've spent years doing the opposite.' Alice laughed.

Lily chuckled. 'Sometimes you have to admit when

you're in front of a superior being, and that was certainly the case last night.'

Alice smiled, shaking her head at her sister's logic. 'Would you like to hold the little man you brought into this world?'

'Of course.' Lily laughed. 'You don't think I'm here to see you, do you?'

Alice frowned as she carefully passed Lily the baby. 'Be careful.' She sucked in her breath. 'Make sure you support his head.'

'Stop fretting, Alice. I promise you, I'll never let any harm come to this little boy.' Lily frowned as she looked down at him. 'I'll protect him with my life.'

A light knock on the open door caught the girls' attention.

'Hello, Grandma, have you come for a hold as well?' Lily smiled at her mother.

'Indeed I have, especially as I wasn't here last night when it all happened, but first I want to see how mum is doing.' Sarah sat on the edge of the bed. She rested her hand on top of Alice's. 'How are you feeling today?'

Alice smiled. 'I'm all right, although I must admit my body feels like it's been run over by a train or something.'

Sarah laughed. 'That'll pass. I'm sorry I wasn't around last night, but I understand I wasn't missed. Mrs Headley, with Lily's assistance, did a wonderful job.'

'Mrs Headley was amazing,' Lily chimed behind her

mother. 'I was in a state of panic, even before I knew you were about to give birth.'

Alice and Sarah laughed.

'That's all right, I thought I just had backache.' Alice raised her eyebrows.

'Never mind. It all ended well, thank goodness.' Sarah patted Alice's hand. 'Right, Lily, let me have a cuddle with my grandson.' She stretched out her arms, while watching Lily kiss him on the forehead.

Lily straightened her lips. 'I don't want to let him go.'

Sarah shook her head. 'Well you have to; Mother has spoken.'

The girls laughed as Lily passed the baby to Sarah.

'He's gorgeous.' Sarah stroked his soft, dark curls with her fingers. 'What are you going to call him?'

'I don't know. To be honest, I haven't thought about names. I was hoping Freddie and I could choose together, but...' A tear rolled down her cheek and she quickly wiped it away. 'I'll have to decide soon.'

Sarah's heart lurched in her chest. 'He'll be home soon.' She looked down at the bundle in her arms. 'And what a surprise he's in for.'

There was a cough from the doorway. 'Sorry to disturb you, Mrs Leybourne.' Mrs Headley stood in the doorway, carrying a tray. 'But I thought you might like some tea, and I've done a boiled egg for you.'

'Come in, Mrs Headley.' Alice smiled at the housekeeper. 'And please, just call me Alice. Nobody calls me Mrs Leybourne. When I hear it, I forget that's me.' Alice grimaced as she tried to sit more upright. She took a deep breath. 'Thank you, Mrs Headley, for the little one's makeshift bed, and indeed for everything. You were a star.'

Lily gave a little cough as she straightened the covers before the tray was laid on Alice's lap.

Alice smiled at her sister. 'And so were you, Lily.'

'Thank goodness you weren't on your own.' Sarah piped up. 'We should have had a rota in place.'

'Well I wasn't on my own, thankfully, so it had a happy ending.' Alice took a sip of the hot tea. 'Thank you for the tea; I must admit I am ready for it. I'll get up in a minute...'

'No.' A shrill of ladies' voices filled the room. The baby jumped at the sudden noise. Sarah rocked him up and down. 'Well, we know there's nothing wrong with his hearing.' She laughed. 'Just take it one day at a time.' Sarah didn't move her gaze away from the baby nestling in her arms. 'Rest for today and see how you feel tomorrow.'

No one noticed the housekeeper shuffle out of the bedroom.

'As much as I don't want to leave you, I have to go to work.' Lily straightened her uniform before strolling around, to give her nephew a kiss on the top of his head. 'I had no idea I'd feel like this about him; it's hard to tear myself away.'

Alice laughed. 'Go on. He'll still be here when you get home.'

Lily frowned. 'I suppose.' She paused, staring down at him. 'You do know I shall tell everyone at work, then Daisy will tell Victoria, and that means you'll have at least one visitor before the day is over.'

Alice laughed. 'I'm under no illusions. Once word gets out, I shall be inundated with visitors, or perhaps I should say baby Leybourne will be.'

Lily gave him another kiss before moving round to give Alice a cuddle. 'See you later, and take care.'

'Hmm, you smell lovely. Is that another Christmas perfume?'

'It is, but I must dash.' Lily rushed out of the bedroom, leaving the door open.

'Bye, stay safe,' mother and daughter chorused.

'I believe the doctor will be in later to check on you both, so get as much rest as you can between this little one's feeds.'

Alice nodded. She finally dipped a small piece of bread into her runny egg that had gone cold. The golden orange of the yolk covered it and she quickly popped it into her mouth. The doughy mixture wrapped itself around her teeth and stuck to the roof of her mouth. She picked up her teacup and gulped the warm liquid, letting it remove the layers of stickiness from her mouth. It was only then she noticed an armchair in the corner of her room. She frowned. 'Why is there an armchair in my room?'

'Mrs Headley insisted on sleeping in here all night.' Sarah frowned as she looked up at Alice. 'It took all my strength to get Lily out of the room and into her own bed.'

Alice's hand rested at the base of her slender neck. 'I don't understand. Why did they both want to stay with me?'

Sarah's lips straightened. 'I wondered if you would remember, but you clearly don't. You were burning hot. The doctor said to keep you as cool as possible and to keep damping your lips, while trying to get some liquids into you.'

Alice stared wide-eyed at her mother. 'I remember being hot when I was downstairs, but—'

'Don't worry, you're fine now and that's all that matters.' Sarah smiled. 'There wasn't a nurse available to sit with you at such short notice, although I have to say there wasn't any moving Mrs Headley. She was determined to stay and watch over you and this little one.'

'Aw, bless her.' Alice immediately wondered how she could repay the woman that had been around her all her life. 'Perhaps, when I am up and about, we should take some photographs of the little man.'

'Now that is a good idea, isn't it, little one?' Sarah smiled.

Alice shook her head at her mother. 'It would be nice

to take one of Mrs Headley holding him, don't you think?'

'That would be a lovely idea.' Sarah laughed. 'If she'll allow it.'

Alice frowned at her mother.

'Mrs Headley is a stickler for the rules.' Sarah rocked the baby in her arms. 'Why do you think we still call her Mrs Headley after thirty odd years?'

Alice shrugged her shoulders. 'I always thought that was more about us as a family, than her.'

*

The china cups were filled to the brim with hot chocolate. Mrs Headley gave them to Alice, who in turn passed them around the family, one by one.

'This is very cosy.' Alice chuckled as she looked around her, everyone cupping their warm drinks. There were makeshift beds on the floor, lined up like horizontal soldiers. Candles flickered, casting shadows around the room. The flames were mesmerising as the thin white wick turned black. Gradually, the melting wax rolled down the sides. She forced herself to look away. 'Ooh, you've added a couple of armchairs since last night. I can see them tucked away in the corner with that old card table.' Alice sipped the hot sweet drink. 'Mrs Headley, you've done a good job cramming in supplies and furniture, so we're all comfortable.'

Mrs Headley smiled and bent her head slightly. 'Thank you.'

Sarah gently blew the steam away from her drink. 'That's a lovely basket for Arthur to sleep in as well. He looks quite content, tucked up in there.'

Luke tutted. 'I wonder how long we are going to be stuck down here this time; we were down here ages last night.'

Lily glared at her father. 'Did you not bring a book to read, or something to do?'

Alice sucked in her breath. 'I've brought my knitting and my old favourite, Pride and Prejudice.' She picked up her book, waving it in the air, before dropping it on the floor and folding her hands around the cup she was holding. The warmth spread through her. 'At least you're safe. I met an old lady at Victoria Station, whose brother had died in the bombings last month. It was heart breaking. Apparently, there was a lot of damage, homes destroyed and people injured. Some inevitably died.'

Sarah shook her head. 'I know the police rang their bells and told us to take cover, but I had no idea. The trouble is, you don't always get to hear of anything.' She paused for a moment. 'It's very sad, but we were lucky not to get hit.'

Lily shook her head. 'We are lucky. Some people have nowhere to go and are apparently hiding under tables, while others try and make their way to the underground stations.'

The floor vibrated. Alice put down her cup. That was something they hadn't experienced before. It shuddered again and was closely followed by a loud thunderclap right above their heads. Then another, and another. Alice physically jumped at the loud noise. Her heart started racing and her palms became clammy. With squinting eyes, Alice looked up at the ceiling as another boom cracked through the air. She grabbed Lily and Arthur's hands. The bombs must be close by. Alice gave a silent prayer, to keep her family safe. She glanced across at her mother, whose eyes were shut, but her lips were moving. She willed her father to give her comfort, by at least holding her hand. He frowned as he caught her stare, his face drained of colour. Was he also afraid? Alice moved her head to silently indicate what he should be doing. He took her lead and took Sarah's hand in his. Her mother gave him a grateful half smile, but fear held her body rigid. Lily squeezed Alice's hand and mouthed, 'I love you.' Tears pricked her eyes until they hurt. She blinked quickly before shaking her sisters hand. 'I love you too.' Everyone sat in silence, each lost in their own thoughts. Arthur slept, as another thunderclap filled the basement.

*

The family emerged as daylight filtered through the

basement door. All were shaken, but in one piece. Alice was grateful that her son had slept through the whole thing, only waking to be fed. She held him tight in her arms as she gazed down at him, stroking his soft skin, not wanting to let him out of her sight ever again. She now understood the love a parent feels for their child, the need to protect at all costs. Alice was thankful he was too young to know the fear they all felt, sheltering in the basement.

Sarah turned and frowned at Alice and Lily. 'The first thing is to find out whether your grandparents are all right.'

Alice took in her mother's ashen features. She had aged overnight. 'I think you should rest.' She frowned as her gaze was drawn back to her sleeping son. She took a deep breath. 'But if you and Father keep an eye on the little one, and promise on your lives to keep him safe, I'll go along to Russell Square.'

'I'll come with you.' Lily's voice came from lower down the stairs.

Mrs Headley eyed her employers. 'I can watch the young sir while Mrs Taylor rests. It will be my pleasure, and I promise nothing will happen to him.'

Sarah smiled at her grandson, but her eyes were cloaked with anxiety and tiredness. 'He's a wonderful shining light in these difficult times.'

Mrs Headley smiled. 'He is that, ma'am.' She glanced towards Alice. 'Shall you be taking breakfast before you go to Mr and Mrs Gettin's?'

Alice turned to Lily who shook her head. 'No thank you, Mrs Headley. The sooner we know everything's all right, the sooner we can all relax.' She bent and kissed Arthur on his forehead, her lips lingering, before she passed him over to Mrs Headley. 'You can sort it out between you.' She laughed. 'Although I do think Mrs Headley is right, Mother, you should go and have a lie down.'

Sarah nodded, unable to deny how exhausted she felt.

Alice and Lily both grabbed their coats from the hallway and rushed out the front door.

Squinting, Alice took a deep breath; smoke hung in the air. The hair on the back of her neck stood on end. Her shoulders were tight, as her gaze darted up and down the road. There was no obvious sign of damage. With silent consent, they sped along Bloomsbury Street, past Bedford Square on their left, before turning right onto Montague Place. 'I should have splashed my face before we came out. I feel a right mess.'

Lily ran her fingers through her hair. 'You're fine. Remember, everyone's had a rough night, so you don't look any worse than they do.'

Alice laughed. 'Thanks for that, you've made me feel so much better.'

Lily frowned as she looked across at her sister. 'Mother looked terrible. I hope she's going to be all right.'

Alice nodded. 'She's exhausted. I think she spent most of the night praying, as I'm sure we all did.'

Lily nodded. 'I've never been so frightened, although this is also terrifying me.'

The old lady immediately jumped into Alice's head. Were they going to find something similar? They turned into Russell Square, both of them gasping as one. The gardens were flooded with water, rivulets rolled down the path. Mud was where beautiful plants once thrived. They were now blackened and strewn across the paths and flowerbeds. The grass was rutted and scorched. They immediately quickened their pace, as glass crunched under their feet.

Alice tried to speak, but nothing came out.

Lily looked down, before quickly taking in the houses around her. 'The houses I can see appear to be undamaged.' She paused and looked down again. 'But where has all this glass come from?'

'I don't know, but it looks like something exploded in Bedford Place.' Alice pointed to the fire damage. 'Perhaps the glass has come from there.'

Lily's lips straightened into a thin line. 'They are going to be all right, aren't they? They have to be.'

Alice nodded, trying to slow down her breathing and ease the pain that was gripping her chest. 'Come on, let's get it over and done with.'

They turned up the other side of Russell Square.

'Thank God, Mother's prayers have paid off,' Lily

yelled as she started running towards her grandparents. 'You're safe, thank goodness, you're safe.'

Residents were busy sweeping the glass off the pavement, while others chatted.

Edward, leaning on a broom, stopped talking to George to look in their direction. 'I was coming round to see if everything was all right with you all, but George waylaid me.' He grinned and dropped the broom handle to wrap his arms around Lily.

George beamed at the sight of the girls.

A man rounded the corner. 'Great Ormond Street Hospital was fortunate. Two bombs exploded nearby, one of them in Queens Square. Everyone's out sweeping the mess up, but there only appears to be broken windows.'

Alice stood and watched Lily throw herself at their grandfather. Tears rolled down her cheeks. They were safe. She didn't care about the house. They were safe and that was all that mattered. The old lady's words echoed in her mind. Life is precious. She hoped she could protect her son from the evil that was in their midst.

Chapter 19

October 1915

Alice had waited until the last moment to register her little boy, in the hope Freddie would come home, or she'd at least have news of him. She had pored over boys' names and had considered calling him Alfred, after his father. That appeared to be the done thing, but she decided to name him after her great grandfather and her husband. Arthur Alfred Leybourne. Despite her grandfather's teasing for not calling the baby Edward, he had been touched by her decision.

Alice scooped Arthur into her arms. She held him close to her, enjoying the warmth and his milky smell. His dark brown eyes stared intently at her, as she sung 'Hickory Dickory Dock' to him, followed by 'Jack and Jill'. A knock on the sitting room door stopped her in mid-verse. 'Come in.'

Mrs Headley opened the door and stepped into the room, closely followed by Victoria and Molly.

'Sorry, Mrs Headley, we couldn't wait to see the little man again.' Victoria smiled, while shrugging her shoulders.

Mrs Headley bowed her head. 'I totally understand that, Miss Appleton.' She stepped aside to allow the two girls into the room. 'Would you like tea, Mrs Leybourne?'

'Yes please.' She turned to her friends as the housekeeper left the room. 'Sorry, no biscuits or cake.'

Victoria sighed. 'I know, what with prices and the shortages, it must be difficult for some. We've had to cut back at home.'

'And us,' Molly piped up. 'Still, it is good for your figure.'

Alice and Victoria laughed.

'Can I have a hold?' Molly ventured.

'Of course. He's awake more now, so I was just singing some nursery rhymes to him.' Alice bent and kissed his forehead before laying him in Molly's open arms.

Mrs Headley returned with a tray of crockery, tea and a small plate of biscuits.

Alice looked down at the plate and arched her eyebrows. 'Mrs Headley, I thought we weren't having biscuits anymore.'

The housekeeper's colour started to rise. 'I made a few this morning, but have only put one each on the plate. I'm not too sure how nice they'll be, because there's less sugar in there than the recipe normally demands.'

'Thank you.' Alice nodded. 'I'm sure they'll be fine,

but we'll report back.'

Victoria watched the housekeeper leave the room. 'You're lucky to still have Mrs Headley. A lot of girls have left service, to be employed in war work. I know quite a few that are travelling to Woolwich Arsenal and Silvertown, to get jobs in the munitions factories; that's supposed to be very well paid.'

'Then there's the fire service and the other factories, like the one Stephen used to work in,' Molly chipped in.

Alice nodded. 'I know you're right, but I think Mrs Headley is happy with us and she's getting on in years, so I don't think she could cope with such physical work.' She glanced across at Molly, who was pulling faces at Arthur. 'Molly, have you heard anything from Charles lately?'

Molly's head jerked up. 'No, and actually I was going to ask you if you had, but I didn't want to spoil your happiness by bringing it up.'

Alice shook her head and a deep sigh escaped. 'No. In fact, there's something I should have told you months ago but...'

Arthur's bottom lip started to quiver.

Victoria stretched out her arms. 'Let me have a cuddle while you talk.'

Molly's colour drained away. Her jaw dropped as anxiety ran across her features. She looked up at Victoria as she lifted Arthur into her arms, before staring back at Alice. She pushed back her shoulders and lifted her head. 'Why do I have a sense that what you're going to tell me isn't good news?'

Alice shook her head. Her hands clung together in front of her. 'There's no easy way to tell you, so—'

'Oh God, he's not dead as well, is he?' Molly burst out, tears already rolling down her cheeks.

'No, no.' Alice ran over to her and knelt at her feet. She grabbed Molly's hands in hers. 'No, but he's missing. I should have told you before. I kept hoping he'd just walk in, but obviously that hasn't happened.'

Molly sniffed. She reached into her pocket and pulled out a handkerchief. 'I thought he'd just got bored with writing to me.' She dabbed her cheeks and blew her nose.

'I've been looking for him.' Alice stood up and paced around the room. 'Of course, he could be anywhere, but I regularly ask at Charing Cross Hospital and check all the men as they arrive at Victoria train station. My mother does the same when she goes, but there's been nothing.' Her eyes glistened as she wrung her hands. 'I don't know what else to do, and with Christmas less than a month away—'

'It'll be all right,' Victoria ventured. 'Remember, you haven't received a telegram saying anything else.

'Well that's good, isn't it?' Molly tried to sound enthused, but failed.

Alice nodded. 'It is.' She stopped pacing and stood by the window. The trees looked bereft without their leaves. The colour of the summer and autumn had long been replaced by the greyness of winter. It matched her feelings at the moment. She couldn't seem to lift herself out of the doldrums, except when Arthur was in her arms.

Molly looked across at Victoria, then back to Alice. 'Freddie was in the same regiment, wasn't he?'

Alice nodded but didn't move away from the window.

'Have you heard from him?' Molly stiffened as she waited for the answer she knew was coming.

Alice shook her head. 'Not since April.' Her voice was barely audible.

Molly poured the tea, which she suspected would be cold, but there could be no wastage in these difficult times. 'Here, drink this before Mrs Headley tells us off for wasting it, or worse, your father comes in and starts ranting at us.'

Alice smiled. She walked over and took the cup and saucer from her friend.

Molly placed her hand on Alice's arm, as she moved to walk away. 'Don't forget the biscuit; you said we'd report back, so you've got to eat it.' She smiled. 'Everything will be all right. Freddie will be home soon.'

Alice's chin began to tremble. 'I keep telling myself that, but it's been months.'

Molly nodded. 'I know.' She paused. 'When I get home, I'll ask my father if he could write some letters to the Home Office, the army or somewhere, to try to find out something for you.'

'Thank you,' Alice whispered. 'But my own father could be doing that.' Her voice rose to a shrill. 'Or he could be asking at that damn club he goes to, practically every day.'

'Come on, Alice, give your son a cuddle.' Victoria offered Arthur to her. 'You have to stay calm for his sake.'

Alice placed her biscuit on the saucer before putting it on the side table. She reached out and held her son close. His small hand immediately wrapped itself around her finger.

'Ah, look, he knows who his mother is.' Victoria smiled. 'He's absolutely wonderful, Alice. It makes me want to have a football team.'

*

'Grab an ambulance. Apparently, a Zeppelin has dropped bombs in The Strand and Aldwych.' The man ran off shouting, 'God knows where it's moving on to next.'

Alice didn't stop to think. She started the ambulance. Her heart was pounding, a pulse thudding in her ears. It was one thing to pick up the soldiers from Victoria Station, but she had never attended a bombing before. She drove at speed, shouting for people to get out of the road, as they stood looking up at the sky. Alice leant forward in her seat and peered up. The Zeppelin was gliding majestically through the darkness, belying the carnage it had caused on the London streets. She pulled up sharp in front of the rubble that blocked the road. Smoke and flames skewed her vision, but she could see bodies lying motionless. She sucked in her breath. *Be professional, get out and get on with it*, a voice shouted in her head. She opened her mouth to speak. Her voice trembled. 'But I've never seen a dead body before, let alone one that has been blown up.'

It was clear a bomb had hit the road outside The One Bell public house, and flames were coming from a large crater, illuminating the street. Where should she start? Alice stepped out of the ambulance. She coughed as smoke caught in the back of her throat, mingling with the stench of charred bodies. She took a step forward, the rubble and glass crunching underfoot.

People stood around, watching in stunned silence. The Lyceum Theatre had an interval, so theatregoers had stepped out to buy refreshments from the street sellers, who were now no more.

'Alice, over here.'

Alice turned at the familiar voice and shouted. 'Lily, what are you doing here?' She carefully weaved between the bricks and rubble scattered around her.

'The same as you. It's terrible. I don't think people know what to do with themselves, so they are just waiting and watching.' Lily looked around her. 'There's some people sitting on the kerb over there that need to go to hospital, so can you take them?'

'Yes, yes of course.' Alice's head bobbed, grateful her sister was taking control. She took a step towards the injured.

Lily grabbed her arm. 'Wait, before you take them, you need to look around in case there are any more urgent cases. They're not dying over there, but some might still be alive in the rubble.' Lily stared at her sister's pale face. 'Look, when you go to Victoria Station, you check all the soldiers first, then decide the urgency. Well, that's what you have to do here, except some will have already died.'

'Of course, yes, that's right.' Alice took a deep breath. 'I know what I have to do, I just have to get on with it. Thank you. It was just a shock, seeing the devastation.'

Lily grimaced as she looked around her. 'It's terrible that you can be having a night at the theatre, come out for refreshments and this happens.'

Alice patted Lily's hand. 'I'll get on, but shout if you need me.' Alice stepped forward, watching her every step. She bent down to a young girl, lying so still. Alice's heart jumped in her chest as she placed her fingers under the child's ear, to check for a pulse. It was there, faint, but it was there. She looked around and beckoned a couple of men standing around. 'Bring something to lay her on. Be quick. I have to get her to hospital.' Her eyes darted between the girl and the men. 'Hurry.' She stared down at the dusty features that were lying so still. 'Hang on girl, you're not dying tonight.'

A man appeared and scooped the girl up, her arm swinging down. 'I'll drive her; my car is just over there.'

Alice didn't know what to say. She was meant to take the injured to hospital. She shook her head. 'Don't hang around. Her pulse is very faint and I'm not sure she's going to make it.'

'She will.' The man wasn't slowed down by the weight he was carrying. It wasn't long before he sped away, with no thought for his own safety.

Alice nodded. Life was precious and some rules were made to be broken. She stood up and moved on to the next. The hours sped by, before she finally stood up and took a deep breath. Alice looked around. Some people had gone home, others had been taken to Charing Cross Hospital. She looked up at the night sky and realised it would soon be dawn.

'What a night.'

Lily's weary voice startled her. Alice turned and smiled as her sister approached her. 'You look a bit of a state.' She smiled at her dust-covered face and the bloodstains on her uniform.

Lily shrugged and glanced down at her clothes, before returning her attention to Alice. She grinned. 'You want to look at yourself, before you say anything.' She gave up the fight and closed her eyes for a moment, before studying the scene around her. 'I've heard they've hit quite a few places in London, but Woolwich has suffered the most. I expect they were after the munitions factory there, but they weren't successful, although, apparently, the army barracks took five hits.'

They both stood in silence for a moment.

Lily broke the spell. 'I think a cup of tea is in order, don't you?'

'That sounds like a grand idea.' Alice licked her dry dusty lips. 'Although I'm not sure where we can get one.'

Lily smiled. 'We've done all we can. Let the others take over now.'

Alice frowned. 'What, just leave?'

'Yes, don't worry, I have permission, and so do you.' Lily winked at her. 'Arthur will be waking up soon and will want his mummy.'

Alice's eyes lit up at the mention of her son. 'Let's go home.'

They walked away from the dust and rubble, towards the ambulance, each holding the other one up as tiredness took over.

'You've worked hard tonight.' Lily yawned. 'I've been told there were at least seventeen dead and twenty-one injured tonight.'

'Oh Lily, all this frightens me. I worry, one day I shall go to work and never see my son again, or he will never know who his mother or father were.'

Lily squeezed her sister's arm as they walked along. 'I

can't offer you any words of comfort, and if I did you'd know they were empty. It's all a chance, but one thing I definitely know is you and Arthur are surrounded by people who love you, and that memory will always be kept alive, no matter what.' Tears dropped onto Lily's cheek. 'Let's not think about it; we are surrounded by doom and gloom. Only happy thoughts from now on.'

Alice nodded, wiping the tears from her eyes. If only life were that simple.

Chapter 20

December 1915

Thick black material covered the large sash window. Candles were lit strategically around the dining room. The silence was deafening. Sarah stood up and placed the first record she could find on the gramophone. Placing the arm of the needle on the edge, she turned the handle several times before it crackled into life. She breathed a sigh of relief as one of the familiar Irving Berlin tunes burst from the trumpet speaker. It was Christmas Day, but there was no celebration. Sarah had only decided to decorate the tree the night before. She told herself everything had to be as expected, in case her boys walked through the door. The girls hadn't wanted to exchange gifts; it hadn't felt right with no news of their brothers or Freddie. Victoria and Daisy sat with Lily, Arthur being a good distraction for everyone. No one spoke of the war, or the boys that were away from home.

Victoria's attention kept being drawn to Alice, wondering how she was really coping. She'd always be grateful that Ted and Stephen both wrote to her regularly and she felt immense relief that no one asked her about either of them.

'That was a lovely lunch,' Edward offered, before sipping his coffee. 'I don't think I shall eat for a week.' He patted his stomach. 'You did well, Sarah, with some food in such short supply, especially sugar and eggs.'

Jane nodded. 'We've practically given up sugar.'

'We're the same. What little we have been able to get, we've been storing for today's meal, but it's probably still better than the boys on the front are eating.' Sarah picked up the heavy teapot, to pour the dark steaming liquid into the waiting cups.

'There's no doubt about that.' Edward reached for a crumb of plum pudding. 'I don't know why I'm still eating,' he chuckled as he popped it into his mouth.

'The way the Germans are bombing our merchant ships, we will soon run out of food supplies.' Luke sighed. 'If you ask me, we need to go back to basics and start growing our own food again.'

Alice stared at her father, wondering what was going on inside his head. He had been subdued all day. Was he finally realising he may not see his sons again?

Edward nodded. 'Well, it was all very nice. I particularly enjoyed the oyster soufflé.'

'It was very tasty, although it has to be said that even oysters are in short supply now.' Luke sipped the tea that Sarah had placed in front of him.

Edward opened his mouth to speak, but quickly

344

closed it again. He looked across the table at Sarah. 'I don't think we will leave very late, with the streets being so dark.' He looked sideways at Jane, before returning to his daughter. 'Your old step-mother gets a little scared these days,' he chuckled into his cup.

Jane nudged him with her elbow. 'Hah, I think you'll find we both get a little frightened. It's amazing how dark it is when there's no light coming from the houses you walk past.'

Alice smiled at the pair of them. 'Grandpa, you are funny.'

Edward smiled. 'I'm very glad you think so.'

Alice shook her head. 'I can't get used to all that hair under your nose; I'm not sure I like the moustache.'

Edward lifted his fingers to smooth it flat. 'My father had one that was described as a large handlebar; he used to constantly tweak it at the ends.'

Sarah laughed. 'That's right, he did. Uncle Henry was always telling him off for not getting rid of it, but I remember him saying the ladies liked it because it tickled.'

Alice smiled. 'Is that what you're doing, growing a handlebar moustache?'

'No, I'll probably shave it off in the summer. I just fancied a change.' Edward smiled. 'How are you getting on with this delightful baby of yours?'

'He's an angel.'

'He certainly seems to be coming on a treat, doesn't

he?'

Alice laughed. 'He is, and he weighs a ton now, not literally, but you know what I mean. He's all that keeps me going, some days.'

Edward frowned. 'I know it's difficult for you, but hopefully, Freddie will be home soon and you'll be united as a family and start your lives together properly.'

Alice nodded. She could feel the tears pricking her eyes.

Jane leant forward in her chair. 'I don't remember seeing the announcement of his birth in the papers.'

Sarah laid a hand over Alice's. 'It wasn't in the papers; we made the decision to go against tradition and not to announce it.' Her hand patted Alice's, before she moved it away.

Jane fidgeted in her seat and raised her eyebrows. 'I see.'

Alice lifted her head high. 'It was my decision. I didn't want Freddie finding out by reading it in a newspaper.' Jane opened her mouth to speak, but Alice held up her hand. 'I know he probably wouldn't have seen it, but I don't know where he is.' Tears rolled down her cheeks. 'I don't know whether he's dead or alive, in England or France. I don't know anything.' She sniffed, before angrily wiping her hands over her cheeks. 'Sorry, but I'm afraid I'm not coping very well. It's the not knowing. I can't sleep at night for thinking about it.'

Jane lowered her eyes and blinked rapidly, before

looking over at Alice. 'I'm so sorry, my dear girl; I just didn't think. Please forgive me.'

Alice nodded. 'There's nothing to forgive.' She gave a watery smile. 'I seem to cry at the drop of a hat since I've had Arthur.'

'That's true.' Lily laughed. 'She cried the other day because she couldn't undo the wrapper around the soap.'

Alice joined in the laughter that was slowly building in the room. 'That's true, I did.'

*

Sarah and Alice removed their gloves and coats, placing them neatly on top of a wooden bench, at the end of the long buffet table on Victoria Station. Alice shivered as she donned her apron, before joining the line of women waiting for the trains to come in. They all busied themselves, preparing cups for tea and slicing cake. Arthur was sound asleep in his pram, tucked in the corner, out of harm's way. He didn't murmur as the trains came and went. Engine noise and the toots of the whistles filled the station, while the grey smoke billowed out of the chimneys. People waited expectantly for them to deliver their heroes home to them. Women murmured to each other as they waited.

'Damned war,' an old grey-haired lady whispered. 'We were told it was going to be over by last Christmas, and yet here we are, over a year later.'

The younger woman pulled at the sides of her headscarf. 'Hah, they got that wrong, didn't they? It's been seventeen months now and we haven't heard anything about it being over.'

The old lady lifted her walking stick and waved it around. 'I come here every day, in the hope my son will be on one of the trains, but it hasn't happened so far.' She pulled out a handkerchief and dabbed at her eyes.

The young woman arched her eyebrows. 'Let's hope he's on today's.' She shook her head. 'I heard someone say they're going to bring in conscription, whatever that is.'

The women stopped talking as they watched a train pull into the platform, casting its shadow over the people waiting. The wheels slowed and the puffing grey smoke gradually lessened. The carriage doors flew open before the train came to a complete standstill. Soldiers in their uniforms stepped off, the first few having to move quickly, as the train was still moving. Their boots and legs were caked in mud. Their weather-worn faces were tanned, each one etched with the pain and gravity of their experiences. Most of them were stooped over, not meeting anyone's gaze.

People cheered as the soldiers approached. Some were waiting, searching the soldiers faces, their eyes alight with the expectation of seeing their man, brother or son.

'Welcome home.' An elderly woman went up to each

man, repeating herself over and over again, guiding them to the buffet table, where they could each get a free cup of tea and a slice of cake.

Alice searched as many faces as she could, looking for Freddie and Charles, but all to no avail. All she saw were bloodshot eyes and faces that appeared rigid and set in stone. Was this how Freddie and Charles were going to come back?

'Welcome home.' Alice frowned at the soldier standing in front of her. 'Have a cup of tea and a slice of cake.' She thrust a cup in front of him, along with the sponge cake. 'You look exhausted.'

The soldier stared at her. 'Not many of us get to sleep properly.' He bit hungrily into the light sponge. 'The trenches fill up with water, rats run around your feet, and that's without the worry that the enemy are going to get you as soon as your eyes are shut.'

Words failed Alice, as she shook her head. 'I'm so sorry. I don't know what to say.'

The soldier let out a humourless laugh. 'Don't worry about it; trust me that's a good thing.'

'I don't know about that,' Alice mumbled. 'I feel quite inadequate.'

'Don't. You're a vision standing there, and will lift the men's spirits.' He laughed. 'The cake's good too.'

Alice smiled. 'Thankfully.'

The soldier raised his cup in salute and drained it before moving off, and she was faced with another soldier. The eyes of a man, but the face of a boy stared back at her.

A couple of hours later, there was a shift change at the buffet table. Alice removed her apron and replaced it with her heavy black winter coat. She glanced across at her mother, who was doing the same thing. 'I feel quite exhausted.'

Sarah's face was ashen when she looked over at Alice. 'They look terrible, don't they?'

Alice nodded, searching for words that accurately conveyed her thoughts. 'It's strange, but I've only thought of them coming back as injured, or not at all.' She paused for a moment. 'I've never thought they wouldn't come back the same men they were.' She shook her head. 'These men today seemed so sad, and yet they were coming home.'

Sarah walked over to the pram and peered inside, before looking back at Alice. 'They probably know they have to go back. It's not over for them and what they've seen will probably never be forgotten. It'll stay with them forever.'

Alice fastened the last of the buttons on her coat. 'I don't know how you do this every day.'

'That's easy. Searching for the boys keeps me coming here.' Sarah paused. 'Just like you.' She shrugged her shoulders and let out a sigh. 'I know why you insist on driving the ambulance here every night. We are both looking for them, in our own way.'

Alice nodded. She blinked quickly as the tell-tale tears began to prick at her eyes. She closed them for a moment, knowing her mother's thoughts were the same as hers; they were with their men. Would they come back the same as the men that had stopped at the buffet table? Would they come back at all?

Sarah grabbed the bar of the pram. 'Come on, we have to stay positive; they deserve that.'

Alice stared at her mother, wondering when she had grown so strong. Perhaps she always had been.

Chapter 21

January 1916

Luke watched Alice over the top of his newspaper. She paced in the hallway, carrying Arthur close, rocking him back and forth, while singing a lullaby to him. His eyes were fighting to stay open, while tiny fingers gripped the sleeve of her loose-fitting cream blouse; cancelling afternoon tea had some advantages. Without looking up, she pushed at the sitting room door, not noticing the usual squeak of its hinges. The low grey clouds created drabness in the room, giving it a sombre feel. She sat on the sofa and laid Arthur against the arm, where she could watch him. He gave a little whimper, so she rested her hand on his chest and hummed for a couple of seconds.

Luke closed his paper, before folding and placing it on the side table, between the sofa and the armchair.

The rustling of pages startled Alice. 'Sorry, Father, I'm afraid I was in a world of my own and didn't realise you were home.'

Luke remained silent as he watched his daughter with his grandson. 'You are going to make that baby soft.'

Alice glared at him, dressed in the usual brown suit, with his white shirt and brown tie. She opened her mouth to speak, but changed her mind and glanced down at the front page of the newspaper that was sitting on the table. 'I heard a rumour at Victoria Station they're introducing conscription; is that true?' Alice glanced across at her father.

Luke yawned. 'Yes, I think you'll find they have already.'

Anger suddenly bubbled inside her. Her colour began to rise. 'For God's sake, when will this end? Enough innocent people have already died, on both sides.'

Luke stared at Alice. 'Don't blaspheme. I understand you and your mother have been serving on the buffet table at Victoria Station.'

Alice nodded and her anger began to subside at the memory of those men. 'Yes, it's heart wrenching.' She sucked in her breath. 'The soldiers look so sad. Pain is etched on their faces; none of them will ever be the same again, you know.'

Luke sighed. 'I don't know why you or your mother do it.'

Alice's lips tightened into a thin line, seconds before she jumped up. 'What? I can't believe you said that. All you do is preach about doing our bit for the war. Charles is missing and it's your fault. He only enlisted because he wanted you to be proud of him, and look where that has got him. What's worse is you don't even care.'

Luke stood up. 'Your mother made him soft, and you are going to do the same to your son.' He took a deep breath as he wandered over to the whisky decanter. 'Women shouldn't be left in charge of boys, because they end up making them soft in the head.'

'I don't know how you can say that. Charles was a bright, happy child, whereas Robert bullied us, forever playing 'the eldest' card, so he could get away with it.' She glared across at her father; his back stiffening didn't stop her. 'And what's more, you allowed it because he could do no wrong in your eyes. You turned him into a bully, Father.' She watched him pour a large whisky into a tumbler. 'Like you,' she mumbled.

Luke turned around and stared at her. He arched his eyebrows. 'Have you quite finished?'

Alice took a deep breath. 'No. No, actually I haven't. You don't care that we haven't heard from Robert since the day he signed up. Freddie was with Charles, so God alone knows what's happened to those two. You want to know why we go to Victoria Station?' She paused, waiting for a response, but he stood in silence. 'We go, so we can look out for the men in this family. There's nothing else we can do to find them, but you on the other hand could be asking your so-called influential friends if they can find out anything. Any news at all would be better than not knowing. You go to that damn club every day, but you offer us nothing in the way of kindness or support. I've had to ask Molly's father to write some letters, because you've done nothing. Charles, and even Robert, deserve better than that. Call yourself a father; you're just a cold fish that's squashed mother's strength for years, with your tyrannical attitude. Well I can tell you, she's got strength I didn't know about, because it was buried so deep. She's the one saying we should stay positive. She's the one out looking for them, not you.'

Luke's jaw dropped. His eyes widened as he stared at his eldest daughter. His body stiffened as he took a step nearer to her. He slammed his glass down; the amber liquid spilt over the sides and dribbled on to the table.

Seeing the glint of steel in her father's eyes, Alice stepped backwards. She ignored the fear that gripped her chest. 'Come on, Father, have you got nothing to say?' she taunted him. 'Tell me, what have you been doing for the war effort?'

Luke's hands clenched and unclenched by his sides. 'I am not answerable to you, or anyone else for that matter, and if you want to stay living in my house, you will watch your tongue.'

Alice pulled her shoulders back and jutted out her chin. Her heart pounded in her chest; the tension was tangible. 'I can tell you what you've done – nothing.' She took a deep breath. 'You know, you could be visiting the men at Charing Cross Hospital. Some of them are so bandaged up, they can't read or see anything. Some of them have no families to visit them. You could be helping with some of the services, or just handing out cups of tea, but no, unless you can do the manly thing of going off to fight, it's beneath you.' Alice saw the pulsating at the side of her father's temple, but the gate had been opened and she could no longer close it.

Arthur gave a cry, waving his arms around and kicking his legs. Alice bent down and picked him up. 'Sshh little one, everything's all right,' she whispered as she rocked him back and forth again.

Luke sped past Alice, as he escaped her onslaught.

*

Sarah rushed into the sitting room. 'What's happened?' Her face flushed as she quickly looked around, before settling on Alice. 'Your father has just rushed past me, with a face like thunder. I tried to talk to him but he ignored me and slammed the front door as he left.' Her hands clenched in front of her. 'He didn't even put his coat on,' she mumbled. 'He'll freeze out there.'

Alice looked sheepishly at her mother. 'I think you'll find that it was my fault.'

Sarah raised her eyebrows. 'Yours?'

'Yes, I'm afraid I actually told him what I thought about him.' Alice bit down on her bottom lip. 'I'd say I'm sorry, but I'm not.'

'I don't know what to say, except that I'm shocked.'

Alice gave a bitter laugh. 'Yes, I think he was as well.'

Sarah stared at her eldest daughter for a moment. 'Nothing has happened has it? I mean, you haven't had any news, have you?'

'No. He told me I was making my son soft, and said you'd done the same with Charles.' Alice sighed. 'I think he may never forgive me, so I shall have to start looking for my own home soon.'

Sarah's eyes widened as she slumped into the chair. 'You can obviously move out whenever you see fit, but it has to be when you want to, and not because your father didn't like hearing some home truths.'

Alice's jaw slackened as she looked over at her mother. 'I probably did go too far, but once I'd started, I couldn't seem to control myself.'

'He was probably more shocked that it was you. He expects it from Lily, although she does seem to have been more settled since she has gained a purpose in her life.' Sarah shook her head. 'I wish I'd seen his face.' She lifted her hand and patted down the back of her grey hair.

'It's better that you weren't here.' Alice frowned. 'I didn't plan it; to be honest, it caught me by surprise. I don't know what got into me.'

Sarah laughed. 'Oh, I expect I can tell you that. You were probably inadvertently protecting your child. It's instinctive.'

Alice nodded. 'Well, I hope you don't get any

backlash from it.' She looked down at her son, before glancing across at her mother. 'He did say if I wanted to continue to live here, I had to be quiet, but I kept going.'

Sarah stood up and wandered over to her daughter. 'Don't worry about it; I'll sort it out.' She smiled down at Arthur. 'You need the support of your family around you, at least until Freddie gets home.'

'Where do you suppose he's gone?' Alice frowned, now wishing she had kept her mouth shut.

Sarah shrugged her shoulders. 'Don't worry yourself. He's probably gone to the club; he'll be back when he's hungry.' She smiled down at Arthur. 'He's such a contented baby.'

Alice smiled down at her son, whose big eyes were staring up at the pair of them. 'Go on, you can pick him up if you want to.' She laughed. 'And you know you do.'

Sarah beamed as she scooped him into her arms and planted a kiss on his forehead. 'It's wonderful having a baby in the house.' She walked around the room, talking to him in a sing-song voice. 'He certainly takes my mind off everything else, don't you, yes you do.'

Arthur smiled up at Sarah.

She screamed with delight. 'Did you see that? I just got a lovely smile.'

Alice laughed as she walked over to the window. She pulled the black material first, to stop any light seeping out onto the street, and then pulled the heavy brown curtains. She yearned for the longer days of spring. Alice looked round at the sound of her mother's murmurings, and smiled. Arthur was sound asleep in her mother's arms and she was still talking to him. 'Shall I take him off you, so you can relax for a little while, before father comes home?'

Sarah looked up and gave her daughter a smile. 'This is relaxing; I'm in my element.' Her gaze went back to her grandson.

Alice sat down and picked up her knitting. She pulled the soft fibres of the pale blue wool flat on her lap and examined the stitches. 'Hmm, I think I'm getting better at this knitting malarkey.'

'What are you making?' Sarah glanced up and frowned. 'That looks too pale to be socks for the men.'

Alice laughed. 'I thought I'd have a go at knitting Arthur a cardigan.'

Sarah nodded. 'You should be all right; just take your time.'

The house shuddered as the front door slammed shut. Alice's head jerked up and she quickly looked at her mother, who had done the same thing. She braced herself for her father's anger, not taking her eyes off the sitting room door. Her body was rigid and, without realising it, she held her breath, waiting, wanting to get it over and done with. The door slowly opened.

'Evening.' Lily flopped into an armchair and closed her eyes, oblivious to the looks of relief that had slowly spread across her mother and sister's faces. 'What a day.

It's quite bitter out there this evening. Sorry about the door, but the wind seemed to whisk it out of my fingers.' It was only then she opened her eyes and looked across at the other occupants of the room. 'What's the matter with you two?'

'Nothing,' Alice answered quickly, forcing her attention back to her knitting.

Lily frowned and her gaze moved from one to the other. 'Come on, tell'

'We just thought you were Father coming in,' Alice answered vaguely, but didn't look up.

'Hmm.' Lily squinted at the pair of them. 'Don't forget I am a police officer and can smell a rat a mile away.' She stood up and began unbuttoning her jacket. 'Come on, let's have it.'

Alice smiled at her sister. 'Are you going all policeman on us?'

Lily pulled her jacket off and slung it over the arm of the chair. 'Policewoman actually, but yes I am, so come on, out with it.'

Sarah sighed. 'It's nothing. Alice had an argument with your father.'

Lily's jaw dropped as she lowered herself back into the chair. 'Well, I'll be...'

Alice frowned as her sister's voice faded away. 'There's no need to be so astonished.'

'You are kidding me, right?' Lily fidgeted in her seat. 'You actually had an argument with Father?' She paused, raising her eyebrows. 'What, a real argument, or did you just ignore some banal instruction he gave you?'

Alice took a deep breath, not really wanting to talk about it. 'You're talking as though I am not capable of such a thing.'

Lily laughed for a few minutes, before wiping the tears from her eyes. 'If I'm being honest, I didn't think you were,' she said, in between gulping for air.

Alice shook her head. 'Well I'm clearly more capable than you thought, thank you very much.'

Lily's laughter stopped and she looked over at Alice. 'Don't misunderstand me, I'm thrilled. It's about time the women in this family started to fight back.'

*

There was a light knock on the sitting room door, before it slowly opened. Alice winced as the familiar squeak became more pronounced. 'We must put something on those hinges; I'm sure they're getting worse.'

Sarah nodded as Mrs Headley walked through the doorway.

'I'm sorry to disturb you, but I was wondering about dinner, ma'am.' The housekeeper stood with her hands clasped in front of her. 'Did you want to delay the evening meal until Mr Taylor comes home, or would you like me to bring the food to the table?'

Sarah glanced at the clock on the mantelpiece. With a

sharp intake of breath, she frowned, before looking back at Mrs Headley. 'Thank you for the reminder. I hadn't realised time had run away so; I think we should eat now.'

'Very well, ma'am.' Mrs Headley nodded. 'If you'd like to make your way to the dining room, I shall bring in the dishes.' She turned and vacated the room.

Alice also stared at the clock, momentarily mesmerised by the pendulum swinging back and forth. She clenched her hands on her lap, before looking over at her mother. 'Where do you suppose he is?' Alice looked back at the clock. 'He should've been home long before now.'

'Stop worrying.' Lily stood up and straightened her skirt. 'He's probably had dinner at the club.'

Alice shook her head. 'I don't think he ever eats there.' She glanced across at her mother. 'Does he?'

Sarah shrugged her shoulders. 'Not to my knowledge, but there's a first time for everything.' She stood up, the soft folds of her skirt dropping effortlessly to her calves. 'Well, wherever he is, we still have to eat.' Sarah took a couple of steps to the door before turning to Alice. 'Do you want to check on Arthur before we eat? Although I'm sure he's sound asleep.'

'I'll do it.' Lily beamed. 'Any excuse to gaze at my handsome nephew.' She sped out of the door, before a response could be formulated.

Alice shook her head, but couldn't resist smiling after

her. As she entered the dining room, she glanced over at her mother and noticed her face was quite pale. Her knuckles were white and her hands gripped each other. Alice reached out and rested her hand on her mother's arm. 'Are you worried about Father?'

Sarah briefly looked at Alice, before lowering her eyes and licking her lips. 'I'm sure he's fine; stop worrying.'

Alice's hands dropped to her sides and she stared down at her feet. 'I'm sorry I've caused this worry. As if we haven't got enough going on.' She squeezed her eyes shut and let out a heavy sigh.

'Don't blame yourself, Alice.' Sarah smiled as she shook her head and walked stiffly over to the table. 'Your father is used to being the voice of authority, so for you, of all people, not to show respect probably hit home a little.' Sarah gave a hollow laugh. 'If it had been Lily on the other hand, he probably wouldn't have batted an eyelid, although he still wouldn't have liked it.'

Alice nodded. 'I'm so sorry; I didn't mean for this to happen.'

Lily grinned. Her eyes twinkled with mischief as she walked in. 'That boy of yours is wonderful; so cute. I could sit and watch him all day.' She giggled as she pulled out a dining chair from the table. 'Right, what are we having for dinner?'

A deep golden-brown pie was sitting on a plate, in the centre of the table. Sarah picked up the sharp knife next to it and cut into the pastry. Crumbs fell onto the white tablecloth. 'It looks like cheese and potato pie, and we've carrots to go with it.' She pulled out a small wedge and steam escaped, as she balanced it on the knife, before placing it on her own plate.

'Excellent, I'm starving. It smells delicious.' Lily passed her plate over to her mother. 'If it's all right, can I have a bigger piece than you?' She laughed. 'That little bit wouldn't keep the mouse in the larder going for very long.'

Alice and her mother shook their heads in unison.

'You get worse instead of better.' Sarah glared at Lily. 'Don't talk about mice in the larder; I hate anything like that.'

Lily raised her eyebrows and gave Alice a knowing look, before glancing back to her mother. 'You know I was only joking.' She grinned. 'I haven't been in the larder to know whether there's a mouse in there or not.'

Sarah's eyes widened. She opened her mouth, but closed it again. She shook her head and continued to cut the pie, placing slices onto the plates.

The women ate in silence. Sarah pushed her food around, eating very little. Alice watched her, with a heavy feeling of responsibility.

Lily put her knife and fork down on the side of her plate. 'Come on, Mother, stop playing with your food. You've got to eat.'

Alice glared at Lily, who proceeded to pull a face

back. Alice tilted her head and rested her hand on her mother's arm. 'You're worried about him, aren't you?'

Lily squinted at her mother. 'Shall I see if I can get someone from the police station to go to the club, to see if he's there?'

Sarah's head snapped up. 'No, no that definitely won't do. Your father would be so embarrassed, and then we'd all be in trouble.'

'I don't know what we can do.' Alice paused. 'We could cycle to all the hospitals, to see if he's been in an accident.'

Sarah gasped. 'I hadn't thought of the hospitals. I just thought—'

'Perhaps you upset him so much, he has caught a train to Sandringham,' Lily threw in, as she picked up her cutlery.

'He wouldn't have gone there; he didn't take anything with him.' Sarah shook her head. 'He was too angry when he left here, to plan where he was going.'

'What's at Sandringham?' Lily arched her brows. 'Why haven't we ever been there, and more importantly, why haven't you ever been there?'

Sarah shrugged her shoulders. 'He has family up there.'

Lily leant in towards her mother. 'Have you met them? Did they come to your wedding? How do you know he doesn't have a second—'

Alice glared at her sister. 'Stop interrogating her.'

'Sorry, I got carried away.' Lily stared at her mother for a moment. 'I'm intrigued why he has kept us all separate though.'

'He hasn't kept us separate.' Sarah took a deep breath. 'He just thinks they'll have nothing in common with us. I think he's a little ashamed.'

Alice tightened her lips. 'If that's true, it's terrible.'

Lily sighed. 'Well, I don't suppose we'll ever know, but whatever you said to him clearly hit home.'

Sarah pushed her chair away and stood up. She gripped the side of the table and closed her eyes, before taking some deep breaths.

Alice stood up, knocking her chair over. 'Are you all right? Do you feel dizzy?'

Sarah fell like a stone, hitting her head on the table on her way down.

Chapter 22

Alice and Lily paced up and down the corridor of St Thomas' Hospital. Neither spoke. The clatter of trolleys rattled in the distance. Doctors yelling orders and people mumbling back rattled their nerves. Alice took a deep breath and the hospital stench caught in the back of her throat. Nurses walked briskly by, but no one spoke to them. Alice bit her lip as she slumped down on an old wooden chair. Blood seeped onto her tongue, leaving a metallic taste in her mouth.

Lily flopped down on the chair next to her. Her hands were clenched in her lap. 'She's going to be all right, isn't she?'

Alice nodded; the colour had long since drained from her face. 'It's a good hospital.' She stood up again, not knowing what to do with herself. Arthur had been asleep when they left and she hoped he had stayed that way for Mrs Headley.

Lily bit down on the side of her fingernail. 'Should we let Grandpa know?'

'No.' Alice sat down, fidgeting on the chair. 'We've both pushed things too far today.' She slumped forward and rested her head in her hands.

Lily nodded. She watched a lady being supported by an elderly man, as they walked past them. He whispered comforting words, while she sobbed in his arms. 'I know. I didn't mean for this to happen. I just can't understand why we've never met the so-called family living in Sandringham, that's all.'

'Just leave it, Lily; you don't always have to know everything,' Alice snapped. 'At this precise moment, I don't care about Sandringham. We don't know what's wrong with Mother, or where Father is. God only knows where Charles and Freddie are, and Robert hasn't been in touch since he left, so in my book, that's more than enough to worry about.'

Lily nodded. She lowered her head and squeezed her eyes shut. Her throat felt restricted as a lump formed and tears pricked her eyelids, pushing to be released.

Alice put her arm around her sister. 'I'm sorry, I shouldn't have ranted at you.'

Lily's head leaned in on Alice's shoulder and she sobbed.

'I shouldn't have taken my worries out on you,' Alice whispered.

'No, you were right.' Lily pulled herself upright and reached for the handkerchief in her coat pocket. 'I've been selfish by only considering what's happening in front of me. You and Mother have much bigger worries. It's probably my fault she collapsed.'

'Don't punish yourself,' Alice whispered as she

looked down at her hands, gripped in her lap. 'I expect it's everything all rolled into one sorry mess. I'm sure things will work themselves out.'

Lily sighed, dabbing her handkerchief on her cheeks and under her dark-rimmed eyes. 'It must be more than a faint because she's been here for some time now.'

Alice nodded. 'I was thinking the same thing, but I know from driving the ambulance that it does also depend on how many urgent cases come in.'

Lily frowned. 'Shall we try and find her, because if she's feeling all right now, we could take her home.'

'No, Lily, we have to let the doctors do their stuff. If we took her home and something happened, that would be awful.'

They sat in silence, each immersed in their own thoughts, watching the scenes unfold in front of them.

Lily gave her sister a sideways glance. 'About Charles and Freddie.' She took a deep breath. 'The thing is, I keep telling myself everyone will come back safe and Charles will just turn up.' Her words began tripping over each other to be heard. She gave Alice a watery smile. 'I haven't said anything before, but I've been looking for him and Freddie as well.'

Alice reached out and covered Lily's hand with her own. 'It's all a mess.' She shook her head. 'Thank goodness for Arthur.'

Lily smiled at her sister. 'He's certainly a wonderful distraction from everything else at the moment.'

The clip-clop of heels on the tiled flooring made Alice swivel in her chair. Molly and Victoria were rushing towards them. She jumped up and tears trickled down her cheeks. Victoria was the first to wrap her arms around Alice, quickly followed by Molly. She found comfort when their soft cheeks lay against hers. Molly let her arms drop and stepped towards Lily, enveloping her in a hug.

Victoria kept hold of Alice's hand as she also swung an arm around Lily. After a moment, she stepped back from the sisters. 'So, do you know what's happening?'

The two of them shook their heads.

'But you've been here hours, and where's your father?' Molly fidgeted from one foot to the other, as she looked along the corridor.

Alice lifted her hand to roughly wipe away the tears from her cheeks. 'That's a long story, but the upshot is that we don't know.' She gasped as she looked from one of her friends to the other. 'How did you know we were here?'

'We knocked to see if everything was all right, because you didn't come into work' Victoria tried to smile but failed. 'I know it was late, but we both had a few errands to do first. Anyway, when we got there, Mrs Headley was going out of her mind with worry, because you had been gone for so long, and told us what had happened.'

'Do you know whether Arthur was all right?' Alice

scanned their faces.

'Don't worry. Mrs Headley is going to stay with him all night, if need be.' Molly repeated the housekeeper's words, while unbuttoning her black winter coat.

'Where would we be without Mrs Headley?' Alice mumbled as she sat down again.

Molly stepped back a little and took a deep breath. 'Look, let me go and find a doctor and see if there's any news.'

Alice shook her head. 'They are so busy; it would be wrong to chase them.'

Molly turned away from the group and started walking down the corridor. 'But if they've forgotten about you, we could be sitting here all night.'

Victoria patted Alice and Lily's arms. 'I hate to say this, but she's right.'

They watched Molly stride away, turning her head one way, then the other, stopping to speak to a nurse, who pointed further away from them. Alice wondered if she'd find her way back. Did everyone who came here get lost? She shook her head as Molly finally disappeared from view.

＊

Luke walked purposefully through the hospital; all thoughts of tiredness had disappeared. It had been a long night, but he felt more alive than he had in years.

When he had first entered St Thomas' Hospital, the overpowering smell of antiseptic caught in his throat. The number of men waiting to be seen shocked him, as did the blood-soaked bandages covering the soldiers' injuries. The patients' screams of agony had him reeling with helplessness. He would have been forgiven for thinking a massacre had taken place and this bloodbath was the result. Nurses and doctors were working at speed, calling out instructions to each other, while trying to make the patients as comfortable as possible. He had read the newspapers every day and seen the Pathé newsreels, but nothing had prepared him for what he saw. He had stood rooted to the spot. He had wanted to run, but something kept him there. Thoughts of his wife and daughters seeing this every day made him nauseous. The reality of the pain and suffering they must have witnessed at Victoria Station, in the ambulance and at the hospital, would be ingrained in their memories forever. Alice had tried to tell him, but he either hadn't listened, or hadn't wanted to hear it. Whichever it was, the outcome had not been good.

He could see Alice and Lily with Victoria, further along the hallway, but they hadn't noticed him. His daughters' shoulders were slumped and their faces were etched in agony. Was this his fault? He took a deep breath and quickened his pace.

Alice looked up. Her eyes widened as she took in his pace and urgency. She stepped forward. 'Where the hell have you been?'

Lily spun round. 'We've been going out of our minds with worry here. We didn't know where you were, or whether Mother is going to be all right.'

Colour rose up Alice's neck and flooded her cheeks. 'I know you don't care about any of us and we are just trophies you can brag about at your club, but have you for just one minute considered anybody else, except yourself.' She turned away from him, as her eyes filled up again. 'I hope Freddie makes a better father than you.'

Luke lowered his head and stared hard at the tiled flooring. He looked up at his daughters with new-found respect. Their faces were etched in pain; he had caused that. 'So do I,' he whispered.

They both stepped back and stared, wide-eyed at him, neither knowing what to say. Alice's jaw dropped. Was this an admission?

'Molly is trying to find out about Mrs Taylor,' Victoria offered, trying to fill the cavernous silence that stood between the girls and their father.

Luke nodded. 'I, um, I passed her in the corridor and she told me you were all up here.'

Alice glared at him. 'I can't believe this. Mother was worrying about where you were, when she collapsed...' She paused. '... Amongst other things.' Her hands clenched at her side as her jaw tightened. 'You left the house angrily and without a word to her about where you were going, or when you'd be back.' She wrapped her arms around her midriff. 'Your argument was with me, not her. If you want to take it out on someone, punish me, because she's done nothing wrong.' Alice looked past Luke and saw Molly walking towards them.

Lily followed her sister's eye-line and swerved past her father to get to Molly. 'Have you found out anything?'

Alice pulled back her shoulders and straightened her lips, before taking a deep breath. 'Is she all right?'

Molly nodded towards Luke. 'Yes, they think it was her blood pressure, but it seems to be fine now, so I believe she can go home.'

Lily and Alice grabbed each other in a bear hug, their tears rolling freely, as they laughed and cried at the same time. Victoria wrapped her arms around the pair of them and hugged them tight.

'So you found them all right, Mr Taylor?' Molly watched him standing outside the circle of relief.

'Yes,' he whispered.

Molly turned sideways from the girls and lowered her voice. 'Do they know where you've been all night?'

Luke shook his head.

'Don't you think you should tell them?'

Luke looked at Molly as if he was seeing her for the first time.

Molly raised her eyebrows. 'Yes, I know I'm just a slip of a girl, but this war has made us all grow up quickly.' She looked over her shoulder at the three girls huddled together. 'Although it has to be said, Victoria was way ahead of all of us there.'

Luke sighed. 'I hate to admit it, but you are right. However, now is not the time or the place.'

Molly watched the fear and anxiety run across his face; he was no longer wearing the tough facade he had portrayed for years. 'Sorry, Mr Taylor, I've always been a bit of a straight talker and yes, it has got me into trouble at times, but in my humble opinion, now's as good a time as any.'

Alice turned to face her father. 'As good a time as any for what?' She frowned at him. Did he have some news that was going to tear this family apart?

Luke cleared his throat. 'To go and get your mother and take her home.'

Lily laughed. 'For once, Father, we're in agreement and it's not every day we can say that. In fact, I don't think we've ever been able to say it.' She threaded her arm through Alice's. 'Come on, let's go and find Mother; she'll be wondering where we are.'

*

Alice draped a shawl around her mother's shoulders as she sat up in her bedroom. 'It's good to have you home; you frightened us yesterday.' She gave her mother a smile.

'I'm sorry. I didn't mean to worry you all.' Sarah sighed. 'To be honest, I don't remember anything about it. One minute I was standing up, and the next, I was at the hospital.'

Alice nodded. 'It doesn't matter now. The main thing is you're all right, but you've to start taking things easy.' She laughed as her mother opened her mouth to speak. 'For a while at least, and no argument.' Alice leaned in to take a closer look at the cut on her forehead. 'Does your head hurt?'

'It's a little bit tender, but not too bad.' Sarah lifted her hand to touch the cut.

Alice smiled as she tapped her hand away. 'Leave it. I'll bring Arthur in to see you later; that'll cheer you up, but in the meantime, be good.'

Sarah smiled at her eldest daughter. 'You're a good girl and an excellent mum. Freddie is very lucky to have you.'

Anxiety chased Alice's smile away.

Sarah grabbed her daughter's hand. 'I'm sorry. I just meant—'

'I know. Don't fret; everything will be all right in the end.' Alice mustered up her smile. 'Just rest. You have your knitting, and there are a couple of books on the side for you to read, so try to relax.'

Sarah smiled. 'I'll be good, I promise. What about Foyles?'

Alice laughed at her mother's reassurance. 'See,

already you've moved on to worrying about my job. Stop worrying.' She sighed. 'I've asked Lily to pop in there and tell them I won't be returning yet, I shall wait until I know you are well enough to be left.'

Sarah shook her head. 'But it's not necessary, I'm not on my own, Mrs Headley is here.'

Alice took the couple of steps towards the bedroom door. 'I'll be back later to check on you.'

Sarah nodded.

Alice checked that Arthur was still asleep, before skipping downstairs to the dining room. She stopped short when her father came into view. He was sat at the table, nursing a cup of something, which appeared to have his full attention. Slices of toast stood waiting for someone to butter them. An untouched boiled egg was on a plate in front of him. Alice took a deep breath, before clearing her throat and walking into the room. 'Morning, Father.' He sat in silence and didn't look up. Determined he wasn't going to ignore her, no matter how angry he was, she raised her voice. 'Morning, Father.'

His head jerked, as if he had been released from a deep sleep.

Alice's eyes narrowed as she watched him. 'I know you are angry with me, but you can't ignore me; that's just rude.'

Luke stared at his daughter, as though he had never seen her before.

Alice sighed. 'I know I owe you an apology for my outburst yesterday, and I am sorry.'

Luke returned his gaze to his cold tea.

'Don't misunderstand me,' Alice continued. 'I'm not apologising for the sentiment of what I said, but I'm sorry for the way that I said it.'

The silence between them seemed to last an eternity. Alice sat down and poured a cup of tea. She knew it would be cold, but she was unable to stand in front of him, waiting to be told off. She lifted the cup and sipped it, trying not to grimace, as the tepid liquid entered her mouth.

'The tea has been there a while; you'll need a fresh pot.' A smile played on Luke's lips as he looked at his daughter.

Alice wondered if he was enjoying her discomfort. Was it all part of her punishment? She shrugged her shoulders. 'It'll do me; it's wet.'

Luke studied his daughter. 'Something has changed you. I wonder if it's being a mother, being married or the extra things that you're doing because of the war.'

Alice frowned as she put her cup back on its matching saucer. 'I think the war has changed many lives. You're the only person I know that appears to be unscathed by it.'

'You are wrong there.'

Startled, Alice shook her head. She raised her eyebrows as she faced him. 'At the risk of making you angry again, tell me how?'

'You and your comments yesterday,' Luke whispered.

'I don't understand.' Alice jutted out her chin. 'I've already apologised for the manner in which I spoke to you, but I'll never apologise for what I said.'

'You don't need to apologise.' Luke sucked in his breath as he looked at Alice. 'You were right.'

'So why didn't you come home last night, instead of letting us all worry about you. I expect you hid in that club of yours.' Alice watched her father shake his head, before frowning. 'Am I missing something here? If I am, please tell, so I can understand.'

'I walked around for a long time.' Luke picked up his cup and went to take a sip, but stopped just before it reached his lips and put it down again.

'You must have been freezing.'

Luke gave a brittle laugh. 'To be honest, I didn't notice. When the daughter you consider to be a mouse starts fighting back, it's usually time to sit up and listen.'

'I'm not sure I like that description, but,' Alice lifted her hand and placed it on her chest. 'I'm sorry, I truly am. I don't really know what got into me.'

'Don't be sorry.' Luke paused. 'It probably should have been said years ago.'

Alice slumped back against her chair.

'Anyway, I didn't go to the club. I walked for what seemed like ages and when I looked up, I was near St Thomas' Hospital.' He looked at Alice and gave a small laugh. 'Someone must have been on your side.'

Alice stared at him. Words were failing her.

Luke sighed. 'Anyway, I went in, and if I'm honest, it all frightened me a little bit. I wanted to run away, but I couldn't. It made me realise the things you and your mother have seen must have been horrendous, let alone the boys at the front.' He stopped and shook his head. He bit his lip and blinked quickly. 'I, er...' He paused. 'I asked the nurse if I could help in any way and she sent me to sit with a man, a soldier. I say a man, although he didn't look any older than Charles.' He sucked in his breath and straightened his lips. 'It turns out they had done all they could and he wasn't going to last the night.'

Alice stared at her father, tears rolling down her cheeks.

'Anyway, I stayed with him all night, well, until he passed away.' Tears rolled down Luke's cheeks. 'I talked to him and held his hand. We prayed a little.' He angrily wiped his tears away. 'He knew he was dying; such a brave boy. I promised to contact his mother, so I shall do that today.' He took a deep breath and shook his head. 'I don't know how you and your mother do it every day,' he whispered.

Alice reached out and held her father's hand. 'It's hard, but you gave that man some comfort. He didn't die alone and that's what you have to remember.'

Luke nodded. 'I felt so helpless.'

'I know; they come back broken. Whether they survive the war or not, none of them will ever be the same again. When I'm at Victoria Station, you can see their experiences etched on their faces. There are no smiles, only bravado.'

'You'll be pleased to know I have arranged to be a helper at the hospital.' Luke gave a little laugh. 'I say helper, but really I shall sit with the patients. The nursing staff will tell me who is in most need, and that's where I shall go.'

Alice smiled at her father. 'It's a good thing you're doing, because it means so much to the men, yet it's only costing you your time.'

Luke nodded. 'So instead of you apologising, I should be thanking you for your outburst yesterday.'

Alice's eyes widened as realisation dawned on her. 'Last night, were you already at the hospital when Molly found you?'

'Yes, he had just died when Molly saw me.'

'But you never said anything. You let me go on at you. Why didn't you stop me?'

Luke shrugged his shoulders. 'Emotions were running high and, to be honest, I didn't really want to talk about why I was there. It suited me to let you think I had just arrived for your mother.' He paused for a moment. 'I'm glad I didn't know earlier, because I wouldn't have known what to do. The boy needed me. He gripped my hand so tight, I am not sure I could have left him.'

381

Chapter 23

Alice stared straight ahead at the dining room window; the black material had been pulled back with the curtains. The wind rattled the frame, making a haunting noise, causing her to shiver. The sun was too weak to break through the grey clouds and drops of rain splashed onto the glass. Alice thought about the men on the front line. She had heard stories of the soldiers being up to their waists in water, with huge rats for company. They were not even able to light their cigarettes for comfort, because everything was soaked. She couldn't imagine the din of being bombarded with gunfire, or bombs exploding all around you, let alone the effect of someone dying next to you. Then there was the poisonous gas. She shook her head, trying to digest her father's words. 'It would have been difficult for you,' Alice whispered, staring at the uneaten toast sitting in the centre of the dining table. 'But we were there for Mother and yes, I was angry with you, but that was because I thought you were just punishing us.' She glanced across at her father. 'Had I known you were giving comfort to someone, I'd like to think I'd have behaved differently.'

Luke arched his eyebrows. 'I can see that, but I suppose I got caught up in the moment and didn't stop to think about anyone else. I just knew I couldn't leave him.'

'I can understand that,' Alice whispered. 'I'd like to think, if any of our men were in that position, someone would show them the same kindness, whichever country they were in.'

Luke nodded, wondering what words of wisdom he could offer, but he knew there were none.

'You know, I've heard some harrowing stories.' Alice looked down at her hands, gripped in her lap. A tear fell onto her thumb. 'And every time I hear one, I hope and pray that everyone is safe and not living through the same nightmares. I can't bear the thought of Freddie or Charles not coming home.' A sob caught in Alice's throat as she gulped for air. Realising what she had said, she looked over at the blurry figure of her father. 'Robert as well.' She swallowed hard, trying to remove the lump that had formed in her throat. 'Obviously. It's just,' she whispered, 'I have a closeness with Charles that isn't there with Robert.'

Luke nodded. 'I understand.'

'The thought of them never meeting Arthur is just unbearable, let alone the thought of my life with Freddie being over, before it actually begins.' Alice pulled out her handkerchief and blew her nose, before dabbing at her cheeks.

'We have to stay positive,' Luke whispered. He wasn't sure what to say or do in this unknown territory.

Alice gave a brittle laugh. 'That's what Mother always says; she said they at least deserve our positivity.'

Luke nodded. 'And she's right. God will bring them back to us, and that is what we have to believe.'

'Will he?' Alice shook her head. 'There are an awful lot of men not coming back. Why should ours be any different?'

'Don't lose your faith, Alice. We have to pray for their safe return, and believe it, because what else is there?'

Alice stared at her father. 'I do try and, as a rule, I think I succeed but sometimes it just gets all too much for me. I look at Arthur and wonder if he'll ever know his father is a wonderful man.'

'He will know. We shall make sure of it.' Luke scraped back his chair and walked around the dining table. He hesitated, before awkwardly wrapping his arms around his daughter. 'I have let you down, but I will start asking questions and writing letters. I know I'm a bit late, but better late than never.' He squeezed his daughter close to him. 'I am sorry.'

*

Luke sat in the corner of the library, in the Gentlemen's Club. Hundreds of books covered the shelves, from floor to ceiling. Only a few men were sitting in there, reading newspapers and books. The woody bouquet of cigars hung in the air, mingling with the rich intense aroma of coffee. Luke twiddled his pen as he remembered this corner used to be where the Gettins sat, when he first joined the family firm. He looked around. It was a good spot, because you could see the whole room and all the comings and goings. He sighed and looked down at his blank piece of writing paper. He looked up again, only to gaze out at St James's Street. Smoke billowed out of chimney pots, only to get lost amongst the grey clouds and the never-ending rain that drizzled down on everyone's umbrellas and hats of varying styles and sizes.

The grey weather seemed to epitomise Luke's mood. He had no idea where to turn next. He needed to ask around, or maybe take an advert out in a newspaper. There must be something he could do. He turned back to his paper and began scribbling a list of ideas.

'Morning, Luke.'

A chair knocked against the table leg, causing it to wobble. Luke looked up, using his hands to steady it. 'Sorry, Edward, I didn't mean to be rude. I was engrossed in making some notes.'

Edward nodded. 'You don't mind if I join you, do you?'

'No, of course not. In fact, you may be able to help.' Luke lowered his eyes to his paper.

A steward came over to take an order. 'Luke, do you

want a coffee?' Edward glanced at his watch. 'Or a whisky? It's lunch time, so it's acceptable.'

Luke looked up. 'Coffee please.' He watched the steward walk away. 'The whisky drinking is going to stop, or at least slow down for the time being.'

Edward raised his eyebrows, while his fingers formed a steeple against his chin. 'I'm pleased to hear it, but I'm intrigued as to what has brought it on.'

Luke put down his pen and sat back in his chair. 'Your granddaughter started it.'

Edward laughed. 'Oh, has Lily been giving you a hard time again?'

Luke's eyes crinkled at the corners as he laughed. 'No. You would expect it to be her, but it was Alice.'

'Alice?' Edward shook his head. 'I find that hard to believe.'

'I know, but they say it's the quiet ones you have to watch.' Luke laughed. 'As shocking as it is, it's true.' He paused, closing his eyes momentarily before looking back at Edward. 'The thing is, everything she said to me was right, but that's not to say it was easy to take, because it wasn't.'

The steward appeared with two cups, a small jug of warm milk and a pot of coffee, and without a word, he placed them on the table between the two men.

'Well.' Edward wrinkled his nose. 'I can't pretend I'm not curious about what was said.'

'To be honest, she told me some home truths, which I

can't pretend I liked. I spent a lot of the evening walking around, trying to take in what she had said to me.' Luke raised his eyebrows. 'I don't think she meant to be hurtful, because Alice isn't made that way, but it certainly hit a nerve.'

Edward shook his head, not sure if he was hearing his son-in-law correctly. 'It sounds like she didn't hold back.'

Luke laughed. 'No she didn't, but the upside is that I think I have found something that was missing from my life, so as difficult as it was, I am grateful to her.'

Edward leant forward, picking up the coffee pot, and began pouring a measure in each cup. 'Which is?'

'I think it's about being useful; you know, being needed again.' Luke paused. 'Everyone around me seems to have outgrown me, and I suppose I felt a bit of a spare part.'

Edward nodded as he stirred some milk into his coffee. 'So what have you found, that has given you a new lease of life?'

'I went to the hospital.' Luke looked at his father-in-law. 'Obviously not intentionally, but when I saw all those men, injured and dying, it just made me realise there was something I could do to help.'

Edward watched Luke pour the milk into his coffee. 'Is that what you are writing about?'

Luke frowned. 'No, what I saw at that hospital will stay with me forever; I don't need to write it down.' He picked up his cup and sipped the strong dark liquid. 'Oh, that's hot.' He replaced the cup back onto its saucer. 'I promised Alice I would try and find out about the boys and Freddie. If I'm honest, I'm not sure where to turn, but I don't want to let her down.'

Edward nodded.

'I have found the address of the War Office and sent a letter there, asking for information about their whereabouts. That has been followed up with a letter to Lord Kitchener, but as yet I have no news to pass on.' Luke picked up his pen again and doodled on the paper. 'I just don't know where to go next.'

Edward watched Luke drawing box after box, wondering if there was any significant meaning to them. 'George might be able to help.'

Luke let out a heavy sigh. 'I don't think he would help; he doesn't like me.'

'It's not that he doesn't like you; he doesn't like what you stand for. George and Emily have a great sense of family, and there's nothing they wouldn't do for Sarah and her children.' Edward paused.

Luke gave a brittle laugh. 'The trouble is, I have always seen George as a do-gooder.'

Edward smiled. 'That's because he is. He owns a house that is used for women and children running away from their violent husbands, so yes, he'll always champion a woman's cause, because he has first-hand experience of how bad a man can be. He doesn't care what people think about him. He's a very principled man and happy with his life's achievements.'

Luke nodded.

'We both see signs that you didn't marry for love, but I know Sarah did, so for her father, that is heartbreaking. I loved her mother with my whole being and when she died, I also wanted to die.' Edward watched Luke almost fold in his chair. 'You have to remember, Emily was there for Sarah when her mother died, not me, because I couldn't cope. Trust me, I know all about letting your family down, but it doesn't mean you can't get that trust back again. It does take hard work though.'

Words failed Luke. He lowered his eyes as shame washed over him.

'For the sake of your promise to your daughter, you need to swallow your pride and pay George and Emily a visit, because they have contacts that might be useful to you. Whatever you think of George, he'll admire you for supporting your family and do his best to help.'

*

Luke took a deep breath as he stood on the opposite side of Tavistock Square, facing the black front door. The five-storey house looked intimidating, with its ornate plasterwork and protective black railings edging the footpath. The front door sprung open; George stood on the threshold. The chill of the breeze made Luke shiver, as his gaze bounced from place to place and he quickly turned his back on the house. The square's garden stood before him. A large mass of grass was edged with wooden benches, either side of the path. Green tips of daffodils peeked through the muddy soil, giving the first sign that spring was on its way. The branches of the tall trees showed there was life, as the leaf buds started to appear, in readiness for the shade they would provide in the heat of the summer. Luke raised his eyebrows; he didn't know what had got into him lately. Here he was, waxing lyrically about the forthcoming spring season. He sighed. Had he even noticed the change in seasons in the past? He thought not. He shook his head and turned, in time to see George walking away from him.

'Right.' Luke steeled himself. 'What are you, a man or a mouse?' His lips straightened into a thin line as the voice in his head echoed, *Squeak, squeak, squeak.* He walked across the road and took a couple of steps to follow him, before stopping to turn and walk away again. He looked at the front door. Perhaps he should talk to Emily; she was always kinder to him, but that was not what this was about. He had to do this, if he was going to gain any respect from his family. Luke pushed his hands inside his trouser pockets as he counted in his head. The urge to run away took hold. *Come on, get it over and done with. The sooner you ask, the sooner you'll know,* the voice yelled in his head.

'How difficult can it be?' He looked down the road and could still see George, dressed in his dark grey winter coat. He had stopped to help an old lady with some shopping. It was now or never. Before he had a chance to argue with himself further, Luke quickened his pace. He had to catch him. He gasped for breath, as every step took him nearer. His lungs burnt as breathlessness took hold.

George looked up, as Luke got nearer. He turned his attention back to the old lady, who gave him a toothless smile before walking on. George took a step towards Luke and arched his eyebrows. 'Afternoon, Luke, what brings you here?'

Luke stopped, thrusting his hands in his trouser pockets as he bent over, gasping for air.

George laughed. 'It looks like you need to walk more often, or maybe just further than the club.' He frowned, reaching out to rest his hand on Luke's back. 'Are you all right?'

Luke lifted his head and nodded, before straightening his body. His heart was pounding in his chest. He took a deep breath. His fingers nervously jingled the coins in his pockets as he glanced up. 'I wanted to talk to you.' His gaze bounced around, as he struggled to look at George. He swiftly removed his hands from his pockets and cleared his throat. 'I was about to call on you, when I saw you leave the house.' He dragged his hand through his hair. 'I hope you don't mind me just dropping by unannounced.'

George let his arm drop to his side. 'No, of course not, but I can't pretend I am not more than a little surprised to see you.'

Luke nodded. 'I know we have had our differences over the years, but I have come to ask for your help.'

George raised his eyebrows again. 'This is clearly going to be a day of surprises.' He paused. 'Do you mind if we talk and walk at the same time, as I am meeting Emily in an hour.' He laughed. 'She is out shopping for knitting wool and threads for her embroidery at the moment, and no doubt Liberty's in Regent Street will warrant a visit.'

'Not at all.' They both stepped forward. 'It doesn't seem to bother you, I mean the shopping, or anything else for that matter.'

George laughed. 'Why would it? I love Emily to bits, and I don't care who knows it either.' His smile faded. 'When you have seen some of the things that men do to women and children, it makes you put things into perspective.'

Luke nodded. 'I suppose I have been very fortunate, but didn't always appreciate it.'

George frowned. 'Didn't?'

Luke kept his eyes on the pavement. He had no desire to bare his soul to George, even if he was a good man. He cleared his throat. 'Edward has advised me to speak to you.'

George stared at Luke but didn't push the conversation he wanted to have. 'About what?'

'Charles is missing.' Luke paused, as a lump formed in his throat. 'We don't know about Robert or Freddie, but Alice hasn't heard from Freddie and he was with Charles. She is tying herself up in knots, worrying about them...'

'So you want me to see if I can find anything out?'

Luke nodded, crossing Bloomsbury Street as they walked towards Regent Street.

George shook his head. 'I'll try, but a lot of the people I knew have popped their clogs, if you know what I mean. I'll certainly try for you.'

'I have written letters, but I have heard nothing.' Luke glanced up at him. 'I wouldn't ask but—'

'You're desperate.' George smiled. 'I know that, Luke.' He laughed. 'You're not the only one to be aware of our differences, you know.'

Luke's lips thinned. 'I am making changes and I hope our differences can be forgotten, along with other things. It isn't going to happen overnight, but coming here is about me swallowing my pride and putting my family first.'

George nodded. 'I'll do the best I can for you, but I can't make any promises. I hope things do move forward because, while she doesn't say anything, I know Emily misses her relationship with Sarah. Over the years, they have seen less and less of each other, yet Emily talks fondly of the time they spent together.' George stopped and studied Luke. 'You know family is everything to me and whether we like it or not, we are family. There's nothing more important, and that includes the ladies and children in our lives.'

Luke shook his head; he had never given Sarah and Emily's relationship a thought. 'Thank you. I can't ask for anything more, and probably don't deserve your help at all.'

Chapter 24

March 1916

Alice sat on her bed, staring out at the blue sky, broken up with its cotton wool clouds. The shafts of early morning sunshine held little warmth or cheer for her. As usual, the tears didn't feel very far away. Her eyes glistened as she looked at Arthur in his cot. 'Hello, my little man.' She scooped Arthur into her arms and he rewarded her with a beaming smile. Alice stroked his soft, tiny fingers. 'So, what do you think of your mother going back to work then? I really don't know if I have made the right decision.'

Arthur waved his arms and kicked his legs frantically, as he gurgled his opinion. His eyes never left her face as she lowered her head, to give him a light kiss on the forehead. 'Your grandma and Mrs Headley are going to love looking after you, all day today, while I shall miss you so much, but as they say, sacrifices need to be made. There's a war on you know.' She stared down at Arthur's chubby face. 'Your father will be home one day.' A solitary tear tripped over her eyelashes. 'I have to keep the faith. I suppose Father's right; without that, we have nothing.'

Arthur's smile disappeared and his bottom lip quivered.

'Don't get upset, Arthur. I have to leave soon and it's going to be hard enough.' She spoke to him in the singsong voice he loved and he immediately smiled. Alice pulled Arthur close. Sighing, she stood up and opened the bedroom door. With one hand gliding across the top of the banister, she walked down the stairs.

There was no mistaking Molly's excitement, coming from the sitting room. 'I can't believe Alice is coming back to Foyles.' Her laughter travelled through the house. 'I'm amazed old Leadbetter asked her; he's a stickler for doing the right thing. I must admit I've missed her.'

Sarah's laughter reached Alice in the hall. 'I think she would have been back sooner if she hadn't been so worried about me, although it'll be hard for her because, while she's always busy, she's never left Arthur all day before. I must admit there's no denying I'm excited at having him all to myself.' The smile gradually faded from her voice. 'It'll do her good to be amongst her beloved books again.'

Resentment gripped Alice. She didn't want to share Arthur; he was all she had of Freddie. She spun on her heels to go back to her room, before shaking her head and turning back again. Taking a deep breath, her nose wrinkled as the faint aroma of coffee caught her. She avoided touching the door as she stepped into the sitting room. The sun's rays reflected off the mirror above the fireplace, spreading brightness and warmth.

Molly jumped to her feet, grinning from ear to ear. 'Morning, Alice, I hope you don't mind, but we thought we'd walk to work with you this morning; you know, keep you company just in case—'

'Morning Alice.' Victoria tilted her head to one side. 'We know it's early and we didn't mean to wake everyone…'

'You haven't.' Alice's dark rimmed eyes bounced from one to the other, her vacant stare giving nothing away. 'I didn't realise I'd have an escort to work.'

'We, we just thought…' Molly bit her lip as she fidgeted from one foot to the other.

'Don't worry.' Sarah stood up. 'Everything's fine and it's lovely to see you girls.' She took a step towards Alice. 'Would you like me to take him?'

Alice stared at her baby and squeezed him close, before giving him another kiss.

'Don't worry, I shall guard him with my life and we'll have fun.' Sarah smiled at her grandson, who was looking at her with wide eyes. 'Yes, we will, won't we Arthur?'

Arthur gurgled his delight.

'I know, Mother.' Alice's vision blurred, as the tears gathered momentum. 'I just hate to leave him for so long.'

Sarah nodded. 'I know, but I promise he'll be fine.'

Alice stretched out to place Arthur in her mother's arms, before turning to Victoria and Molly. 'I suppose we should be going.'

They both nodded as one.

Alice looked back at Arthur and her mother, but they were already lost to each other. 'It doesn't look like I'm going to be missed.' Her hands twisted together in front of her. 'So we had better get going.'

Victoria touched her arm as she walked into the hall. 'At least you know he's in good hands,' she whispered.

Alice nodded and picked up her grey lightweight jacket. She pulled it together to fasten the buttons. She turned to glance in the mirror. It had been her favourite jacket for years, but for the first time, she wasn't happy with the way it hung so loosely on her. She shrugged her shoulders and grabbed her handbag. 'We are off now.'

'Bye. I hope your day goes well,' Sarah chirped back. 'Molly, give my love to your parents.'

'Will do, Mrs Taylor.'

The three girls left the house and walked a few steps in silence.

Alice frowned and pushed her hair away from her face, as she stared down at the pavement.

Molly broke the silence. 'It'll be lovely to see you behind your counter again.'

Victoria followed her lead. 'Mr Leadbetter only told us yesterday he'd asked you to come back. He said he couldn't get the staff, what with all the extra war work being done by everyone.'

'I expect it'll be strange at first,' Molly chimed in. 'But you loved working there, so I'm sure you'll soon get back into it.'

'I'm sure,' Alice mumbled, concentrating on the way ahead.

Victoria placed her hand on Alice's arm and stopped walking. 'What is it? Is it leaving Arthur? I'm sure your mother will look after him. Is it—'

'No.' Alice's lips straightened into a thin line. 'I'm pretty sure Arthur will be fine.' She sucked in her breath, through pursed lips. 'He looks more and more like Freddie every day; the constant reminder that he's all I have of him. What happens if he doesn't come back, or doesn't return the same man I married? I see it all the time at the station and the hospitals. The men are broken.'

Molly turned and glared at her friend. 'Stop feeling sorry for yourself; at least you have Arthur. Women have lost sons, husbands and brothers. Some people have lost loved ones and are left with nothing at all.'

Victoria frowned at her friend's outburst. 'Stop it.'

Molly ignored her. Her eyes glinted as she stared at Alice. 'If Freddie returns home broken, be grateful he has come back to you, and help stick him back together. Some people aren't that lucky. Some people have no one.'

'Molly.' Victoria raised her voice.

'Well, what do you expect?' Molly glared at Victoria, before turning her anger on Alice. 'If he came home right now, what use would you be to him? You're not even holding it together for your beautiful son, let alone for someone that has seen horrific things that he quite possibly will never be able to remove from his mind. Instead of feeling sorry for yourself, you should be grateful for the good things you still have in your life.' A tear slid down her cheek. She turned and carried on walking.

*

Sarah stood in the hall, holding a brown envelope in her hand. She stared down at it, instantly recognising Robert's handwriting. She pulled it to her chest and breathed a sigh of relief, before stepping quickly into the sitting room, not noticing her heels clicking on the tiled floor. Struggling to catch her breath, she reached out to grip the back of the nearest armchair. Her attention was immediately drawn to Arthur, who was fast asleep in his chair. She stood still for a moment, closing her eyes as she gasped for breath. The scent of the potted lavender Mrs Headley had left on the sideboard the previous day filled the room, distracting Sarah as she breathed. 'Stay calm; you've your grandson to think about,' she told herself. She took deep breaths, in a bid to control her breathing and the light headedness that was creeping over her. Slowly, she lowered herself onto the chair, leaning back to rest her head, not loosening her tight grip on the letter.

'Is everything all right, Mrs Taylor?'

Mrs Headley's voice found its way through the fog that had gripped Sarah. She opened her eyes and gave her a weak smile. 'Indeed, Mrs Headley.' Sarah lifted her hand holding the letter. 'It looks like we've a letter from Robert.'

The housekeeper nodded. 'If you don't mind me saying, ma'am, it doesn't look like it's done you much good; you look quite pale. Can I get you a drink or something?'

Sarah gave a feeble laugh. 'It's probably shock. He's been away nearly two years and it's the first letter we've had.' She looked down at the envelope and turned it over in her hand.

Mrs Headley didn't take her eyes off her.

'I think I'll have some tea, please.' Sarah smiled up at the housekeeper. 'Thank you for the lavender.'

'I've heard said that it has healing qualities, ma'am.'

Sarah nodded. 'Yes, I think I was told that once.' She paused as her mind wandered. 'Poppy always grew it in the garden.'

Mrs Headley nodded. 'It is popular, and I believe easy to grow.'

'I didn't realise you were into gardening, Mrs

Headley.' Sarah arched her eyebrows. 'Is there nothing you don't know?'

'Plenty, ma'am.'

Sarah laughed. 'Well, I hope you know we appreciate everything you do for us, and we all regard you as family.'

Colour flooded the housekeeper's face and neck. 'Thank you, ma'am.' She gave a slight bow. 'I'll fetch your tea, ma'am.' Mrs Headley spun on her heels and left the room.

Sarah looked around for the silver letter opener, but she couldn't see it, so she slid her finger under the envelope's seal and ran it along its edge. She pulled the opening apart and peered inside, before pulling out the single sheet of paper. She unfolded it. The paper was stiff, and brown rivulets ran, where it had got wet.

Mrs Headley came in and, without a word, left the tea things on the side table.

Dear All,

I hope everyone is safe at home. I hear snippets about life in Blighty, but not very much. Thank you for the parcels I have received, particularly the socks and balaclavas. They have helped keep me, and some of the others, warm. I particularly enjoyed the book you sent me, The Thirty Nine Steps. It helped keep me occupied so I've passed it on for some of the others to read. We all get quite excited when a parcel arrives and tend to share out the contents. I actually had some chocolate yesterday, which was wonderful. Yes, I have come to appreciate the simple things in life, like chocolate.

I keep a diary now; it helps to keep my sanity and I know it's a cheek to ask, but when you send another parcel, could you include writing paper for me please.

I know I haven't been a very good son, particularly with my letter writing, but I find it hard to think about you all at home. The last thing I want to do is cause you worry.

It has been freezing here in St Eloi, that's near Ypres, in Belgium, Mother.

Sarah smiled at her son's cheekiness; geography had never been her strong point, despite her extensive travels with Poppy, in her younger days.

We are continually wading in water and I don't think my feet will ever be the same again. I can't pretend I don't miss the normalities of life in London, or all the things I used to moan about, including my brother and sisters. On the one hand, I try not to think about it because then it becomes too hard to deal with, but I do fear I will forget what normal life is. Tell Charles not to rush into enlisting when he is eighteen, because the reality is horrendous. I am lucky to still be alive; I have seen plenty going to meet their maker.

A lump formed in Sarah's throat. She blinked several times to hold back the tears, pricking at her eyes like hundreds of needles.

I am hoping the powers that be will let me home on leave soon. I miss Mrs Headley's cooking and the thought of just sitting and doing nothing, which I do here, but it's hard to relax, not knowing when the next bombs or gunfire are going to rain down on you.

I have run out of paper, so I will sign off now. Don't be surprised if my letter has been censored when you receive it. I hope the others are all behaving themselves while I'm away.

Miss you all, keep safe and keep writing.

Robert xxx

Sarah's hands flopped down onto her lap. 'He's alive,' she whispered. She looked down at the letter. The tears coursed down her cheeks, coming to rest on her lips. 'He's alive.' The saltiness coated her tongue as she spoke. She leant over and picked up her cup of tea and sipped it, grimacing as the lukewarm liquid filled her mouth. Replacing the cup on its saucer, she hugged the precious letter close to her chest. How she'd love to share it with the others, but she enjoyed the time she had alone, so she could read it as many times as she liked.

*

George had been tempted to have lunch at the club, but he had looked in the restaurant area and the tables were all occupied. Edward had warned him more men were eating their meals there these days. He had thought it was because of the reported food shortages. George sighed, silently berating himself for not having thought of it earlier and reserving a table.

'George.' A grey-haired man waved from inside the restaurant.

George smiled and waved back, not convinced he knew who it was. He kept walking towards the library.

The club was as busy as usual, but the atmosphere had become subdued over the last few months. As he walked past, George glanced into the gaming room. The large windows were open and the dark green curtains billowed into the room, as the breeze caught them. It wasn't full, or as raucous as it had been a year ago. He looked around, not really expecting to find Luke in there. Men were playing cards, but there were no cigars burning away in ashtrays and no money piled high on the tables.

A middle-aged man laughed, as he laid his cards out for his opponent to see. 'Right, I think you'll find your tab has gone up; you now owe me sugar and cigarettes.'

The older man ran his fingers over his greying moustache. 'Don't tell the wife, whatever you do. She'll skin me alive.'

'Don't worry, I won't hold you to it.' The younger

man smiled. 'After all, if she does you in, who else am I going to play cards with?'

George chuckled at the banter that was being exchanged, but he did wonder if the shortages, and everything going up in price, were beginning to bite, even for the more affluent. Were they feeling the pinch along with everyone else, or did they just think it was inappropriate to be having fun? He shrugged his shoulders as he walked away. Luke was a lot of things, but a gambler he was not.

George walked into the Library and frowned as he spied Luke sitting reading his newspaper, in the usual corner, by the window. He began weaving between the tables and chairs, nodding his hellos to their occupants as he passed.

Luke peered over his newspaper, in George's direction. The pages rustled as he shook it a little, to straighten them. He closed and folded it, before placing it on the centre of the table.

'Good day, Luke.' George pulled out a chair and sighed as he sat down.

'Morning, George.' Luke pulled a fob watch from the pocket of his tweed waistcoat. He sprung the cover and studied the time, before snapping the lid shut again. 'Perhaps I should say afternoon, George.'

George gave a weak smile, before picking up the newspaper, unfolding it and glancing at the headlines. He shook his head and without a word, folded it and put it back down.

Luke glanced down at the table, staring at the paper for a few minutes, before stretching out his hand to touch the corner. He pushed it slightly to the left, so it was straight and central to him. He pulled in his lips, before raising his eyes to look at George. 'Is there any news?'

'Shall we order coffee?' George twisted in his seat, to get the steward's attention.

Luke sucked in his breath and his body tensed in the chair. 'That doesn't sound good.'

George looked back at him, squinting as the sunshine caught him. 'Not at all. To be honest, I don't have much in the way of news.'

The steward cleared his throat.

George looked up. 'Can we have two coffees, strong ones please.'

The steward nodded and walked away.

'I can't abide weak coffee.' George raised his eyebrows. 'As I said when we spoke, a lot of the people I knew have died or retired. I've spoken to friends of friends and they are going to try to find out some information, but you need to know they are inundated with work, so it'll take some time.'

Luke arched his eyebrows. 'Ridiculous, I know.' He looked down at the table. 'But I had been hoping for a speedy outcome.'

Without a word, the steward placed their coffee cups

in front of them and walked away.

Luke glanced at George as he opened his mouth to speak, but he held up his hand. 'I know what I said was unreasonable. It just goes to show I didn't think about others being in the same position; you know, looking for news of loved ones.'

George nodded. 'Apparently, there are hundreds of people writing to Kitchener's War Office every day, hoping to get news.'

Luke nodded. 'It stands to reason, doesn't it?' His chest tightened. He held his breath. 'Thank you for trying though. I know you didn't have to.'

Pity swept over George, as he watched the disappointment and worry chase across his face. He had never seen this side of Luke before and he realised something fundamental had changed in him. 'I'll stay on it, I promise, and as soon as I get news, I will let you know.'

'Thank you.'

A middle-aged man rushed in the doorway of the library, gasping for breath. 'There's been an accident,' he yelled, while holding his chest. 'I don't know the details, but an ambulance crashed near Victoria Station. I was told the woman was in a pretty bad way, and apparently it doesn't look good.'

Murmurs travelled around the room.

Luke jumped up, knocking the table and spilling coffee into the saucer. 'Was the woman driving it?' he yelled, not stopping to think about the consequences of his outburst.

The man frowned. 'I believe so.'

Luke's eyes glistened, as he stared down at George. 'I have to go.' He turned and grabbed his jacket from the back of the chair. 'Sorry, but I don't know whether Alice was on duty today.'

'Shall I come with you?' George shouted at Luke's back, as he hurried out of the room.

'I can't wait; I need to find Alice.'

Chapter 25

Foyles was as busy as ever. There was a constant noise of conversation. Some customers were talking to staff, seeking directions to find books, but not knowing who the publisher was. Many just wanted to talk to someone. Paper rustled, as books were wrapped, ready to be delivered to customers. New and used books were constantly arriving, ready to be catalogued and crammed onto the shelves. None were ever turned away.

'Alice?' a man yelled. 'Alice, are you in here?'

'What's happened? Are you all right? Can I help?' The lady's voice tried to calm the man.

There was so much he hadn't said or done. Panic coursed through his veins. He was a child standing there, not the man who had once ruled with an iron fist. 'No, no, I need Alice.' His head frantically moved from left to right. 'Alice, are you here?' he shouted again, making sure he could be heard above the growing interest he had created, as it travelled around the shop.

The raised voice caught Alice's attention. Had someone called her name? She twisted right and left, but didn't have a full view of the commotion, by the entrance to the store. Her thoughts immediately went to

Arthur and her mother. She stood frozen to the spot, as fear gripped her heart. She gasped as he ran into view. What was her father looking so agitated about? He was flushed and gasping for breath. She ran around to the other side of the counter.

'Alice.' Luke lowered his head and rested his hands on his thighs, as he tried to catch his breath.

Colour drained from Alice's face. Her eyes were dark with anxiety. The walls of the store were closing in on her. 'What is it? Is Arthur all right?' Alice ran towards him, her heart pounding. 'Is it Mother? What's happened?'

Luke tried to take a deep breath, but his lungs were on fire. 'You're safe.'

'What?' Alice held his arm, as she stood in front of him. 'Tell me what's wrong.'

Luke stood upright and took a deep breath. 'I was at the club, talking to George, when someone came in and said there had been accident near Victoria Station, involving an ambulance and I thought...'

'Oh my goodness.' Alice paled. 'And you thought...'

'Yes I did.' Luke's eyes dampened as he looked at his daughter. 'It was just unthinkable,' he whispered. He licked his dry lips, as his eyes darted around.

'Oh Father, I'm so sorry.' Alice stroked his arm; the handmade jacket was soft under her hand. 'I've been here all day.'

Luke gave a shaky laugh. He reached out and pulled

her to him, wrapping his arms around her. The woody scent of his cologne caught in her nose.

'He said it didn't look good for the driver, and I just ran.' He squeezed her tight. 'The thought of—'

'I know. Don't say it.' Alice returned the hug, ignoring the glances from the customers moving around them.

Luke pulled back and stared at Alice. His chin trembled. 'I came here first, because it was nearest. I was so frightened you wouldn't ever know how much I love you, and all my children.' He paused, watching Alice's eyes well up. 'You and this damn war have made me realise a few things, and the thought of—'

'Sssh, everything's all right.' Alice took half a step back, to look at him properly. 'You don't have to explain; I do understand. I've been an emotional wreck since I've had Arthur.' She gave a shaky laugh. 'I wasn't great before, but having a baby, and with the boys being away, I've turned into a constant worrier.' She looked down for a moment. 'It's the fear that does it.' She glanced back at her father. 'The fear that you'll never see them again, and all the things you haven't said, that you wished you'd been brave enough to say before they left.'

Luke nodded. 'You are very wise for someone so young.' He sucked in his breath through pursed lips and shook his head. 'Some poor family and friends will be living the same fear I felt, before I found you.'

Alice frowned. 'That's true. We're all ultimately living

the same life, one that is filled with fear. The rest doesn't matter.'

Luke pulled Alice towards him and held her tight. 'I had better let you get back to work. Let's hope you don't get into trouble because of me. I just didn't think, when I came running in.'

'Don't worry, everything will be fine.' Alice patted his back, before drawing away. 'What did you say to me, "keep the faith," and that's what you must do.' She laughed. 'Practice what you preach.'

Luke smiled. 'All right, I'll try.' His hands dropped to his sides. 'I'll see you after work.'

Alice nodded. 'I'm at Victoria Station after work, working on the buffet table, so I'll be home later than usual,' she whispered.

Luke nodded, before giving her a last squeeze. 'Stay safe.'

Alice nodded as she watched him turn to walk out of the shop, before returning to her counter. Her legs were trembling. She sat on the wooden chair, wondering if she had fallen asleep and dreamt what had just happened.

*

Alice straightened her white apron, protecting the good clothes she had worn at Foyles earlier. There had been no time for her to go home and change. She began busying herself, placing cups on the buffet table and slicing cake, noticing there was less since the food shortages had hit the shops. She could no longer bring herself to look at the expectant upturned faces of the women and children waiting for the trains to crawl into Victoria Station. It broke her heart to see the chins wobble, as disappointment crept across their faces, when their loved ones didn't appear. She knew the sadness would be quickly chased away by a determination to be strong and protect their children from the disappointment, but Alice wondered how long the families could keep living that way. She jumped as a train gave a long whistle, on its approach to the station platform. Everyone stopped what they were doing and looked up. Women bit hard on their bottom lips, studying the occupants of each carriage as they disembarked. They clung on to their children's hands, as they hoped today would bring good news for them. Alice carried on working at the buffet table. Her mind drifted to Robert's letter. It saddened her to realise he didn't know about Charles and that fear kept him company in the trenches. She had always thought nothing ever got under his skin. A smile crept across her face; her mother had been beside herself with excitement, when Alice had arrived home from work. Robert was alive, and that was all that mattered.

'Am I allowed some tea and cake?'

Alice didn't look up at the man who spoke to her. 'No, these are for the returning soldiers.' She carried on cutting the cake, trying to make the slices smaller, but without much success.

'I am a returning soldier,' the man whispered.

Alice lifted her eyes slightly, noting his grey trousers, before going back to slicing the cakes. 'No, that can't be true, sir, you're not in uniform. It's a terrible thing to try to take food from this country's fighting heroes.'

The man gave a little chuckle. 'I couldn't agree more.'

Alice squeezed the handle of the knife. A vein was pulsating in her forehead, as her colour rose. 'Are you making fun of me, sir?' Her lips thinned as she looked up. Her eyes widened and her colour disappeared as quickly as it had arrived. Her hand loosened its grip on the knife, which thudded onto the table. She blinked rapidly as her jaw dropped open.

The man adjusted his hat. 'Aren't you going to say something?'

Alice was struck dumb, as she stood rooted to the spot, staring up at him.

He smiled. 'Well?'

'You, you look taller,' she whispered. 'And you're not in uniform?' Her fingers clung to the table edge, as everything began to spin around her.

'That's right. Does that mean I can't have the tea and cake then?'

'You didn't come on the train that brings the soldiers back and forth every day.'

Charles smiled at her. 'No, and yet here I am.'

Alice dropped like a stone.

'Alice, Alice, can you hear me?' Charles leant over her crumpled body.

She fluttered her eyelashes and shook her head, trying to evade the overpowering smell of ammonia that was wafting under her nose. Alice opened her eyes, startled to see Charles' weather-beaten face staring back at her. She tried to pull herself upright.

'Take your time, lovey. You fainted, so give yourself a minute.' The old lady had a tight grip on the smelling salts as she looked across at Charles. 'I take it you know Alice?'

Charles studied his sister, before looking at the grey-haired lady. 'She's my sister.'

'Aah, that explains everything. She has been looking for you for months.' The old lady straightened her back. 'Can I leave you to look after her?'

'Of course.' Charles frowned from one to the other.

'Alice, we can manage without you today.' She paused, before turning to Charles. 'I expect you've a lot to talk about, so you might want to take her home.'

Charles nodded, before turning to Alice. 'Can you stand, if I help you?'

Alice nodded.

Charles wrapped his arm around her and pulled her to her feet. 'Hold on to me; I don't want you fainting again.' He grinned at her. 'I thought you might have recognised my voice.'

Alice slapped the arm that wasn't around her.

Charles let go of her and doubled over in agony.

'Oh my God, what have I done?' Alice lifted her hand to her mouth. 'Are you all right? I'm sorry. I didn't mean to hurt you.'

'I have to go to the hospital to get it looked at. Something exploded around me and I think something is lodged in my arm.'

Alice frowned and she ran her dry tongue over her lips. 'What do you mean "something"? Perhaps we should take you straight there.'

'Don't look so worried.' Charles' shoulder nudged her. 'I don't remember much about it, but I don't suppose a few more hours will make any difference.'

'I'm so sorry,' Alice whispered. She shook her head, wondering if she could ask him about Freddie.

Charles lifted one eyebrow. 'Do you think I should go away, and we should start again?'

Alice wrapped her arms around her younger brother. 'No, definitely not. I've been searching for you since that awful telegram arrived, telling us you were missing.'

Charles held his sister tight. Their tears mingled on their cheeks.

Alice pulled back to look at Charles. She ran her hands roughly over her face. 'I can't believe you are here; am I going to wake up and it will all have been a dream?' There were so many questions running around her head, but she knew she had to be patient. 'Everyone will be so happy to see you.' She grinned. 'I can't wait to see their reaction when you walk through the front door.'

Charles frowned. 'Even Father?'

'Even Father.' Alice laughed. 'He's been writing letters, trying to track you down.' Again her thoughts were filled with Freddie, but she told herself he'd eventually tell her, if he knew anything. She stared, wide-eyed at him, drinking him in, unable to believe he was standing next to her. 'What made you come here?'

Charles laughed. 'The train I was on came into Charing Cross Station, so I walked up to Foyles to find you, but some old chap told me you'd left for the day and would probably be here.'

Alice nodded as she looked around her. 'I try to help out most days; it's heart-rending.'

Charles stood in silence. He followed her line of vision, watching the faces alive with hope, as people searched the crowds for their loved ones, only to have that hope doused in cold water. 'This war has a lot to answer for,' he mumbled to himself, before taking a deep breath and forcing a smile to his lips. 'Well, as you are able to go, let's get home.'

Alice took off her white apron, while Charles held up her coat, for her arms to slip into. She buttoned it up and slid her arm through his, her hand gripping the rough wool of his black jacket. 'I can't believe you're here.' Alice giggled. 'Mother will be so thrilled and shocked to see you. We've only just heard from Robert, the only letter since he joined up. I thought he'd forgotten all about us.'

Charles gave Alice a sombre look. 'Don't judge him. It's not how we all thought it was going to be. A bloke I met thought he'd be able to meet some French girls; actually, so did I.' He gave a shallow laugh. 'He was shocked, to say the least, because we never saw much, outside of a trench, except when we were charging at the enemy and being shot at.'

Alice nodded. 'At least you've survived it all.'

Charles gave a long low sigh. 'Yes.' His voice thickened. 'He didn't survive it, so I suppose I'm one of the lucky few, although at times it hasn't felt that way.'

Alice could feel the tears pricking behind her eyelids, as she quickly blinked. She repeatedly shook her head. 'I can't begin to comprehend what you've been through.' She closed her eyes and sucked in her breath. 'I come to this station most days, to either take the injured to hospital or,' she gave a little laugh, 'feed the soldiers tea and cake.' Her eyes became cloudy as she looked at her brother. 'But either way, I've heard some horror stories, although most of the time, the men act with great bravado and bravery.'

Charles gave a little chuckle. 'I can imagine. I suspect most of them probably haven't seen a pretty girl for a long time, so you'll be a sight for sore eyes.'

Alice smiled. 'I can't wait for everyone to see you.'

Charles closed his eyes for a moment and lifted his face to the sun, soaking in the warmth of the early summer. He looked around at the fine architecture of the tall buildings, seeing everything with new eyes. The barren landscape he had grown used to seemed a long way from the intimidating tall buildings and the general hubbub of people going about their business. It no longer seemed the colourful, exciting place to be. The ladies they passed were mainly dressed in brown or black uniforms. Women police officers walked along the street in pairs, some nodding as they walked by. He shook his head; things had changed for everyone. 'I had forgotten how noisy London is. If you took away the gunfire and bombs exploding, you could've heard a pin drop, on the front line.'

Alice glanced around, trying to see everything through his eyes. 'You are here now.'

'I don't know how long I'll be here for.' Charles squeezed her hand with his arm. 'I need to check in with the regiment and the hospital.'

'But,' Alice's eyes widened, 'they have you as missing, so you could stay here with us. They don't need to know you're home.'

'What, hide me in the attic?' Charles laughed. 'I'd be lying if I said it wasn't tempting, but this isn't about me or you, Alice, it's about the greater good and the men that have already died. If we give up, they'll have given their lives for nothing.'

They walked slowly down Bloomsbury Street. Alice bit her lip. 'You know, once the family have got over the excitement of having you home, they're going to want to know why you didn't write, to let us know you were safe.'

Charles laughed. 'Nothing really changes, does it?'

Alice shook her head. 'I know you've had a hard time but, for very different reasons, it's also been hard for us. When you stand on the train station and watch all the women waiting and hoping, it breaks your heart.'

Charles nodded. 'I suppose; I never really thought about it.'

Alice laughed. 'And there's no reason why you should have. It's more important that your focus is on you and staying alive.' She paused. 'I'm just trying to prepare you for the questions that will inevitably come.'

'The truth is, I don't really know what happened.' He paused for a moment, staring down at the pavement. 'The last thing I remember is Freddie falling on me; I think he saved my life.'

Alice could feel her eyes filling up. She came to an abrupt standstill, jerking Charles backwards. 'Does that mean he's...' She gulped hard. 'Dead?'

Charles took a deep breath and stared at his sister. 'I don't know what it means.' He pulled in his lips tight for a moment. 'When I came round, I was lying in a barn, on some straw. I don't even know how I got there. There was an old guy with a pitchfork who used to come in every day, and I felt certain he was going to stick it in me. It was terrifying. I didn't speak French and they didn't speak English, so communication between us wasn't great, but they nursed and fed me, before getting me to England. I owe them and Freddie for my life.'

Alice slowly nodded. No words would come, as she watched the emotions chase each other across his face.

Charles glanced at Alice with watery eyes, as he pulled her forward. 'Freddie will be back. He has to be, even if it's only so I can thank him.'

'He has a son.'

Charles stopped dead. 'What?'

A tear tripped over her lashes. 'He has a son, Arthur.' She wiped her eyes. 'You're an uncle.'

His eyes filled up. 'Wow, I can't believe it. I'm an uncle.' He pulled her towards him and held her tight. 'I'll make it my job to find Freddie; he's alive, I know he is.'

He stepped back and they walked on in silence for a moment.

'How old is Arthur? Oh wait, I can probably work it out.' Charles laughed.

Alice couldn't help joining in. How she'd missed her brother. 'He's almost six months old. Mrs Headley and Lily delivered him.'

'Gosh.' Charles smiled. 'Lily must have settled down; no more demonstrating then.'

Alice's eyes sparkled as she looked at him. 'Oh, are

422

you in for a shock.'

'What?' His eyes clouded over as they came to a standstill, outside their home. 'She's all right, isn't she?'

Alice laughed. 'She's a policewoman.'

Charles looked stunned for a moment, before breaking into a hearty laugh. They walked up to the front door and Alice inserted her key, quietly turning it in the lock.

Alice gently pushed the door open and a strong aroma of coffee greeted them. She turned to Charles and put a finger on her lips. 'I've a surprise for you all,' Alice yelled out, before she had walked through the front door. 'I hope you're sitting down.' She ran down the hall and into the sitting room, where Sarah was just rising to her feet. Her father looked up from the small writing desk he had recently bought. Lily was already wrapping her knitting around the needles she was holding. 'I think you need to sit down for this, Mother.' Alice laughed. 'Trust me on this one, you are all going to love it.'

Sarah frowned, but lowered herself back into the armchair. 'You look too happy for it to be bad news.'

Alice grinned as she waited for her mother to get comfortable. 'A surprise isn't bad news, and I've already told you, you'll love it.' She clapped her hands together and did little jumps on the spot, as the excitement became too much to bear.

Sarah laughed. 'Oh yes, you're quite right, how silly of me.'

'What is it?' Lily asked, a smile spreading across her thin features. 'It must be big for you to be this excited.'

'Stay there,' Alice instructed everyone, as she briskly walked into the hallway. She grabbed Charles' hand and pulled him into the sitting room. 'Ta da.' Her arms made an exaggerated introductory movement towards her brother.

Sarah's hand rested on her chest, as she gasped for breath. 'I can't believe it.' She quickly stood up, as he bounded towards her. 'Charles, is that really you?'

Lily's eyes widened, as she stared at the man who had walked through the doorway. She jumped up and grabbed Alice's arm, as her vision became blurred.

He wrapped his arms around his mother. They clung to each other. She didn't notice the jacket scratching her skin, as she sobbed into it. Charles pulled away and stared at her. 'It's unbelievably wonderful to be home.' He pulled her back in his arms. 'Don't cry.' He rubbed his hand up and down her back. 'I'm here now, safe and sound.'

Unable to contain herself any longer, Lily threw herself on them both. Her arms stretched around them. 'I can't believe it. Thank God you're safe.'

Alice smiled, as she watched them all laugh and cry at the same time. She noticed pain flicker across Charles' face, but he never said anything. She tightened her lips; perhaps she should have warned them about his arm. Alice glanced over at her father, who was also on his feet smiling. The sheet of paper was screwed up in a ball, on his desk.

Charles pulled back from Sarah and Lily, his eyes feasting on them, before he turned. 'Hello, Father.' He frowned as he looked at the man grinning, not knowing what he expected from him. Charles wanted a hug, but he assumed he'd prefer a handshake. He stepped towards him and held out his hand.

His father looked down at Charles' hand.

Alice held her breath. His smile had vanished and her father's expression was unreadable.

'I don't want to shake your hand.' Luke looked tight lipped at Charles as he dropped his hand. 'I want a hug.'

Luke pulled Charles into his arms. 'I am so sorry,' he whispered. 'Thank God you are alive.' His arms tightened around his youngest son. 'I am so proud of you.'

Charles' throat tightened. He tried to take a deep breath and swallow, but a lump had formed.

Luke pulled back. 'Not because of the war, but because you are my son.' He snatched him back into his arms and squeezed tight.

Charles tried to hold back his tears, but failed.

*

'Do you feel better for your bath?' Luke couldn't take his eyes off his son. His face was gaunt, although his frame had filled out, and he appeared to have lost the boyish charm the ladies had loved. His tanned features looked older and etched with pain.

'Much, thank you.' Charles sat in the nearest armchair and looked around the sitting room. Nothing had changed, yet for him everything had changed. He looked down, wondering if he'd ever fit into his family's lives again.

Luke watched Sarah. She hadn't stopped smiling since Charles had walked through the door. He looked across at him. He was blankly staring into his teacup, while his mother and sisters chatted around him.

'Charles.' Lily stood in front of her brother, holding a plate of biscuits. 'You were miles away.' She put the plate down on the side table next to his armchair, before kneeling at his feet. 'I'm sorry. I've been wittering on. Are you all right?'

Charles mustered up the smile everyone expected from him. 'Of course; why wouldn't I be? I'm home, drinking cups of tea.' He picked a plain biscuit from the plate. 'And I'm about to eat this.' He laughed, but his eyes were dead.

Alice glanced at her brother. 'Would you like to meet your nephew?'

'Most definitely.' Charles placed his cup down on the table. 'Where is he?'

'Stay there and I'll bring him to you.' Alice jumped up from her seat and walked out of the room.

Lily twisted round on the floor. 'Arthur is lovely. I helped deliver him, you know.' Everyone laughed. 'What?'

Charles' laughter gradually faded away. 'I've missed you all so much.'

The sitting room door gave the inevitable squeak, as Alice pushed it open with her elbow. Arthur sat up, proud in her arms.

'Can I help introduce him to Uncle Charles?' Lily stretched out her hands to take him.

Alice shook her head and laughed. 'It's about time you found your own man and had a baby, then I might get to keep mine for more than ten minutes at a time.'

Lily smiled at her sister. 'That's a little bit difficult these days. In case you hadn't noticed, all the eligible bachelors are off fighting the Germans. We weren't all lucky enough to find a good man before it started.'

The room fell silent.

Luke stood up. 'Perhaps it should be Grandpa that holds him first.'

Shocked, Alice moved her attention to her father.

'What do you say Arthur, are you going to come to Grandpa?'

Arthur giggled at Luke, as he spoke in a musical voice. He took him and held him close. Soap and talcum powder wafted around him. Arthur fidgeted to be free, so he could try to crawl around the room. Luke sat down, before putting him down by his feet. 'Go on then little man, be free.' He laughed as Arthur stared at him, with his big wide eyes.

Alice sat on the arm of Charles' chair and tapped her brother's leg. 'Do you know who this is?'

Arthur's gaze bounced from Alice to Charles. His arms stretched up to her. She picked him up and sat him on her lap. 'This is your Uncle Charles.'

Arthur clapped his hands and shouted. They all laughed, mainly because no one understood what he was saying. He reached forward. His hands gripped Charles' trouser leg.

'Do you want to come and say hello?' Charles frowned. 'Erm, I could use some help here. What do you do with babies?'

Lily smiled. 'He likes it if you talk in a sing-song voice.'

Charles arched an eyebrow. 'Oh yes; I wouldn't feel an idiot doing that, would I?'

Luke stared at his son. 'There's no need to feel an idiot. You are among family.'

Charles nodded.

Alice laid a hand on her brother's lower arm. 'Just let him take the lead. He'll soon let you know if he isn't happy.'

'Hello, little one. I'm your Uncle Charles and I'm going to be your favourite.' Charles smiled as Arthur gurgled and shuffled further onto his lap.

Lily laughed. 'You can't possibly be, because that's

me.'

Charles stroked Arthur's hand and the little fingers clasped his. 'Well, Arthur, your aunt has to prepare to lose her crown.' His face softened, as his eyes became watery. 'Such innocence.'

Arthur yawned, before snuggling into his uncle's chest.

'It looks like it's time for his afternoon nap,' Alice said. 'He has snuggled in very nicely, thank you very much.'

'Charles.' Luke coughed, while he seemingly examined the carpet. 'I shall be going to the hospital shortly.' He looked directly at him. 'I wondered if you would like to come with me?' He watched his son's head jerk back and he swore his body tensed.

'Here, let me take him upstairs for a sleep.' Alice gently lifted Arthur, making sure his head was resting on her shoulder, as she carried him to bed.

'Is there...' Charles took a deep breath. 'Is there something wrong?'

'No, no.' Luke stood up and gazed blindly out of the window. 'I visit patients nearly every day.' He turned to face Charles. 'Alice suggested, rather heatedly I might add, that it was something I could do to help, and I have to say she was right. I just wondered if you would like to join me?'

'He's only just come home,' Sarah admonished. 'Why would he want to go to the hospital and see all that pain and suffering?'

Luke shrugged his shoulders, before shaking his head. 'Sarah, our sons have already seen all the pain and suffering. This will help him see that some come home and survive. Admittedly, they are not the same men that went away. That will take time, if they ever get back to it at all.' He thrust his hands deep into his trouser pockets and turned back to the window.

Charles stared down at his hands, clasped together in his lap. 'When I went away to war, it was exciting. I thought I was going to be back in a few months. It hasn't turned out that way and I've prayed more in the last eighteen months than I have in my whole life.' His throat tightened and tears pricked at his eyes. The sniffing into a handkerchief made him glance up at his mother. 'I'm sorry, I didn't mean to upset you.' He turned to his father, who was staring at him. 'Thank you. I'd love to go with you.'

Chapter 26

Alice's feet were aching. She eyed the old wooden chair, which stood adjacent to her counter at Foyles. It looked inviting. Did she dare to sit for five minutes? She looked around and there was no sign of Mr Leadbetter. Alice flopped down on the chair and straightened her legs, wriggling her toes inside her black court shoes. Looking up, she glanced at her counter and the stack of books waiting to be collected. She had written out a lot of bill payment slips, but they were mainly for second-hand, rather than new books. Her mind wandered to Robert's letter and Charles being home. Things had changed for them both, so if, 'no when' a voice screamed in her head, Freddie came home, would he be a different man to the one she fell in love with?

'Excuse me.'

Alice looked up.

'I'm sorry to disturb you.' A young woman stood at the counter. 'But I wondered if you could help me.'

It took a few seconds for Alice to digest the words. 'Of course.' She stood up, despite the pulsating of her aching feet. 'I'm sorry, what can I do for you?'

'I'd like to buy a second-hand book for my five-year-old niece. Is there anything you can recommend?' The customer's friendly smile readily appeared.

Alice returned her smile. 'Come with me and I'll take you to someone who can help you.' She led the lady to the children's section, and Molly's capable hands.

Alice returned to her counter and began tidying up the shelves that stood behind her. She sighed as she perched on the edge of the wooden chair again. Her mother had been right about being back amongst the many books the shop held. She never tired of the musty smell or the smokiness that some of them carried, where they'd been stored in people's homes. If they could talk, each one would have its own story of how it ended up in Foyles, whether second hand or new. Alice took a couple of deep breaths, before slowly standing up to tidy the books on the shelves. She ran her rag over the spines and covers, not giving the dust time to settle. The temptation to buy more books was as overwhelming as ever, but she had to refrain from spending her money. The savings were steadily growing, so when the war was over and Freddie came home for good, they'd have enough to buy their own place. Her mind kept drifting back to her father, and how he had acted so out of character. She found herself running over it, time and time again. She frowned as she tried to remember if he had ever hugged her before.

'Hello, miss.'

Startled, Alice turned around. An old lady was

grinning in front of her. Her time-ravaged face was lit up with a smile that showed off several crooked brown teeth with intermittent gaps, while her smoky-grey hair had been combed into soft curls. One gnarled, weathered hand held the edge of the wooden counter, while the other rested heavily on a walking stick. Her brown tweed coat was almost threadbare.

'Good afternoon, and what can I do for you?' Alice looked at her, wondering how warm her coat was, and why she looked familiar.

'I don't expect you to remember me, but I remember you and the wonderful police sergeant who was so chivalrous to me. He made my day.' The lady giggled. 'Mind you, I did flirt outrageously with him.'

Alice frowned for a moment, before the memory came flooding back. How things had changed. Tears glistened on her eyelashes. 'Yes, I do remember you.' She gave a watery smile. 'You did flirt with him. I think you were trying to steal my man.'

The old lady cackled. 'He was very kind to me and, if I'd been forty years younger, you'd have had a fight on your hands.' Her eyes twinkled. 'You know, it stays with me, because it isn't something you witness every day; such kindness.' She stared at Alice. All signs of the smile had vanished. 'I suppose he's with all the other brave men, fighting the bloody Germans.'

Words failed Alice. Her breath caught in her throat. She couldn't trust herself to speak. Tension formed a band around her chest.

The old lady nodded. 'I'll be glad when it's over; it's just wrecking lives and families. Do you write to him?'

Alice nodded. 'We got married,' she whispered.

'Ahh, is that why I haven't seen you in here for a while?' The old lady leaned heavily on her stick. 'I've been looking out for you, wondering where you were.'

'That's very kind of you.' Alice smiled. 'It's nice to be missed.'

The lady's eyes clouded over. 'We all want to be missed by someone.'

Alice wanted to ask if she'd be missed by anyone, but didn't. 'I must admit, I've never really thought about it, but I suppose that's true.'

The crooked teeth showed, as a smile spread across the lady's face. 'I think it's something you think about more when you're coming to the end of your time.'

Alice shook her head and frowned at the woman standing in front of her. 'Don't say things like that. You've many more years of flirting in you yet.'

The old lady cackled loudly and customers looked around to see what was happening. 'You could be right.' She grinned as she turned to leave the shop. 'Take care of yourself, young lady.' She held up her hand to wave, as she hobbled forward. 'I'm sure your man will be home soon.'

Alice waved, but the lady didn't look back.

Victoria caught Alice's attention and waved from the

payment booth. 'All right?' she mouthed.

Alice nodded and waved back, fighting the urge to cry.

Molly gave a spluttering cough from behind one of the racks of shelving, stacked high with books. Her eyes flitted around, as she pulled at her neck. 'Oi, old Leadbetter's on his way.'

'Old Leadbetter's right behind you, Miss Cooper.'

The deep voice made Molly jump, and the urge to fan her face told her she had gone a lovely shade of red. 'Yes, sir, sorry, sir, I was just...' She bit down on her lip.

'I know what you were doing, but more importantly, I know what you weren't doing.' Mr Leadbetter gave her a stern look, his jaw clenched tight.

'Sorry, sir, I'll get on. It won't happen again, sir.' Molly turned and quickly moved amongst the customers.

Mr Leadbetter raised an eyebrow, as he tried to contain his laughter. He felt sure it would happen again, and probably before the shop shut that day. He strolled over to Alice. 'Entertaining the customers, Mrs Leybourne?'

Alice smiled. 'Apparently, I've been missed, or at least Freddie has.'

Mr Leadbetter glanced towards the entrance of the shop. 'I don't know who she is, but she does come in here regularly; mind you, she doesn't always buy anything.'

'Sometimes, people just want some company, sir. It must be hard, living on your own.'

'I'm sure.' Mr Leadbetter nodded. 'How have you found coming back to work here?' he asked, lowering his tone. 'Is everything all right? You seem to have been miles away today.'

Alice blushed as she picked up her rag and turned back to her dusting. 'I'm fine, sir, quite tired, but it is good to be back.'

Mr Leadbetter eyed her closely. 'Who was that man yesterday, the one who caused the commotion by the door?'

Alice blushed as she turned to face him. 'Sorry, sir, that was my father.' She took a deep breath. 'There was a misunderstanding and he thought something had happened to me.'

Mr Leadbetter raised his eyebrows. 'No wonder he was agitated.'

'Yes.' Alice sighed. 'I've never seen him act that way before. It was most out of character.'

'That's what the war is doing to us. He must have thought it was serious.'

'Apparently, there was an accident and he thought it was me driving the ambulance involved in it.' She paused and looked up at him, wondering whether to apologise, but not wanting to.

'Well, it caused a stir, but all's well and that's the main thing.'

Alice returned to her dusting.

Mr Leadbetter started to walk away, but someone caught his eye. 'Mrs Leybourne, you might as well pack up and have an early day. I think you are going to need it.'

'I'll be all right,' Alice quipped, concentrating on the dusting.

Mr Leadbetter sighed. 'I'm sure you will, but I insist.'

Alice looked round. Her eyes widened, as her gaze became full of wonderment. Her mouth dropped open. She dropped the rag, as her hand flew to her chest. She heard the yelp of a dog being trodden on; was that her? She took a step forward, but stopped. Her eyes didn't stray from the man in front of her. He was leaning heavily on a walking stick and his head was bandaged over one eye. She shook her head, in disbelief. 'Is... is it true?' Alice covered her face with her hands, squeezing her eyes shut. 'Is... is it really you?' Her voice shook and her body trembled.

Freddie hobbled towards her. 'Yes, it is.'

Molly watched wide-eyed. Her mouth dropped open, just as her eyes glistened with unspent tears, she yelled, 'Victoria.'

Alice ran forward and threw her arms around him. His walking stick crashed to the ground, as he picked her up and swung her around. He trembled in her arms. Their heads clashed as their lips passionately sought each other's, over and over again. A groan escaped. He squeezed her tight, taking her breath away. His facial stubble scratched at her skin, but she didn't care. They cried and laughed at the same time. Their tears mingled, as they stayed wrapped in each other's arms.

'I didn't think I was ever going to see you again,' Freddie gasped.

'Nor I,' Alice whispered. She pulled back to look at him, but became aware that they had an audience who were cheering and clapping. The old grey-haired lady, with her crooked brown teeth, grinned at her, before turning to walk out of the shop.

Mr Leadbetter gave her a rare smile. 'I expect you want to go home now?'

*

Alice and Freddie walked slowly along Bloomsbury Street. Alice was bursting to tell him about Arthur. Every time the urge came over her, she bit down hard on her tongue until she could taste blood.

'It's wonderful to be home.' Freddie stopped to take in the buildings and the trees. 'Everything feels so different. Perhaps tomorrow, we could sit in the park, any park, just so I can watch the world go by and admire the colourful flowers and blossom.' He laughed. 'I sound like a right one.'

Alice smiled, as she rested her arm in his. 'You can do whatever you want tomorrow. I can't believe you're here.'

'No, nor me.' Freddie looked down at his walking stick. 'Have you had any news of Charles?'

Alice followed his gaze, wanting to ask about the limp and the damage to his eye, but that could wait until tomorrow. She wanted to enjoy the little time they had together, before the family took over. 'Oh yes. Sorry, with the shock and excitement of seeing you, I forgot to say, Charles is home.' Alice paused. 'He has to have an operation on his arm, but the main thing is he's alive. He says he owes you his life.'

Freddie's face lit up. 'Thank goodness he's safe. I don't really have much recollection of what happened.'

Alice laughed. 'It doesn't matter, and maybe it's better that way.' She squeezed his arm. 'Charles doesn't remember much either. He said you saved his life by throwing yourself over him, but he remembers nothing after that.'

Freddie's eyes clouded over. 'You know, one thing I have learnt, war is about innocent people killing innocent people.'

Alice looked up at him with troubled eyes. There were no words to offer reassurance. The black front door came into view. She wanted to help him forget. 'I've a surprise for you.'

Freddie looked down at her. His eyes had a distant look in them and his lips were set in a grim line.

'You'll love it.' Alice cleared her throat. 'At least, I

hope you will.' She pressed her lips together, as anxiety ran across her face.

'It doesn't look like a pleasant surprise,' Freddie whispered.

They reached the front door. Alice turned to him. 'I love you, Mr Leybourne, and don't you ever forget that.' She leant in and kissed him. All fear and doubt was forgotten, as the butterflies in her stomach took control.

Freddie pulled her in tight. His lips pressed hard on hers, as the urgency grew between them.

Alice reluctantly pulled away, flushed with colour and her eyes full of passion.

'I love you too.' He smiled, wondering if they could book in somewhere for a couple of days.

'Are you ready?' Alice held his hand tight. She had no urge to let him go, ever again.

'I was born ready. What did you have in mind, Mrs Leybourne?' Freddie grinned, as Alice's colour became heightened.

She shook his hand. 'You'll see.'

They stepped inside the house. Alice was tempted to sneak him upstairs for a few days, but they were not alone in the hallway.

'Oh my God, Freddie.' Charles blinked and rubbed his eyes. 'I'm not hallucinating, am I?'

Freddie laughed. 'No, it's me.'

Charles ran forward and hugged Freddie. 'I can't believe it.' He pulled back, to stare intently at his brother-in-law. 'Thank God you're all right. You are all right, aren't you?'

Freddie laughed. 'I'll live, and I'm certainly better off than most.'

Charles nodded. 'That's very true. It's good to see you, and to have you home, looking so well.'

'Hopefully, things can only keep improving, although Alice said she had a surprise for me, but her face told me otherwise.' Freddie laughed, as he turned to see Alice shaking her head at her brother. 'What's going on?'

Charles laughed as he stepped aside. 'Nothing. My sister is warning me not to spoil things, that's all.'

Freddie arched his eyebrows, giving them both a suspicious look. 'Why don't I believe you?'

Alice stepped forward. 'Your leg must be aching; let's go into the sitting room.'

Freddie laughed. 'Mrs Leybourne, are you trying to change the subject?'

'No.' Alice grinned up at her husband. 'I am trying to guide you to your surprise.'

'Hmm, I'm not so sure.' Freddie followed her into the sitting room.

Alice immediately saw Arthur lying on the floor, happily kicking his arms and legs. She stepped aside, allowing Freddie to see inside the room.

Freddie stepped inside and his mouth dropped open.

Charles grabbed an armchair, manoeuvring it behind Freddie's legs, so he could drop into it.

Alice's eyes filled with tears. 'We have a son.'

Freddie dropped like a stone, thankful for the chair behind him.

Alice walked over to Arthur, who squealed with delight at seeing her. His arms and legs thrashed about with excitement. 'He's called Arthur, after my great grandfather.'

Freddie held out his arms.

'Arthur, allow me to introduce you to your wonderful father.' Alice placed him in Freddie's waiting arms.

'I'm a father.' He looked down at the boy that was staring at him intently. 'Hello, Arthur.' Tears rolled down Freddie's cheeks.

'I know I should have told you, but I wanted you to concentrate on looking after yourself, and not worrying about me or Arthur.' Alice rambled; she had thought about this moment so many times.

Freddie stroked Arthur's hand and kissed his forehead. 'It doesn't matter.' His gaze never moved from his son. 'He is handsome.'

Arthur gurgled and gripped his father's hand.

Alice beamed at the pair of them. While she had stumbled a couple of times, she had kept her faith and now she felt like the luckiest girl in the world.

Chapter 27

The unfamiliar steady breathing, and Freddie's arm resting across her stomach, told Alice it hadn't been a dream. She opened her eyes and blinked at the early morning sunshine peeking through the edges of the bedroom curtains. Arthur gurgled in his cot, peering through the wooden slats at them. She snuggled further into Freddie's body, enjoying the warmth of his skin next to hers. After a few moments, Alice slowly rolled over, so she could gaze at her husband and touch his soft skin, to soak up this moment of heaven. He looked so peaceful, so rested. She fought the urge to touch the rough bristles on his face, not wanting to wake him. The lines that were etched on his face the day before were no longer visible; sleep had given him the release he needed. Alice smiled, knowing Mrs Headley wouldn't be able to wait to fuss and build him up again.

Alice leant forward, giving in to the urge for her lips to brush his forehead. 'I love you, Freddie Leybourne.' She pulled the blanket up over her bare shoulder and snuggled down again, not letting her gaze leave him. Was it wrong that she didn't feel guilty for having this happiness? Images of Molly and Victoria popped into her head. She frowned.

'Morning, Mrs Leybourne.' Freddie peeped through half opened eyes. 'What's wrong?'

Alice smiled. 'What could possibly be wrong, I'm lying in bed with the man I love, and our son is content in his cot.'

Freddie scanned her face. 'And yet you were frowning.'

Alice's lips straightened into a thin line for a moment. 'Just guilt, for not feeling guilty about being so happy.' She took a deep breath. 'I have it all, when Molly and Victoria have been having such a miserable time.'

'Their moment will come, you'll see, and it'll be when they least expect it.' Freddie's lips lifted. 'Look how we met. If I hadn't had to come to give Victoria news of that terrible tragedy, we probably would never have found each other.'

'Yes, I know, but that makes me feel worse, we are a constant reminder of her loss. The three of us have always been there for each other but the war has made that bond even closer, if that's possible.'

'And I'm sure you will all continue to do that.' Freddie wrapped his arms around her. 'It's all out of our control, sweetheart. Their time will come, you'll see.'

'I know, I'm sorry.' Alice smiled at him. 'I love you so much. I can't believe you are here in my arms.'

Freddie closed his eyes and breathed in her scent. 'I've not thought about anything else for so long.' His voice was husky as his hand caressed her back. 'This feels so good.' He pulled back, to look at Alice. He brushed the hair from her face. 'I love you so much. I never want to leave you and Arthur ever again. We're going to have hundreds of children, and if we don't, we will have fun trying.'

Alice giggled as he pulled her in close.

Acknowledgements

I have had a lot of help, encouragement and support since I started writing, so I would like to thank everyone in the order they have joined my journey.

Firstly, I would like to thank my wonderful family for their support, encouragement and role-playing that took place in my front room. My son started my creative journey by finding an on-line course and The Write Place creative writing school, which was held just up the road from where I live. It was there I met the tutor and author Elaine Everest. She, and her students, have encouraged, and supported by giving critical feedback on my writing. Elaine has always led the way by example and always been there when advice has been needed. It was through her, I joined the Romantic Novelists' Association (RNA) New Writers Scheme, which gave me valuable feedback and introduced me to many budding and established authors. It was also with Elaine's encouragement that I started blogging, on the WriteMindsWritePlace Blog. The original cast was Elaine Everest, Vivien Brown, Natalie Klienman, Francesca Capaldi Burgess and of course me. I would like to thank them for their endless encouragement and support. Viv also had a big part to play in encouraging me to join the Society of Women Writers and Journalists. I am lucky to be a member of such supportive organisations and groups.

I have attended many talks, events and conferences, locally and through the RNA. It was through a local talk that I met Ian Castle, who was a font of all knowledge when it came to WW1, so I owe him a big thank you. It was at an RNA event that I met and want to thank Felicity Trew, of the Caroline Sheldon Literary Agency, and Natasha Harding, of Bookouture. They both gave me valuable advice at different times in my journey. The RNA conferences gave me the experience of having one to ones with agents and publishers. It was through those that Natasha was the first industry professional to love this story and I can't thank her enough for passing her wisdom on to me. It was also through the one to ones that I met Rosie de Courcy (Head of Zeus), who loved my writing and suggested I send it to a contact at Aria, which is also part of Head of Zeus.

A huge thank you must go to my editor Lucy Gilmour and the team at Aria, who are publishing this book. They have been a pleasure to work with and have fine-tuned my novel. I truly hope everyone who reads it enjoys it.

If you wish to talk to me, get in touch.

HELLO FROM ARIA

We hope you enjoyed this book! Let us know, we'd love to hear from you.

We are Aria, a dynamic digital-first fiction imprint from award-winning independent publishers Head of Zeus. At heart, we're avid readers committed to publishing exactly the kind of books we love to read — from romance and sagas to crime, thrillers and historical adventures. Visit us online and discover a community of like-minded fiction fans!

We're also on the look out for tomorrow's superstar authors. So, if you're a budding writer looking for a publisher, we'd love to hear from you. You can submit your book online at ariafiction.com/we-want-read-your-book

You can find us at:
Email: aria@headofzeus.com
Website: www.ariafiction.com
Submissions: www.ariafiction.com/we-want-read-your-book
Facebook: @ariafiction
Twitter: @Aria_Fiction
Instagram: @ariafiction

Printed in Poland
by Amazon Fulfillment
Poland Sp. z o.o., Wrocław